Abby's Theory

Abby's Theory

L. C. Paoletti

A Novel

LCP

Abby's Theory

L. C. Paoletti

A Novel

This novel is dedicated to those who already know and are willing to share their knowledge.

Chapters

Abby's Theory

Nexus I

The small, single dorm room at American University was purposely kept on the warmer side of comfortable. During the fall semester Abby Lark slept naked except when she was on duty as a resident assistant, a once a week task. On duty nights she wore a sports bra and running shorts in the event of an emergency that required her to leave the room quickly. Most evenings during the cooler winter months Abby wore only a large, loose fitting shirt that had become even roomier since she arrived on campus six months ago. The combination of having to constantly study for her own coursework, combined with daily preparations to fulfill her role as a teaching assistant, coupled with a light workout regimen resulted in weight loss that was at long last, real and sustained. For the first time in her life she felt as though she owned her once plump and frumpy body instead of it owning her.

Abby adapted quite well to the hectic pace of her first semester as a newly minted graduate student. She was living on her own for the first time, away from her insignificant father, who was over 400 miles away—a distance that was becoming more distant with each passing week. She did not live with him in Massachusetts anymore and thankfully so. Her life was finally coming together after the sudden loss of her loving mother at a young age, followed by the cruel social drama called high school. The stigma of attending Wilmington College on a hardship tuition waiver was not overcome until she reached her senior year so yes, leaving the familiar landscape of semi-rural New England to attend graduate school at American University in undeniably urban Washington, D.C., was just the life-altering change for the better Abby needed. Finally, she was in control of her life. It was defined, simple and focused. Now she owned her life as well as her body.

By the beginning of the second semester Abby had settled into the role of a graduate student in the Advanced Communications department. With the exception of new courses and the several fresh faces in the classroom where she taught, everything was becoming routine. And as a professional student with a few dollars from her teaching stipend securely deposited in her first checking account, along with new responsibilities and new friends that mostly lived within the confines of the now familiar campus, Abby slept soundly. That usually peaceful rest was disrupted during the course of one uncommonly warm night in early January.

It's...it's...it's you! You're a young man she thought to the thirty-something who stood in front of her as if he had been there, somewhere, in the darkness all along. Yes, it happens he responded wordlessly. She thought, it does? Yes, more often than anyone knows. The answer Abby is so simple. The answer? The answer to what? So simple and you already know it. You just have to realize that you already know it. Suddenly, the man left as mysteriously as he had appeared.

Abby's eyes popped open. They stared at the nondescript, pale white ceiling of her dorm room. It had been a long time, and the experience reminded her not only of her former professor but of her mother as well. Oh how she missed them both! Along with the odd, dreamlike experience came a flood of memories—a barrage of wonderfully vivid yet achingly painful snapshots—and a torrent of tears.

The Press Conference

1

It began at exactly 12:10 p.m. Eastern Time on a sunny Wednesday, the twenty-third day of January. The feed from the small MIT pressroom was carried live to all major news networks as well as to the smaller regional outlets. The timing of the event was the idea of the MIT publicity director who had been frantically fielding phone calls and email inquiries since the embargo on the *Nature* paper was lifted, not more than twelve hours ago. She wanted to make sure that west coast viewers were able to receive the press conference live, during normal business hours.

The bulky television cameras operated by overweight cameramen, invited guests, and a small group of local reporters filled the windowless room outfitted with crystal clear acoustics and versatile, adjustable lighting. Four paper name tents were evenly spaced on the small rectangular table loaded with microphones; they read: Dr. Huntington, Dr. Kianamann, Dr. Sukawa, and Dr. Ito. The backdrop that hung tightly on the wall behind the table was a sharply arranged photographic mural of key MIT discoveries made over its storied 150 year history, along the familiar logos of companies launched from those that walked the hallowed halls of the Cambridge, Massachusetts center of academic and entrepreneurial excellence. The mural's visual message was clear. Discoveries made at MIT translate into products you use every day, made by companies you readily recognize.

The press conference was opened by a distinguished looking, silver-haired statesman named Dr. Malcolm Huntington, the President of MIT.

"Good afternoon. I'd like to welcome you to witness today's spectacular announcement from our research community. Here at MIT we strive to create an atmosphere of innovation and collaboration, and today's announcement is a testament to the virtues of these endeavors. I'd like to turn the microphone over to Dr. Jane Kianamann, MIT's Provost for Research, who will provide background and context to the discovery; she will also introduce the principal investigators. Dr. Kianamann?"

The tall, thin South African native appeared much younger than her actual age of fifty-five. Small frameless round glasses were almost invisible against her smooth, pale, thin face adorned by brown short-cropped hair. She approached the podium with an air of superiority that was all but confirmed by her proper British accent.

"Thank you, President Huntington," she began. "Each and every day, here in Cambridge, throughout the Commonwealth, across the United States and indeed around the entire world, scientists unearth new knowledge. New information that, in one way or another, be it overt or subtle, affects your daily lives. Scientists persevere through years, indeed decades of failure to arrive at a single moment of discovery. Our brief history as a species is replete with discoveries and understandings that have altered the trajectory of our existence—the geocentric model of our universe, gravity, magnetism, microscopy and the structure of cells, vaccines, penicillin, evolution, quantum mechanics, the theory of relativity, nuclear fission, DNA, transistors, the Higgs boson, and proof of universe inflation are some ready examples. However, what separates the discoveries detailed in the *Neurogenic Transformations at the Moment of Death*, from all others is that it brings us to the edge of what can only be described as the true last frontier. What unfolds at the moment of our death, what we choose to believe, what we choose to accept, what we choose to dismiss, has occupied our imagination for millennia. These beliefs have been the foundation for entire civilizations and cultures, rituals, traditions, all in the absence of a real understanding of what actually occurs at this defining moment of our lives. And now, with the discovery that the majority of our genetic makeup and most of our vast brainpower is held in reserve for this defining moment, we are poised to cross this last decisive threshold. Ultimately this research will serve, as Dr. Dante Paolo, a co-investigator stated in an article published posthumously this week in *The Atlantic*, 'to reconcile what was once thought to be irreconcilable—that is, nothing less than our place in the universe.' We are pleased to have the lead authors of the study with us today, both with MIT ties. Dr. Jin Sukawa, MIT Professor Emeritus in the Integrative Biology Department, and Dr. Jainbin Ito, a pioneer in DNA sequencing technology who received a Ph.D. from MIT and is now the Chief Innovation and Technology Officer at Codex. Let's start the questioning with you, Carolyn."

Carolyn Jacobson, the senior science correspondent for the AP bureau in Boston, was seated in the front row in clear view of Dr. Kianamann, her longtime friend. The portly, middle-aged brunette had a sound reputation for publishing complete and accurate biomedical research news articles. Rumors that her first draft was not a draft at all but a polished, error- free composition that was readily comprehensible to the layperson and expert alike, were true.

"This paper began with a hypothesis born from an idea. Which one of you had the original idea, the key insight that launched this research?" Carolyn asked.

The two professors looked at each other momentarily until one nodded, a signal that yielded the question to the other.

"Neither one of us," replied Dr. Sukawa indifferently. The response drew a few muffled snickers from the audience. "The initial idea and hypothesis were developed by Dr. Dante Paolo, along with the student co-authors of the paper, Ms. Abigail Lark, Ms. Amy Ito, Mr. Brad MacIntyre, and Mr. Phillip Hess."

"For the record doctors, neither of you initially conceived this research?"

"As you know Ms. Jacobson," Dr. Sukawa responded, "my research career has focused on the many facets of human neural pathway development. One of my longstanding interests has been to map areas of the brain associated with various processes, so when members of Dr. Paolo's class asked for some assistance with a project they were conducting at Wilmington College related to telepathy, I was more than happy to assist. Telepathy was not a topic I had considered studying, but one that had interested me for quite some time."

The AP reporter's third rapid-fire follow up question was her last. "So did you have anything to do with the initial telepathy mapping experiments or the moment of death experiment?"

"No. Dr. Paolo and his students performed those experiments with assistance from Dr. Robert Wyle, a Howard Hughes investigator in my laboratory. My direct contribution to this work was in providing the laboratory environment and the analytical software to measure brain activity. I also provided a critical analysis of all the data including those obtained with a nonhuman primate."

Dr. Kianamann called on the next reporter, a young upstart from the Boston Globe, "Paul?"

"Dr. Ito, the publication has two authors with the same last name. Any relation?" A low rumble of chuckles again echoed across the room as the question appeared to have an obvious answer. The odds were low that the two individuals were related, as there must be a thousand people surnamed Ito in just the greater Boston area alone.

"Yes, Amy is my daughter," Dr. Ito replied to a surprised audience. "She asked if I would sequence the DNA from cheek cells of individuals involved with the study. We at Codex had recently developed a new sequencing technology and we used that new technology on these samples. The samples arrived coded, that is we did not know the identity of the individuals, nor did we know the nature of the experiments. We simply purified and sequenced the DNA and annotated the data, that is, we identified the location of known genes."

"When did you know that those DNA samples were different?" was Paul's follow up question.

"Codex had been developing technology to visualize epigenetic events, modification of DNA that can occur slowly over time or suddenly due to an acute environmental exposure. A key epigenetic occurrence is the addition of methyl groups to specific sugars on the DNA molecule. This process is known to control a whole host of cellular processes including chromosome stability. In human DNA, the pattern of DNA methylation is found sporadically throughout the entire genome and that's exactly what we found for most of the samples we analyzed. But then, one human DNA sample looked like it came from a nematode worm *Caenorhabditis elegans*, or from the common yeast *Saccharomyces cerevisiae*, because the entire DNA was unmethylated. Suddenly all of the genes were active—the genetic brakes for all of these genes were off. Repeated tests confirmed this bizarre finding and it was much, much later that we learned that this one sample came from Dr. Dante Paolo; it was taken at the precise moment of his death. DNA prepared from his cells before he died showed a normal pattern of methylation. What I just described was actually the second remarkable finding. The first discovery was made when we annotated the DNA from those involved with the telepathy experiment. Suddenly, and well as you now know from the publication, an entire new set of genes was turned on in cellular DNA isolated from telepaths in a region of the genome previously thought to be quiescent."

"And expression of those genes was temporally associated with activity in the parahippocampal gyrus," added Dr. Sukawa, "a primitive region of the brain that has been well studied; we thought we knew everything that was controlled by this region. We were very surprised to find telepathy associated with PHG because it is the part of the brain that essentially makes us human. We are very excited about this unique finding."

Impatiently, a young reporter seated to the back of the room blurted the next question.

"Could someone explain how Dr. Dante Paolo was able to essentially perform a self-experiment with the neurotracer *RW88*? And did it kill him?"

The provocative and insinuating question spread quickly across the room like a wind-swept ocean fog. It instantly created a tense atmosphere but, remarkably, it was the one question that the MIT panel had been forewarned by their team of lawyers to expect. Although they all had been briefed and all were prepared to respond to this exact line of questioning, the legal team thought that if possible, Dr. Kianamann should address it, and that she should address it head on.

"I'm sorry, I did not hear your name," said Dr. Kianamann who sought to make the upstart earn his way into the ring.

"Kingston. Lee Kingston, *Rolling Stone*."

The Provost launched into the scripted reply, "Dr. Paolo was suffering from late-stage pancreatic cancer when he self-administered *RW88* obtained previously from Dr. Sukawa's laboratory. That he self-administered *RW88* was included in the publication as supplemental information in the materials and methods section available online. There is no evidence to suggest that *RW88* was lethal for Dr. Paolo. His official death certificate states that he died from cancer of the pancreas."

"But *RW88* was responsible for the death of a rhesus macaque, correct?" Lee Kingston interjected.

"Yes, that's correct," replied the Provost without hesitation. "But we know that the unfortunate event with the nonhuman primate was due to an error in dosage. It was the wrong amount on a weight basis. What is not known is the amount of tracer Dr. Paolo administered to himself. All we know is that he acted alone and with an enormous amount of bravery, I may add."

"But surely Dr. Paolo's students must have known what was happening if they recorded the events when he passed, right?" asked the persistent reporter.

Inside the Provost was ablaze with anger, but outwardly she remained steadfastly cool and poised. "At the time of Dr. Paolo's passing, the Wilmington College alumni involved with the study were indeed his students; in fact, since they had already met the requirements for their respective degrees, they would have been considered his former students. The class he taught had ended and, remarkably, the students left their own graduation ceremony to be with their friend and his wife at their moment of great need. Dr. Paolo's wife told me afterwards that the student's presence when her husband passed was an extraordinary display of affection. It was Dr. Paolo's wish that his brain activity be monitored as he passed. So while it is true that he wore a brain activity transmitting cap, no one, including Dr. Paolo's wife, the hospice care provider that had been with him throughout, nor anyone associated with the study saw the tracer or knew anything about it. No one. Is that clear? The first time that any of the investigators associated with the study learned about the use of the tracer was when they read Dr. Paolo's original draft of the manuscript, or when they reviewed his brain images after he died."

Content with her replies and before the *Rolling Stone* reporter tried to slip in another question the Provost quickly pointed to a young lady seated to the far right side of the room. "Yes? Go ahead."

"Linda Marne, *Reuters*. This question is for both investigators. I'd like for you to explain what this research means for the everyday person. How will it affect their lives?"

Since the question was directed to the study's authors, Dr. Kianamann allowed them to answer it first, but she was ready to append their answer. She was armed.

"From a geneticist's point of view," started Dr. Ito, "the iceberg is now completely exposed, we no longer only see its tip. That most of the genome is held in check until the moment when biological processes ends tells us that there is something greater in store. What events could these obscure genes encode? Is this some last ditch effort at survival? Preservation perhaps? What are we missing? What questions haven't we asked? No one saw this coming. No one predicted this finding nor can anyone presume to know its meaning. And we've now shown that this event also occurs in other animals—mice, rats, cats, dogs, rabbits, monkeys, fish—we are led to think about this challenge globally, across the entire animal kingdom. It's no longer just about us humans. Most likely it never was."

"And from a neuroscientist's view," continued Dr. Sukawa, "these data will spawn new fields of exploration unlike any mankind has before witnessed. Think about it this way. Each and every one of us performs a wide array of tasks each second of every day. Some of these assignments are hardwired, meaning we don't think about them, like the beating of our heart, or the mechanics of breathing, or the constant surveillance and protection by our immune system against harmful organisms. They just happen. Other assignments are deliberate—lifting a glass, smelling a rose, reading a book. Now consider for a moment that all activities are programmed, learned, stored, monitored, regulated and retrieved from only two percent of your brain. It would be like we only have been studying the peel but not the pulp of a pear. Now we're at the very starting line of a long journey to understand the pulp, a new voyage with an undefined destination. Just think of the possibilities."

The two learned professors were working very hard to convey the importance of the finding in a way that would be easily assimilated by the general public. And while they were somewhat successful—judged by Ms. Marne's nodding as if she clearly understood the still abstract nature of the discoveries—Dr. Kianamann had the very writing that would drive the message home.

"If I may," Dr. Kianamann said, "I'd like to read an excerpt from Dr. Paolo's *Atlantic* article as I think it will compliment the answers just given. He wrote: 'Imagine the shock and sadness of the infant who just saw a ball roll under the couch and out of sight. In her underdeveloped brain it simply vanished until one day, during a period of rapid intellectual development, without warning or drama, the evolving infant brain correctly deduced that the ball has a permanent physical presence. The infant's keen ability to bridge abstract and physical worlds is a unique aspect of her hungry mind. A bridge created without the use of spoken language, yet her mastery of object permanence is readily conveyed and appreciated by the perceptive parent. The findings in *Neurogenetic Transformations at the Moment of Death* will not cure diseases, prevent wars or disasters, nor will it make people smarter. But it will serve a single purpose—it will bring us back to reexamine the conundrum of our infant mind: Is the object truly permanent?'"

———•———

The hospital's doctor lounge was known among its privileged users as the Oasis. Furnished with a black leather couch, a coffee table, a kitchenette, a computer and a printer, it was a retreat where physicians could sit quietly to read or to have a cup of coffee without being assaulted by a nurse, a patient or worse, a member of a patient's family. The wall-mounted flat screen television, tuned to one of Boston's four local news stations, was always on, but most of the time the sound was muted.

Dr. Laura Kean had only fifteen minutes during the noontime hour to relax before her presence was expected at the monthly hospital staff meeting. So instead of the usual brisk walk to her nearby condo for lunch she opted instead for a cup of black tea at the Oasis. She sat towards the corner of the couch, picked up the remote control and scrolled through the television stations in hopes of catching the rest of the week's weather forecast, however, what she saw on the screen in place of a meteorologist made her straighten her back in attention.

The voice of the elderly Asian in the white lab coat seated behind a line of microphones was soft but audible, "... and hypothesis were developed by Dr. Dante Paolo, along with the student co-authors of the paper, Ms. Abigail Lark, Ms. Amy Ito, Mr. Brad MacIntyre, and Mr. Phillip Hess." Her mind raced to remember. Hadn't Abby told her in the Happy New Year email that the manuscript had been accepted for publication? *Yes, yes she did*, the internist thought to herself. *She said it would be published soon but did she mean soon, as in within the month, soon?* Laura tried to recall the rest of Abby's email when she heard the hard question from Lee Kingston. Her heart rate leapt and she froze in place transfixed at what was unfolding in front of her very eyes. She couldn't believe what she was witnessing—the story of her husband's premeditated death, described on live television in front of the whole world. There was Dr. Kianamann, whom she had spoken with only briefly by phone just a couple of weeks ago, handling the reporter's question so self-assuredly, so convincingly that it almost made Laura forget how the events actually occurred.

She was so spellbound by the events on the television screen that she didn't hear the door to the Oasis open.

"Laura," was the only word her colleague uttered that caused the widow to spring up from the couch visibly alarmed and bewildered. "Oh, I'm so sorry. I didn't mean to startle you," her colleague said. "Coming to the meeting?"

"Um... yes. Thanks. Go ahead, I'll be there in a few minutes," replied Laura as she stepped closer to the television screen while simultaneously blotting the spilled tea from her white lab coat with a napkin. The interruption caused her to miss the next question but she gathered from Dr. Ito's lengthy response that it had something to do with the importance of the findings. She was holding herself together quite well until the Provost began quoting from her husband's eloquent and thought-provoking magazine article.

His spoken words were the emotional tripwire.

As Dr. Kianamann brought the give and take to a close on the wall-mounted television, Laura backed herself into the folds of the couch at the Oasis where she wept alone into her moist hands. The gains she'd made over the past eight months to move beyond the death of her husband were unraveled by a 15-minute televised news conference.

2

Bradford MacIntyre didn't check his email that morning until he was sitting in the classroom in the Medical Education Building at Harvard Medical School where the Human Anatomy tutorial would start promptly at 10:30. The second message that had arrived that morning was from Robert Wyle and it was also addressed to Amy, Phil and Abby. The email read:

> Hey,
> Dr. Sukawa wanted me to drop you a line to let you know that there will be a press conference here today around noon to announce our paper. Dr. Ito is in town and he'll also be there. Hang on to your hats gems and gents; the knockers will be knocking hard once they hear this. I recommend deferring questions to the big guys here at MIT.
> Later,
> Bob

Brad grabbed his phone, swiped it on, tapped in the required four-digit passcode and switched off the mute button. That's when he saw that the others had been texting for three hours already. The most recent one from Phil screamed: BRAD! WAKE THE FUCK UP! After glancing at the string of messages exchanged between Amy, Abby and Phil, Brad typed:

> I'm here, late night. Holy cow is right. In HA tutorial till 12
> then I'll watch. Good advice from Bob

Amy Ito was not sitting in Human Anatomy tutorial, nor would she be attending the Medical Biochemistry, Medical Embryology, Human Genetics classes that were scheduled for that day. The entire campus of the University of Minnesota was closed due to a ferocious blizzard unlike any she'd experience during her prior four years in Massachusetts. Duluth had already received 10 inches of snow with another foot expected before the winds arrived. By the next morning, when classes would resume at nine, the air temperature would be 20 degrees below zero with a wind chill that seemed better suited for those living in the Artic.

Wrapped in a down comforter on the sofa in the shared common area of the three-person graduate suite, Amy was relieved to see Brad's text. She missed him terribly. She could not comprehend what it would be like to be so far away from the person you love without modern electronics to help bridge the divide. While it was no substitute for the real thing, their before-sleep video love sessions were full of steamy visuals and endless tease. Amy already knew that last night was a late one for Brad and she also knew that he would not complain about it. Just weeks after they started their online erotic sessions as a part of their New Year's resolution to make love long distance—one resolution they would definitely keep—Amy had become extremely comfortable in front of the laptop's tiny camera. Her strip tease was so erotic, so sensual, so smooth in low light that at times she'd barely touch the top of her red lace thong before Brad, who was fourteen hundred straight miles away, erupted. But on this morning, at the start of a blinding snowstorm, Amy yearned for more than soft sounds and visuals. She planned to watch the press conference live online on a Boston news site, and she also wanted to stay connected to the others via text. She was glad her dad was able to be at MIT for the press release. She had never seen him on television before, but she was confident that he would know how to handle the glare of the bright lights.

———•———

Staring out at New York's gray January skies Phil Hess thought, *Algebraic Number Theory itself isn't boring, it's the person trying to teach it who is.* He did quite well for himself during the first semester at Rensselaer Polytechnic Institute, a respectable 3.7 GPA. "Drink beer and study. What the fuck else is there to do in Troy?" he lamented to Abby more than once. But with the press conference due to begin in less than thirty minutes, Phil left the Algebraic Number Theory class, grabbed a meatball grinder at

Sammy's lunch truck, then settled into the best room in the library to be by himself, and the entire World Wide Web. Surely he would be able to patch directly into the video feed from MIT. From his phone he texted: Abby, let me know if you need help finding the MIT link. I found it easily.

There was no instant reply from his close friend.

There was no two ways about it. Abigail Lark loved American University. She loved graduate life. She enjoyed her professors, her peers, the staff and the entire structure of the doctorate program in Advanced Communications, and she especially enjoyed the responsibility of being a teaching assistant to the Introduction to Communications course. By all accounts, American University and the metro D.C. area loved her back. She felt safe in the suburb, in the classrooms, and in her dorm room. Once she told Phil that she was undergoing a metamorphosis, becoming a new person, to which he replied, "I wish you were metamorphosing right here in my bedroom. I'd cocoon with you any day."

She was in Spaulding 122, the office shared with three other graduate students reviewing an assignment when Phil's text message arrived. She responded: Thanks. Let you know if I have trouble. Logging onto MIT now.

A flurry of text messages ricocheted between the former Wilmington College classmates during the MIT news conference.

> PH: Holy shit. Get a load of this coverage
> BM: No kidding!
> AL: Anyone read the Atlantic article?
> PH: Didn't know about it
> AI: Me neither
> PH: Just found it @Atlantic online
> PH: Downloading it
> BM: Please send

PH: K

AI: Dr. Kia, laying it out nicely. Hi Dad!

BM: Gotta love Dr. S

PH: Hey! We're famous!

PH: Ajay no about this? He's right there @MIT

AL: Haven't heard a word from him

AL: The Ito connection made!

AI: Odds were high, right?

BM: Didn't know about nematode and yeast.

AL: Me neither, cool

PH: Is Stones fucker a conspiracy theorist?

AI: Oops did anyone tell Laura about publication?

AL: I did by email a couple of weeks ago. Man this stuff is personal

BM: Love the iceberg analogy

AI: Me 2

AI: Excellent Dr. K. Dr. Paolo has last word

PH: Ha!

AL: Gotta run. Stay in touch

BM: Me 2 Later

PH: Ciao

AI: K-SIT

————•————

Still he had no regrets.

In the month since he left the United States, a life that began as a neuroscientist turned academic leader at Rockefeller University, then as a Dean at Wilmington College in New England, Lorenzo Benedetti, the world renowned *Professore* Benedetti, was more than ready to return to his Tuscan childhood home and to an unnecessary, but appreciated, small town hero's welcome. The unusually mild winter was matched by his dear cousin Rosa's warm, loving embrace, punctuated with tears of joy because he would leave her no more. The view from their portico was spectacular; a magnificent vista of rolling hills each harboring a village or two carved out of the mountainside with solid homes made of stone walls that supported red clay-tiled roofs. Tradition, folktales, and aging power lines connected independent villages to each other. They were also linked to the rest of the globe with new satellite relay towers that carried the latest Internet service to anyone who could afford the small access fee.

Lorenzo rose slowly as not to disturb the warmth trapped by the blankets on the bed he shared with Rosa. He loved her love, but he also enjoyed the solitude of the early morning. Although it wasn't necessary, he lit the small cast iron woodstove in the kitchen to add new warmth to the spacious living room before the gas furnace turned on once again. There, with a cup of hot black coffee and the first dim rays of sunlight, amid the crackling sounds of the burning wood, Lorenzo was content to learn, at a leisurely pace, what had transpired in the world while he slept. He opened his laptop and launched the browser that revealed headlines from *Ansa*, the online Italian newspaper that he read daily in an effort to relearn the subtleties of the language, and also the names of current soccer players. Listed among the articles related to the new Dengue outbreak in Kenya, and the small tsunami that struck the northern coast of Australia was a short article from Reuters about a press conference held the previous day at MIT in the United States. Lorenzo's 70-year-old eyes skimmed the article for familiar names. Listed were Dr. Sukawa and Dr. Ito as well as the now familiar and, in his opinion, overly verbose title of the *Nature* publication. *Surely*, he thought, *somewhere during the press conference my efforts must have been acknowledged.*

He went directly to the MIT website and easily located the entire length of the prior day's new conference. Also available were post-conference interviews with MIT's President Huntington and Provost Kianamann. Outside, another Tuscan dawn exploded with streaks of orange and red over the eastern horizon that foretold of another beautiful day in the mountains. Inside, Lorenzo listened intently to the video recordings. He focused not on the strange series of questions posed by reporters but on details of the answers provided by the two professors. He too had often wondered if *RW88* had caused Dante Paolo's death but routinely dismissed the notion given the late stage diagnosis of pancreatic cancer that plagued the former Harvard Medical School and Wilmington College professor. The video recording of the press conference brought back memories of his time with the researcher-professor, not all of which were pleasant.

He recalled the first time he met Dante Paolo. It was in his Dean's office at Wilmington College where the recently retired Harvard biochemist interviewed for an unadvertised teaching position. Jean Holliday, the College's president, also attended the meeting. "She liked him immediately," Lorenzo said aloud as he placed a piece of chestnut wood in the stove. "I didn't."

Staring out the window at the now brightened morning sky he recalled how he disapproved of the proposed senior-level course, *Teach the Professor*. How the course attracted only a handful of students but, against his advice, was allowed to continue under the guise that it would test a new teaching method. He recalled the research talks presented at the end of the year by Dr. Paolo's students and his outrage that the telepathy experiment was performed without written consent nor human subject approval, a clear violation of federal regulations but one that garnered no reprimand whatsoever. And then he recalled the odd sense of pleasure he enjoyed upon hearing that Dr. Paolo had cancer, and only a short time to live.

His marginally high blood pressure rose further making him feel flush and his palms became moist as he recalled the moment that was the beginning of his undoing. He lapsed into a trance as his memory replayed the events that transpired after the death of Dante Paolo beginning with the brown envelope and the letter.

"*Buon giorno Lorenzo mio*," said Rosa whose presence severed the memory-induced trance. Rosa Benedetti was a healthy, stout woman with plain soft features. Her old eyes were sad but true and as sharp as those of a young falcon; her demeanor was gentle yet firm. She was one of those persons who made everyone feel welcomed while dismissing outright, and often openly, those she distrusted for one reason or another. Unlike her famous cousin who travelled extensively, Rosa never left the mountain village for any durable length of time. A weekend in Rome with her elderly parents had fulfilled the one and only request she made of them. And other than short distance forays to Lucca to celebrate a festival or to attend a wedding, her world was contained within a five-mile radius of where she now stood. The old woodlands comprised mostly of chestnut, elm and hickory trees were her world.

She adored her cousin Lorenzo who was five years her elder. That neither of them had siblings did not matter because they had each other. They were constantly together as children right up to the day that Lorenzo left for Bologna to attend college followed immediately by what Rosa would say was a "painfully long stay in America." Bologna was one thing, but leaving Italy would have crushed Rosa completely had it not been for Lorenzo's promise of weekly letters.

Their correspondences became an obsession, a religion, with them. As it turned out, documenting their weekly lives served as a form of therapy for each of them; personal and intimate written accounts of their lives that spanned five decades. Letters to Rosa described life in New York City at Rockefeller University, of his steady rise as a world-leading neuroscientist, then later as Dean both in New York and in Massachusetts. His letters read like grand adventure novellas to Rosa. She lived the world vicariously through him, and in turn she, oddly enough, became his long distance confidant and the one person he trusted with his most private thoughts. Later in life, after he'd left the Rockefeller and moved to Wilmington College in Massachusetts at the behest of his longtime female companion, was when he realized that he never intended to settle down with anyone in America. His deep-rooted devotion to Rosa stemmed from the fact that she never left their childhood village; she was his anchor and his foundation. Her Italian words and stories of the simple events in the villages became his escape from the ugly realities of his so-called 'real world'—a cherished lifeline back to simple, stress free times.

With refreshed memories evoked from the MIT press releases, Lorenzo wondered if he should share the one secret he steadfastly withheld from Rosa. Given her deep-rooted religious beliefs he knew that her cheery morning greeting would rapidly deteriorate if he revealed the secret; his hidden horror would haunt her exhaustively. If she knew what had happened to him during those last few months at Wilmington College she would never again see him as she now did. She would fear him forever. And then, after a day or so of contemplation, she would conclude that he was possessed by *il diavolo*, the devil, then she'd fear for her very life.

"*Ciao bella*," he replied as he stood, smiled and slipped his moist hands under the back of her nightshirt where they found the soft folds of skin by the small of her scapulae. She drew towards him and placed her head on his chest, and there they stood for a full moment in a morning embrace that had become a part of their daily routine. In the past she cried when he left for Bologna, when he left for America, and when he left after each visit. She had lived with, cared for, and then buried his mother and father and her parents as well. Rosa tended to the house and to the animals and she walked alone in the woods while patiently waiting decade after long decade for Lorenzo's permanent return. She lived each day for this time in her life; this time right here, right now, in his arms.

If Rosa heard Lorenzo's heart beating faster than usual, she didn't mention it.

3

Dr. Franz Albracht shunned technology whenever possible. He enjoyed the sounds of his bustling Munich rather then placing little speakers in his ears, he preferred to walk to his office at Ludwig Maximilian University instead of taking the subway, and he desired to read the daily news from a paper rather than to see it on a shiny screen. It was in his relatively small and plain office where the 78-year-old current Secretary General of the Nobel Committee unfurled the morning edition of *SZ* and read the press release from Cambridge, Massachusetts. He glanced at his watch, it was 9:02 a.m., too early to phone so, reluctantly, he opened his tiny laptop and composed an email to his colleague at Johns Hopkins University.

The message to Richard Johnson, the newly minted Nobel laureate in Medicine and Physiology was pointed: MIT press release. Call LMU.

The formal dinner at MIT's Faculty Club was a private, intimate affair. Only three were invited at the request of Dr. Kianamann.

"Gentleman, I think it all went quite well today," she said to her guests. "Other than the *Stones* reporter who was annoying, but manageable, I think the others were actually quite helpful."

"I concur," replied Dr. Sukawa who raised his glass of red wine in the direction of the Provost. "And I think that the post-conference interviews were an effective way to expand the message in an informal way."

"I'm still quite impressed that Dante Paolo had the forethought to write the article for *The Atlantic*. Not only did he accurately predict the results and interpretations of the final set of data, but he also anticipated the public's interest and skepticism. "To professor Paolo," Dr. Ito said as he raised his glass before continuing. "I spoke with Amy just an hour ago. She said that the conference was very exciting for her and her college friends, and that the University of Minnesota PR department has already contacted her for an interview."

"Did any of you know Dr. Paolo?" asked Dr. Kianamann.

The question transported Dr. Bob Wyle back to the last time he saw Dante Paolo in person. It was the day his daughter Erica was born, a cold and snowy Saturday almost one year ago. The Howard Hughes researcher in Dr. Sukawa's MIT lab took a chance that morning and met Dr. Paolo and the students in Cambridge. On that morning his wife was in early stages of true labor, but since she had slept well through the night and also because her sister had arrived in anticipation of the big event, Bob didn't see the need to stay home. He heard about that poor decision later when he met his wife and sister-in-law in the delivery room just in time to witness his daughter's birth. Although she never bought it, he goodheartedly told his wife that her delivery was short because her anger towards him translated into powerful pushes, like a boxer unleashing his fury on a sworn enemy.

"Yes, I did. I met him," replied Bob. "Well, sort of. He came by the lab a couple of times."

"And was he the type of person who touted his intellect? Wore it on his sleeve for all to see?"

"No, not at all; in fact, just the opposite. He was unassuming and curious. And he must have known that he had cancer when he took *RW88* from the lab."

"I agree. He was quite unassuming. Not Ivy League at all," added Dr. Sukawa.

"I did not meet him directly but Amy spoke very highly of him. She told me that he was an inspirational teacher; he molded her scientific mind," said Dr. Ito. "It's really too bad that he isn't here to see the outcome of his profound insights."

"Which brings me to the next topic, gentlemen. Now that the lights and cameras are gone, what is the big advance that will come out of this research? I'm not asking about the nickel and dime stuff, I'm looking for the big prize. What will it be?" Dr. Kianamann asked her guests.

The two elder scientists knew that the question was loaded. They also were well aware that speculation led to trapdoors more often than it did to golden staircases, and while they were interested in marshaling research endeavors forward, they were not keen to voice wild theories.

After a full moment of heavy silence Bob Wyle, who was staring at his wineglass, looked at Dr. Sukawa, then to the Provost and said, "Access."

"Pardon me?" asked Dr. Kianamann quickly as if she didn't hear him.

"Access. Communication. Intelligence. It may sound like science fiction but it's highly likely that we now have the blueprint to understand how to access those..." he trailed off before continuing in a slower, more deliberate voice. "To communicate with those that are not here physically; how to access the proverbial 'other side'. And nothing but pure intelligence will result. It will be the ultimate discovery. Other than revealing a true understanding of what happens when we die, when our heart stops, this research is the very key to our past, and more importantly, to our future. There is no doubt that most of our DNA and brain power is dedicated to..."

Dr. Wyle stopped as soon as he heard the door to their private dining room open. A trio of waiters had arrived with the main course, and with more wine. Once the servers left the room, Dr. Kianamann nodded to Bob to continue. "Most of our DNA and brain is dedicated to... to interacting with the other side, with others that have gone before us."

"Communicating with the dead? Is that what you mean?" asked Dr. Kianamann with a whiff of arrogance before turning to the other scientists. "Are you buying any of this?"

Dr. Ito recalled his earlier statements and rarely did he retract or mix messages. "As I said earlier today, no one saw this coming, it wasn't predicted and it's a stretch to instantly understand its meaning. I mentioned survival and preservation, but of what and why I simply don't know. We'll have to take the methodical approach and move cautiously step by step down this path to find out."

"Preservation, some sort of SOS survival mechanism, access to other worlds, I think everything is on the table. These discoveries will occupy the thinking of scientists for generations. It's very likely that none of us will be around to see the full answer. This will take time," added Dr. Sukawa.

"I don't have a generation of time. Knowledge is power and if there is new and potentially powerful information here I want to see it. MIT started this work, now lets finish it. I'm making one million dollars available immediately to initiate work in this area. The monies will be discussed with no one, but if someone asks, it will be deemed a gift to Dr. Sukawa's lab from an anonymous donor. Bob, if you are committed to this project, I will relocate the other laboratory on 6-2 so you could expand. There will be more money where the million came from provided you show me plans and data. This is my doing and my doing only. Huntington knows nothing. Dr. Ito, we can keep you on board as a consultant unless you can think of a way to keep you more directly involved, a way that would be acceptable to Codex. If so, please let me know. I sense that there is something big here and I don't mean just chatting with ghosts. I'm counting on all of you to figure it out," proclaimed the stern, outwardly determined Provost.

———•———

Richard Johnson's daily routine was as rigidly structured as a Catholic mass. He rose no later than five o'clock, urinated, brushed his teeth, dressed in sweats or shorts depending on the season, then he would go for a brisk 20-minute walk without accessories. He used this sacred time to plan the rest of the day or to mentally review his often packed schedule. After the walk, he showered then ate a cup of oatmeal with one cup of black tea for breakfast while still in his white cotton bathrobe. He dressed in plain white Oxford button down shirts with black trousers and comfortable black leather shoes. Like Einstein, he wore the same outfit every day as to not waste time contemplating attire. By six he logged onto his laptop to review the headlines of the *New York Times, The Baltimore Sun, The Washington Post,* and *The Wall Street Journal.* He glanced at the RSS feeds from the top science journals before checking both his work and personal email inboxes. As time allowed, he would respond to one or two personal emails before leaving the house promptly at 6:45 a.m. for another brisk two-mile walk to his office in the Medical Research Building on the West Campus of Johns Hopkins University. Each weekday, and many Saturdays as well, Dr. Johnson was in his office and seated at his desk by 7:30 a.m. with another cup of black tea in hand. The five technicians and five postdoctoral fellows who worked in his laboratory duly noted his efficient manners. If a meeting with Dr. Johnson was scheduled for 9:00 a.m., it started exactly at 9:00 a.m., no sooner nor later. Folklore in the lab told of Dr. Johnson's impulsive rage when someone arrived late to a meeting, a tale that made everyone without an excused absence arrive at least ten minutes ahead of schedule for a meeting with their boss, just to make sure they didn't trigger another tirade.

By this Thursday morning, Dr. Richard Johnson had read not only the original *Nature* paper and the *Atlantic* article by Dr. Dante Paolo, but he had also watched the MIT press conference online, and he had read several news reports on the discovery.

He was well informed by the time he read the pointed email from Munich—that had arrived exactly as expected. He then dialed the long string of numbers that connected him to the small office in Germany.

"Franz? Richard. How are things at LMU?"

"Forget LMU," replied Dr. Albracht gruffly.

The old neurologist had all Thursday morning and a part of the early afternoon to remember when he first read the article weeks ago, before it was published, before the whole world knew. And it all started with his wife who found the unmarked envelope that held the small SD card snug in it's little plastic container. The envelope was tucked deep in the inside pocket of his tuxedo jacket that had been tossed on the downstairs sofa in the early morning hours after the Nobel Prize Gala Dinner. The jacket, along with the pants and white shirt, was destined for the dry cleaners, and had it not been for his careful wife, the envelope from Dr. Lorenzo Benedetti would most likely have been discarded or irreparably damaged. Instead the tiny computer disk along with a few paper business cards from individuals he had met that evening was saved and placed appropriately on the black writing mat of the antique cherry roll top desk where she was sure her husband would find it. He recalled slipping the thin wafer-like disk into the only slit opening on his laptop where it fit to find that the little plastic piece contained two document files. One file, labeled *'primo'*, was a short note from Lorenzo that described the soon-to-be-published manuscript. Of the eight typed sentences, only the last one was of interest:

> In light of your lifelong research interests, and due to your esteemed position at the Nobel, I thought to present this manuscript to you not only for personal, but also for professional reasons.

It didn't take long for Franz to decipher the vaguely worded statement. His friend wanted to be nominated, or rather simply chosen, for next year's prize. Unbeknownst to Lorenzo Benedetti, his old German colleague had already used the unpublicized, once-in-a-lifetime privilege on a scientist; an American named Richard Johnson.

The other file, labeled '*secondo*', was the uncorrected galley proof of a manuscript. It was the near-final version of a scientific report that required one last review by the lead authors before heading to press. Only the authors, the journal editors and two outside reviewers, who were handpicked by the editors and sworn to secrecy, would have seen the manuscript. The results and interpretations contained within the pages of the report would be considered highly confidential as it contained new and original information.

"What have you done now, Lorenzo?" the Secretary General whispered aloud as he opened the not-yet-public manuscript.

As he stared at the laptop screen, it was what Dr. Albracht read, and also what he didn't read, that stunned him. Towards the inside of the antique desk, where words were trapped within the dozen small square cubbies, the old yet sharp neurologist partly-mouthed, partly-whispered the manuscript's audacious title: "*Neurogenetic Transformations at the Moment of Death.*" He then read aloud the names of the authors listed below the title: "Phillip J. Hess*, Abigail Lark*, Bradford L. MacIntyre*, Amy Ito*, Robert Wyle1, Jainbin Wu2, Jin Sukawa1,3, and Dante Paolo4."

The superscripted symbols and numbers were explained underneath the line of names. The asterisks meant that the person contributed equally to the project with the numbers indicating the academic affiliation of the author and the identity of the corresponding author. Superscript number 4 denoted that the person was deceased. And, as if the title wasn't intriguing enough, the name of his friend, the deliverer of the SD card, his esteemed colleague Lorenzo Benedetti, was nowhere to be found in the list of contributors nor was he listed anywhere else on the important title page.

What the devil? Franz thought to himself as he scrolled to the next page that contained the paper's brief account of the findings; the so-called abstract:

> From the beginning of written history, humans have been intrigued with mortality. During this same time, tools needed to explore complex molecular and chemical events have been invented, refined and perfected. Herein, we describe, through use of extended DNA sequencing technology, and a novel single cell, neuronal tracer, two distinct and potentially interrelated findings: Nonverbal communication occurs via the parahippocampal gyrus, a region previously thought to be quiescent, and the gene for this sense located at position Xp29.47 on the X-chromosome; all brain neural nets are active at the moment of death, an event concomitant with total DNA demethylation signifying transcription of every gene. Collectively, these results imply a coordinated, transformative event at the moment of death; an event that requires most, if not all, of the information encoded in our DNA, and virtually all of our brain capacity.

Dr. Albracht read the short synopsis not once, not twice, but three times before the full impact of the stunning results sunk in. He spent the rest of that sunless morning reading the still private manuscript with a keen interest in how the experiments were performed. He was especially interested in the chemical makeup of the tracer *RW88*.

"What did you think of the press release?" The Secretary General impatiently asked Dr. Johnson. "Did they give anything away? Are they thinking like us?"

"Yes, yes, and maybe," Dr. Johnson replied quickly before he went on to explain. "Yes, they are on the same track and probably further ahead because apparently they've shown the same DNA demethylation pattern in laboratory animals so once those data are released then others will have ready model systems to test anything they want. But Sukawa's tracer is the key element in all of this. By the way, do you know this guy Sukawa?"

"No, never heard of him."

"Neither have I but in any case they use the word 'preservation' which is a potential clue that perhaps, well maybe, they're thinking along the same lines we are."

"Have you started? How far behind are we? What the hell have you been doing since you left Stockholm anyway?"

The condescending tone did not sit well with the Nobel laureate but he knew better than to push back, or to let Franz get to him. After all, he owed him. Richard Johnson took great comfort in the fact that there was a high probability that he would outlive the old man; all he needed to do was to be patient.

"It's been nonstop since we left the gala. Remember you sent me to lecture at a dozen colleges around Sweden and Germany?"

"Not bad work for a cool million and a lifetime of worldwide fame."

Sensing that he needed to pull back, Dr. Johnson ended the short call on a more positive note, something he knew Franz Albracht would want to hear.

"The monies arrived last week and a special subaccount in my discretionary spending account has been set up. We're hiring and moving along as we discussed. I think I have a bright chemist hooked. I'll tell you more about him when he's signed on."

"Listen, I didn't bust my backside to get you the prize for nothing. Sick on her deathbed my mother told me 'while the doctor studies the patient dies' which reminds me to remind you that I won't live forever, but I intend to see this project through. Move your labeling technology out of infectious diseases and onto something meaningful. I'll call again soon." The old German neuroscientist hung up just to make sure that he had the last word.

As he peered outside his office window at the snow covered Freshman Quad on the sprawling campus of Johns Hopkins University, the American scientist gently placed the receiver back on the base of the phone, sat back in his leather desk chair and softly said, "Kiss my golden ass."

———•———

Rarely are two individuals instantly compatible, but that was the case when Abby first met her dissertation advisor, Dr. Alexa Goldberg. Alexa Goldberg, who wanted to be addressed solely by her cherished first name, was at 49 the youngest tenured faculty member in the entire American University system. The Professor of Advanced and Alternative Communications was a cross-disciplinary thinker, a dynamic lecturer and skilled teacher. Her specialty was in building bridges not only between people but also between various subspecialties related to the understanding of a wide range of communication disorders. Her research integrated speech pathologies with population genetics, advanced communication with multimedia-based interpretative sign language, and pathological verbal constraints with disorders of the brain, to name a few. She sought to bring together as many different ideas as possible, various technologies as required, and all types of expertise to tackle a single problem. Scientists in and outside the University wanted to collaborate with Alexa on these difficult problems—clinically-important issues that mainly affected children—not only because she was smart, but also because of her overriding optimism and enthusiasm for the discipline.

So, with no trepidation, Abby knocked on Alexa's partly opened office door the morning after the MIT press conference with an issue of *Nature* in hand.

"Published!" exclaimed Abby with a broad smile.

"What?" asked Alexa, who did not know that the research Abby had been involved with while at Wilmington College had even been cleared for publication. When the acceptance notification arrived via email from Dr. Sukawa earlier that month, Abby shared the news only with her diary. She wanted to surprise her new mentor but only when the research article was physically real, when it was in print and on paper. Today was that day. Abby had already opened the journal to the first page of the article when she handed it over to her advisor. Alexa sat in her black leather office chair and read the title, the names of the authors and the abstract before looking up at Abby.

"Cool beans Ab!" was the uniquely enthusiastic reaction that Abby would remember for the rest of her life. "This is unbelievably wonderful—a co-authored *Nature* paper as an undergraduate? This is not common Ab. No way. Actually, it's extremely rare. Like it doesn't happen. This is so supercool."

"Yeah, I lucked out. Simply lucked out," was Abby's honest reply.

"Listen I have a conference call in fifteen minutes. Are you free tonight for dinner? We'll celebrate. Just the two of us, if that's okay with you. We'll discuss your research project and this paper. It may be just the thing we'll need to raise some funds. How's six?"

"Um, great. Sure. I teach until 4:30 then I'm free. I'll swing by at six."

"Great Ab. Wow, this is great stuff. Congratulations again. See you then."

The Beltway Bistro was pricey but not as pretentious as other eateries around D.C. and although Alexa wasn't a regular, she wasn't exactly a stranger to the popular pub located within a mile east of campus either. As a single professional she loved dining out not for the sake of eating *per se*, but for the one-on-one conversations with close friends and colleagues. Rarely did she attend large dinner parties or was she seen with in a crowd, she simply sought the company of a few people, especially those that would provide stimulating intellectual discourse. On this Thursday evening the honors went to Abby Lark, her newly published graduate student who had yet to seriously start her own dissertation research.

"Care for a drink ladies?" asked the waiter with the dark complexion.

"Ab, have you ever... never mind. We'll have two Old Speckled Hens. On tap, right?" replied Alexa.

"Yes ma'am. I'll bring them right over."

"Two old what?" asked Abby.

"Old Speckled Hen. No, it's not me, at least not yet! It's a British beer. I hope you like a good draft."

"I do."

"Great. It goes well with their grilled eggplant and mozzarella panini." The waiter returned with two tall, frosty glasses filled with the British beer, set them carefully on the table as not to spill any, then took their orders.

"Cheers to you Ab on a unbelievably wonderful paper, in *Nature* no less!" Alexa said as she raised her glass.

"So tell me how that paper came to be. Who initiated the research? How did it all happen?"

For the next ten minutes Alexa listened intently to Abby's story. She told her about the older professor that joined Wilmington College and of his experimental course. She detailed Dante Paolo's teaching style, the makeup of the class, and of the many lessons learned from a simple walk in the woods. Abby told Alexa about everyone's chosen topics starting with Amy's research into the human genome and its importance in the development of personalized medicine. She described Brad's good looks and his interest in the human brain, and also of Phil's interest in quantum physics and high order mathematics. Then she described her study on telepathy and the first classroom demonstration where she easily read everyone's mind.

"Wait, wait. Hold on. Let me get this right. So you accurately read their thoughts? Right there in class? How'd you do that?"

"Easy really. I dressed up provocatively and shocked everyone. I wore a tight dress, showed cleavage, put on makeup—which I hate—strutted into class and read everyone's silent reactions. It was quite amusing actually. Their responses were instant and easy to sense. And that led to my design of an experiment where everyone participated but no one knew ahead of time what was going to happen. It was a pure blind study."

Abby described Dr. Paolo and his strong ability to send thoughts as a transmitter and how she accurately captured them as an able receiver. She described how they—the professor transmitter and student receiver—were in prefect harmony during the first experiment and also during the second experiment that was performed with special wireless brain scanning caps developed at MIT. She did the best she could in describing the findings of the DNA samples taken when they did the telepathy experiments, and how Amy's father worked at Codex and sequenced the samples for free. The only person she omitted from the story was Dr. Benedetti. The lapse was unintentional. There was no way Abby could forget what transpired the last time she saw the former Dean, when the entire group met in the library to discuss the manuscript. Perhaps Abby subconsciously repressed the dramatic effects of her unleashed rage.

It wasn't until they were served a frozen concoction called 'the kitchen sink', an overly generous combination of six different flavors of homemade ice cream over a warmed fudge brownie topped with whipped cream, walnuts, and molten butterscotch, that Abby told her mentor about Dr. Paolo's encompassing hypothesis. She described how it brought together the unusual facts about DNA, as described by Amy, about the brain, mentioned by Brad, and the wild world of quantum physics, as described by Phil.

"Dr. Paolo also integrated my telepathy into his hypothesis. Once he put it all together, he knew he was right," Abby said. "It was like he had an epiphany or something. He wrote the first draft of the manuscript and the insightful article for *The Atlantic* too, all while dying of pancreatic cancer. At the very end, Dr. Paolo performed his last experiment on himself, the one with *RW88*."

"That is an unbelievable story Ab..." Alexa started to say, but she then stopped after she realized that Abby's face had suddenly turn focused and pensive.

Abby stared at the remaining fluid at the bottom of the beer glass and said, "We all went to his house just as he had asked. We didn't know about the tracer and..." her voice trailed off. "And when he died..." Abby again stopped speaking and became even more separated from the moment.

She had just made a connection. Abby just made a link to the dream she had just a few weeks ago. Was it really a dream? The dream with the young man came back to her like a jolt from a thunderclap that exploded directly overhead.

"Ab, what is it?" pleaded Alexa.

"He said. He said that I already know."

"Know what?"

"The answer."

"The answer to what Ab? To what?"

"To how it all works. He said that it was simple too."

"Who said what Ab? Who said that the answer was simple?"

Abby hesitated for what seemed like an eternity to Alexa who appeared to be unsure if there would ever be a response.

"Dr. Paolo," Abby said, her voice reawakened. "I remember now. He told me that the answer was simple." And with an uncanny level of certainty Abby looked across the table at her mentor and stated, "Alexa, I know the studies that need to be done."

Directions

It was no longer business as usual for Dr. Bob Wyle after the private dinner with the Provost. In fact, events unfolded so quickly for the Howard Hughes investigator that he often thought that they were too good to be true. For starters, he was promoted to Associate Scientist, an event that rarely occurred at MIT. Now he was junior faculty and no longer under the direct supervision of Dr. Jin Sukawa. The promotion paved the way for MIT to dedicate laboratory space to their new faculty member, and although he didn't have a say as to where it would be located, the specialized space was ideally situated on the second floor of Building 6, right next to Dr. Sukawa's lab; just as the Provost had demanded. Money was no longer an issue, it just appeared in a special account for him to spend as necessary.

Bob couldn't believe his good fortune. He had the support of the university's Provost, a sizzling hot topic to explore, and a world-renown mentor who doubled as a collaborator right next door. His future at the world-class institution was secure and to top it off he didn't have to teach for two full years. When the news of Bob Wyle's promotion reached the folks at the Howard Hughes Institute, it confirmed that they had backed the right horse; the prestige of the Maryland-based institution would be elevated along with their new rock star. By early April, when snow was becoming a distant memory to those who lived in Cambridge, Massachusetts, Bob looked around his new office and spacious laboratory and thought that he'd died and gone to research heaven. But even heaven has its share of problems and it wasn't long before the first one walked in through the door of his freshly cluttered office.

———◆———

Their young relationship was held together by fiber optic tethers, but only barely. Both Amy and Brad knew that the long distance that separated them would challenge their commitment to each other. Along with the warmer winds of spring and the pressures that accompanied the end of their first year of medical school came concerns that their once infallible bond was beginning to weaken. With each video chat, the upcoming summer months that they had hoped to spend together was also becoming increasingly fragmented. Brad's excitement over landing a job as a summer intern in the laboratory of a Harvard neurosurgeon did not sit well with Amy. While she loved the University of Minnesota's campus, its professors and its international blend of students, she desperately wanted out of the university town often referred to as "dull-ooth."

But Amy needed to do something meaningful over the summer. Wasting time was not in her blood. She needed to make the most of long breaks if she was going to maintain a competitive edge and it seemed like her best options were right where she was in Minnesota, even if the town did not have the allure of Boston. Going home to her parents in California was a consideration, although not her first choice, and going to Boston to wait for Brad to come home from work each day would simply not suffice. However, what Amy was about to learn was that sometimes, albeit rarely, serendipity has a way of solving dilemmas.

The solution to Amy's dilemma appeared on her laptop's screen, in an email from Abby that was also sent to Brad and Phil:

Hey everyone, check out what Ajay's been up to.

Below Abby's single sentence was a forwarded email from Ajay Adani:

Hello Abby,

I apologize for not having written to you sooner but I have been buried under a tremendous workload. Your paper with Dr. Paolo was a big hit on campus. It was front-page story of the MIT student newspaper and there is plenty of stuff on the MIT website too. Let me know if you need the links but I assume that by this time you have seen everything. Thank you for telling me before the publication that I was listed in the acknowledgments; even that wasn't necessary but it was very cool. It was my mistake to drop Paolo's course in the first place. I should have listened to you and stayed. Anyway, classes are fine and challenging, but I'm not really happy with my current mentor. He's never around and I need a project to break the classroom routine. I'm thinking of visiting Bob Wyle over in Building 6. Maybe he has some suggestions. Do you think he'll remember me? I hope you are doing well and let the others know that I said hello to them too.

The email from MIT was signed "aj".

Amy wasted no time. Her email to Bob Wyle was pointed:

Dear Bob,

I plan to spend the summer in Boston and I'd like to work in your lab on the research Dr. Paolo started. Let me know if this is possible. I'm into genetics and I'd like to know if telepathy is an inheritable trait. I have some ideas. I hope you, your wife and baby Erica are well.

All the best,

Amy Ito

She thought to end the email with a personal touch in an effort to take the edge off the direct request for a summer job.

———•———

"Aaa...Bob?" The young man's broken dictation had become such an everyday occurrence that Bob Wyle no longer recognized it as such.

Jo Jung-Zoo had been in the department's graduate program for about two years although Bob had actually lost track of the thin Korean's academic progress. Jo was as constant a presence in the laboratory as a glass beaker—a true lab rat. He was there every day and most evenings until midnight. Weekends and holidays meant nothing to the industrious student who, at a young age, was a standout among exceptionally gifted and highly competitive peers in South Korea's most southern school district. As a budding molecular chemist, he had become a valuable part of Dr. Sukawa's laboratory, but Jo joined Bob's new laboratory from the start. Jo worked closely with Bob Wyle in the refinement of the now famous neurotracer *RW88* as well as with the latest, and less toxic, formulation called *RW96*.

"Yeah, what's up?" Bob asked without even looking up from the manuscript he was editing.

"Soon I leaving MIT. In two months I must leave MIT and go work with Richard Johnson at John Opkins. He called me and offered me job at John Opkins."

"What? Are you talking about Richard Johnson, the Nobel laureate?"

Jo nodded quickly, once.

Bob did not know Richard Johnson personally although he had heard the entrepreneurial scientist deliver the plenary talk at a national scientific meeting not long ago. He read Johnson's publications not for the infectious disease aspects *per se*, but more to understand the details of his new labeling technology. Jo's decision to leave felt to Bob like a solid punch to the gut not only because he was a good and careful chemist, but also because he had spent quite a bit of time nurturing Jo's scientific ways and as such he was counting on the smart Korean to anchor the chemistry part of his research. Bob also knew that as an academic, who needed to uphold the freedoms inherent to academia, he had no say in Jo's decision. He could try to change Jo's mind but life at an academic institution meant that talented individuals come and go as regularly as undrafted rookies in NFL training camps.

Upon learning of Jo's recruitment by Richard Johnson from a distraught Bob Wyle, Dr. Sukawa quietly suspected that there was more to the story. Indeed, Dr. Sukawa was surprised to learn that the Nobel laureate who had made his mark in the world of infectious diseases was the same Richard Johnson that had presented the good, but not remarkable, seminar in Boston so many years ago. He recalled having heard the young upstart Johns Hopkins neuroscientist present his latest research findings at the meeting, but then he didn't hear of him again. He did not attend scientific gatherings nor did he publish extensively as was expected. It was as if he went underground to work secretly. Dr. Sukawa's apprehension about the targeted recruitment of Jo Jung-Zoo was heightened when he learned that the postdoc had received a direct recruitment call from Richard Johnson. The customary permission seeking and competence vetting practiced among academicians was suspiciously and audaciously circumvented.

For Jo Jung-Zoo, the opportunity was a golden one. For Jin Sukawa, and more so for Bob Wyle, Jo's departure was a disappointment, a true setback. For Dr. Richard Johnson, it was a clever and cunning coup.

Jo's unforeseen announcement derailed Bob's ability to focus on the manuscript. He now needed to think about hiring and training someone to fill Jo's position and he had to do it quickly. The transfer of techniques from one person to another was important for continuity and productivity in any research laboratory, but especially so for one like Bob's that was not yet fully established. What he needed was to get out of his office to clear his mind. A walk on the footpath of the Memorial Drive side of the Charles River was in order, but as soon as he stepped out of Building 6 and onto Milky Way, a relatively short, dark-skinned young man who looked vaguely familiar met Bob.

"Bob? Aren't you Bob Wyle?"

"Um, yeah. Who are you?"

"My name is Ajay Adani and I don't want to make the same mistake twice."

"What?"

"I helped Dr. Paolo and Abby and the others do some computer work for the *Nature* paper; I am in the acknowledgements. I am a student here at MIT and now I need to choose an advisor as I am almost done with the core requirements and I need to start my research project very, very soon in order..."

"Whoa, time out. Slow down. Right. I remember you from some meetings. Come on, I need to walk. Follow me."

Ajay spent most of the half-hour walk recounting how he dropped out of Dr. Paolo's course after the first day, but then was asked for help with a part of Abby's telepathy experiment. He also described the first time he visited Building 6 on a very cold day as if the climate detail itself would jog Bob's memory of him. Ajay also told Bob that they had reviewed for the first time the rendered images from the key telepathy experiments with Dr. Paolo and Abby in his apartment on a very snowy and cold night, again using the weather as some sort of a bookmark.

"So you're a student here now?"

"Yes, in the computer science department. I'm a programmer."

"And your advisor is?"

"On sabbatical. I haven't met him yet."

"And you want to join my lab at the Integrative Biology Department?"

"Yes. I'd like to work with you on the telepathy work, if you are still doing it. I assume that you are."

"Do you know chemistry?"

"No. I just took Chem 1 and 2 at Wilmington College."

"I need a chemist."

"You need a computer geek."

"No, I need a chemist interested in neurobiology."

"How about a computer geek who can learn chemistry and who also is interested in neurobiology?"

"You're not going to go away, are you?"

"No sir."

"Let me think about this and get back to you."

"Thank you sir. I don't want to miss out again. My name is Adani, A-D-A-N-I. Ajay Adani."

Back in his office, Bob leaned back in his chair and woke his computer to see that a dozen emails arrived in the short time that he was out of his office.

Among the nonsense requests to join another scientific social media website and official, but meaningless announcements from MIT, was an email from: aito at uminnmed. The subject line simply read: job.

Hmm... Amy, he thought. *Right. The cute one.* He leaned back in his chair, stared out the window and thought. *Inheritable trait, genes, RW96, computer geek, programmer, algorithms, Xp29.47, population, it's a long shot but maybe....* Bob pulled himself closer to the wireless keyboard and typed a short reply to Amy. He then found Ajay's MIT email address and sent him a pointed email as well.

Minus one, plus two. Keep it rolling Bob, keep it rolling.

2

It was five-thirty a.m. and Abby was sitting on the back of Phil's bare thighs. She was about to put her strong hands on the lower part of his narrow back when she glanced out the east-facing window of Flatbread, Phil's one-bedroom apartment above a bakery in Troy, New York; a rust-colored barge was slowly heading upriver.

"Wow, that's huge!" Abby commented as she began to message the thin muscles of Phil's back. The RPI student was still in a quasi-dream-like sleep and he loved every minute of it. Abby's arrival from D.C. the night before had been a long anticipated event and the full evening of unencumbered sex was worth every minute of the months of over-the-top, red-hot buildup. Neither let the other down as they continued to honor their year old vow to keep it simple, sexy and monogamous. Their adage—no commitment, no disease—was alive and well.

Their words, his which were partly muffled by the side of the pillow, crossed in mid-air:

"And..."

"You..."

"...it's..."

"...can't..."

"...loaded!"

"...even see it from there."

"What?"

"Sure is!" Abby then slid off his legs and leaned forward to let her swollen breasts rest on the top of his firm buttocks as she reached under his pelvis and gripped his erection.

The loaded barge had barely left the narrow field of vision of the east-facing window before she had flipped him over. She rode him for the fourth time in twelve hours, and had they not spent two hours at dinner and almost six hours asleep, the number of pleasurable events would surely have been higher.

"Now that's the right way to start the day," he said afterwards knowing full well that she could read his mind with ease. "It's good to see you again, Abby."

"Remember, I can tell when you're lying... and this time, you're not lying," she remarked as she popped off of him and onto her back as she drew the thin bed sheet up to her chest. She closed her eyes to bathe in the soft post-climax calm while Phil turned to his left and stared at the soft features of her profiled face.

"You're right," she said without opening her eyes. "I have lost weight since you last stared at me like this and it does show in my face, mainly around my eyes."

Phil simply smiled.

"I'm so easy..."

"Easier than anyone I've ever met."

"Can you believe that we're already done with our first year of graduate school?"

"I know, right? It was just yesterday that we took that spontaneous road trip to D.C. and it seems like just hours ago we watched the MIT press release and now it's summer again."

"Hey, by the way, have you started your research?"

"Well sort of. My advisor is so great. Her name is Alexa and she is so cool. She knows everything about communication and it seems like she's interested in anything and everything related to it, even telepathy. Her specialty is communicative disorders, but she has an all-encompassing approach to everything she does."

"You call your advisor by her first name?"

"She insists on it. No Dr. Goldberg for her."

"Not here; it's old school formal. So have you started your project?"

"No, not really. Alexa has asked for an outline of what I'd like to do and I'm almost done with that. I don't think I could have handled one more thing last semester, classes and teaching were enough, but as soon as I return it'll be nothing but research until I teach again in the fall. And you?"

"About the same. I've got to get moving on it, but with mathematics it's more about the problem then it is about the math itself. There are some here that are studying trends in global currency fluctuations or modeling copper futures, water usage, cancer rates over the last 200 years, you name it and they're trying to figure it out using mathematical formulas. Some projects are related to solving a theorem someone proposed hundreds of year ago. So fucking abstract, so complex that no one is even convinced that it'll ever be solved, yet there they are scribbling out formula after formula on the whiteboard all night long."

"Still into the multiverse?"

"Yeah, but I'm kind of alone here. No one in the department is really into astronomy or physics for that matter. They're pure number people. I did read about one prof in the physics department who was involved with the SETI Institute when he was younger. I'll..."

"Seedy Institute?"

"Not seedy, SETI as in search for extraterrestrial intelligence. They've been waving their arms to the universe for decades hoping for a return wave. Maybe this guy will have some ideas on what would be the most important question to ask for my dissertation project."

"So we're both at the beginning of our research, how romantic," Abby said without really thinking of the connotation of the reply.

Phil, however, caught the word immediately. "Romantic? What's romance got to do with anything?"

Abby smiled and slowly leaned over him, her right breast pressed up again the side of his chest and whispered, "Did I say romance? Silly me. Of course romance has nothing to do with us. Nothing what-so-fucking-ever." And as she reached up to kiss Phil deeply, the young mathematician thought, "I think I love this woman."

Abby didn't respond. She just smiled through her kiss.

3

The deputy editor of the *Rolling Stone* had heard enough.

"Listen Lee, there's no story here. A dying scientist refuses hospitalization, he wants to die at home and he injects himself with some tracer chemical thing that lights up his brain. Where's the story? Where's the angle? I think the exciting parts have already been published in *The Atlantic* and in that science journal."

"Wait, wait. Hear me out again. Paolo purportedly injects himself, right? At least that what he wrote earlier in the year, long before he actually died. If so, then was it a form of suicide, right? Or was it self-experimentation? Or was he murdered?"

"What? Murdered? You told me that he died of advanced pancreatic cancer, correct? And his wife is a physician? Where in the hell are you getting this wacky idea? Listen Lee; what I don't need is another reporter chasing his tail. Now get out of here, I've got things to do."

"Fact: Dr. Paolo had advanced pancreatic cancer. Fact: he died at home under hospice care. Fact: there was no autopsy performed. Fact: his brain activity is recorded at the time of his death. Fact: he was cremated immediately after he died. There was no wake, no funeral nothing. Fact: his wife Laura signs the next of kin on his death certificate and she records the time of his death. A hospice care provider named June Kennedy signed as a witness to the death. Problem is, she never actually saw him die nor did she see him dead."

The deputy editor was losing patience with his young understudy. "You just said that Kennedy signed as a witness, but then you said that she never saw him dead? That makes no sense and anyway how do you know that?"

"I know. I interviewed her."

"You did what?"

"I located June Kennedy and called her. She works for a hospice firm in Massachusetts. I spoke with her about Dr. Paolo's death. She sounds young."

"I didn't authorize you to work on this story..."

"She said that the whole thing was a blur that she was too distraught to watch her first patient die, and that she did in fact sign the death certificate as a witness because she saw the paramedics carry him out of the house on a gurney. She said, and I quote, 'he was dead all right. As dead as they come.'"

"So what are you thinking?"

"I'm thinking that Dr. Paolo was too sick or too feeble to injected himself. He wouldn't have had the strength or the dexterity even if he had the will. I'm thinking that his wife administered the tracer that killed him. That's what I'm thinking. Dr. Paolo was murdered. Murdered, or euthanized, or whatever you want to call it by his wife, a physician who certainly would have known how to jab someone with a syringe. For either reason, it's a crime, wouldn't you agree?"

"Yes but apparently there are no witnesses and there's no body. So even if you're right, and I'm not saying you are, then how do you plan to prove this?"

"She'll have to confess. I want to interview her under the assumption that I'm doing a piece on her famous husband. Then I'll manipulate the good Dr. Kean into confessing her crime."

"Lee, I've been in this business for a long time and no one has ever volunteered to having committed a murder to a reporter face-to-face. I like the idea of learning more about Dr. Paolo and about the tracer at the time of his death. After all it is an important part of their big splash, right? But I doubt you'll get anyone to confess to murder."

"There's nothing like a challenge," said Lee Kingston as he left his boss's glass-walled office.

———— ‖ ————

Abby lucked out both going to, and returning from, her trip north. With high anticipation she boarded the Thursday afternoon bus at Union Station and sailed to Albany in just under eight hours. The return bus she road on Tuesday morning to D.C. required exactly nine hours. On the northbound trip Abby slept sporadically in preparation for what she knew would be a long night, followed by a long weekend of overdue sex, while on the southbound return leg she slept soundly for at least two hours, and through two city stops due to outright physical exhaustion.

On her returned ride to D.C., the confinement of her seat in the roomy bus gave Abby space to think about how far she had progressed as an individual since she left her father last summer—almost a year ago. She didn't miss him or his probing family. Looking at her clenched fist she extended a thumb, then a forefinger, "Twice," she said aloud to her shadowy reflection in the small dark monitor mounted on the back of the seat in front of her. That's exactly how many times she called him since leaving Massachusetts, once when she arrived at school to let him know that she was okay, and the other for Christmas from Phil Hess's home. The Christmas message Abby left on her father's answering machine was short, and it didn't reveal her whereabouts. "Merry Christmas Dad. I hope you are okay. Bye. Abby." The closed fist remained closed as she counted how many times her father had called her over the past year. Obviously, he was content to have shed his fatherly duty. With his only child out of the house, the now childless widower could spend more time with his bar buddies, his booze, his empty television shows and his vast array of deep-rooted childish insecurities.

She also had time to think about Phil. Their crazy relationship was becoming as emotional as it was physical with each passing visit. While their mutual hunger for pure carnal experiences was what initially attracted them to each other, something much more substantial seemed to be brewing. Were they using sex to cloak, or perhaps ignore, deeper more meaningful feelings for each other? Abby clearly had enjoyed her time in River Bend, Massachusetts, a sleepy town near the Berkshires with the Hess family over the Christmas holiday. They were real people, not shallow sugar coated Hallmark greeting card types at all. They were a down to earth, *bone fide* family of four with a sober and caring father who was a self-made electrician, and a doting mother who taught at the local grade school, and two healthy children, Phil and his younger sister Judy, who immediately considered Abby her long lost sister.

Staring out the window of the bus and thinking about Phil's family brought her back to when she was nine, to the day when she asked her mother if she could have a sister.

No sweetheart. That's not going to happen. You'll have to get on by your-self and in order to be happy in this life you have to be happy with yourself first, Abby. Her mother's response was so prophetic, so memorable that Abby wondered if her mother somehow knew that she would not be around much longer. Certainly little clueless Abby couldn't have known then that she'd have only a few more glorious years with her mother. No one could have known.

Abby was in mid-thought when it suddenly happened.

An elderly man was making his way to the back of the bus, steadying himself with both hands on the top of the seats when Abby turned to her left and saw him.

That's when time twitched.

Abby knew—a split second before the event actually happened— that the old man would harmlessly jerk to his right and come perilously close to falling before regaining his balance. She watched the scene unfold before she identified the unique instant as an episode of *déjà vu*. Although she had heard and read about these strange situations Abby had never before experienced one firsthand. She quickly reached for her diary, tucked deep in her knapsack and recorded the unusual event and the feeling that followed.

> Wow. For a moment I knew what was going to happen im
> mediately before it happened. Then after it happened—that
> is, what I knew was going to happen—everything returned
> to normal and I was left with a residual feeling of having
> experienced something that I either shouldn't have or...
> or...or what? Should have? Should I have experienced that
> déjà vu moment at all? My first ever and it was really odd.
> Really odd.

The last two words were double underlined for emphasis.

With just an hour remaining in her return trip Abby thought about the upcoming research filled summer. How was this all going to work? She knew what she wanted to study and she had some idea on how to start but what actually would it entail? How would it work? The upcoming meeting with her advisor would end the suspense and answer many questions; the fun, she knew, was about to start anew.

The platform at the bus depot was crowded with passengers that had just arrived crisscrossing through those who were about to board. Despite the chaos, Abby had a clear view of the struggle that unfolded in front of her. A woman, who appeared to be a mother, was tightly holding a little girl's left hand while the thin child's free right hand gestured wildly. Obviously, the mother was not paying attention and the little girl began to cry strange sounds as she tried to stop their progress away from the bus by attempting to sit on the cement walkway. The quick jerking of the girl's hand as the mother tried to pull her up to her feet made Abby flinch. Halfway up to a standing position the little girl's head turned to the left and her eyes made contact with Abby. That's when it happened.

"Excuse me ma'am. Your daughter left her blanket on the bus. She wants to go back to get it." The woman stopped, looked at Abby then over to her daughter who was now standing calmly.

"Is that true?" the mother asked her daughter.

The little girl nodded and signed Y-E-S.

The woman, still clutching her daughter in her right hand, turned and hastily made her way back to the bus, rudely ignoring Abby in the process. The little girl looked over her right shoulder and again spotted Abby.

Thanks, thought the little girl with a smile.

Anytime, Abby thought as she smiled back.

That evening, in her dorm room and after a refreshing shower, Abby wrote a lengthy entry in her diary, the second one of the day. Her research goals were no longer a mystery.

The incoming caller interrupted the usual greeting from the hospital's main operator.

"Hello," Lee Kingston said in his best direct, matter-of-fact voice. I'd like to leave a message for Dr. Laura Kean. Would you please patch me to her voice mail? Thank you very much."

"Certainly. One moment, please." And within seconds the young reporter heard Dr. Kean's recorded message with instructions to leave a name, a short reason for the call and a phone number where the caller could be reached.

"Hello Dr. Kean. My name is Lee Kingston and I'm a reporter with *Rolling Stone*. I'd like to do a follow up piece to *The Atlantic* article your husband wrote. Given the high interest in his *Nature* article, I think it would be good to know more about the scientist who started it all. If you agree, I'd like to set up a time when I could interview you for the article. I understand that you are very busy. I will make myself available to you anytime. Please call this number to arrange a meeting. Thank you in advance. Lee." The young reporter gave the widowed physician 72 hours to respond.

The voice message from Lee Kingston appeared in Laura's email inbox at the hospital's computer terminal. She had just one more patient record to update before making the short walk home to her condominium and the last thing she needed was another crisis—the day had seen its share of them. It was already seven p.m. and she'd been with patients or attending meetings for 13 seamless hours. It was time to go home, but she couldn't resist listening to the new voice message from someone with an out of state area code. Such calls were usually from a relative of one of her patients seeking answers on mom or dad's latest medical dilemma. But after Laura listened to the message and realized that it was from someone who did not require an immediate callback, she ignored it and headed home.

Lee Kingston, she thought as she exited the hospital for the eight-minute walk to her luxury condo located towards the center of town. *Where have I heard that name before?*

Although time seemed to have accelerated for Laura since Dante's death, she frequently reminisced about the last few months of her husband's life. From the day they learned the shocking diagnosis of pancreatic cancer to his refusal of treatment, his work on the manuscript at all hours of the day and night, the conversion of the downstairs bedroom to a makeshift hospital room, and the hiring of a young hospice care provider named June Kennedy or Jumpin' June as he called her, all of these memories were still quite vivid even in the absence of a wake, or a funeral, or an urn filled with his ashes on the mantel. But the change of season, from winter to spring with brown sticks sporting small, green buds and daylight crowding out the dark night refreshed memories of those last months, weeks, and days. Those tortured last days when she would listen to the sounds of Dante's pain that forewarned his death; sounds of pain that were building, building like the rolling, long-rolling, rumble, deep-rumbling, clap of humid summer thunder. Until finally Dante's last day arrived—a day when his agony unabashedly surrendered to lifelong serenity. Along side her dying husband in the makeshift hospital room, Laura watched. She was strangely disengaged as the stringent pain ripped through his defeated, internally deformed, body that caused him to thrust his torso upwards in a final arch of apparent defiance. Then Laura remembered the after-death time; how he was so very quiet, so calm and still. There was the cap, the samples, and students in graduate robes giving each other tight hugs. Also there were the tears, the gurney rolling out of the house followed by the vacuous feeling of being all alone after the students and June left. She was completely, all alone. These vivid recollections appeared in rapid-fire sequence through Laura's mind, memories that were still fresh, as though they happened from a very long ago yesterday.

Get a grip, she thought as she poured herself a glass of white wine. *He's suffering no more.* Laura walked to her bedroom where she removed her white cotton sweater, navy blue dress, panty hose, black bra and lace underwear. Before heading into the adjoining bathroom she stopped to look at the reflection in the full-length mirror that doubled as the sliding door of her closet. Her posture was straight and sure. Her legs, more muscle than fat, were portioned appropriately with her slim torso. Her hips were wide but not outwardly so, and her backside was round and firm. Twisting to the left gave her a great view of her waist, buttocks and the side of her still firm breasts. She smiled at the thought of how Dante often sang, *From C to shining C* as he gently cradled and fondled each breast in his warm hands. She raised her glass towards the mirror and toasted her naked self at the amusing memory and said to the empty room, "Fifty and fabulous, as they say." Then she slipped into the bathtub full of steaming hot, soapy water.

"Where have I heard that name before? Lee Kingston. *Rolling Stone.*" Laura couldn't place the name as she wondered what harm would come of granting the reporter an interview. She'd been interviewed before for a medical journal after she treated a patient with a rare illness, and that experience wasn't so bad. *Actually being interviewed was quite easy and harmless, she thought.*

4

Rosa knew that something was bothering Lorenzo Benedetti, but despite her best efforts to draw him out, to make him lean on her for a change, to share his inner thoughts with her, he remained unmoved and uncharacteristically moody, even outright miserable at times.

Lorenzo desperately wanted to tell someone about his bizarre experiences for the sake of freeing his mind but there was no one with whom he could confide. In some ways he was trapped in the small village where knowing everyone else's personal comings and goings is a time honored social sport. Indeed, only those that were in that room in the library at Wilmington College—Amy, Brad, Abby, Phil, Dr. Sukawa and Dr. Ito—and Bob Wyle who watched via a video feed—knew, or at least they understood to some extent, the kind of mental anguish he suffered. The rest of his frightful experiences were his, and his alone.

The night after watching the MIT press release, Lorenzo rose from bed leaving Rosa sound asleep. In the nearby bathroom, with the moon providing just enough light to guide him to the toilet, he sat, opened his tablet and started a new note. Carefully he typed the first 're-' word that came to mind: r-e-a-s-s-u-r-e. To his delight, 'reassure' remained as such. His heart would race each time he recalled when every word he typed that began with 're-' automatically changed to "reconciled." Clearly it was Dr. Paolo communicating with him, controlling him if you will, from the beyond. Until he followed through with the directions Dr. Paolo penned while still alive would he be relieved of the constant torment that expressed itself through the written word. He often reflected on how many remarkably common words began with those two letters. Satisfied that he was still freed from the controlling powers of the deceased Dr. Paolo, he closed his eyes, exhaled deeply and returned to bed.

While currently not in Dante Paolo's control, Lorenzo still worried about his vulnerability. Would his one-time nemesis return and again plague his body and mind? Would he be perpetually plagued by the possibility that one day, with no forewarning, his movements would not be his—a prospect that terrified him more than death itself? What could he do to alleviate his angst? Could he find out if the departed Dante Paolo still had designs on him? If so, who would know? These questions swirled in his mind like tiny tornadic tempests as he slowly drifted into a restless sleep.

———— ◆ ————

Jo Jung-Zoo loved the combination of heat and humidity. The bone penetrating heat of Baltimore, Maryland's summer sun reminded him of his childhood home outside of Busan, in the southeast region of Korea, and for the first time since arriving in the United States several years ago he was hot enough to be outside without a shirt. For the thin chemist the feeling of the summer air on his pale skin was complete bliss, and along with it came certainty that his move from MIT to Johns Hopkins was a good one. Not only would he be working in the laboratory of a Nobel Prize winning scientist, but also he would no longer have to wear so many layers of clothing just to stay warm.

The first meeting with his new mentor, Dr. Richard Johnson, was a lengthy one-on-one and it was held in the faculty lounge, away from the hustle and bustle of the laboratory. It was the strangest meeting Jo had ever had with a scientist.

The Nobel laureate began by stating a scientific fact related to the research Jo would be involved with; a fact that was common knowledge to anyone who knew anything about science. Dr. Johnson then moved on to say more about the research project that was again overtly obvious to anyone who was well read. But then deftly, Jo's new mentor said something that was involved and complex; Jo wasn't sure if he was being tested or challenged, but he listened intently nonetheless and said nothing.

"The discoveries of your MIT colleagues have already shifted paradigms," the Nobelist began, "but there are more to be shifted; they've just touched the surface. In some ways one could say that they unearthed the eyetooth of a new type of dinosaur and the rest of the beast remains buried. Our job is to be the first to reveal the whole damn thing. It was my laboratory that started the entire tracer movement in biomedicine that has now become somewhat of a cottage industry across many scientific fields, including neurobiology. Wyle merely modified what I pioneered and applied it to Sukawa's brain imaging work. The rest was luck on their part. Luck and smart experimental design. And Paolo was astute enough to simultaneously seize the technology, and his fate, to get those fantastic images of his brain at death—again that was mostly luck. Damn luck. So what we're going to do is reveal the rest of the buried fossil. And to do this, my friend, we won't need luck."

Jo didn't recall Bob Wyle or Dr. Sukawa mentioning luck when they constantly refined and repeated experiments.

"Everything is traceable," Dr. Johnson continued. "And we've already shown how diseases progress by following the electrochemical signals in bacteria that are hiding in other organisms. Okay, now, since our resident bacteria are critical for our very existence, then there must be an important connection between them and the human neural network, including the brain itself. It could be that bacteria control the functions of the brain not directly, of course, because the brain itself is sterile, but indirectly via chemical signals that could move across the blood-brain barrier. Bacteria may even control our natural death, and if we find that part of the fossil, why, why then we would have found the key to immortality itself! Bacteria can be manipulated to do whatever we want them to do. We could then engineer them to control that signal, that chemical. To turn it on to die, or to turn it off to circumvent total system collapse. You've got to find this connection, that chemical. Since these bacteria evolved with us there must be significant cross-kingdom sharing of chemistry. Shared chemicals. And because we can't live without them and they can't live without us, these chemicals—or there may be a master universal regulator type of signal—must be mutually accessible. I bet it's that simple Jo. It's probably that simple."

The meeting with Dr. Johnson to discuss the research strategy lasted for just over one hour on a Friday morning, but a full day later Jo, amid young joggers and young parents pushing their infants in strollers on the busy walkway that surrounded the National Aquarium, was still trying to understand the scientific rationale behind the task he was assigned to tackle. He knew little about bacteria, but what he did know made him question Dr. Johnson's logic. *Maybe that's what makes a good scientist great,* Jo thought. *The ability to take something that seems wild, bizarre, and even illogical and show that it's right, that it works.*

Jo was also bothered by the condescending tone Dr. Johnson voiced against his former teachers at MIT. Staring out at the sailboats in the protected cove, Jo was trying to recall what someone said about luck. *It was Pasteur who said that luck, no not luck but chance, chance favors the prepared mind,* he thought. *But Bob Wyle and Dr. Sukawa have great minds. Why is Dr. Johnson so angry? Is he afraid of them or maybe in competition?* With tiny beads of sweat forming on Jo's lean hairless chest, he momentarily second-guessed his departure from MIT. *No,* he concluded after dismissing such thoughts while encased in the heat of the day. *For me this was a good move. It will be good for me when I go back to Korea. I must do what Dr. Johnson wants me to do. First, I will locate the chemical, then identify its structure, and finally purify it to its crystalline form. He said it would be simple, so it must be simple.*

———◆———

Lee Kingston arrived at Myer Memorial Hospital an hour before his scheduled meeting with Dr. Laura Kean. He wanted to have some time to re-review the synopsis he had prepared on Dante Paolo and his wife, including a web search that led him to Laura's high school yearbook. After a quick review of 1981 edition of The Topsfield Pioneers, Lee learned that young Laura was involved with music (Strings 2, 3, 4), sports (Tennis 3, 4), student government (2, 3, 4 Class President), and a community elderly service program (Healthy Pioneers 1, 2, 3, 4). She was an attractive teenager who was beyond cute, but less than beautiful, although her brown hair, dark eyes and smooth angular jaw with a slight, yet real, smile showed promise that the popular student would blossom into a beautiful woman one day. Only two additional items from the quick Internet search indicated that the promise was kept. One item was a four-person photograph of a Dean at Boston University Medical School presenting awards to three graduates including Laura, and the other was a close-up of the internist on her group practice's webpage. There was no doubt in Lee's mind; the good doctor was a very attractive woman—a very attractive *widowed* woman at that.

The interview took place in the Oasis as Laura knew that the lounge would likely be deserted at half past six in the morning on a Saturday. Lee would have preferred a later time and a more private setting, especially after he met Laura and felt firsthand the unmistakable aura of her strong confidence and steadfastness that accentuated her natural sensuality. He knew she was twice his age yet he was instantly drawn into her physical presence. If he could he would have made love to her right then and there with no hesitations, but what he needed to do was to focus on the task at hand that unfortunately had nothing to do with sex.

"Dr. Kean, thank you for granting this interview. Do you have any questions before I start the tape recorder?"

"Yes. Why do you need to tape this conversation?"

"Well it's a matter of protocol to ensure the accuracy of quotes."

"Won't I be able to make corrections or edits to your article before it's published?"

"No, that's not commonly done."

"I did that the last time I was interviewed. I edited several lines for clarity. The article was much more accurate."

"Are you saying that I can't record this conversation?"

"No, you can. I guess it'll be fine. Let's start. I have to make rounds in 25 minutes." Lee tapped the green button on the small digital reorder and set it between them.

"Lee Kingston interviewing Dr. Laura Kean. It's Saturday July 27, 2013. Myer Memorial Hospital. Dr. Kean, I read the article that your late husband Dante Paolo wrote for *The Atlantic* with great interest. It seems to have been written in a way that makes me think that he knew he would not be alive when it was published. Would you agree with that assessment and what can you tell me about his mindset when he wrote it?"

"Dante worked on the scientific manuscript, the *Nature* article, with great passion and dedication during his final months. He was up all hours of the night researching various aspects of the paper, revising, editing and rewriting. And yes, I would agree with your assessment that he knew he wouldn't be alive when it was published. I actually didn't know that he wrote *The Atlantic* piece until much later."

"How much later?"

"My husband had always been a meticulous planner, a trait that even pancreatic cancer couldn't alter. He left a series of items that needed to be done after he passed and submitting his article to *The Atlantic* was one of them."

"So you learned about the article after he passed?"

"Yes."

"Was submitting the article the only thing you had to do on his behalf?"

"Well no, there were many other things left in my care."

"Such as?"

"Well, they're really not important."

"Did any of the tasks surprise you?"

"No, and they were quite personal and no one's business so you can move onto the next question."

Lee had to back off the quick hard approach and try to get his answer using a different angle.

"Dr. Kean, were you your husband's caregiver at the end?"

"No, that's not medically ethical. Dante had a wonderful hospice care nurse named June. She was a thoughtful, caring person, a sweet person. Dante loved having her around."

"Was she present when your husband died?"

Laura became suspicious of the line of questioning.

"Yes, she was. Why?"

Lee sensed that he had blown the soft approach and now he had only two moves to consider. He could either drop it completely or come straight out and ask if she gave her husband a lethal injection. But for a brief moment he said nothing. Laura's soft angular face hardened, her eyebrows knitted slightly and her eyes unleashed a pointed, intense glare, a look that turned him on and decidedly threw him off course. He was solidly in her spell. If she wanted to get angry with him, to slap him around, to dominate him, to make him her sex slave, it would be fine with him. She could whip his bare ass as much as she wanted, he wouldn't care. In his mind she wore nothing more than a black garter belt and a silk black bra. She knelt over him on a soft bed with her head held high as if she had just tackled her prey to the ground and was about to deliver the final blow—a slow, soft, open mouthed kiss aimed directly at his tensed inexperienced lips.

"Yes. June was there as were the students from Wilmington College."

Her voice startled him back to the Oasis and to the business at hand, but as he tried to straighten up in his seat he felt the awkward sensation of a progressing erection. This was not going well and suddenly he felt like he was in trouble. He had blown this assignment and there was no turning back now, especially given the effects of his hyperactive imagination.

Not used to wasting time, Laura took charge and ended the awkward interview ten minutes early. "Mr. Kingston," she said, reluctantly addressing him like an adult, "I have a full day ahead of me and so if you don't mind, I'd like to end this now. Perhaps we can pick this up another time?"

Lee couldn't believe his luck. She gave him a way out and another chance. "Sure, that would be fine with me," he replied as he tapped the off button on the recorder. "I'll call to schedule a follow up."

Laura stood to show him out of the lounge but Lee needed another moment to avoid the embarrassment of having to stand with an awkward bulge. He used a question as his delay tactic. "Is there a number where I can reach you?"

"The main line at the hospital is fine."

Lee's ride back to his tiny office in Boston was pleasurably slow amid heavy Cape Cod-bound traffic. The idle time gave him an opportunity to replay the interview and to listen to Laura Kean's silky voice over and over and over. He would now have a crystal clear vocal to accentuate the dream scenarios with the hot, foxy doctor he'd invent anew night after night after night.

———•———

"Abby Lark, this is fantastically wild," was Alexa's initial reaction.

The meeting with her dissertation advisor to discuss a research project was decidedly more formal than their dinner out to celebrate Abby's first publication. The starting point of any project is critical but when it could last for four or five years it is of particular importance. Today's errors in planning are next year's disasters and significant setbacks.

Abby presented Alexa with a broad outline of research questions and experiments as she had done for Dr. Paolo as an undergraduate. "The overarching theme can be summarized in one sentence," Abby stated. "The devolution of communication."

"Yes, I recall your interview when you and I first chatted about these ideas. Have you refined your questions?"

"Somewhat. And I think I have a great study population with interesting control groups," Abby said before telling Alexa of the recent encounter with the deaf child at the bus station, and how effortlessly she connected and communicated with the little girl. "Lets suppose that her inability to hear and thus to imitate sounds and the spoken word, was replaced with telepathy. Perhaps the ability to telepathize is as necessary for those who are deaf, as is the increased sense of touch and smell is for those who are blind. Her brain developed new ways of getting a message to another person. Her verbal pathways were blocked so she turned to non verbal ways to communicate."

"Abby, there has been some research published recently on the plasticity of the human brain and its wild ability to adapt to new stimulations and inputs."

"Right. I've read some of those papers. It's called 'cross-modal neuroplasticity' and you're right, it's really cool, but with telepathy I bet the whole thing hinges on age. It's a primitive sense but one that can still be developed during one's youth. I'll hypothesize that the ability to communicate nonverbally follows both phylogeny and ontogeny. It is an information exchange mode that is evolutionarily conserved, and it is, at it's most heightened state when we're very young say from newborn to about—and I'll take a stab here—about nine or ten. Over time spoken language displaces and diminishes our telepathic ability until it's essentially lost for good, like a battery that can no longer hold a charge. I'll bet that the little girl I met the other day has been deaf from birth, thus her brain has not been exposed to spoken language. Therefore she is using the only other innate way to exchange information—telepathically. Her only problem, and it's one that must be extremely frustrating for her, is that essentially no one, at least not her mother, is able to receive her thoughts. When I stumbled on the scene and silently communicated with her, the look on her face was one of relief and also one of disbelief."

"Well, that is very intriguing and interesting. It's definitely a testable hypothesis Abby," Alexa said as she glanced down at the rest of the research outline.

Abby was filled with excitement over her original idea and the process of describing it, even in broad strokes, to her mentor only heightened the positive experience. "I think we'll need three groups," Abby continued. "The test group will be deaf children, then an age-matched control group of non-deaf children. Perhaps we'll also need a subset control group of children that are blind but not deaf. And I'm also hopeful that some of the parents will allow us to do functional MRI scans on their child's brains so we can see how the signaling of the neural pathways differ between age groups."

Alexa placed the papers with the research outline on her cluttered desk and leaned back in her chair. "So far I see one problem with this entire study Ab. Where in the world are you going to find telepathic receivers? As the researcher you can't be the only one to do the experiment. You'll have to have receivers, several of them."

"Right. I think I know where to find them and when I do, it will lend support to my hypothesis right off the bat."

"Really? Where?"

"Do you want to know now? Don't you want to be surprised?" Abby's voice rose teasingly.

Alexa folded her arms, knitted her eyebrows and waited for Abby's response. Her answer was as clear as it was certain. "In places where those like me frequent."

———•———

Amy and Brad survived their first year apart, but not without emotional challenges. Now, with Amy back in Boston and Brad's roommate off to the Azores for the summer, there was plenty of space and privacy in the two-bedroom apartment on River Way for the medical students to re-stoke the embers. But after their first full afternoon together, when for a few hours it felt like the old carefree times they had enjoyed in the old Victorian house in Winchester as undergraduates, they knew that their lives had changed.

Their passion for each other just wasn't the same. The distance had indeed dulled their relationship around the edges and aside from discussing medicine and medical school they seemed to no longer share each other's interests. Not even the bustling atmosphere of life in the inner city that streamed through the living room windows of the brownstone apartment on hot summer evenings—the sounds of the fans reacting to the home run hit at Fenway Park or music from a nearby concert hall—helped. For Brad the city sounds only added to Boston's allure while Amy now found them annoying compared to the relative quiet surrounds of 'dull-ooth'. Little things were adding up for the young couple and unfortunately, not in a positive way.

It would take them some time to understand that their relationship had simply matured. It was transitioning from the physical, impulsive and emotional to the cerebral, steady and rational. They were unaware that they were, in fact, building a solid foundation for a long-term relationship, and what would anchor them solidly was each other's interest in medicine, medical research, and overall intellectual curiosity. The little things that seemed to divide them would eventually become unimportant. This summer of research in Boston for Brad, and across the Charles River in Cambridge for Amy, would unwittingly serve to forever reunite their minds, as well as their hearts.

Hiring and training formalities consumed most of Amy's first day at work in Bob Wyle's lab at MIT. It wasn't until 5:30 in the afternoon when she finally met with Bob to discuss her research project.

"So I like your idea of determining the frequency of Xp29.47 in the general population because it would be interesting to know how many among us harbor this gene for nonverbal communication," Bob rambled while admiring Amy's beauty.

"And while I was waiting at the ID office to get my badge, I found a way to obtain human DNA samples for this study," Amy responded. She opened her small laptop and continued, "Harvard and MIT have had a joint program to collect and store cells for use in population-based studies. They have thousands of samples from people all over the city, and from across the country. All of the samples are anonymous, that is we do not know the identity of the donors. It says here that we have to submit a short summary of the research plan, a protocol, and pay a small processing fee to start the process. If approved we can obtain up to 100 samples at a time."

Bob was thrilled with Amy's aggressiveness. "Sounds great. Yeah, I heard that they were going to start this tissue-banking program, but I had not kept up with it. I'm glad to see it's finally launched. So will you..." Again, Amy anticipated the question and continued on.

"I'll work on the research plan and protocol this week. I'll have something for you in a couple of days. One question. Will we have access to the probe for Xp29.47?"

"Yes, I think so. I'll ask Dr. Ito, umm, your father, tomorrow, but I think he'll provide the probe for that gene."

"Terrific. I'll build that into the proposal."

"Amy, you know that this is an epidemiological study, a look-and-see-what's-out-there type of study and that's fine, you'll definitely get an answer, but I want you to think about the next step too. What will you do with that information?"

"Right. What's the value? I get it. Let me work on it. It'll be a written into the proposal."

"Great. Amy, I'm glad you decided to come here this summer," Bob said in all honesty.

"It's good to be back in Massachusetts," the medical student replied.

"Oh, I almost forgot to tell you that one of your classmates from Wilmington College has recently joined the lab."

"Really? Who?"

"Ajay Adani."

"Oh sure, I remember Ajay. He was Abby Lark's friend. He was into computers or programming, right? Didn't he come to MIT for graduate school?"

"Right he's a computer geek and yes, he's already here. He just transferred into my laboratory the other day. He's out today, but he'll be in late tonight or tomorrow. I think your project will need his expertise in building computer algorithms. You're going to need to organize and condense your data, so you don't get swamped."

"Okay. Thanks again for the opportunity," Amy said as she packed up her laptop, slipped it into her satchel and turned to leave his office.

Bob watched intently as Amy departed, and he would have day-dreamed a bit longer had the wall clock not been hung right by the door. His wife expected him home by 6:30 at the latest. He had twenty minutes to meet that curfew, if he hustled.

——•——

No matter how well Brad's day went Amy's day was better. She was always animated and full of energy in the evenings. Amy was excited about what she had accomplished or learned that day especially since Bob Wyle's laboratory received institutional approval to use the banked human tissue samples for her research project. And in some ways, Brad felt left out and somewhat envious that Ajay was also involved with Amy's Xp29.47 project. Brad liked Ajay even if he didn't fully appreciate how one could be so enthralled with computers and computer programs. Brad thought of computers like someone thinks of a screwdriver—a tool to be bought and used. How could a computer geek contribute intellectually to Bob's biology-based laboratory? Moreover, Brad wondered, what specifically will he do to help Amy with her research?

"Ajay is not just about computers," said Amy. He's also into electronics, so he's going to try to build an optical detector that will scan the entire chromosome to find a single gene of interest. Apparently he has a friend who works with nanotubes and, well, I really don't know the engineering details, but these nanotubes will somehow use light scatter and something else that I don't quite understand to scan the entire length of DNA until it finds that one gene. Wouldn't that be so cool? I hope it works because then it'll save a lot of time and I'll be able to run more samples and increase the statistical power of the study."

"This sort of sounds like what your Dad was doing with DNA sequences, right?" asked Brad who couldn't recall the details of Dr. Ito's sequencing technique described in the *Nature* paper.

"Not really but I've already volunteered my father's help if Ajay needed it. That reminds me that I have to call him after dinner and let him know that I offered his services," Amy laughed.

"I have to say that your day in Wyle's lab sounds much more interesting than what I've been doing in Shulman's. The guy is always in surgery and his laboratory has only one animal technician who spends most of his time in another building, and a graduate student who is trying to grow mouse brain cells on a special matrix to give the cell shape and form. And the only postdoc is a biomedical engineer whom I've rarely seen."

Amy listened intently then asked, "What does Shulman do? I mean I know he's a surgeon, but what is his main area of research?"

"Yeah, well sort of. When I met Alex, the postdoc biomedical engineer, he told me that Shulman is trying to find ways of repairing brain tissue that's been damaged. And what Alex is trying to do is to make an implantable device for the brain that will repair damaged electrical signal transmissions. The hope is that when the device fixes one part of a damaged area it will then maneuver to another part of the brain that needs repair on it's own. A self-homing, nanodevice of some sort."

"That'll be amazing if it works. It could be used to treat Parkinson's, Alzheimer's and hey, maybe," Amy paused for a moment to consider the viability of her next question. "I wonder if it'll repair lost memory, like what people experience after a stroke or a coma?"

"Who knows?" replied Brad sullenly. He knew that he needed to get more active in the laboratory if he was going to get anywhere this summer but exactly how to accomplish this was not obvious. It was only an hour later, as the couple walked the Back Bay Fens towards their favorite ice cream parlor, that Amy had the winning suggestion.

"I bet the bioengineer guy Alex could use an M.D.," she said matter-of-factly.

"What?" asked Brad.

"Just that. I'll bet you one scoop of pistachio that he needs someone with the skill to implant those devices he's making."

"Don't you think Shulman will do the surgeries?"

"Yeah, when it's perfected and ready to go into humans. But until then, I bet Alex will need a set of steady hands to get those things he's making into the brains of small lab animals, right?"

"Hmm...I guess so. That's a good idea. I'll get ahold of Alex tomorrow and ask him if he could use a hand."

"That's taking the bull by the horns," Amy said.

"That's your *forte*," replied Brad.

"Correction," said Amy with a grin. "That's our *forte*."

Nexus II

The August humidity made the heat intolerable for Abby. It was suppose to be a quick walk to the streetcar diner for a hummus pita pocket then back to the office to continue writing her research proposal when the midday sun altered the course of her afternoon. She asked for lunch to be placed in a bag then decided to bring it to her dorm room where she would get back to it after a quick nap. The heat index was a blistering 112 degrees Fahrenheit and the air conditioning in most buildings, including Abby's dorm, was unable to keep up with the rising temperature. A city wide electrical brownout only added to the miseries of a weeklong, mid-Atlantic heat wave.

She placed the lunch bag in the cube-sized refrigerator and drew the sole curtain that hung above the only window in the small room. In the darkened room, Abby peeled off her clothes that clung annoyingly to her damp body and collapsed on top of the bed in a wave of exhaustion. The small clip fan provided little relief but it was the clicking sound of the rotator arm ratcheting the fan back and forth that Abby last heard as she lapsed into a deep sleep.

Be careful who you work with warned the young Dr. Paolo. Not all have good intentions. How will I know the good from the bad Abby asked still unaccustomed to seeing her former teacher as a young man. Be critical and stay vigilant. Ask yourself why the question was posed. What is the motive behind the smile? Am I on the right track? Yes. It's simple. The answer is simple. Can I ask you about my mom? No because the answer will not make sense to you. You must experience it to comprehend it. I miss you Dr. Paolo. There are a few things I miss too, but only a few. Now, as before, he vanished. *Wait. Dr. Paolo. Wait! Wait!*

Abby awoke somewhat dazed, with sapped energy and with beads of sweat rolling off her body like little ball bearings. The air in the room was thick despite the constant swirling of the small fan. She forced herself to eat lunch and also to drink water to avoid dehydration. Abby showered then returned to campus to resume her writing. That evening, turbulent thunderstorms marched across campus towards the bay like wanton mammoths, ahead of a weak cold front. It was a disorganized weather system that did little to change the week's bewildering atmosphere or Abby's sullen mood.

Encounters

1

Dr. Richard Johnson ran out of patience with the MIT recruit. He had given Jo one full week to come up with a plan on how to isolate the mysterious factor responsible for total DNA demethylation at the time of death, and so far Jo had not produced anything. Not even an outline.

"Look," said Dr. Johnson directly to Jo who was standing among others in the laboratory. "How simple can this be? Do I have to spell it out for you? All you have to do is to kill some mice and immediately rip out each organ, then do the same for other mice while they're alive. Then you prepare protein samples from each organ taken from the live and dead mice and compare them. From an organ or two, you are bound to find the enzyme that's expressed or overexpressed precisely at the time of death. Then, once you find that enzyme, purify it, sequence it and use it to find the regulator molecule that controls its expression. How tough can that be? Do I have to do everything around here? Christ! I thought you were an MIT whiz kid."

Inside Jo was burning with anger. He was raised in a culture, and in a household, that respected their elders and as such he was not about to dismiss that clear social ideal. But he was bothered by the reprimand dished out in public, in full view of his new laboratory friends. He was not skilled in killing animals, or in harvesting organs from them. Nor did he have experience isolating proteins from tissues or organs, for that matter. He was a pure chemist and what he did know is that nothing in science is simple. In fact, it's always more complicated that it appears to be on paper, or spouted wildly by someone, even if that someone happened to be a Nobel laureate. So as it was, with eyes and head lowered, Jo said absolutely nothing. And even if Jo were going to answer his boss, he certainly wouldn't have done it in front of an audience.

"When I come back from South America, I expect to see some progress here. Understood?" barked the Nobelist directly in Jo's downturned face. Richard Johnson left the laboratory for the office where he grabbed his packed suitcase. He proceeded out of the building and to the idling limousine that took him to the airport.

What happened next was nothing short of the yang to Dr. Johnson's yin. Each member of the laboratory—from the wide-eyed undergrad to the crusty, senior lab manager—approached Jo to voice support. One by one they offered to help him accomplish the goals of his research that had been, just a moment ago, broadcasted loudly and for all to hear.

"He's a bigger asshole now then he's ever been," commented the crusty, old lab manager. "Yeah and if his fucking ego gets any bigger his fucking head's gonna fucking explode, that's for fucking damn sure. Hang in there bro," declared a postdoc who liked to turn up his inner city vernacular whenever the opportunity presented itself. "He used to be different," recalled an older postdoctoral student. "He's like a crazy man now. It's not like it used to be. This used to be a nice lab with a lot of support and interactions. Now he's made it like a cutthroat business. Like he's trying to get another big fish, another Nobel Prize."

That the group offered their support made Jo feel better but the task at hand was still virtually insurmountable. Jo was still feeling quite gloomy until he heard one last comment by a postdoc who stood to the back of the group. "I'll help you with the animal work," said the petite young Asian woman with jet-black hair and brown eyes. "I work with mice all day. I can do what he wants done and in a humane way too." That's when Jo breathed a sigh of relief. Later that evening, to show his gratitude for their kindness and support, Jo bought the lab members a round of beer at the local pub. The tide, he correctly thought, was turning.

———•———

After Abby submitted the application to the University to use human subjects in her study, she sought to address the challenge that Alexa post from the start—specifically, the need to find individuals that were telepathic. Abby thought that those like herself who suffered a traumatic experience during childhood and thus felt alone in the world, were likely to reignite quiescent telepathic capacities. It would be their way of interacting with others without having to be fully engaged. Such individuals, she reasoned, would seek solace in quiet places like libraries or art museums, or in places of worship like churches or synagogues. After generating a list of the libraries, museums and churches in the greater D.C. metro area, Abby then wondered how she would approach a stranger who was telepathic. What would be a professional approach? Abby had several ideas that, in retrospect seemed lame, but she ultimately settled on a tried and true old-fashioned method. Abby printed business cards with her name, university and department affiliation, as well as her degree program and her academic email address. The American University's logo, placed in the upper left hand corner gave the cards a look of authenticity. On the back of the small rectangular, off white card was written:

> My research goal is to understand the biology of telepathy.
> I am also a telepath so I understand your concerns. Your
> identity will be kept private if you choose to participate in

a study I am conducting. Please contact me if you are interested in learning more about my study.

To use the new business cards with the American University red, white and blue logo as a method of recruiting telepaths also required institutional approval, but Abby was anxious to see if the method was going to work at all. With a few cards in hand Abby rode the subway to the National Art Museum. There she paid student rate admission and entered a new exhibit named *Pissarro and the Birth of Impressionism*. Abby thought that only those like her would attend such an exhibit in the middle of a hot summer, in the middle of a large city, in the middle of the week, and during peak rush hour. She was totally wrong.

The exhibit was packed. The waiting line that led into the specially prepared gallery extended some twenty yards towards the inside café. Patiently she stood in line and slowly inched forward to the entrance of the exhibit hall. There, Abby observed individuals among the mainly middle-to-late aged crowd staring intently at Pissarro's carefully mounted and thickly framed works. The pieces ranged from his early gray pencil sketches of people going about their business in the city and in the fields to the full-colored *Landscape in Chaponval* mounted in full glory on the far wall of the third, and last, massive viewing room. Whereas sounds in the gallery consisted mainly of incoherent murmurs and *sotto voce* comments aimed towards straining ears, all telepathic signals were nonexistent. Abby sensed not a single transmitter among the patrons, as she exited the through the one-way door that led to the exhibit-accompanying gift shop. Although she usually did not spend time in gift shops, Abby spotted a cashmere scarf wrap of a Pissarro landscape among others hanging from a display in the far corner of the small room. She picked up the wrap and admired the softness of the material, the roughened edges and the colors of *The Red Roofs*; the tag read $142.95. *A bit pricy*, she thought.

"But lovely," said a young lady with closely cropped red hair. Abby turned to her left, faced the stranger and, quickly held her tongue.

You read my mind?

Si bambina my/as easy as pie/with an eye to the sky/oh me, oh my/who are you and just as important, who am I? The young lady with the sweet smile and the closely cropped red hair replied without uttering a sound.

Well, that's a new one on me; a telepathic poet, Abby smiled and thought before extending her right hand and saying aloud, "Abby Lark."

Abby hit the jackpot. The young lady, with the sweet smile and closely cropped red hair, introduced herself simply as Rosi.

Over coffee in the museum's café Abby learned that her new friend was not only a telepath but also an interior designer by day and an artist by night, weekends, and holidays or whenever she found a spare moment to take paintbrush and colors in hand. Her art blended scenes from old masterpieces with modern day counterparts. Rosi readily showed Abby photographs of her art that were stored on her cellphone. Abby was stunned at what she saw and quickly understood what the young artist meant when she said that her work could be considered a blend of two different situations or conditions; she called it 'amalgamart'. Abby slowly flipped through the small set of photographs and while they all were very clever and interesting it was the second to last photo of Rosi's amalgamart that was poignant for Abby because she saw its inspiration in the exhibit just moments ago. On the left side of the canvas Rosi had beautifully recreated with impressionist's strokes the dim scene of Pissarro's *Red Roofs, Corner of a village, Winter* with it's simple homes peacefully clustered closely together behind a leaf-less forest—a small group of buildings bravely bracing for the season's cold winds. Melded from that well recognized landscape to the middle and extending to the right edge of the canvas was a continuation of the scene, also painted in the same impressionist's strokes, of a Red Roof Inn, with it's brilliant white façade and shiny plastic-appearing, bright red shingles, complete with countless tiny windows and a covered entranceway. It was as if Saint Denis had always had the modern hotel situated right in their wartime village that Camille Pissarro simply decided to omit from the canvas.

But it was the last painting in Rosi's cell phone portfolio that impacted Abby the most. It incorporated Dali's *Christ of Saint John of the Cross*, one of Abby's all-time favorite works of art reproduced brilliantly. It was the iconic bird's eye view of the faux-crucified Jesus, with his head down and arms outstretched to his back, in front of a wide, perfectly finished, dark-wood crucifix. The crucifix itself was positioned against an even darker background with light-thrown shadows cast to the left. The piece clearly demonstrated Rosi's breadth as an artist. But if the death scene demonstrated her talents, the rest of the painting revealed her genius. Instead of a tranquil lake with blue skies and rugged mountains of Dali's original creation, the base of Rosi's thick wooden cross morphed seamlessly into a steel beam that was firmly planted among the twisted concrete and metal remains of the Twin Towers at Ground Zero. An enlarged photograph of the sordid scene was placed carefully at the bottom of the canvas and lightly stuccoed to create a surreal texture—one that leapt from the canvas. Abby studied the painting's powerful imagery when she noticed something written towards the top of the cross. Engraved vertically in pale gold lettering was written, *In Deo Etiam*?

Abby asked, "God something?"

"In God We Must?" replied Rosi. "It's the title of the piece."

"Rosi, this is really amazing work. You are very talented. How did...."

Abby didn't need to complete her question. Rosi already knew what she was going to ask. *The ideas come to me in a flash, in a moment that has neither rhyme nor reason*, Rosi thought. *With no rhyme or reason/but always in season/for life eventually ends for all/be they Christians, Jews, Muslims or heathens.* And before Abby even had a chance to complete the formulation of the next thought Rosi transmitted a question. *I'm the inventor/free so free thanks to my benefactor/my benefactor, you see?*

Abby took a sip of coffee to clear her mind and to slow the rapid pace of Rosi's telepathic comebacks.

"Wow," Abby said aloud. "Are you saying that you have a benefactor? For your art?"

"Yes I do," replied Rosi who sensed that she was being way too animated and forthcoming with Abby. "I'm very lucky to have met him and fortunate that he likes my work. In return for sponsoring my art, he gets the right of first refusal. If he doesn't want to buy it then I'm free to sell it on my own."

"And the interior decorating job?"

"I do it whenever I feel like it. Clients galore here in D.C and in New York City too."

"Where did you meet this benefactor?"

"A friend in New York had a party and invited only telepaths. He was at the party."

For the third or fourth time that afternoon, Abby was in shock by what she heard from this young lady named Rosi—the talented artist with red hair and a cute smile. And before the telepath said another word or read another thought, Abby produced an unapproved AU business card then launched into a succinct but complete overview of who she was and why she was at the museum. Abby explained where she was doing her research and the outline of the project itself. For her part, Rosi listened intently. After listening to the details of Abby's study, Rosi took a sip of tea then said, "Love it. I'm in. And I can get as many telepaths as you need. Every telepath I know is an artist. Are you an artist, Abby?"

"No, well at least I don't think so. No, definitely no."

"I bet you are and you're not even aware of it," Rosi said aloud before thinking, *Abby the professor/had childhood stressors/that act like repressors/ but the fire within/wild with sin/is alive with love-passion-creativity akin.*

This red-haired, young telepath was bright, beautiful, sensitive and talented. She opened her very soul to Abby and its affect was as numbing as it was alluring. Unexpectedly, and for the first time in her life, Abby felt the undeniable desire to make love to a woman, and to not just any woman but to Rosi who was, by all measures, a stranger.

Rosi, still seated across from Abby at the small, round café table, smiled as she drank the rest of her now tepid tea.

———•———

In the soft palm of her small left hand, Mi-Ok cupped the small mouse with snow-white fur and pink eyes as if she was holding an exquisitely delicate pearl, the very meaning of her name. Her calm, peaceful demeanor soothed the mouse to the extent that it did not even flinch when she shaved the back of its head between the ears to the base of its neck with a small electric razor to expose its smooth skin. Jo watched intently as Mi-Ok silently placed the razor on the stainless steel table, one of many in the animal surgical suite. By feel alone, she then deftly opened a small, hard plastic case that was also on the table. The case held three tiny acupuncture needles. Jo had seen acupuncture needles before but these were unusually small; they were at least one-quarter the length of those used on adults. Mi-Ok pickup up one of the needles by its thicker end with her thumb and forefinger and, with the ring finger of the same right hand, she located the shaven base of the mouse's skull. With a gentle but sure move, the small Korean steadied the head of the still tranquil animal and swiftly twisted the sharp, hair-thin acupuncture needle into the base of its brain. The mouse immediately became flaccid in her hand.

Mi-Ok looked up at Jo with her tender eyes. "Not dead," she softly said to Jo who seemed to be holding his breathe in fear. "She is in a deep sleep. She will feel no pain now." Mi-Ok then slowly placed the shallowly breathing mouse with the small needle still in its brain, on its left side, atop a blue adsorbent pad on the stainless steel table. She then pinched the little animal's toe—not even a twitch was induced. Jo, who had never before been so close to an animal of any kind, was stunned.

"Will it die?" he asked.

"No. Not unless I place one more needle in the other side of her brain. When I do that she will die instantly. But if I take out that one needle, she will be just fine."

"But I will need the organs at the moment of death. How will that be done?"

"I would simply open her up surgically, then insert the second needle and harvest the organs that you need. I can do it all in less than a minute. My furry friend will feel no pain at all."

"This is incredible. Where did you learn this?" Jo asked.

"My grandfather taught me how to do this when I was a little girl. He said that it works on any animal. I've done this to dogs and cats and even chickens. As a child I raised mice on our farm in Korea. They were brown with black eyes and more difficult to handle than these white laboratory mice. Lab mice are very calm compared with mice I caught in our barn."

Mi-Ok continued to prepare the small placid animal for surgery. Before Jo the chemist who hated to even think about animals, let alone tissues and organs, could come up with an excuse to leave the quiet animal facility, Mi-Ok inserted the second needle into the mouse's brain and in rapid succession deftly removed the it's thymus, heart, liver, spleen, stomach, intestines, and lungs. She placed each organ in a separate tube that contained a solution that instantly stopped metabolic

95

processes. These seven vials were then placed in a bucket of ice. They were labeled with the organ, the date, and 't=o' to signify that they were harvested at the moment of death. These vials were clearly distinguished from the vials labeled 't=5' and 't=30' to identify the specimens recovered from mice 5 minutes and 30 minutes after insertion of the second, fatal acupuncture needle.

It was 11 p.m. when the two Korean lab mates exited the basement level animal facilities and rode the elevator to Richard Johnson's laboratory located five stories above ground. By this time Jo was not only impressed with Mi-Ok's skills with animals he was also smitten with her intellect and self-assured manners. He was, however, cautious with expressing his feelings towards her since he was unsure of how she viewed him. Jo simply kept his emotions to himself. He was also aware that virtually every square inch of campus, including elevators, was under video surveillance. He did not want to get in trouble, but he desperately wanted to get closer to her. A friendly thank-you hug, or any other sign of thanks, would have to wait—their hands were filled with racks of test tubes containing mouse organs suspended in a special fluid. Time was of the essence.

After a quick stop in the laboratory to flash freeze and store the mouse organs, Jo asked Mi-Ok if he could walk her home. Her apartment was only five short blocks north of campus. Mi-Ok accepted his offer and the two scientists stepped out of the temperature-controlled building and into the summer's night air that was heavy with heat and humidity. When they were clear of the watchful eyes of campus cameras, Mi-Ok took Jo's hand into her own and held it tightly for the remainder of the ten-minute walk. Jo smiled. He loved her aggressiveness. And when they reached the front of her apartment building, in what would normally be an awkward moment, Mi-Ok turned towards Jo, pushed up on her toes and gave him a quick kiss on his unsuspecting lips. He watched flatfooted as she scampered towards the front door of the apartment building, flashed her security card that released the door's latch, and promptly disappeared inside.

Jo smiled as he turned and headed back towards campus and in the direction of his own apartment. He couldn't wait for the morning when he'd return to the laboratory to process the frozen mouse organs, for then he would be reunited with his newfound pearl.

———•———

Alex Rudman was a thinking man's man. Tall, lanky with closely cropped curly brown hair he immediately conveyed an air of authority and knowledge—traits common to everyone that entered the field of surgery. But the soft-spoken Alex was not your average uptight surgical intern; he was also working towards a Ph.D. in bioengineering. He wanted to be more than a brain surgeon; he wanted to work on a cure for neurological problems, especially those that manifest later in life, such as memory loss.

"What can be more devastating than to lose one's memory?" Alex asked Brad. "A person spends an entire life building a database of memories and then gradually, in most cases, or acutely, in some cases, these memories are irretrievably lost forever. Alzheimer's patients can't even remember their own names or recognize their own children. They forgot when or where they were born—things that have been driven into their memory since childhood are lost forever. They can lose their entire identity and, ironically, they don't even realize it. I watched my grandfather go down this one-way road. It was very sad. He taught chemistry to generations of children, and then towards the end of his life, he couldn't even recall the name of the school that bears a plaque to honor his 45 years of dedication. I'd like to try to find a way to prevent or to cure this horrible disease, and others like it."

Brad was taken by Alex's passion and focus.

"I want to help," Brad said. "I've just completed my first year of medical school here at Harvard and I'm here as a summer intern, but I've only seen Dr. Shulman once, on my first day. I don't really have a project to work on so I do not have much to do."

"I see," replied Alex. "Follow me." The two men walked through the deserted Shulman laboratory, down the hall and into different type of laboratory.

The tissue culture suite was a brightly lit room with six shiny, sterile, stainless steel biocontainment cabinets. The purple glow from inside the cabinets came from the tubes of ultraviolet light that kept the inside surfaces sterile and ready for use by investigators. Located next to the biocontainment cabinets were incubators maintained at exactly 37 degrees Celsius, the temperature of the human body, and at a carbon dioxide level of 10%, a level that helps human cells grow outside of the body. Alex opened the larger, outer insulated door of the incubator then he opened a second, thin Plexiglas door and rapidly retrieved a rectangular flask that contained a small amount of pink fluid. He closed both doors to keep the inside temperature and carbon dioxide level from dropping too low. The sounds of the temperature and gas solenoid valves opening and closing to readjust the internal atmosphere could be heard as Alex placed the flask on the black metal stage of an inverted microscope. He turned on the light source and looked through the microscope's eyepieces at the cells contained within the flask. With his right hand Alex adjusted the fine-focus adjustment knob of the microscope and with his left hand he slightly repositioned the rectangular plastic flask that contained pink fluid.

"These are brain cells at twenty-four hours post-seeding straight from a mouse. Here, have a look." Alex moved away from the microscope and Brad looked through the eyepieces and made slight adjustments until the cells were in sharp focus. What he saw was an array of differently shaped cells, some long and thin with smooth edges, some round with barbs, and still others that were more rectangular with convoluted edges. Most of the cells were attached to the bottom of the plastic surface where they formed little patches, like disconnected islands in a vast ocean. But there were some cells, essentially round balls that floated freely above the islands. Brad knew enough cell culture to realize that the free-floating cells were dead. When Brad looked up from the microscope Alex picked up the flask and gently returned it to the incubator while retrieving another rectangular flask containing pink fluid. He placed the second flask on the microscope's stage and nodded for Brad to have a look.

"Seventy-two hours," Alex said simply. The cells in the flask were no longer separate islands. They were three-dimensional structures, like many islands squeezed together to form a single, multidimensional mass.

"The cells are coming together," said Brad.

"That's right. Viable brain tissue."

"But in three dimensions? How's that possible?"

"You can't see them but the culture medium also contains billions of nanotubes that provide a scaffold for the cells to adhere to and grow. We then add a chemical when the cells reach a certain mass. This critical signal prompts the cells to self-assemble. This self-assembly process results in a tissue that contains a series of small but intact neural nets."

"And then do you implant this tissue back into the mouse to repair damage? Isn't that the goal of your research?"

"Well, yes, but not exactly that way. After the tissue is fully formed, that takes about ten days or so, I then injure it."

"Injure it? How?"

"I injure it by limiting a nutrient in the growth medium known to be critical for neurotransmission, like calcium. It models a dietary imbalance in humans that could lead to brain damage and disease states. It can lead to irreversible damage in synaptic junction connectivity and permanent memory loss. That's when I add the nanoparticle-tethered homing virus."

"A what?" Brad asked.

"It's a simple concept and its really simple to make. It's a nanoparticle that has surface structures that lock on to damaged neural tissue like a magnet to steel. The nanoparticles ferry an inactive adenovirus that contains genes necessary to promote stem cell production of new neurons at the site of injury. Once the nanoparticle binds to the damaged target tissue, the adenovirus becomes activated via an internal chemical released by the covalent binding interaction itself, and the virus infects a nearby cell and undergoes a single round of replication. The virus takes over that cell's machinery that allows it to make millions of copies of itself until the cell bursts. The new virions attach to the nearby damaged tissue, an event that causes the virus to weaken. Genes that promote stem cell production, that were once inside the virus, integrate with DNA in neighboring healthy tissue, and a cycle of cellular repair is initiated."

"That's brilliant!" exclaimed Brad who clearly followed the rationale behind the complex molecular concepts.

"Well, almost brilliant," replied Alex who replaced the seventy-two hour flask with another from the incubator that was labeled 'day 17'. Brad looked at the tissue matrix inside the flask then looked up at Alex. "These structures look like their falling apart, collapsing. It's almost looks like their melting or something."

"Right," replied Alex. These cells were artificially damaged with chemicals, then treated with the adenovirus-containing nanoparticle and, well, as you can see it's not working. The cells are initially responding to the repair process but then something is missing—something critically important." Alex placed the flask back in the incubator, turned off the lights to the inverted microscope and left the room with Brad right behind him.

"Have you considered damaging the cultured brain tissue with prions?" asked Brad as they walked down the hallway to Shulman's laboratory.

Alex's sure stride came to a sudden stop. "Prions? Prions are bits of self-replicating proteins that cause scrapies in sheep and CJD in humans, right? Real nasty brain diseases are caused by these prions. You know Brad I think you might be onto something here. What we may be missing is not a chemical or an artificial form of injury *per se*, but a natural way of causing injury, something that can, and does occur in nature. Brilliant!"

2

The ringtone on his cellphone irritated him to no end, yet he never bothered to change it. The call was from Munich, and Dr. Johnson decidedly ignored it because he was still on his way to the comfort and privacy of his office. Once there, the red light on Richard Johnson's desk phone flashed, an annoying signal that meant that there were unanswered voice messages that required attention. As was his custom, the neuroscientist Nobel laureate deleted all messages without bothering to listen to them. He then he dialed the old German.

"You answer my goddamned calls," spouted Franz Albracht from halfway around the world. Richard Johnson instantly wanted to hang up, but then he thought better of it. "I was outside. The call would not have been private," he replied.

"It's been a month and no word from you. You better have something good because I'm in no mood for bullshit, Richard."

"Well Franz, your going to have to cool your jets and relax. I've been out of town for most of August. South America. Argentina. Buenos Aires. Peru. You've been to Buenos Aires, haven't you Franz? The place is full of beautiful people. It has great wines and without question, it also has the best beef on the planet. Beats Europe in many ways, Franz."

Dr. Albracht did not want to relax or to cool his jets. He simply wanted sound data, and not preliminary or half-baked results either. He wanted something he could use, something tangible. He knew that his mind was deteriorating; he was slipping away, a fate suffered by both his mother and grandfather before him. He wanted none of it. The tracer that he wanted Richard Johnson to perfect would reveal areas in the brain where misfolded proteins turned smooth well-bundled, high-functioning neurons into clumps of sticky spaghetti, a condition known to lead to memory loss. It was obvious to Franz that Dr. Ito's tracer was able to rapidly race through the brain's entire network of neurons thus providing an important clue on how to penetrate the deepest regions of the soft organ. But then the next trick was to untangle the damaged neurons—the clumpy spaghetti—and restore them to their original form and function. Repairing memory loss was an intermediate and an absolutely necessary goal if he was going to think clearly enough to ensure that he would attain his lifelong dream. What the old German neurologist wanted more than anything was the same singular goal others have sought since the beginning of time: cognitive immortality. He knew that his body would continue to decay and to eventually whither away, but he wanted his mind to live on forever. The findings published by Ito, Sukawa, Paolo and the others provided important clues towards reaching his lofty goal. But it was too late to support those scientists, he had already placed his bet on a horse named Richard Johnson, and he was cautiously optimistic that the Johns Hopkins researcher would deliver. Had Franz Albracht known about Dante Paolo's work only a year earlier, the Nobel Prize in Medicine would have been awarded to a different American.

"I assume you'll be meeting with your lab rats today. I expect a call back with a full report by this exact time tomorrow. It better be good." The call ended abruptly, and for the second time in as many calls, the old German had the last word. The wonderful memories of warm weather, fine wines, beautiful people and succulent beef that Richard Johnson enjoyed during his month long excursion to South America dissipated with one very short phone call. Nonetheless, he gently returned the phone to the receiver and leaned back in his large office chair. The meeting with members of his laboratory was scheduled to begin in exactly twenty minutes.

———•———

Abby was pleasantly surprised to see an email from Phil. It read as if he was in mid-thought and needed to get the information in writing quickly before it dissipated:

> I finally met that professor that used to work at SETI and I found out that he was just asked by that same group to mathematically model the likelihood that our galaxy spawned a solar system identical to our own, and also within the conceptual framework of parallel galaxies. I told the professor (more about him later) that I'm his man and guess what? He accepted me right on the spot! So just like that I have a dissertation project. Can't wait to see you so we can celebrate, you know, our way.
> Phil

Abby knew that this was a big moment for Phil and she wanted to respond with a lengthy congratulatory email, but she had little time to spare and since she also wanted to fill him in on her new friend Rosi, she simply sent a short reply:

> That's great news! Let's chat later. Will you be around tonight?

———•———

Ajay Adani washed his hands whenever he entered Bob Wyle's laboratory. He again washed his hands when he exited the laboratory and whenever he thought to do so throughout the day. Even when he typed on his own laptop he wore latex gloves, "Just in case something escaped," the germophobe said to Amy.

"You're so paranoid," Amy told him more than once since they started working together. "Nothing's going to jump out of anything. A couple of dangerous chemicals are all we have to be worried about with this experiment. Purified DNA is harmless."

"Yes, but what about the cells where the DNA came from?"

"Ajay, you worry about nothing. Even if, and I repeat, if the cells had something nasty in them they would have been destroyed long ago by the chemicals used to extract the DNA. You're being silly. Just stay focused and tell me if the detector is doing what it's suppose to do."

"Well I scanned the samples you ran three days ago and here's what I got." Ajay opened a file on his computer and waited for the very large data set to become visible on the screen. Four large panels appeared. Each panel showed a different view of the same set of DNA that had been prepared by Amy. The picture on the upper left panel looked familiar to Amy. It showed an image of the ten DNA samples cut with enzymes into thousands of gene fragments that created a ladder-like pattern. The DNA fragments were separated by size with the smaller, fluorescently stained pieces creating the lower parts of the ladder. The upper right panel also looked familiar. It was an image of the same gel as in the left panel but the DNA had been probed to look for a single gene; Xp29.47. The image showed some faint lines where the probe may have found the target gene but they were not at all clear. In contrast, the data shown in the lower left panel was crystal clear. The sharp bands in DNA samples 1, 5, 8, and 9 indicated that these were the genes that reacted with the probe. The lower right panel graphically depicted the intensity of the strong reactions seen in the four DNA samples.

"Are these the results you were expecting?" asked Ajay. Amy opened her laboratory notebook.

"Let's see," she began. "Lane 1 was DNA from Abby. That's our gold standard. That should always be positive. Lane 2 was DNA from me—it should always be negative because I'm not a telepath. Lanes 8 and 9 were DNA samples that were also from me but blended with some DNA from Abby. Lane 8 contained only one-tenth of Abby's DNA and lane 9 contained one-one hundredth. All of the other lanes were DNA from the repository. Wow! Ajay, it looked like it worked! It looks like you've developed a very sensitive technique to identify Xp29.47. Wow!"

"So do you think we're ready to scale up? To do a hundred samples at one time?" Ajay asked as he rubbed hand sanitizer on his recently washed hands.

"I think so but let's check with Bob first. I think this is awesome, Ajay. Good job."

"Thanks. And just so you know, the optical scanner worked perfectly too. It accurately measured the amount of the gene in the sample, exactly as you had prepared in lanes 8 and 9," Ajay said as he pointed to the graph in the lower right panel of the computer screen.

Amy was nodding in agreement. "True enough. The only bummer is that I'm leaving for Minnesota this Saturday, so I won't be here to see the results from the large number of samples. And from this small sample size, we already have one positive hit, in lane 5. So someone out there is telepathic, or potentially telepathic."

"That much we already know," remarked Ajay.

"True enough, true enough."

Amy and Ajay presented their findings to Bob who was impressed with both the accuracy and sensitivity of the new search tools. He gave them approval to test the DNA samples they had received from the repository. He also made a call to MIT's office of information technology and requested that Amy Ito be allowed access to the computer located in his laboratory, the same computer where Ajay will keep the results of the study. Bob wanted to ensure that Amy could review the data at anytime from anywhere. He wanted her to be engaged with the project at all times.

———•———

There would be no television, no dinner out, no movie nor would there be a visit to their favorite Back Bay ice cream parlor, Amy and Brad spent the last evening of their summer alone, together. They simply sought to feel each other's skin, to stroke each other's hair, to remember the past, to enjoy the present, and most importantly, to plan their future. They've been meaning to have this discussion for the past few months, but the long, bright days of Boston's summer actually seemed to accelerate time, as opposed to the long, dark days of winter which seemed to reduce it to a painful crawl. Summer weekdays for the couple were dedicated to work, and weekends were spent visiting Brad's family in Rockport, a schedule that left virtually no spare time. But now, in Brad's apartment in Boston, the two medical students were beginning to feel the full weight of their future. In three short years they will have earned medical degrees, and again be faced with life altering decisions. They needed to think seriously about each other, and of their respective long-term hopes and desires.

It came as no surprise to Brad that Amy knew what she wanted. In short, she expected to have it all. "I will become a pediatrician. I will be married and I will have not one, nor three, but two healthy children. And I will marry my soul mate, whom I can confidently say, is already holding me in his arms." Amy was less certain about her future as a researcher. If it fit into her work as a pediatrician, then fine. If not, then that would be fine too. Either way, she'd be the best at what she did.

Brad was only certain about one thing. He loved Amy with all of his heart and he wanted to be her husband. All else in his life was a distant second. He knew that he would be a successful doctor, probably a surgeon, but he was also hooked on research, so that too had to fit into his life. There was no doubt that he also wanted children, and although one child seemed plenty he wouldn't be opposed to raising two. Brad would prefer to spend their post-graduate training years as residents together, preferably in Boston where they would likely settle down given its vibrant healthcare industry. Amy agreed. They would only need to endure three more years apart. Then they would be together forever.

Early the following morning Brad gave Amy a long hug outside the security checkpoint at Logan International Airport. With a heavy heart he watched as she went into the full body scanner with her arms raised. He watched as she gathered her belongings and walked away towards the gate. Brad was glad that she didn't turn back to see if he was still there for he already memorized the delicate details of her saddened face.

It was the first day of September and unbeknownst to Amy and Brad events were already underway that would alter their lives forever.

———•———

Answer the phone you old fuck, Dr. Johnson thought to himself as he sat in his office.

"Richard?"

"Yes Franz, it's me."

"Good. What's the news from the cutting edge?"

Dr. Johnson spent most of the previous day reviewing data that his laboratory generated during his month-long absence. Predictably, most of the experiments needed to be repeated, and collectively they were not all that exciting save for one bright spot. Of all people, it was Jo who dropped the bomb of the day. He reported a potentially important breakthrough in his research. His new results showed that at the exact point of death, the experimental white mice produced either a single novel chemical, or two existing chemicals that combined to form a new product—a result that occurred in all of the ten mice tested. Richard Johnson knew that Jo's results could be quite significant, a rare finding. But he wasn't sure if he wanted to share the exciting results with Franz Albracht, who had become nothing more than a time-consuming annoyance.

"As you know," started Richard Johnson in a condescending tone of voice, "a key to understanding what occurs at the exact moment of death requires a method to reproducibly capture that fleeting moment. Humane killing methods are often too gentle, and take too long, to freeze that moment. Plus, many of these methods use a chemical or some sort of a gas, or it involves a technique that would trigger a systemic alarm—a survival, fight-or-flight-type response. All of these methods, and the reactions they'd induce, would confound the value of any finding. It would muddy the waters and it would not provide us with a crystal clear answer."

"Yes, yes, yes. Get on with it," shouted Franz Albracht impatiently.

"So we've developed a new technique to kill mice that uses no chemicals, no gases. It kills them predictably, controllably and rapidly, and..."

"Every goddamned scientist on the planet is hell bent on working with mice, which is fine if you're trying to cure a mouse! But this method has to work on humans. Richard, will this method work only with those goddamned rodents?"

"Are you ready to let me finish?" asked Dr. Johnson impassively.

"Get on with it."

"What if I told you that the roots of this technique sprouted at least three centuries ago, is extremely inexpensive and, I'll predict right now, it will be applicable to all mammals, including humans. Now what would you say?"

"Prove it. That's what I'd say, prove it," grumbled the old German.

"You know that the key to isolating the chemical signal is to capture the exact moment of death. To freeze it in time, right?"

"Of course."

"Well, that's not as easy as it sounds. As I said earlier, one cannot use chemicals, like morphine, because they may interfere with the signal. You can't use gases for the same reason, and other ways simply take too long or they are messy. Besides all of them take too much time; they are not quick at all. So, I had a brilliant idea of a way that would circumvent these issues, and the lab gave me the results of my brainstorm just yesterday."

"Yes? Would you get on with it? I haven't all day."

"Well, it worked just like I knew it would," Richard Johnson said without even as much as a trace of dishonesty. He proceeded to describe in detail—which was part fact, part fabrication—the acupuncture procedure pioneered by Mi-Ok's grandfather and proficiently executed by his granddaughter on laboratory mice. What Dr. Johnson didn't reveal to the German neurologist was the truly groundbreaking finding Jo described at the prior day's lab meeting. Jo had shown convincing evidence for a small molecule that was detected in organs at the moment of death. This small molecule did not exist either five minutes before the animals died, nor did it exist just after the mice expired. Jo's astounding revelation prompted Dr. Johnson to order an entire new set of experiments using different animals. He also assigned a small team of chemists the task of purifying the small molecule so its structure could be determined. When the chemical structure of the small molecule is revealed then it could be made synthetically in large amounts.

"This technique involves acupuncture to first sedate then passively kill. The first needle is inserted into the brain at the…"

Franz Albracht was not amused. "All this time to tell me that you pithed a goddamned mouse?"

"It's not exactly pith…" Richard Johnson said in defense of the technique, but the only thing he heard from the telephone's ear-piece was a hard click followed by a steady tone.

Once again, the Johns Hopkins scientist remained calm. Dr. Johnson leaned back in his chair, swiveled to the right and focused on a newly framed picture that had been recently hung on the far wall next to the small conference table. In the photograph, alongside Franz Albracht who was dressed in a black tie tuxedo was the newly crowned recipient of the Nobel Prize in Medicine wearing the oversized gold medal bearing Alfred Nobel's profile. Both men beamed brightly at the official Swedish photographer as if there was nothing but harmony between these two worldly scientists.

You'll die soon, Dr. Johnson thought. *If I have to pith you myself.*

3

Rosi's studio apartment in Georgetown was as vast as it was breathtakingly chic and stylish. The twenty-foot tall ceiling of the spacious, single level room was made of old wood post and beam construction. Exposed industrial-sized aluminum ducting, snaked neatly along the ceiling, maintained a comfortable and constant seventy-two degrees and fifty percent humidity year round. Solid oak flooring met red brick interior walls that held ten-foot tall thermal-paned windows that faced east and south. Although natural light was maximized, arrays of individual lamps suspended from the ceiling added a wide range of lighting possibilities.

The cavernous room was divided roughly into thirds. To the east and left was Rosi's art studio. It was denoted not only by its contents but also by the thick Plexiglas sheet that covered the entire section of the floor. Two easels supported one large canvas that was ten feet in length by six feet in height. A solid wooden table positioned to the left of the easels held an array of paints, brushes and different sized palettes. The far corner of the art studio was where Rosi sculpted. Two unfinished marble pieces, each approximately five feet tall, were draped in a thick canvas cloth. A long, sturdy, stainless steel table with a wide assortment of art supplies—several chisels, various wooden mallets, sponges, clay, spatulas, plaster of Paris, mixing bowls—was positioned against the wall opposite the huge windows.

The central third of the room was a living area. It contained two plain futon couches, a black leather recliner, a glass-topped coffee table and an oriental rug. The living room did not have a television, or an entertainment center. Instead, it contained a long built-in bookcase made of hickory that fit cleanly underneath the tall windows. Most of the books in Rosi's collection were related to art, art history, philosophy, poetry and psychology.

To the right and west was an open bedroom alongside a marble bathroom. Clear, thick glass separated these rooms from the rest of the apartment. The toilet was positioned in the corner of the bathroom besides the shower. It was not meant for the modest as it faced towards the bedroom, and was clearly visible from the living room. A kitchen with appliances positioned against the interior wall was situated to the left and right of the entrance door. The efficient kitchen had green granite-topped counters and a plain dining room table with several chairs.

Abby was speechless as she viewed the apartment. The setting sun sent its last rays of the day into the apartment. It was a calm light that illuminated the contents of the interior while yielding to the darkness in the far eastern corner of the room where draped sculptures stood somewhat eerily. Rosi placed the apartment keys on the kitchen counter then promptly returned to Abby. As Abby turned her head to the right, towards the direction of the open bedroom, her mouth was unexpectedly met by the softness of Rosi's lips. The kiss was not one that Phil—the only man who had ever kissed Abby—had ever, or could ever, have delivered. Rosi's lips seemed to have a mind and a sensuality of their own, and Abby who was momentarily shocked, neither recoiled nor resisted the bold advance. The minds of the two young women—unified and convivial—catalyzed the passion to a height that was all too familiar to the artist but one that was completely new to the graduate student.

The long, hot shower in the clear, open bathroom was as soothing and as welcomed as the loving caress of a new mother's hand. Their minds led the way. Each knew what the other was thinking and exactly where and how the next touch would land. Abby's inexperienced tongue circled the firm, resilient nipple of Rosi's right breast as her own slightly larger breasts were supported and fondled gently by the artist. Their soft moans rose in synchrony as they lay on the bed, one atop the other; their eyes wide open to accept the light that bounced off the folds of their soft skin and their sensitive regions. The two telepaths were not on that king-sized bed, in that studio apartment, on that street in Georgetown, in that state, or in this country, nor were they on this planet. With minds and bodies interlaced, they were in their own universe and as such their multiple orgasms seemed to have, ultimately and predictably, combined to form one powerful sensation. At that moment, both women took the other's face into their hands, and kiss it with the highest level of awareness of each other's physical and emotional existence humanly possible.

Silently, with limbs entwined, they lay still.

That was... Rosi quickly usurped Abby's brief thought.

Your passion, your love has been repressed/it's something you need not to me confess/for that was then and now is now/you are forever released from that dark cloud/of the past/not nice/your mother dead/your father ice/you are now free/to forever be/the intellect full of curiosity/and love, Oh Dear Love/how beautiful your skin/it senses, it moves/with no chagrin/a reluctant virgin from deep within/perplexed you are about women and men/accept them both/it's not a sin, no my love/My Dear Love/it's not a sin.

In the museum Abby told the artist-stranger about her experiment. In her new lover's bed and within her arms, Abby told Rosi everything.

In the museum Rosi told the graduate student-stranger little. In her new lover's arms, amid the flicking glow of candlelight, Rosi told Abby everything.

Each had no choice. There are no secrets among telepaths.

———◆———

Laura knew that she had to follow through in order to get the guilt out of her head and to move on with her life. She and Dante had planned to spend at least a month, preferably an entire season in Tuscany when they retired. It was a dream he'd never realize.

Dante wanted to absorb the culture, to know the people, to go beyond being a simple, wide-eyed tourist; he want to be a part of the countryside. He spoke of volunteering at a small vineyard to learn, to work, and to be a member of a family when they harvested the grapes from the rolling hills and deep valleys of Tuscany. He wanted to feel the pressure of the handle on his hands as he ground the purple clusters of grapes into the old oak wood barrels. He heard his grandfather's voice, and his father's voice too, describing how it was done in the old days with everyone in the village participating in the harvest, everyone lending a hand to each other so that the pressing and the second fermentation could begin before the cold winter set in for good. As a child, he heard the stories often and now, as an adult, he wanted a chance to live them. Dante also realized that details of the stories were fading and he desperately wanted to restore them because they meant the world to him. But, as with many things in a life cut short, it would never be. He would never step foot in Italy. He would never experience wine making or anything else in Tuscany for that matter. Countless lonely days, as he lay on his deathbed in the guest bed-room that had been turned into a makeshift hospital room, were spent looking out the window wishing he had taken the time to trace the well-worn paths of his ancestors.

Laura had listened to Dante's stories on many occasions. After Dante's passing, she still vividly envisioned his desires. She promised that one day she'd retire and follow through with his dream. She would travel to Italy not as a reluctant tourist or as a pitiful widow, but as some-one who would honor her long time partner. She would live in Italy, at least for a short time, and enjoy *la dolce vita*. Indeed, she must go and she would go. Not to make wine but to drink it, not to become a peripheral part of the culture but to experience it—to breathe it. She would go by herself and she'd stay in a small flat in Florence, far away from her heavy patient load and the never-ending circus of the hospital. She couldn't bring her husband back from the dead, but she'd go in his memory and she'd carry his gold wedding band, the sole piece of jewelry he always wore. The same ring that had slipped off of his withered finger and wobbled to the middle of the room when his arm drooped to the side of the bed one evening as he was actively dying. The same gold band that was found by Jumpin' June Kennedy and given to Laura for safekeeping just a week before the professor died. Laura would bring the small circular symbol of their lifelong commitment—in sickness and in health and now, in death too—to Florence and she'd throw it as far as she could downstream in the Arno River from the famous *Ponte Vecchio*. She would do this painful, final act of their shortened marriage in dim light just before daybreak, alone.

———•———

It was surprisingly warm in Florence for October and within a week of her arrival Laura seemed to have its local residents at her beck and call. Tomasso Montecatini, the chef-owner of *Palato dell'Artista*, a *trattoria* located directly beneath the second floor flat Laura rented, enjoyed catering to her dining needs. With the pleasurably sweet and spicy aroma from Tomasso's kitchen infiltrating her flat each morning, Laura was drawn, like a child to *gelato*, to the small table for two by the front window of small restaurant that faced the narrow *via Palazzuolo*. Smitten by her natural, mature beauty and self-assured manners, Tomasso offered to be her personal tour guide to Florence, a proposal she politely refused at least once a day for most of a week.

She spent those early days in Florence alone acclimating to the Italian way of life with its slow starts, midday chores and activities, followed by a long evening finish that was squarely centered around food, friends and family. It was as if Italy's clock was adjusted several hours ahead of the rest of the world so that the Italians could enjoy quality dinnertime for themselves without intrusion from the outside.

During her first week, Laura visited its well-known art treasures and she began where she knew Dante would have started. The unassuming exterior of the *Galleria dell'Accademia* sharply contrasted with the unique sculptures it housed. Inside, the four powerful captives that seemed to struggle mightily to emerge from the block of solid white marble lined the hallway that led to the magnificent *David*—the highly polished, young man who emboldens the visitor to stand tall, firm and defiant with him.

And outside of the *Galleria dell'Accademia*, in the distance, Laura could see Brunelleschi's famous dome, *Il Duomo di Firenza*. It remains not only a dominant symbol of both the city and of Christianity but also as a monument to the architectural brilliance of Renaissance architects and engineers.

It wasn't only the oft discussed and photographed works of art that Laura viewed. She also absorbed mannerisms and everyday gestures of contemporary Florentines. She quickly understood that Florentines have a deep respect for individual privacy—an age-tempered tradition that respects the fine line between caring for someone and being intrusive. While elders are resolutely passionate about their religion with its daily rituals and weekly celebrations, the younger generation is relatively indifferent to Christianity's lofty demands and strict rules yet both young and old shares one common cause—they are steadfast stewards of the city's countless treasures and traditions.

Laura discovered that the people of Florence, especially women close to her own age, were cautiously warm to her. Instinctively, they knew that she did not belong to the class of clumsy Westerners who bumbled through their town like they were on Main Street, Disneyland nor was she a quick-hitting, rude, boastfully wealthy tourist from the Middle East seeking fine jewelry or leather jackets, but rather she was genuine in every way. From the nonthreatening looks and only casual stares from the city's inhabitants, the widowed physician felt accepted and oddly enough, at home in Florence.

Perhaps for the first time in her adult life, Laura was experiencing time—luxuriously free, untethered time. Not the type of time that ticks towards a certain end date but a gentle time, a slowed time that allows one to reflect and to think clearly. And so it was at this point when Laura began to carefully think about herself, for a change. Where had she been? What had she done with her life? And now, where was her place in the world? This sort of inner self-analysis was completely foreign to the good doctor. Most of the time Laura's energies were spent caring for others, asking them questions about things that impacted their lives. She always put herself low on the priority list, third or fourth perhaps, after her patients, her parents, and her husband. Other than the monthly visit to the hairdresser that she deemed to be a necessary burden, Laura did not indulge in massages, pedicures, manicures or time at the spa. For others she'd recommended therapy, but never sought it herself. For others she'd recommend taking time off to relieve stress, yet she was never away from the hospital, or her patients, for more than a week at a time. For others she recommended sound lifestyle choices, vaccinations, and regular checkups while she never made the effort to take her own pulse. She gave constantly yet sought no rewards, no medals, nor certificates of appreciation to hang on the wall, in return. Each day she did her very best to listen, to heal, to soothe, or to fix the heart, the toe, the mind, or whatever needed repair. And although Laura was dedicated, she was not a sufferer to her profession.

Overall, Laura Kean's life was like an EKG of a dead man who was momentarily brought back to life—steady but with a few surprising spikes. The loss of each of her parents, as difficult as they were to experience, were relatively small spikes. Their prolonged illnesses made their passing not unexpected and, in some ways, welcomed. But the loss of her twins, those full-term, ultrasound-confirmed perfect children—a boy and a girl—that she unselfishly incubated for nine straight, uneventful months, created the most damaging spike she had, or will ever have, to endure. Not even Dante's passing, a significant peak in and by itself, could match the profound pain she experienced with the loss of her children.

But it was not a life absent as a mother that Laura contemplated as she walked down Florence's narrow cobblestone streets and across the wide opened piazzas, or as she stepped into and out of the ornate churches, each with its own bank of lit candles and unique solemn ambiance, indeed, Laura thought of her husband. There was no doubt in her mind that he would have, by this point, become friends with several Florentines, and he most likely would have aligned himself with someone, an entire family perhaps, who was in the midst of winemaking. Her thoughts at that moment were strengthened by what appeared to be several generations of men piled in pickup trucks filled with presses, wooden barrels, and grinders. The men seemed to be leaving the city in the cool early morning hours, for what Laura could only image was a hard day's work in the fields and cellars of a local vineyard. They seemed happy enough dressed in their worn hats and warm overcoats that would be shed in time as the sun warmed the crisp autumn day.

And it was during these times of fantastic projection that Laura poignantly felt the loss of her husband. *Isn't that the reason I'm here?* She thought. *To live it. To reflect on our life together? So heal and move on already—right? Isn't that what he'd say? Move on Laura. I'm yesterday's news. You're in Florence. You're alive today! Have fun! Get laid for Christ's sake. Isn't that what he'd say or am I saying this to myself?*

Laura smiled coyly at the thought of Dante urging her to again have sex, or perhaps to tease a Tuscan, someone like chef Tomasso? He's been the only man who has flirted with her in ages. He's someone who is roughly her age, perhaps slightly older, with dark Mediterranean features and honest, truthful way. Chef Tomasso was not unattractive to Laura, but could she ever flirt with him to the point of having to make an adult decision? Laura's thoughts spun. *No, that just wouldn't be right. Right? Wrong? You're thinking too much, he'd say. Just jump his bones, that'll show him who's boss. Take charge. But why should I? And just for one night or should I have him every night? Maybe just a weeklong fling before I leave then, arrivederci Tomasso, you were good but not great. Is that it?*

Laura had not been intimate with anyone since Dante passed. She really hadn't missed sex until this very odd moment surrounded by the majesty of medieval structures. And in the context of Dante's dead voice ringing in her head, she also thought of her own mortality. At fifty, she felt young yet vulnerable. She was experiencing the same reluctant realization she had when she turned forty, namely, that fifty was the age of an old person. The next milestone, now less then a decade away, is sixty; a prospect that seems more frightening to her now then fifty did a quick decade ago. And she also came to the cold realization that she essentially was alone in the world. Other than her colleagues at the hospital with whom she maintained a professional relationship, Laura had no true friends. Those she thought were her friends—both women and men that she had spent considerable time with in college, and later, those she met while in medical school—ended up to be lifelong disappointments. She had already lost touch with Robert and Beverly Pierce, who were good friends and neighbors. The loss of their friendship was an unforeseen consequence of selling her home for the convenience of a condominium situated closer to the hospital where she worked. And the passing of her parents several years ago meant that Laura also had no family, immediate or otherwise. She was independent, self-assured, fifty and in Florence.

Laura was ready for a new beginning but the beginning of what exactly was not readily apparent or obvious, at least not yet.

———•———

For two solid weeks Laura resisted the impulse to open her small laptop because it meant that she was getting back into work mode. But then suddenly, when she did lift the small computer off of the small night-stand next to her bed, Laura remembered what had occurred—it all came back to her in an instant. It happened when she left for her morning walk that very day. After she locked the door to her apartment and made her way down the short flight of stairs, Laura reached with her right hand for the curved handle of the metal gate that opened directly to the narrow alley adjacent to *via Palazzuolo*. What happened next seemed like it had happened before. Laura watched her left foot land softly on the smooth cobblestone of the narrow alleyway when the odd sensation occurred. When she looked up and to her right she saw an old lady carrying a bag by its paper handle. There was no time for Laura to react or to warn the old lady that her bag would be struck and torn. A young boy on a bicycle would startle her from behind and hit her bag causing its contents of fresh vegetables to spill on the ground. Laura felt numb as she gathered the peppers and onions that rolled in her direction because she realized that she foresaw the occurrence unfold in real time, yet she knew it would take place before it actually had. The lady's voice yelling at the fleeting boy was muted as the scene came back to focus in Laura's mind. Then, as mysteriously as it happened, the scene dissipated and was forgotten for most of the day.

Having returned to the moment, Laura hesitantly logged onto to the hospital's secure website where she checked the status of some of her patients. Having spent most of the day immersed in quiet self-reflection,

Laura now felt the need to be needed, and there was no doubt that her patients needed her. But it wasn't Mrs. Moore's high fever, Mr. Landrum's arthritis, or Ms. Greer's appendicitis, nor was it the long list of backlogged, urgently flagged messages from her colleagues who were covering the care of her patients that caught her attention. Among the bold-lettered list of unread messages, were two emails that had arrived one week ago, one from Abby Lark and the other from L. Benedetti.

> Dear Dr. Kean,
> It's me Abby. I am now in my second year at American University and I have a great mentor and a very interesting research project. How are you? I hope you are well. The other day I received an email from Dr. Benedetti, the former Dean at WC. He asked if I had your email address, so I sent him this one (actually its the only one I have for you). I hope you don't mind. Please write when you have a moment.
> Love, Abby

Apparently, Dr. Benedetti was ready to strike as the very next email had arrived in Laura's inbox one hour after Abby's.

> Dr. Kean,
> Although we have never met formally, I knew your husband very well when I was the Dean of Academic Affairs at Wilmington College. Later, as I'm sure you know, I assisted in ensuring the publication of his manuscript that, I was pleased to see, was very well received by the scientific community. I am sorry to have never had the opportunity to covey my condolences to you after Dante's death and now that I have permanently relocated to Tuscany, I am afraid that I will not be able to so in person. However, I would appreciate

the opportunity to speak with you by telephone, if possible.
Please let me know your availability.
Sincerely,
Lorenzo Benedetti

Laura read both emails again, ignoring altogether the other parts of the hospital's portal that showed a long list of patient issues for her to address. She replied to Abby without hesitation.

Hi Abby,
Thank you for writing and for letting me know how things are going for you at AU. I can't believe you are already in your second year, my how time flies. All is well with me, especially at the moment as I am out of the country on vacation. Please keep in touch and no problems regarding Dr. Benedetti.
Affectionately,
Laura

The response to Dr. Benedetti's message required more thought. Laura knew that the Dean and her husband did not see eye to eye, but that was all she knew. And it could very well be that he lived in the very city that she's been enjoying for the past two weeks. *How big is Tuscany anyway?* She wondered. After a quick Internet search Laura learned that Tuscany encompasses a large area of northern Italy with coastal regions to the west and centrally located mountainous regions. *Where in Tuscany does the Dean live?* She thought before replying.

Dear Dr. Benedetti,
Thank you for your kind words and also for your help with the publication of the manuscript. I think Dante would have been pleased with how it was received by the scientific community. I am currently on holiday in, of all places, Florence. If you'd like, I could call you. I did not bring an international

cell phone, but I am sure I could arrange to use my neighbor's phone if necessary. If this is acceptable, please provide a number where you can be reached. I arrived in Italy two weeks ago and I have another two weeks remaining before I return to the U.S. Perhaps we could meet for lunch?
Laura Kean

Nexus III

1

Abby was in a deep, early morning slumber as dark overruled dawn at least for a few more minutes. Her breathing was shallow, and her heart rate steady; she was warm, comfortable and at peace. Her mind was floating. She heard nothing. She was unaware of her physical surroundings.

Dante approached Abby but this time she was not shocked to see him as a young man. It's not all that it appears to be. What's not? What you think it is, it is not. Be vigilant. Always be vigilant.

Abby's eyes opened abruptly. The ceiling of the dimly lit room was not readily familiar, but she regained her bearings when a soft hand under the bed sheet move slowly upward, caressing the left side of her torso and settling at the underside of her left breast. Her mind heard, *There's more to know that's not of our world/and you've found it, that's true, our universe unfurled/how long have you known of this place in our midst?/it's both terror and joy like a woman's first kiss/and the boy with a warning was he special to you?/the message clear but why the clue?*

In the dim morning light, Abby saw Rosi propped on her right shoulder. The artist slowly leaned over and softly kissed Abby on the lips as her thumb and forefinger gently twisted her erect nipple—sensations that sent shivers of anticipation through her newly awakened body.

Immediately Abby focused on the pleasure of Rosi's wandering hands that purposefully and effectively steered her mind away from Dr. Paolo's message, a message that was clearly channeled to Rosi who sought to know more. Abby needed to review her former mentor's message, and to do so meant that she needed to be alone. She was anything but alone at the moment, as Rosi had now positioned herself even closer to Abby. With ever-so-light fingertip touches, Rosi nimbly located each of Abby's many pressure points, creating wave after wave of excitement that radiated throughout the graduate student's highly sensitized body.

Numbers

Sextillion is incomprehensible. Other than reading it, saying it, writing it as the number one with twenty-one zeros after it, or seeing it written exponentially, ten to the power twenty-one, it has no meaning, no logical context, and no reasonable framework in reality. So, to offhandedly say that there are some sextillion Earth-like planets in the universe means absolutely nothing to anyone with the possible exception of planetary scientists or computer geeks who are use to working with large, bizarre numbers. It's like saying that helium is lighter than air, for most people, this fact means nothing.

So wrote Phil. It was his turn and his first time to write an article on his research project aimed to the general public. What began as an opinion piece published in the *Albany Tribune* penned by Phil's mentor to dispel a flagrant myth about the connections between space and time turned into a weekly science column in the *New York Times*. As the gate-keeper for the column, Phil's mentor screened submissions from peers across the United States, and he also made it a required writing exercise for everyone that performed research in his laboratory. "We have to be better at letting the public know how his or her tax dollars are being spent," he'd say forcefully to anyone who challenged him on the assignment. "Scientists have to use the media to promote themselves, and their research interests, as effectively as fashion designers use the catwalk. We have to strut our stuff often and with passion, intent and above all, with conviction. We have to use new fabric, new styles, new designs, anything that would work, to let them know how we think, how we plan experiments, and why we believe in what we do each and every day. We have to look straight into the camera and tell the audience how our research impacts their everyday life, and the lives of their children, and even their children's children. By the time they've reached the end of the article—the end of the runway—each and every reader of your article should not only understand the topic presented, but they should want to be involved in your studies—to buy the outfit—no matter how seemingly esoteric or abstract its pattern or purpose."

His mentor's words echoed loudly in Phil's head as he continued to write his piece.

So rationally speaking, if there are Earth-like planets then there must be entire solar systems similar to the one we live in. These solar systems must exist in the same way that supports life, at least life as we currently define it. But while we pretend to be interested in finding life no matter how you define it, what we really care about, what really interests us is whether or not we exist elsewhere. By 'we' I don't mean chemical building blocks like amino acids, nor am I referring to single-celled organisms. I am not going back to some beginning point where life began to evolve, but I am describing an exact clone of each of us doing precisely the same things that we are doing now but somewhere else in the universe, on a Earth clone. Does it sound improbable? Unimaginable? Exactly. It's sort of like comprehending the number sextillion.

The key question is not whether parallel galaxies exist—because strong data all but verifies that they do—but whether or not randomness, inherent to the laws of probability, can dismiss the concept of the existence of multiple forms of the same human being. In other words, can high-order mathematics predict if the universe allows us to exist at the same time in different worlds simultaneously? Or does such vast randomness possess firm boundaries? These quests, these questions, are not posed as an exercise in futility, but as a matter of future utility. To reconcile...

Phil stopped typing in mid-stroke. He looked up from the keyboard to the monitor because oddly, he already saw the next words, not because he was stringing them together now, but because he had seen them before.

> To reconcile what was once thought to be irreconcilable.

As he reread the sentence, he knew it would be shortened.

> To reconcile the irreconcilable.

Phil paused and again read the shortened sentence. He tried in vain to remember where or when or how he knew that sentence, those words. The phrase itself had been previously written, right? Had he heard it? Said it? Then the odd, trance-like moment passed and Phil carried on with his writing. He reread the entire paragraph and realized that the last sentence needed to be lengthened not shortened.

> To reconcile what was previously thought to be irreconcilable: we exist in the exact same form, in the exact same condition, under the exact same set of rules, structure and order as we do here and now on this Earth, as well as on another Earth located elsewhere.

Phil reasoned that the probability model he was developing needed to describe how the slightest variation in events to one person on a given Earth would alter events to clones located elsewhere. How would subtle, virtually immeasurable and unperceivable differences affect each clone? And how many clones are there?

Abruptly, Phil had a revelation, an intellectual lightening strike. He closed his eyes to focus and to think. He needed to crystalize the new concept as a real, if not fantastical, possibility. The sooner he wrote it down the less likely he was to forget it.

A mathematical model to describe multiple universes was not comprised of a single line but of a central one with several new branches emanating from it like tributaries to a great lake. The mathematical branches, if they held up to scrutiny, could explain a great deal. Phil jotted down his thoughts using a pencil and loose papers that were lying idle on his desk. He filled three sheets with notes and sub-notes, edits and arrows that looked like complete gibberish with logical and non-logical mathematical equations filled with quantifiers and odd symbols that seemingly led nowhere. He even added a rationale for each new equation. At times he wasn't sure where these ideas were coming from, but they kept coming and coming in waves, one after the other like a midsummers night deluge. Question marks annotated with vague references to something he had heard or something he had read in the past covered the margins of the papers of what would one day be regarded as priceless.

When he felt as though he had adequately documented his thoughts, Phil looked at the papers starting with the page that had the number one circled in the upper right hand corner and read what he wrote. By the end of the fourth page he knew he had something quite special, something that undoubtedly needed to be signed and dated, photocopied and stored electronically for safekeeping.

Above all, Phil needed to speak with someone about what he had just discovered. Someone who would not think he was crazy, delusional, or touched with fire. Instinctively he knew that no one he had befriended at RPI would do. Although his RPI pals were smart in that they aced every exam and they could memorize facts by the truckload, they uniformly lacked the ability to string together what they had learned to form a cohesive, novel idea. In essence, they lacked imagination. None of them, as far as he could tell, had the capacity to push the boundaries beyond those that had already been cemented in the literature. He needed to speak with Brad or with Amy, and without a doubt he needed to speak with Abby, too. Perhaps he could speak with all three of his former Wilmington College classmates at the same time. Phil hastily arranged a four-way video chat before he had the chance to relinquished his idea, haphazardly scratched on four pieces of paper, as nothing more than wild fiction.

———— ● ————

Inconsistent with her self-assured and independent nature, Laura was actually thankful that chef Tomasso would be in *Palato dell'Artista*'s kitchen during her lunch date with Dr. Lorenzo Benedetti. She simply didn't know what to expect. Other than the glowing Internet articles pertaining to the former Dean of both Rockefeller University and Wilmington College, she knew nothing else about Dr. Benedetti. During his time at Wilmington College, Dante shared little about the college dean with Laura. She was even less certain why the now retired professor would want to travel to Florence to meet with her. Was he just being a gentleman or did he really want to express his condolences in person as he stated in his email?

Tomasso, for his part, would not have missed this day at the *trattoria* even if God himself made the request for him to be elsewhere. He was decidedly protective of Laura despite the fact that she effectively dismissed his good-hearted advances from the start. Her dismissals meant little to him. In fact, her reluctance to immediately accept him only added intrigue to her beauty. She was lovely, smart, and sexy too, and the chef tried repeatedly to convince himself that the last trait was not as important as the first two.

He would be presiding over her special luncheon because he was unusually anxious about Professor Lorenzo Benedetti, a fellow Tuscan. Laura had shared little information on the exact nature of the meeting, so it was up to the Tomasso to put the puzzle pieces together. By this stage in his life, he knew all too well that Tuscan men sought only three things from women, and the chef and self-anointed protector of Laura, Tomasso Montecatini, felt that it was his job to make sure that the good professor received not one of them.

Laura sat at what Tomasso had referred to as "her chair for life". The chair that accompanied the table by the window, had it's back to the corner wall. It was a position that gave Laura a sense of security, as well as a clear view of the entire *trattoria*. She also had a clear front row seat to the pedestrians traversing *via Palazzuolo*. From this vantage point Laura would be able to spot Dr. Benedetti as he entered the building from the street. Laura thought to add ten years to the photos of him posted on the Internet. She was on the lookout for an older man with white hair and a salt-and-pepper beard with slightly hunched shoulders and sadder, distant eyes.

Laura spotted Dr. Benedetti instantly when he entered the *trattoria*. Not only had she accurately guessed his physical features, but also she also correctly predicted what he would wear. He was dressed not overly formal but rather warm, sharp and appropriately informal—in line with the look of Italian men, regardless of age or social status.

Laura rose and stood by the table as Dr. Benedetti walked into the dimly lit eatery shortly after one o'clock in the afternoon. Instinctively, he glanced to his right where he spotted an attractive single woman rising from her seat.

"Dr. Kean, I presume?"

"*Buon giorno* Professor Benedetti," Laura replied using both languages in a single greeting while extending her right hand. Lorenzo held her hand and bowed his head slightly as a sign of respect. He would have preferred to kiss each of her cheeks in a customary sign of friendship but then thought better of the idea. He didn't want to presume that they were, or even would become, friends.

Lorenzo carefully removed his black scarf and light brown overcoat then took his seat opposite Laura at the small table. Initial impressions of one for the other couldn't have been more different. He was taken by her natural beauty that was accentuated by her poised mannerisms, whereas without his coat and scarf, and after a closer look, he appeared older than he did just a moment ago. Laura correctly placed Dr. Benedetti in his mid- to late-seventies but in overall good health.

"What good fortune, *buona fortuna*, that you are here in Italy. I am delighted to finally have a chance to meet you Dr. Kean..."

"Laura, please," she interrupted.

"*Bene*, Lorenzo is more than adequate for me. I'd like to personally convey my sincere condolences on your husband's passing. He was taken from us much too soon."

Before Laura had a chance to respond to Lorenzo's sentiments, Tomasso, who wasted no time, made an abrupt appearance at the table. He introduced himself as chef and as their server for the afternoon. He went on to tell the couple that being a server was not his usual job, but that he had no choice because they were busier than usual that day, which was far from the truth given that there were only four other individuals seated in the *trattoria* that held twenty. Tomasso's pleasantly pretty niece, who worked as a server at the *trattoria* on occasions while attending school, couldn't believe her eyes. Her uncle the chef was assuming the menial task of waiting tables even if it was only the lowly table for two by the window.

He, Tomasso Pietro Antonio Montecatini and none other, would be Laura's guardian and protector. He made it his personal responsibility to make sure that she was safe from the dangers that lurked under the skin of every man. The owner-chef-waiter-protector offered each of the two guests a menu that consisted of nothing more than four items hastily written in pencil on thin, tan paper the size of a playing cards. *Insalata, fusilli con burro fresco , pollo arrosto con patate, pere con formaggio,* 20 €. As if in a silent movie-era comic skit, Tomasso set a bottle of mineral water on the table, picked it up again, unscrewed it then set it back down on the table. After wiping his dry hands on his chef's apron and without hesitation, he rapidly picked up the now opened bottle of water and poured some into the glass of each guest before again setting the bottle down in the center of the table. To further prolong his stay and to get a better look at the old Tuscan from the mountains, he once again picked up the now half-empty bottle and topped off each of their water glasses that had yet to be touched by the patrons. Again he wiped his hands on his apron before replacing the cap on the bottle.

"*Un po di vino?*" Tomasso asked Dr. Benedetti in an effort to get a good look at the old Tuscan's eyes.

"*Per me, sì,*" replied Lorenzo. And although the upward glance was quick, Tomasso saw the tired eyes of the old Tuscan. They appeared to be apprehensive, not in an eager way like those of a fisherman's face before his first cast, but troubled like those on the face of a child on the first day at school.

"*Signora*, would you also like some wine?" As a general rule, Laura did not drink alcohol before evening, but since arriving in Florence she had grown to enjoy a small glass of wine, usually red, with lunch.

"*Sì, grazie.*"

"*Prego.*" Tomasso retreated to the kitchen to gather a bottle of wine and also to tend to the orders that had arrived from the other patrons while he was being Laura's protector. *Why is the old man so concerned?* Wondered the chef as he peered at the table by the window through the small space between the swinging doors that separated the kitchen from the dining area.

"Have you been enjoying your stay in Florence?" asked Lorenzo.

"Yes, very much so. I wasn't sure what to expect when I left Boston, but everyone has been so friendly and the city is simply beautiful. Not only because of the remarkable art and the architecture, but also the people. They have been very accommodating and welcoming. I guess I expected Florence to be a cold, perhaps standoffish, like New York or Philadelphia, but it's been just the opposite. And the weather has been warm and welcoming too."

"I've always held Florence close to my heart. As a child, it would be a special treat to visit this city. My family traveled here once a year during the Christmas season when festivals were plentiful. Indeed, this is my first time to Florence since I returned to Italy, and the experience has brought back wonderful memories of my childhood."

"Are you glad to be back? Laura asked."

"*Sì.* I very much needed to return to Tuscany, to a simple life. Only rarely do I miss the United States and the demands of my career. I still make an attempt to keep up with science, but I find myself becoming more and more detached with each passing month."

It was not difficult for the retired professor to tell that underneath Laura's firm exterior layer of self-confidence was a sensitive and caring woman. Acting on an instinct that Laura had a true soft side, Lorenzo, who was anxious to get a female's approval for his recent purchase, reached in his pocket and retrieved a small black box. "Forgive me for changing the subject, but I've just made a significant purchase and I would value your opinion of it. I bought this for my cousin Rosa just this morning from a jeweler here in Florence. Would you be so kind as to tell me your opinion of it?"

"Why certainly," responded Laura who was taken with Lorenzo's comfortable manners. He seemed to be a genuinely nice person.

Tomasso was as nervous as an expectant father in a waiting room, and he was stunned at what he saw when he peered through the space between the swinging doors. Laura had just opened a little box given to her by the old Tuscan. Then, she gently removed a rope necklace made of pure gold from the little black box. Tomasso watched in horror as she held it up to her neck then pressed it against the thin skin of her delicate throat as if assessing the length of the deeply intimate gift. Laura's face was positively radiant but the chef's eyes, along with anyone else that might have happened to be looking in that direction, were easily drawn to the lowest most part of the gold chain that rested comfortably at the very top of her cleavage. The scene froze Tomasso in place. And if his alert niece who was carrying a tray full of dishes had not, at the very last moment, noticed that the light from the seam that separated the side-by-side swinging doors was abnormally obscured, the *trattoria* owner-full time chef-part time waiter and self-anointed protector of Laura Kean would also have been a patient in a nearby hospital sporting a broken nose to accompany his tormented heart.

Back at the stove full of boiling pots of water and simmering sauces Tomasso's mind spiraled out of control. In rapid Italian he mumbled, "What gall! Why is this old man who knows little of my precious Laura... why is he trying to win her over with gold? Of all things, why gold? She knows, I know, that life is not made of gold. Gold is temporary, but food, ah yes, food is, well...food is permanent. Lasting love is cemented in food, not gold, you foolish old man. How trivial that hard gold when compared to my soft *gnocchi*, for example my soft, golden *gnocchi*. Not a simple chain of gold. Why a chain? Go ahead! Try if you must old man because you will lose. I will win her love with my golden, perfect *gnocchi*. Yes, it's true we have *fusilli* today, but tomorrow, ah, tomorrow, *gnocchi*. You will see, old man. Foolish old man, go back to the mountains."

And with two plates of fresh green salad crowned with cherry tomatoes and small pepperoncini in hand, the chef headed back to the window table. To his surprise there was no sign of the gold necklace, not a trace. It's disappearance led the owner-chef-protector to conclude that the old man was planning to place it around the American beauty's neck when they were alone and out of the public's envious and spiteful eye.

"It's absolutely lovely..." was what Tomasso's straining ears heard before he reentered the noisy kitchen that masked all dining room conversations.

"She'll adore it. What a nice thought," said Laura.

"*Grazie*. Now tell me, what brings you to Italy?" asked Dr. Benedetti as he slipped the jewelry case back into his coat pocket.

"Well you may find this crazy but it was my husband who led me here," Laura replied nonchalantly.

This time it was Lorenzo who froze in place. Unlike the *trattoria's* owner who was startled by what he saw from the kitchen, the old professor was rattled by what he had just heard from the widow of his one-time nemesis. Lorenzo thought, *Was it possible? Could her dead husband manipulate her as effectively as he had manipulated me?*

"Your husband?" asked Lorenzo nervously.

"Yes. Dante had always wanted to live in Italy for an extended period of time. We spoke of it often and I agreed to the idea, but we just never made it a priority. So here I am fulfilling his dream as a way of understanding what it was about this country that interested him. From what I've experienced here in Florence, I now know that Dante would have become one with Tuscany."

Clearly, Laura was speaking to him in code. Her cryptic words evoked vivid memories that made the professor perspire in fear. He recalled the time when the dead Dr. Paolo had become one with the former Dean. When, from another world, Dante took control of his arm, of his hand, of his fingers leaving him helpless in full view of everyone in that library room in Wilmington College. He felt the powerful control from the beyond. Authoritative control, a true commanding force like the raw energy of a rogue tsunami. And now, here in this little *trattoria* in Florence, dead Dante was sending him messages. The codes from Laura were coming as rapidly as were the plates of food from Tomasso. Two small bowls of homemade fusilli glistening in butter were placed on the table. Tomasso also left a piece of pecorino Romano with one end wrapped in cloth along with a small grater.

"*Grazie* Tomasso," Laura said cheerfully.

Lorenzo, who was desperately trying to ignore his thoughts, asked, "How do you know his name? Did he tell us and I missed it?"

"I'm sorry. I should have introduced you to Tomasso. He is the owner as well as the chef. I am renting the apartment above the *trattoria* and Tomasso has prepared most of the meals I've had on this trip. Francesca, his mother, makes pasta every morning. '*Francesca fresca*' is how Tomasso like to say it. She uses eggs from the chickens she's raising in her yard," Laura added with a smile.

"Well, this is indeed excellent. It is as good as Rosa's pasta. The texture is perfect. Forgive me, Laura, for probing, but what did you mean when you said that 'he would become one with Tuscany'? Is it just a figure of speech?" Lorenzo Benedetti did his best to not ask the list of questions he so desperately wanted to ask Laura. He would have preferred to be more direct: *Laura does your husband control you and others from the beyond? Does he dominate your every move?* And most pointedly: *Will your dead husband manipulate me again? How can you be sure of it? I must know to preserve what I have left of my waning sanity.*

But those thoughts remained trapped in his mind as he was trying to maintain a degree of calm sophistication. He was unsure of what she knew about Dante's plans or of his powers. The once steadfast Dr. Lorenzo Benedetti, who had become increasingly paranoid with each passing month of retirement, even considered the possibly that Dr. Paolo's wife not only communicated with, but also provided targeted directives to, her late husband. Thus, Lorenzo took precautions to make sure not to anger the good doctor.

Laura considered Lorenzo's questions after she savored the entire plate of Francesca's delicate fusilli. She wondered, *what exactly did I mean? Was it simply a figure of speech or did I mean to imply more?*

"Lorenzo, I don't know you very well and it's difficult for me to share my emotions with others, but since you asked, I'll tell you outright," she said in a firm, clear voice. "Dante's dream was to come here to Italy. I was the one who put up roadblocks to that dream. I'm making myself feel better by coming here and trying to understand the magic of this land that so much interested my husband. Now, after having spent time here, there is no doubt in my mind that he would have controlled the machine, he would have partaken in any and all events, activities, festivals, and he would have been a central figure—the organizer, the manager, the doer, the sweeper—he would have made sure it was all done right. He would have become one with all Tuscans. He could easily work with farmers that live in small villages on hillsides as well as those who live and work in big and small towns alike. He would have embraced them all like the great stonewalls that encircle and protect these cities. Like a dutiful father, he would look over them. And I now know that he is still able to do this because I did something I never planned to do in my life..."

"*Pollo arrosto con patate per la principessa*, and the same for the gentleman, roasted chicken with potatoes," described Tomasso as he set down the warm plates while removing the empty pasta bowls.

"Oh Tomasso, this looks exquisite," Laura gushed. Her enthusiasm for his cooking made the chef smile broadly while he thought about the waning value of gold.

"*Grazie*," the owner-chef-protector replied.

Lorenzo was eager to hear Laura complete her sentence. "As you were saying?"

The aroma from the roasted chicken coated with fresh rosemary and black pepper surrounded with golden, roasted potatoes filled her senses and distracted her from her line of thought. She couldn't immediately recall what she was saying or even where she'd left off.

"You were saying that you had done something that you never "

"Oh yes. Right. What I never planned to do was to discard the only tangible item that belonged to Dante, a symbol of my enduring commitment to him—the gold ring I gave him when we were married. But I did it. I threw it in the Arno. I realized that I don't need it anymore. We are forever united no matter where he is. Indeed, he is here now," she said placing her open right hand across the top of her cleavage, where the bottom of Rosa's gold necklace once hung. "And he is here, everywhere. In this city, in this building and in everyone I meet," she added.

Twitching tremors—like those felt after drinking three double espressos in rapid succession—began in his toes then traveled across his feet to his lower legs. The odd sensations migrated upward through

Lorenzo's body until it reached his eyelids. Now he had no doubt that the physician's dearly departed husband controlled her often and apparently at will. But, there was a new and terrifying revelation—one he had never considered, was completely unforeseen, and went against all unscripted rules of the flow of invisible powers. Laura, it appeared, was able to control her dead husband. Upon reaching this conclusion, Lorenzo turned pale and he experienced a sudden loss of appetite. The once aromatic and succulent meal instantly became just dead poultry and starch on a plate.

Laura delved into her lunch with zest, but then looked up at Lorenzo and noticed, as only a skilled physician would, the subtle signs of sudden distress. She set her fork gently across the plate, reached across the small table with her right hand and took the professor's left hand into her own. She was certain that the sensitive Dr. Benedetti was distraught over Dante's unfortunate passing.

"Don't despair," she said reassuringly with a slight smile. "He's still with us and in more ways than you know."

The extremely sensual *mano nella mano*, Laura's hand wrapped around the old man's hand, was too much for Tomasso to witness. The pendulum had swung in the favor of the old Tuscan and the chef needed a way to regain control, to turn Laura's attention back to him. He had one last chance—with *dolce*—a sweet dessert must be his winning move. However, pears and cheese offered little in the way of evoking affection, therefore, he had to be inventive without altering the written-in-pencil but set-in-stone lunch menu. The peeled and cored pear halves lay in a yin-yang, side-by-side position on the small light-blue plate; their flat sides up. Tomasso filled the small center craters of the cored pear halves with syrupy limoncello. He then wedged between the halves a generous slice of cave-ripened Asiago cheese alongside a thin slice of fine, dark chocolate. Drizzled around the pears on the small plate was deep red strawberry syrup, an accent that provided the final stroke to the perfect harmony of seasonal colors.

After clearing the plates from the small table, Tomasso returned with his aptly named *dolce* invention.

"*Voilà!*" exclaimed Tomasso cheerfully as he careful delivered the two small plates of pear. "*Pere riconciliati.*"

Laura gushed at the site of the special dessert. "Oh my! Tomasso, why how beautiful! How lovely. Let's see. Pears and cheese and, and is that a sliver of chocolate? What did you call this?"

"*Principessa,*" replied the beaming owner-chef-self-anointed protector of Laura. "I call this *dolce* 'reconciled pears' because the pear that was once whole is brought back together despite the attempt by the cheese and the chocolate to keep them apart. The center of each half is filled with *dolce amore*, sweet love. It is famous limoncello from Ravello."

While Laura was enthralled with the dessert and Tomasso's eloquent, if not overreaching, personification of the unassuming pears, Lorenzo Benedetti was rapidly becoming unglued.

He could not have used the word 'riconciliati' by chance, thought the professor. *The chef must also be 'one with Dante' and he must have been directed by the manipulative dead man to torture me, to send me a message, to remind me that I am not free, as I had assumed. Or perhaps it was the lovely, innocent-looking Laura who sent the clear sign to me via her dead husband via the chef?*

'Reconciled' was one word that the old Tuscan never wanted to hear again. He never wanted to see the word, to speak it, or to write again, neither in Italian or in English or in any other language for that matter. He had his answer. Now it was time to leave the *trattoria* and to retreat back to the relative safety of the mountains and to Rosa's soft arms before it got any worse. Lorenzo Benedetti looked at his watch and feigned the need to leave immediately in order to catch the train back home. In a rather lively and animated moment, Tomasso and Lorenzo settled the bill with an exchange of rapid, breviloquent Italian sentences, and it was with pure delight that Tomasso, who was still beaming at the symmetry of his dessert creation, watched the hasty departure of the old man. Lorenzo left the *trattoria* with coat in hand and without as much as a second glance at the table.

Laura was startled by the sudden departure of her lunch date. She did not comprehend what the two men discussed, but it appeared as if Tomasso waved off the lunch debt convincingly and without reservation. The clear victory of food over gold, young over old, urban over rural Tuscan, satisfied the owner-chef-waiter and self-anointed protector of Laura who then proceeded to help himself not only to the old man's vacant seat across from the just rescued princess, but also to the untouched plate of perfectly presented pears.

———◆———

Phil's oversized, high-resolution computer monitor had plenty of room to accommodate live streaming videos of Brad in Boston, Amy in Minnesota, and Abby in Washington, D.C. The virtual meeting program also allowed the initiator to use a whiteboard that could be seen by all participants. Phil was genuinely pleased to see everyone. It brought back memories of their good times together in Dr. Paolo's class.

"Nice to see you all," Phil started. "Thanks for accepting the invitation. How are things?"

"Just straight out here in lovely Minnesota," replied Amy, who looked even prettier than Phil remembered.

"Same here in Beantown," answered Brad.

"Never a dull moment in D.C. where the action happens everywhere but in the Capitol Building," Abby said with a broad smile.

Phil and Abby hadn't video-chatted before, but seeing Abby live had a physical effect on the conference call initiator. Phil quickly refocused his thoughts.

"Listen, thanks again for taking time to hear me out. I recently had a brainstorm that I'm about to tackle mathematically, but before I do I would like your frank feedback on how it comes across to you. I simply don't trust anyone here to keep it a secret or even to comprehend my idea fully, and given what we've done together as a team, well, I thought you'd be the best ones to hear this first."

"Go for it," encouraged Amy who was sipping a hot cup of tea alone in her apartment.

"Okay. So this all has to do with proving mathematically, or rather, providing the probability values to show that we are not as unique as we think we are. Let me start with the universe and our own solar system. I'll start with an analogy. If a gust of wind drives a few grains of sand in your eyes, the tremendous pain could lead you to imagine that your eyes are filled with all of the sand on the beach. Similarly, when we look at the evening stars, the sheer number makes us think that we're seeing all of the total celestial objects when in fact, like the few particles of sand in your eyes, we're only experiencing a tiny fraction of the total. Long way to say that the probability is quite high that Earth-like planets exist in the universe. For now, just accept that as a given. Not known however, is whether we exist elsewhere. And by 'us' I don't mean multi-cell organisms or mammals or humans, but us. You and you and you and me exactly as we are here and now—exact replicas. And not just one clone, but rather hundreds perhaps thousands doing the exact same thing that we are doing now, just elsewhere. The Big Bang may have been a random event, but the result of that event was anything but random. The fact that we are all built with just four DNA bases and that we rely on just a handful of elements to survive makes the likelihood very high, at least on a cosmic probability scale, that we exist identically elsewhere."

"So," interrupted Amy. "Even if you can show this mathematically, say if there are one hundred Amys doing exactly what I'm doing right now at this moment then how could it be proven and what are the ramifications of such a theory?"

"Right. That's exactly why I wanted to talk with the three of you. I need your help to figure this out. The mathematical models will need to be substantiated with something quantifiable and Abby, isn't that what you want to do with telepathy? Quantify telepathic ability and telepathic episodes?"

"Yes, that's right Phil," replied Abby. "At the moment I'm trying to test whether or not telepathy is an innate sense that is lost early in life due to the development of speech that, as you know, relies heavily on being able to process sound. If this is true then I should be able to quantify the gain or loss of telepathy with age." Abby stopped short of describing details of the experiment because she didn't want to tell the group about Rosi. She wanted to speak privately with Phil first and she knew that it was going to be a complicated discussion at best, and a contentious one at worse. She also didn't want to tell the others about the sleep-state interactions she's had with the young Dr. Paolo but she knew that these episodes might be relevant to Phil's research. Abby made a mental note to discuss them later with Phil, clearly now was not the right time.

"But how is the ontology of telepathy going to help you, Phil?" questioned Amy. "Oh and I almost forgot to tell you that we worked out a way to quickly scan individual DNA sequences for the Xp29.47 gene in Bob's lab, and we identified that gene in the DNA of an anonymous donor. How exciting is that? Ajay is ramping up the process to screen as many DNA samples as possible. So soon we'll know the distribution of this gene in a larger sample size then perhaps we'll even start to understand how the expression of this gene is regulated. Abby, this may fit well into your study. Don't you think?"

"Yes. Absolutely. Let's keep each other posted on progress. I'm sure there's a collaborative study here. That's so cool Amy," Abby said excitedly.

"To be honest I'm not sure how telepathy fits into the multiverse scenario," said Phil in response to Amy's question. "I could imagine that if telepathy is indeed a primitive form of communication as Abby suggests, and you Amy are finding the gene for it in our DNA, then perhaps it's a universal mode of advanced communication, one that transcends time and space. In fact, this may be one of the branches off the main mathematical formula I'm developing. Communication is a major, if not a very important branch, and who knows maybe it will turn out to be *the* main branch after all of the other parts are assembled."

"And don't forget our brain," added Brad who had been listening and watching the discussion intently. "I'm working with this amazingly smart guy named Alex and I think he's onto something big. We'll soon know how, or rather if, the brain can repair itself and if so, we hope to develop this further. Think Alzheimer's disease here folks."

"Brad, did you say Alex?" Abby asked.

"Yes. Alex is his name."

"That's odd. My advisor's name is Alexa and well, that's one hell of a coincidence. Don't you think?"

"I guess so."

"Is that it guys? I have to go. I have a hematology exam tomorrow," said Amy.

"Thanks everyone," replied Phil. "I'll be in touch again soon."

"Later. Good luck," Brad said as he signed off. Amy had also signed out of the video conference call leaving just Phil and Abby in each other's view.

"Hey. How've you been? It's been awhile since I've heard from you," Phil said. Abby had to think quickly. She preferred not to tell Phil about her personal life while on a video call, telling him without cameras would be much better.

"I've been straight out here, no break whatsoever. Sorry. Listen, I need to go to the ladies room," she lied. "Can I call you back in just a few? There's something I'd like to tell you."

"Yeah, sure," replied Phil who was going to suggest a first-ever long distance video sex but decided against it after hearing the seriousness in Abby's voice.

2

The only thing Alexa enjoyed more than dinner at *The Beltway Bistro* was lunch at the comfortable pub. The best time to arrive for lunch was before noon when the tables were mostly empty and the wait staff was low key and barely awake. Abby thought that the atmosphere at the *Bistro* would be the best place for Rosi and her telepathic friends to meet Alexa, and to hear the details of the experiment they would help conduct with children.

Aside from discussing the goals of Abby's experiment, Alexa could hardly wait to meet Rosi and the other telepaths. Nonverbal communication has been a topic of great curiosity for Alexa, as well as for many of her peers. But studies on telepathy were performed with a short list of nonhuman primates—rhesus monkeys, baboons, and tamarins—kept in captivity. There was also one natural field study with great apes published by the ageless observer, Jane Goodall. Studies with humans have been observational as in let's see how newborns and young infants wave their arms and flail their legs in response to a sad face or a happy face made by their mother or by a complete stranger. Never before had a telepathic study been designed using minors. Alexa wanted to make sure that the study personnel understood the importance of what could become a landmark event. She also wanted to make sure that everyone understood their unique role, and that they were willing to see the experiment through to its completion.

While Abby told Alexa how she met Rosi at the National Art Museum's gift shop and how the two had hit it off, she kept the other, more personal details to herself. The professor urged Abby to document her silent discovery of Rosi not only because it was quite unusual, but also for posterity should her research prove to be revolutionary.

"Future generations always want to know how specific situations evolved, how events unfurled, how one thing led to another. This story starts with a chance meeting between two telepaths in a gift shop. That, my friend, is not your average we-were-working-in-the-same-laboratory kind of story. Your story is all about timing and chance. Love it," remarked Alexa who had just taken a seat next to Abby when Rosi arrived with two friends in tow. Abby introduced Rosi to Alexa then waited for Rosi to introduce her companions. Olysia was an unassuming tall, thin, strawberry blonde who outwardly seemed to be shy and guarded. Johanna was shorter than Olysia; at five foot six inches she was the same height as Rosi and Abby. Johanna was a Brazilian beauty with a dark, alluring complexion, a long thin face and jet-black hair.

It was the first time Olysia and Johanna met Abby and they wasted no time in evaluating her inner sensuality. Silently, they readily agreed with Rosi's description of the graduate student as a *diamond whose many angles have yet to be viewed.* Abby felt flush, but she roundly dismissed the distractions and got down to business. Rosi, Olysia and Johanna got the message and they soon turned their full attention to Alexa who was more than happy to address the young women.

"Okay ladies. First I'd like to thank you for coming to hear about our study and your role in it, should you agree to participate. If Abby hasn't told you already, I am broadly interested in understanding alternative forms of communication as a way to help those with communicative disorders. These disorders can range from the inability to speak at all—a condition that commonly manifests in very young children—to the decline of clear sentence structure due to brain diseases that manifests primarily in the elderly. The spectrum of this latter syndrome is as wide as it is important, especially today because the general population is shifting, in pure numbers, towards the older. Now, along comes Abby with this idea of how to study telepathy, a form of nonverbal communication that is, at best, a nebulous concept to both the general public and to those in my field as well. We're hoping to change all of that, right Ab?"

A response from Abby would normally have been delivered without hesitation, but there was a longer than usual pause because she knew that the three telepaths were not completely comfortable around the Alexa. Abby sensed that all three had bad experiences with teachers at some point in their lives and Alexa's forthright introduction to the study was making them feel as though they were back in a classroom. After a few pensive moments, Abby restructured the lead-in to the study and softened the tone of the discussion.

Abby told a personal story in a slow and calm voice as if she was speaking to young children. "I always knew that I had this unique talent, but my telepathy was something that I did not share with friends nor discuss openly or even secretly for that matter with anyone. And it wasn't until I was in college and took this amazing senior-level class that allowed me to explore new ideas that I revealed my gift. What I realized while taking that class was that I wanted to know everything there is to know about telepathy. I want to quantify, to measure, each and every last detail of how telepathy evolved and how to perfect its use. I want to understand what happens at the molecular and cellular levels that regulate and control it. I even want to know what parts of the brain are active during telepathic events and, if I can, I also want to know if telepathy transcends time and space. I want to do all of these things using the latest and the greatest technology available.

"Until I met Rosi, I thought I was a one in a million. I knew that I had this special sense, a special ability that has no apparent use in today's society. But then Rosi told me that other telepaths exist and the simple fact that you three are not only telepaths, but you are also artists, is an important connection and a potentially huge clue with respect to understanding the areas of the brain involved with communication. Understanding telepathy is my life's work and this clinical study is an important step in what I hope will be a long, productive journey." Abby continued as she correctly sensed that Rosi, Olysia and Johanna were warming up to the study. Although not a telepath Alexa knew exactly what Abby was doing and where she was going.

"So a small step in understanding telepathy is to determine if it exists in other people, specifically in those that either don't know they have it or those that are unable to understand what it is and how to use it. And I decided to start with children, specifically deaf children, children born with the inability to assimilate sound that clearly impact their ability to develop verbal language skills." Abby then recounted the story of the young deaf child who left her blanket on the bus and how frustrated the child was with her inability to communicate with her mother.

"That little girl was silently screaming. She wanted her mother to understand her inner plea. That episode, that chance encounter with that little girl, was the clue I needed to devise the set of experiments we're about to initiate," Abby said. "And these studies...not only are they very important, but they will require your participation, patience and devotion. We hope you are willing to join us and to be a part of our team."

All activities of the restaurant—a waitress taking an order, the bartender filling a mug with beer, the new patrons being seated—all disappeared into the background, into the shadows, as if a bright spotlight in the middle of an otherwise empty stage illuminated the table of five women. Each was focused on the other and on the topic at hand yet only one of these women, Alexa, had ever undertaken such a serious project that involved human beings—and a study that naturally had high risks.

Abby's soft approach and personal story put the telepaths at ease. There was no doubt that they were going to participate in the study as receivers of telepathic signals. Rosi's fondness for Abby's intellect heightened as the graduate student outlined the test group of congenitally deaf children and the control group of children with no outward signs of hearing impairment.

"There may be other groups we want to study, but for now we'll keep it simple. We start recruiting subjects next week. Are there any questions, comments or concerns?" Abby asked.

But before the telepaths had a chance to answer, Alexa added, "From what I understand from Abby, some telepaths are better receivers than transmitters and vice versa, while others are proficient communicators in both directions. For these studies, it is imperative that you receive information, and you should keep to an absolute minimum the amount of conversation you have with each subject because it could, if anyone could verify it, be considered a form of subject manipulation. Should that happen we would have to dismiss the result obtained with that child from the rest of the dataset."

"Right. You are only to read and to receive. There should be minimal two-way communication with the child," added Abby.

"I learned just this morning that I'm able to offer you a one-time payment for your involvement with this study. It won't be much, but it's better than nothing," added Alexa.

Although all three guests had questions and comments, Rosi was the *de facto* spokeswoman for the group. "So none of us has ever done anything like this before and we think it's really a great study. We, and other telepaths that we hang with, always considered ourselves privileged to have this ability. So one major concern, that may not be a concern at all, is what happens if the study shows what you want it to show, then what? Will we be marginalized by society? Cast off? Chastised? Will our names be associated with this study in any way? On one hand, this is very cool Abby. On the other hand, we were happy being who we are. We don't want others interfering with what we do. Our art is our form of expression. Our telepathy is our sacred sanctuary. It's our way of ignoring the common person whose spoken words are often not worth the air used to create them. Can we participate anonymously? And we don't need to get paid either. We'll volunteer our time."

"Let me see if I can address your concerns, and Alexa, please feel free to jump in," said Abby who was clearly in her element. "I'll begin with the hypothesis. We hypothesize that telepathy is an innate form of nonverbal communication that is more completely developed in those unable to processes sound, those that are born deaf. They are known to have speech delays or impairments relative to those who are not deaf. It also states that telepathy is present in young children and that telepathic skill improves with age. A deeper part of the hypothesis, and one that we probably won't be able to answer for some time, is that telepathy is a primitive, yet higher, type of communication and that verbal communication, despite it's complexity, is a devolved human trait. It's backwards compared to the more efficient and universal language of telepathy. My hope is that our research will bring this intrinsically human sense out from the shadows and allow telepathy to become more accepted, even mainstream perhaps. So no, I don't think telepaths will be marginalized by individuals, but I can't promise what greater society will say, or do, with our findings should the data support the hypothesis."

"If you decide to be an active member of this study group, you will have to sign a confidentiality agreement. We need to make sure that the identities of the study subjects are not disclosed to anyone," added Alexa who wondered if the telepaths were communicating to each other as she spoke. She searched for cues like eye-to-eye contact or shifts in body language but none were obvious.

"That will be fine," said Olysia who, until that moment, had not said a word. Johanna looked at Rosi and shrugged to accentuate the point she had already sent silently.

"That's acceptable to us," Rosi replied. "You know, it's not like we're some secret society that wants to take over the race, it's just that we enjoy our uniqueness, away from the spotlight and we don't want this luxury to be compromised in any way. We think the study goals are great and, well, as you mentioned, one never really knows where this will lead. Let us know when we start and what we need to do. We're all in and we're ready to help out."

"Thank you," said Alexa. "This study is going to be a lot of fun, and I think it has tremendous potential. It couldn't happen without you. All of you."

Rosi turned towards Abby and smiled: *Go now my dear/without worry or fear/to your world where you look beyond the frontier/when you return/ tonight should you yearn/we, yes we/all three of us will be here/waiting for you with candlelight and cheer.*

Abby was instantly aroused. And from across the table she also knew that Olysia and Johanna matched, if not exceeded, her state of excitement. Alexa was unaware of the sexually charged atmosphere, which was a good thing.

Abby was accompanied her mentor back to the university where a very busy afternoon awaited. "That went well, don't you think?" Alexa asked her mentee as they walked away from the *Bistro*. "They seem like very nice women. I hope they are enthusiastic about this study. Do you think they are the type to be passionate?"

"Oh yes," replied Abby assuredly. "I think they are passionate. Very passionate."

———•———

Why did it feel like she was cheating on him? They weren't married nor were they dating. Phil was her first and only boyfriend and she enjoyed his company, his intellect, his humor and his sexuality very much. But were they really a couple? Did she care for him more than she wanted to admit? And what about Phil? Did he care for her more than he let on? Did he have other female interests? Or were they simply each other's form of entertainment and pleasure until mister or miss perfect came calling? Why is she feeling so guilty for having to tell Phil that she'd made love, and perhaps is even in love, with Rosi? Why? Where did this guilt come from?

"Hello," said Abby cautiously.

"So hi. How are you? It's been a long time and I've missed you," replied Phil with levity in his voice. This is not what Abby wanted to hear, but in a real way it was exactly what she needed.

"I've missed you too," she replied half-heartedly. "Listen, I've been meaning to call but it's been absolutely crazy here with teaching duty, classes, and now my project is off the ground and there just doesn't seem to be enough hours in a day. Sorry."

"No need to be sorry. I hear you. Same here. You kind of wonder where the day goes. It's totally non-stop."

Abby thought to be direct and forthright and to just say it, just blurt it out.

"Phil I want to tell you that I met someone. She's an artist, a telepathic artist named Rosi. She's about our age and she's awesome and she's going to be involved with my research study on telepathy in children."

"That's great!" Phil replied almost too quickly.

"And I made love to her. I mean we made love to each other. It was mutual."

This time there was no quick response. Phil was silent. A woman? Abby made love to a woman? He was taken aback by what he'd just heard. He was instantly bewildered and simultaneously perplexed. What did he care who she made love to? It's not his business to care or to know, is it? But wait, weren't they a couple? And why was she telling him this and why did it bother him when it really shouldn't matter?

"Um, I kind of don't know what to say Ab. I thought we had something here, something unique, something special; I mean how did this happen? Where did you meet her?"

Abby calmly recounted how Rosi read her thoughts in the museum's gift shop and how one thing led to another. She spared no details on how she ended up in Rosi's bed. Through Abby's words Phil was taken inside Rosi's beautiful loft apartment and art studio. Abby detailed some of Rosi's amalgamart and how the artist blended two different concepts into a single painting or sculpture. Abby voice was calm and sure. She even described her lovemaking with Rosi as quite different than what she experienced with him. In some ways it was completely different while in other ways it lacked what only he could provide. She told Phil, quite offhandedly, that she thought Rosi was bisexual, but that she wasn't completely sure. Abby ended the synopsis by describing the beautiful physical features of Rosi, as well as Olysia and Johanna, and the role the telepaths were going to have in her upcoming experiment.

Phil heard most of what Abby was saying. He was distracted and decidedly turned on by images of Abby making love to a woman. Her full breasts fondled by small soft hands that instinctively knew their way around the creases and folds of a woman's body. He saw her strong back arching in rhythm like it did when she was close to reaching an orgasm, and the passionate kissing and the gentle pull of a woman's lower lip as Abby had so often done to him when she was in that zone. He wished he knew exactly what Rosi looked like so that he could have a more accurate picture of how these telepaths looked together. And did Abby just say that Rosi was bisexual? Did she actually mean bisexual in the way that he thought of bisexuals as having sex with both a man, or men, and a woman, or women, simultaneously, as in at the same time? Is that what she meant. Did Abby just say two women? He wondered if he'd be invited to join them someday, perhaps?

Abby interpreted Phil's silence to mean that he was upset. She wished she could read his thoughts across the great distance that separated them, but she could not. Thus she was left with trying to make things a bit better for the young mathematician whose company and touch she still desired. Interestingly, it was at this exact point in time when she wondered if she too was bisexual.

"Phil?" she said choosing her words carefully. "I think you should come down for a visit and meet Rosi and the other telepaths. I think you'd enjoy them."

Phil was still silent on the other end of the line. Should he fake being turned off by the entire situation or should be tell her that he's in fantasy heaven with the potential of being invited to a threesome, or better yet, a fivesome! But he thought better of it. He didn't want to let on for fear of overreaching and ruining his big chance at an all out wild orgy.

"Sounds good Ab," he said in his best-deadpanned, voice. "Things are quite busy here so I'll have to get back to you."

"Okay," Abby replied. She almost added, "You do know I love you, right?" But she decided against it mainly because she wasn't sure if she meant it. Instead she said, "Think about joining us for Thanksgiving. We're celebrating at Rosi's place."

3

"Jo, this is beautiful. Simply beautiful."

Dr. Johnson held the small glass vial that contained a dram of pure white crystals shaped like tiny spears up to the mid-day's sunlight. For a moment, the professor marveled at the accelerated speed of modern day research compared to how it occurred over three decades ago when he was a postdoc, like the thin Korean standing on the other side of his desk. From identifying the chemical compound expressed in mice at the exact moment of induced death to the synthesis of pure material in a glass vial had taken Jo just two months. This same process would have taken the Nobel laureate several years, if not a full decade, to accomplish and the end product would not have been as pure.

"Never seen before?" he asked Jo.

"Aaa...no. The structure is not in any chemical database. Not in the natural or in the synthetic databases."

"And the Hopkin's chem synthesizers? Confidentiality agreement in place, right?" Jo nodded hesitantly because he knew that it was not his job to secure the legal document

"Aaa...you, you did agreement."

"Right. So I did," replied Dr. Johnson who promptly placed the vial on his desk then scribbled a note to have his secretary make sure the legal paperwork was in order.

"What do you think this stuff does Jo?" Jo shook his head from side to side.

"All I know is that it is... aaa... made by all organs. The muscle heart, the stomach and the bowels too, as well as all of the organs of the immune system: spleen, thymus and lungs. Aaa...liver too. They all made, but only right after death. No trace of chemical five minutes later or even thirty minutes later. Just at death time."

"And did you put this back into mice?"

"Aaa...yes. Like you say, like you said. Mi-Ok injected mice, different amounts of chemical into mice, like you say, aaa...said."

"And? What happened? What did the mice do? Did they survive the injection?" Dr. Johnson asked excitedly.

Mi-Ok who was standing next to Jo answered the professor's questions meekly but firmly. Her command of the English language was clearly superior to that of the thin postdoc. She looked at Dr. Johnson and replied, "When placed back in the cage after the injection, each of the ten mice per group were perfectly still for a moment. Then their little bodies twitched once, as if all of the muscles in their forelimbs, in their back, and in their hindlimbs simultaneously contracted. But only once, then they again were still for another moment before resuming normal behavior. They were as active as ever. This behavioral pattern occurred after each of the three doses." Mi-Ok reached into the pocket of her lab coat, took out her cell phone and handed the device to Dr. Johnson. The short video clip showed exactly what Mi-Ok had just described. He watched the eleven-second recording, and then returned the cell phone to the technician who, after a deft flick of the screen with her thumb, returned it to the professor.

"This is what usually occurs," she said. The second clip showed mice that had just been injected with harmless salt-water then placed back in their cage where they actively scurried about without hesitation, as if nothing had happened to them at all. Differences between the two groups could not have been more striking.

As the cell phone was again returned to Mi-Ok she added, "And there were no deaths. Not even at the highest dose as you instructed—the mouse equivalent of two grams per kilogram or about ten times a typical human dose for other chemicals."

"Does the chemical linger?" Dr. Johnson asked Jo but Mi-Ok answered quickly.

"As instructed, I surgically excised a piece of liver from a group of mice within a few minutes after the chemical was injected then again the next day. Jo found no trace of the chemical in these samples. The chemical appears to be very short lived. There was none in their blood, urine or feces, either."

"Which group?" Dr. Johnson asked.

"The highest dose group, as you instructed," she replied. Mi-Ok wanted to make sure her boss understood that she was following his directives. "Jo also put the liver cells from mice that got the chemical, and liver cells from mice that received saline into culture. He then made an observation."

Jo was not expecting Mi-Ok to tell the head of the laboratory that he had, on his own accord, performed this small but potentially very important, comparative experiment. Ever since Dr. Johnson lashed out at him in front of the whole laboratory, Jo was very careful not to do anything other than what was asked of him. But driven by the desire to learn a new technique and to fulfill a nagging curiosity, Jo decided to ask Mi-Ok to show him how to make cells grow in culture, in plastic flasks with nutrients that sustained them. It was also a way for Jo to spend more time with the person he was growing to admire not only for her technical skills and sharp mind, but also for her strong, sure and level-headed personality. He simply wanted to be with her as much as possible. Mi-Ok was, for the most part, always neutral towards him. She never expressed any feeling for the thin Korean postdoc one way or another; she neither flirted nor rebuffed his subtle attempts at making a pass at her. She was just Mi-Ok. She was what she was and she felt what she felt. Jo accepted her ways, but he now had to reveal preliminary data on an experiment that needed to be repeated again, if not several more times, to confirm the findings. He had to say something as Dr. Johnson's eyes were now firmly fixed on him.

"Aaa...I wanted to put the liver cells in culture to see if the chemical made a difference."

"Yes," the professor said with an inflection suggestive of a question rather an answer.

"The liver cells from the mice that got the chemical lived for tree weeks but the liver cells from the control mice died in just two days."

"Three weeks?" the professor asked.

"Aaa, yes th-ree weeks," Jo said annunciating the word carefully. "Th-en when the cells began to die I added some of the chemical and they started to grow again and divide again. They are still alive now four weeks all together."

"Let me see if I have this right," Dr. Johnson began. "The chemi-cal, when given to mice at the highest concentration, was not toxic. The

160

mice responded by becoming momentarily still followed by a single, transient twitch before returning to normal behavior. The chemical had a very short existence in mice, as it was undetectable in their liver, blood, secretions and excretions within moments after administration. Liver cells from mice given the chemical, but not from the livers of control mice, grew robustly and for several generations *in vitro*, and the chemical, when added to the liver culture media reignited growth and cell division." Jo and Mi-Ok nodded affirmatively as Dr. Johnson listed each result.

This time, the Nobel laureate and head of the laboratory didn't appear angry or upset or even disappointed. Dr. Johnson was simply pensive as he leaned back in his chair and pivoted towards the office windows and the day's bright sunlight. He left the two lab mates standing awkwardly in front of his desk awaiting permission to leave. They looked at each other briefly then back to their boss whose side profile was dark against the outside light behind him. He was breathing shallowly and regularly while apparently in deep thought. Finally, after what seemed like hours to the young scientists, Dr. Johnson spun back, leaned forward and looked squarely into Mi-Ok's large dark eyes.

Dr. Johnson's question was as direct as it was forceful. "What is the largest animal you've put to sleep with acupuncture needles?" Mi-Ok was so startled by the suddenness of his movements that she popped up in place like a partially heated corn kernel.

"A cat. A small cat, a kitten," she answered.

Dr. Johnson didn't want to spend all day asking question so he went directly to his bottom line. "Will it work on primates? Mi-Ok, do you think it will work on humans?" Before she had a chance to answer, Dr. Johnson rose from his chair and asked Jo to have a seat in one of five chairs that surrounded an oval, glass-topped table located on the far side of his office. Obediently, Jo sat in the chair.

"Can you show me where you would insert the needles?" asked Dr. Johnson as he pointed to the back of Jo's naturally hairless thin neck.

Jo was now placed in the second awkward situation of the day. Mi-Ok's warm fingers gently palpated the base of Jo's neck just below the hairline. As her thumb climbed the large trapezius muscle up to the base of his skull, Jo felt a tingling sensation in the upper part of his inner thighs. *This can't be happening*, Jo thought to himself. *It mustn't.* But the oddly timed tingling sensation radiated all the way to the tip of his erection that was now on a trajectory of its own. It started to build as Mi-Ok silently placed her left hand next to her right so that the tip of each thumb barely touched each other at the base of his cranium. Ever so slowly Jo made deliberate moves to cover his growing groin with both hands as Mi-Ok's middle finger on her right hand and the outermost fifth digit—the pinkie—of her left hand, pressed firmly into his neck.

"Here and here," she said looking up at Dr. Johnson who, thankfully, was focused not on Jo's crotch, but squarely on the back of the postdoc's neck where Mi-Ok had left only two fingers pressed in place. "Only the right one for sleep," she said with authority.

"And the left one, the pinky finger?" asked Dr. Johnson who pressed his right index finger just above Mi-Ok's pinky finger. "Is this one for death? Both are needed for death, right?"

The sensation of Dr. Johnson's relatively large fingers on his neck combined with his repeated use of the word 'death' counteracted Mi-Ok's simulating touch such that Jo's erection reversed course and retreated rapidly, much to the postdoc's great relief.

"Yes."

"Would you try this technique on a monkey if I can arranged it? I mean, the sleep part only?"

Mi-Ok stood firm and stared blankly at the intricate pattern of the Oriental rug on the floor of her boss's office. She blinked four times while weighing her response. Although it should, Mi-Ok was not completely sure if the technique would work on large animals. The last thing she ever wanted to do was to do harm or inflict pain with acupuncture needles. It would violate her grandfather's creed. His sage voice, long silenced, rang repeatedly in her head. *These ancient needles are to be used properly, with precision and with purpose to heal, to soothe and, if necessary, to end suffering. Should you use them to cause harm, it would reveal a deep personal flaw.*

"Yes," she answered tentatively. Mi-Ok was overcome not only by the challenge, but also by the pressure of having to please her boss.

"Good. I'll let you know when I've lined something up. Thank you."

And with that statement from Dr. Richard Johnson, the two lab mates left the office in silence. Neither said another word.

————•————

The oversized computer screen in the small cubicle at the Boston branch of the *Rolling Stone* displayed all of the emails sent and received by Dr. Laura Kean over the past several months. Gaining access to the hospital's email server was easier than the self-taught, opportunistic hacker-turned-investigative reporter expected. In fact, hacking the email server was so easy that he made a quick note to do an article on other potential electronic security flaws in healthcare-based computer servers.

"So doctor hot ass, you are out of the country, aren't you? In Florence no less," Lee Kingston whispered to the glowing screen as he read each of Laura's email messages one at a time. "Lorenzo Benedetti. Hmm...who is this person, Lorenzo Benedetti?"

Trials

1

"Well Brad, there's no two ways about it. Prion-injured brain tissue can be repaired with the adenovirus-containing nanoparticle. This is remarkable. I would have never thought to use prions to repair damaged brain tissue. But it looks like it worked. Great idea Brad, just great," Alex said as he sat on the stool in front of the inverted microscope and peered inside the small tissue culture flask. From one end of the special plastic flask to the other, cultured brain cells that just a few days ago showed obvious signs of damage from exposure to harmful prions, were once again looking healthy and robust just forty-eight hours after treatment with the adenovirus-containing nanoparticle.

"This is five of five, right Brad?" Alex asked in reference to the number of times they repeated this experiment. Brad couldn't have been more excited to see these results. It was the first time he had made a significant contribution to this research project, and now he felt as though he was an important part of the team.

"Yes, that's right," said Brad with high excitement. "And remember the last time we did this experiment? I was blinded as to which culture plates received the adenovirus treatment from those that received the sham treatment and it was a slam-dunk. I scored them perfectly. I could easily tell which flasks had the brain tissue that recovered from the insult, from those in the control group. Those cells that got the sham treatment were hosed, essentially nonviable, almost all of them dead." But just when Brad thought that he had made an iron-clad, earth-shattering finding that would be the scientific breakthrough of the year, Alex calmly dropped a bomb.

"Okay," started Alex. "So this shows that prion-induced brain tissue injury could be rescued by treatment with the adenovirus-containing nanoparticle, but will this work *in vivo*, in a live animal like a mouse? Also, if these stem cells are promoting neuronal growth, is there a key factor that is making the whole thing work? A signal, a chemical signal of some sort?"

Brad took a deep breath. He thought that all of the questions for this experiment were answered, that the puzzle was solved. But what Alex was asking opened up a whole new line of experiments that would take months to complete. He also knew that Alex was digging deeper into the mechanism behind the results. Alex was trying to understand exactly what was happening to these cells, and to also make sure that they weren't missing something important.

"Let's repeat this study one more time with one exception. Let the control brain cells that didn't get the adenovirus-containing nanoparticle get to the point of becoming nonviable, then collect and chemically analyze the growth medium. Compare that profile with the chemical profile from the adenovirus-rescued and repaired, healthy cells," Alex said to Brad who instantly knew how to set up the experiment without having to write down details. "We're also going to want to do this same experiment in mice. Let me chat with some folks over at the hospital who are studying Alzheimer's and maybe we can collaborate with them on studies in animals. Meanwhile, I'll start writing the manuscript with the data we already have in hand. No doubt, we're off to a solid start."

Brad enjoyed working with Alex and he was learning a great deal about basic research. He also liked spending time in the quiet, aseptic world of the laboratory. If Brad's parents didn't have their hearts set on having a physician in the family, he would consider dropping his pursuit of a medical degree and enter a Ph.D. program. That's how much he loved the research laboratory. As a way to potentially please everyone, he made a mental note to meet with his adviser to discuss entering the most demanding, and perhaps the most competitive, of all graduate programs offered at any medical school. The combined M.D.-Ph.D. program is how the most ambitious, driven and dedicated biomedical students satisfy their desire to practice traditional medicine while also embark on a career of science inquiry. If successful, the dual degree recipient traverses seamlessly between the patient and the laboratory, the malady and the microscope, the disease and the discovery. Like all graduate programs, the desired outcome is not automatically guaranteed but what is certain is that the added degree will require time, lots of time. Even if he passed the requirements to enter the M.D.-Ph.D. program, would Brad be willing to tack on an additional four or five years of study? And what about Amy? Would she be supportive of such a shift in his educational commitment, especially after she spoke so passionately about their future? After graduation they were going to get married, settle down and start a family. It was as simple as that.

Unlike men of any age, women are acutely aware of time, especially those of childbearing age like Amy. Women often feel the rapid pace of life and the eventuality of death; time impacts their very being. But when it comes to that same commodity, most men and especially young men like Brad, are clueless. Although they are physically the stronger of the two genders, men are mentally weaker and thus more vulnerable to the not-so-obvious traps of time.

I'll discuss it with her over Thanksgiving break, Brad thought. *Whenever that is.*

———•———

Dr. Richard Johnson, the esteemed Johns Hopkins professor and Nobel laureate was going to lose it. The old neurologist Franz Albracht, in his signature raspy voice, left a lengthy voice message on Dr. Johnson's office phone and it wasn't pretty. "Richard," the message began, "you leave me no choice. I must play my final card. I would rather not go down this road, but you've left me no choice. You have disappointed me beyond belief. What you fail to realize is that time, ah sweet time, is the only thing precious to me now. For me time is short and so too is my patience. I want to reverse this plague and regain my youthful brain. I am becoming increasingly forgetful and I don't like it at all. I will not become a pathetic, brain-dead invalid. I know you have an answer, if not *the* answer and I sense that you are not forthcoming with me. Indeed, I think that you are using time to your advantage and I will not sit by idly and whither away, as you so hope. Richard, hear me once and hear me clearly. I will tell the world that you bribed every member of the Nobel committee to get your award. You made me promise the heavy hitters on that committee that in return for their vote, they would be the first to take advantage of your discovery to reverse and to repair neurological damage including Alzheimer's. That's what you promised me and that's what I promised them. And I, like the head of some sort of twisted medical Ponzi scheme, not only persuaded the other old goats that I would personally see to it that you delivered, but that they, for the sake of their own mental well being, should fall in line and support your rogue nomination. Of course, I will just tell the press that you bribed us with cash. Instantly you will be deemed guilty in the definitive court of public opinion and your professional life, as well as your personal life, will be destroyed. Even if you are eventually exonerated, it won't be in time to rescue your career. That will be irreparably ruined. I trust I have your attention, Richard? My wife and I will plan to visit the United States, specifically Washington D.C. to see the cherry blossoms in April. At that time I plan to visit you at Hopkins. I will instruct my wife in writing of this plan should my mental capacity by that time deteriorate to the point that I am not able to say it to her directly. The letter to my wife has already been written. When I see you in April of next year I will receive the treatment. Only then will I consider withdrawing this warning. I will have backup plans in place should you attempt to back out. So Richard, don't do anything foolish. You have far more to lose than I. Time can be my friend too."

Dr. Johnson listened to the message three times before deleting it. He also ensured that it had not been inadvertently archived in the university's electronic phone system's mailbox. Then he picked up a pen and he wrote one word on his notepad—April. He had about six months to come up with a plan. Then, in a moment of clarity, a plan appeared in his mind like a white dove from a magician's black hat. His inward rage turned into outward calm.

The simple yet rational idea began with a short email typed with purpose to Dr. Albracht.

> Dear Franz,
> Thank you for the succinct voice message. I look forward
> to hosting you and your wife during your visit to Baltimore
> next April.
> All the best,
> Richard

That evening the Johns Hopkins professor lay flat on his back on his bed in his pitch-black bedroom and refined the plan in his mind. *No serious threat goes unpunished*, he thought.

———•———

Franz was still a bit fuzzy after his afternoon nap when he checked his email for the last time that day. His eyes sharpened on the text of Dr. Johnson's message.

"I knew it," he whispered to himself. "The bastard already has the answer."

2

On several occasions, Alexa had worked directly with humans. These clinical studies were mainly observational and noninvasive. They involved adults older than 18 years of age, which meant that the person could agree to participate in the study and sign the Consent Form on their own. Abby's study would be the first one done under an Institutionally approved protocol that focused primarily on deaf children between the ages of four and ten. The narrow age window sought to capture the period of time between the earliest age that non-deaf children develop oral language skills, to after the point when they comprehend and master the written language—commonly by the age of seven.

Children cannot sign Consent Forms. This important paper work describes the parameters of the research, the potential value of the study to the individual and to society, possible ill effects from the treatment, and remuneration for expenses associated with travel to and from the clinic. In order for a child to be enrolled in the study, the Consent Form must be signed by a parent or a legal guardian who clearly understands what the child is getting into. A member of the study team reviews each main point on the form with the adult and ensures that the parameters of the study are understood. They are also told that while they could drop out of the program at any time, compensation would be paid only after they completed the entire study. Per university rules, Abby had to advertise the clinical trial using multiple means. She designed posters, wrote announcements for local newspapers, recorded a radio spot, and she also advertised the study using social media.

The first recruitment day finally arrived. Judging by the crowd in the waiting room, Abby was not going to have a problem reaching their recruitment goal of between 100 and 150 children. As per written protocol, only the intake nurses knew the fine details of the child's hearing or sight deficits. Whether the child was blind or deaf from birth, or if they had lost these senses during their short lives, was not revealed to the rest of the study team. This common approach to behavioral studies serves to eliminate bias.

Guardians of potential children had been asked by phone to attend an interview session to review eligibility. Two interview sessions were held each week, on Tuesdays and Thursdays.

Alexa and Abby watched nervously as the two intake nurses calmly escorted hopeful participants, and their adult legal guardians, into small rooms where they privately conducted the screening interview. Only four parents decided not to have their children participate in the study due to the lengthy time commitment rather than to any of the procedures. Each approved child-adult pair was instructed to arrive at a specific time the following day at one of three rooms at the University's clinical study building. The special building consisted of a series of versatile rooms that could be easily structured to accommodate different types of clinical studies. Rooms could be transformed into bedrooms to study sleep patterns, comfortable rooms with a simple table and chair to conduct interviews, or simply clean rooms for blood draws or for administration of investigational new drugs.

For Abby's study, three rooms were converted into observational rooms with one-way mirrors complete with hidden video and sound recording devices. Two chairs were placed on each side of a simple round table with one camera aimed at the interviewer, and the other focused on the child. The child could sit alone at the table and the adult would be seated in a nearby chair against the back wall located behind the child. If the child preferred he or she could sit on the lap of the accompanying adult, but the adult was instructed not to interfere in any way with the interactions between the interviewer and the child.

The experimental protocol was simple, almost too simple as commented by an institutional reviewer who, after some hesitation, voted to approve the clinical study. Abby, Rosi and Johanna would be in the interviewer's seat in one of three rooms that were situated next to each other in the short hallway. When given the signal from Alexa, who monitored all three separate rooms on a single computer screen via live feeds, a nurse would escort a child with the accompanying adult into the room and situate the child across from the interviewer. The adult would then sit in the chair behind the child or with the child according to his or her wishes. The nurse was instructed to introduce the child and the adult to the interviewer, to seat everyone, and then briefly chat with the guardian. The idle chat was an effort to put the child at ease and also to allow the cameramen behind the mirrors to make final adjustments. The faces of both the interviewer and the child were recorded. Before heading into the room, deaf children were told via sign language, that they were going to play a game with a friendly lady. Blind children were told the same thing verbally. On the round table in the center of the room where the interviewer and the child were seated was a pad of plain, unlined paper and two pencils. The experiment started when the nurse left the room and closed the door behind her. She would then wait in a nearby intake room for instructions from Alexa.

Abby's first subject was a blind little girl who started chatting right off without prompting.

"My name is Fortune. I'm six and I can't see." Abby didn't respond, but instead looked directly into the wayward eyes of the dark-haired girl and waited for a silent message. There was none. The short silence was not appreciated by Fortune who sought help. "Momma? Did she leave? Momma?" The mother looked at Abby and as instructed, she did not say a word.

"Hi. I'm here Fortune. You have a lovely name and I love your long hair," said Abby aloud. Abby's words caused Fortune's mother to relax especially since she wasn't exactly sure what would happen in a telepathy study, and for that matter neither did Abby. Quickly, Abby telepathically asked Fortune her age. The child responded only by asking, "What game are we going to play?" When a child was deemed to not be telepathic, the interviewer was instructed to do a quick task with the child.

"I'd like to trace your beautiful hands on this paper with a pencil. Is that okay?" asked Abby.

"Okay," echoed Fortune who slammed both hands flat down on the table and waited for Abby to do the tracing. When the tracing was done Abby wrote Fortune's name on the bottom of the paper, dated it and wrote:

Thank you, Fortune.
Abby

That was the cue to Alexa that the interview was over and that she should send in the nurse to retrieve Fortune and her mother, which is exactly what happened. The nurse then led the pair into the next room where she asked Fortune to show the tracing to her friend, Johanna. Telepathically, Johanna quickly asked Fortune her age. There was no telepathic response so Johanna proceeded as instructed and simply complimented the little girl's tracing. "Why, that's awesome! Good job." That short phrase cued the nurse to take her to the third room where Rosi sat waiting. After experiencing an identical response from Rosi the nurse was instructed to discharge the child using all of the predetermined exit formalities.

A second nurse repeated the process with Abby and a second child. The nurse introduced Lilly and her mother to Abby. Instantly, Abby knew that tiny Lilly, with her thin face and stringy brown hair, was different than Fortune. Very different.

----•----

Tomasso was gentle and patient with Laura. He let her make all of the advances, choices and decisions as they made their way to her rented apartment above his *trattoria*. Although he had indeed been with women before, he roundly renounced Laura's assertion that he has escorted many female tourists to this apartment after seducing them with his sensual meals and desserts.

Lorenzo's sudden departure from their lunchtime get-together left Laura in an oddly giddy, almost childish, mood. That wild scene with it's sudden shifts in male lead roles, the give-and-take in rapid Italian language complete with wild hand waving, could have been taken directly out of a classic foreign tragicomedy where the lowly chef trumps the lofty professor to win the heart of the fair maiden. But now the giddiness faded and Laura's demeanor turned quite serious. For the first time in many decades she was about to make love with a man who was not her husband.

As much as the physician was confident about her looks she was equally unsure about the state of her psyche. Could she discharge the past and make love to this man? This nice man who befriended her for most of the past month? And what if she did embrace the moment and rode it for all it's worth? What then? Would she emerge a new person or would she drown in guilt over participating in such carnal pleasure after having injected the solution that ended, definitively ended, her husband's life? The dying man begged her and she delivered, right? Was she now an evil person, especially if no one knew what she did? And perhaps most importantly, while lying besides Tomasso in nothing but her silk bra and panties, Laura wondered if she, a murderess, could ever love again?

Tomasso's light strokes on the right side of her face and neck made it impossible for Laura to sort out her convoluted thoughts. The chef was intensely studying the profile of the physician's face. It was the profile of a middle-aged woman whose skin was not taunt but slightly puffy with tiny hairs that were not of uniform length and skin with creases that deepened at the corners of her eyes and on her upper lip. With each stroke Tomasso wanted to rise above her and kiss her with all the passion he had, but he knew he needed to be patient. It would be in his best interest if she moved beyond the halfway point and removed the rest of her garments. She could continue to undress him too, if she so desired. He must show restraint with the most alluring woman he had ever met.

Suddenly, Laura's mind replayed Dante's imagined words. Four short sentences that first rang when she arrived in the ancient city. *Move on Laura. I'm yesterday's news. You're in Florence. You're alive, today!* And as if propelled by the declarative words themselves, Laura slowly turned towards the kind and patient chef and kissed him ever so tentatively on his lips. Afterwards she withdrew and looked at him. His eyes were lightly shut in an effort to freeze the moment he had envisioned for an entire life and dreamed of for weeks. Laura did not wait for his eyes to open before she kissed him again, this time with significantly more meaning.

3

Lilly separated easily from her mother. She sat motionless across from Abby as the nurse went through the routine, stating matter-of-factly that Lilly has been deaf since birth. The thin child's brown eyebrows were knitted tightly, and her unflinching eyes were squarely focused on Abby's lips. Lilly's mother shifted nervously in her seat as if she was in dire need of a cigarette. And as she had done previously with Fortune, Abby started the interview by not saying a word. Instead of empty silence, however, the graduate student's mind was receiving messages from Lilly at a rapid, manic rate. It was difficult for Abby to keep up with the flood of emotions emanating from Lilly. The transmissions were not delivered in a childlike manner nor were they clear, but they were unambiguously frightening.

Through a series of expressive thoughts and scenery Lilly conveyed a message of a life filled with torture and abuse. The sound of thunder filled Abby's mind accompanied by a child's icy-loud, panicked scream along with that hauntingly terrifying jack-in-the-box jingle. Lilly sat motionless as she sent another wave of thoughts Abby's way. The child knew exactly what she was doing and why she was doing it. This time she sent brilliant images. A wind-swept firestorm engulfing a house, a gold door latch, and that strange clown face of the newly sprung jack-in-the-box, Jack.

Abby was completely unprepared for such a violent assault. The hidden camera suggested to Alexa that Abby was interviewing a telepath but that something was not right. Suddenly, Abby looked up at Lilly's mother. The nervous woman, in a breach of rules, walked over to the small child and signed, "Tell her how old you are Lilly."

Go away! Lilly silently screamed to her mother. Then she turned towards Abby and opened her left hand.

"She's telling you that she's five. She's five years old even though she looks like she's two or three or something like that because she was born early, like a runt or something," said Lilly's mother as she back-peddled to her seat.

Abby did not want to speak. She simply nodded and gestured to Lilly's mother to remain silent by bringing her index finger to her closed lips.

Lilly sent more. Images of a large black spider, an opened door leading to a dark room, and a green-faced witch filled Abby's mind. The interviewer had to focus her energy beyond the dreadful images to ask Lilly to write her name on the piece of paper in front of her. Instantly, the child picked up the pencil and wrote her name on the paper using all lower case letters. When she was done she slapped the pencil down on the table and again focused on Abby's lips.

Abby looked directly into the lens of the hidden video camera located behind the mirror. That was the cue to Alexa that the session was over. A moment later, the nurse that had escorted Lilly and her mother into the room knocked twice then entered.

"Oh," the nurse both said and signed. "You wrote your name. Let's show this to someone else. Follow me this way." And with that Lilly and her mother rose to leave the room. As Lilly was heading out the door she turned to Abby and transmitted an image of a large lion, with its full orange mane and it's mouth opened as if it was about to bellow a guttural, ferocious roar typical of a protective alpha male. The roar, however, was not that of a lion but of a child's high-pitched, body-piercing scream of sheer terror. Abby took out the small notepad she had in the table's drawer and jotted down some quick notes as the scream echoed in her head.

Even before she was seated in the adjoining room, Lilly frightened Johanna. The artistic telepath had all she could do to focus her thoughts on moving the child along, and out of her sight. On the video display, Alexa spotted Johanna's response immediately, and instructed to the nurse to move Lilly along. That the tiny little girl is a telepath was all but certain. When the nurse closed the door leaving Johanna alone, Alexa watched stunned as the artist broke down and openly sobbed.

Rosi knew what to expect even before the nurse opened the door to her room, and even before she laid eyes on Lilly. Rosi sensed Johanna's distress from the adjoining room and as such she braced herself for what was about to transpire. Rosi decided instantly to go on the offensive even though she knew it would be a breach of protocol.

Fear not my child/I am your friend/I will know you better if you don't pretend/tell me the truth/I will not tell/have they been mean/do they scream and yell?

Rosi did not hear the nurse go through the introductions and Lilly who was now familiar with the shuffling routine took her seat across from Rosi.

Lilly nodded twice as she focused on Rosi's lips.

The silence, and indeed the entire situation, had become too much for Lilly's mother. She was full of anxiety and virtually twitching with agitation; she also was in dire need of a cigarette and a strong cup of coffee. In the third room, Lilly's mother leaned against the wall beside her chair in anticipation of another short visit. Rosi completely ignored the older woman.

Lilly's response was delivered neither in sounds nor images, but in clearly transmitted unspoken words: *They hurt me. They hate me. Help me.* Rosi was momentarily taken aback by the tiny child's crystal clear, forceful silent voice. *You hear well without your ears/you are a very smart girl despite few years/do you speak this way with others/perhaps your sister or brother or even your mother?*

With focused eyes, Lilly quickly responded. *No you are number three. Abby was number one. Help me! Help me!*

The camera that was focused on Lilly also showed, in the background, the lower half of Lilly's mother who was still standing nervously behind her daughter. Alexa could see the erratic movement of the adult's legs and she correctly anticipated that the thin woman would intervene again. The silence, coupled with the lack of signing by Rosi, drove Lilly's mother crazy. Alexa motioned to the nurse to enter the room just as Lilly's mother took two steps forward and with a quick grab jerked Lilly's left arm and pulled the child off the chair to her feet while stating, "This crap is over. We're outta here."

Wisely, Rosi did not move. The nurse opened the door as Lilly and her mother were heading towards it. "Where's my money? We're outta here. This is bullshit!" The nurse led Lilly and her mother away from Room 3 and into a separate room. There the experienced clinical study nurse calmly explained that Lilly was required to return for follow-up visits in order to receive compensation.

"Fuck that!" Lilly's mother said. "This is just bullshit!" While Lilly could hear not a sound, she knew from the formation of her mother lips what was implied. She also knew from the color of her mothers forehead that it was going to be a bad night, a very bad night.

Hurry, Lilly aimlessly transmitted as she left the facility with her highly agitated mother. *Hurry! Please hurry.*

The team was scheduled to interview five of the thirty young subjects deemed eligible by a pre-screen. Roughly half of the thirty were deaf from birth and the rest were legally blind. But on that first day of the study, the three telepaths had agreed to see only five recruits as a way of getting a feel for how the process would flow, however no one had anticipated meeting someone like Lilly. While Abby and Rosi, although stunned by the little telepath were ready to continue. However, Johanna was already spent and she wondered whether or not she could continue at all; Lilly had been too much for her. But before she could call a time out, a maneuver that was not in place, she heard the door in Abby's room close. Johanna had to quickly get herself together before the next subject arrived.

Although he was only ten years old, Javier already had features of a prepubescent young man. His dark complexion, brown-black hair, lengthy sideburns and a whisper of whiskers on his upper lip made him appear older than he claimed to be. It made Abby sad to think that he will never see his handsome face, a sentiment that she transmitted to the second blind subject of the day. Nothing. Abby did not evoke a silent reply, but she gave it one more try by sending a message that was sure to evoke a response in any male telepath of any age, *Would you like to feel my breasts?* Again, there was no response from Javier. He did not even smile and thankfully so because Abby knew that the question was dangerously way out of bounds.

"Javier? Thank you for coming in today," Abby said aloud in her soft kind voice.

"Sure. What would you like me to do?" He asked under the watchful eye of his lovely, dark haired mother.

"Tell me three things about yourself. I'm going to write them on this piece of paper so you can discuss them with my friends."

"Um. Okay. Well, I like chess, Shakespeare and football. My team is the Ravens." Abby wrote his answers on the paper and read them aloud just as the nurse entered to escort the young man and his mother to the next two rooms in rapid succession.

Barbara was eight years old and she was also blind. Like Fortune and

Javier before her, Barbara showed no indication that she was telepathic. None of the three interviewers could elicit a telepathic response nor had they received a silent message from them.

Kenny was altogether different than Fortune, Javier, Barbara, or even Lilly who was in a category of her own. The slightly overweight seven-year-old was as outgoing as anyone Abby had every met. Kenny had already become best buddies with the nurse who had her arms around the jovial child.

"Abby, this is Kenny and his step father," said the nurse.

"Yeah, he's my old man," said Kenny in amazingly clear speech.

The well-dressed man approached Abby, "Hi, pleased to meet you. My name is Charlie. My wife and I adopted Kenny five years ago when he was two. We were told that he has been deaf from birth. The nurse instructed me not to interfere, so I'll just take this seat." Abby silently shook Charlie's hand then the pleasant man sat on the chair and folded his overcoat across his lap.

"Yeah, have a seat big guy, get some popcorn, enjoy the show," said a smiling Kenny to his stepfather who replied, "You got it champ," both aloud and with hand signals.

Abby perspicaciously noticed that Charlie and his step son were using cued speech and she quickly sought to learn if there were any other ways that this seemingly bright child communicated.

Cued speech? Abby transmitted to Kenny, referring to the use of phoneme hand signals and mouth movements to build words and phrases.

Instantly, Kenny's face changed from jovial to quizzical. And like dipping one's toe cautiously in a lake, Kenny responded telepathically. *Yes.*

Again, Alexa who was glued to the camera feeds knew something was happening with Kenny that differed from what had occurred with the others.

Abby silently fired back a question. *Am I the first person you've communicated with this way?* As before, the bubbly boy appeared dumbstruck. He momentarily looked at his stepfather, who did as he was told and just looked on without making a gesture of any kind, then he turned back to face Abby.

Yes it is. And I think this is very strange. I didn't think it was real.

With the line open Abby transmitted: *It is certainly real. Would you write your name on this piece of paper for me?* Charlie watched as his stepson, who he raised with all of the love and attention that any father could give to a child, picked up the pencil and wrote something on the paper; all without the exchange of a sound or a hand gesture of any sort. Abby picked up the paper—that served as Alexa's cue to send in the nurse—and looked at it. In uppercase letters Kenny wrote his name followed by a heart and an exclamation point. The nurse knocked twice and walked into the room. Abby stood up and displayed her skills at cued speech. "Thank you both for coming in..." but Abby was interrupted mid sentence by a silent plea from Kenny. *No. I don't want to go yet. I want to do this some more.*

Abby responded to young Kenny privately, *I'll see you again and before you leave you will meet other interesting people.* Then Abby continued to interact verbally and also by cueing from where she'd left off, "It was a pleasure meeting both of you. I'm sure I'll see you again." The nurse then escorted Kenny and Charlie into the next two rooms. It did not take long for both Johanna and Rosi to independently confirm what Abby already knew. There was no doubt, Kenny was telepathic, but he had used it only rarely, perhaps even accidentally.

It was close to 4 p.m. when the nurses departed leaving the three telepaths and Alexa alone to review the tapes and to discuss what had transpired that day. From a technical standpoint, it took close to four hours to conduct the interviews from start to finish.

"From my perspective, things went quite well today," said Alexa as she uncapped cold bottles of Old Speckled Hen and passed them around the room. "The cues went well, the participants, for the most part, behaved and the little ones were amazing. Let's go through them one by one, shall we?"

Abby pulled out her small notepad and took the lead. "Fortune, Javier, and Barbara were all legally blind from birth and I did not receive any messages from them nor did they send anything to me. These three were like many people I've met, they were not telepathic." Johanna and Rosi nodded in agreement. "Then," Abby continued, "there were two telepaths that were quite different from each other. "Kenny is deaf. Perhaps he was born deaf. He was highly vocal and he spoke exceptionally well. He also was learned in the art of cue signing, as was his father, I mean his stepfather. When Kenny received my telepathic message, he froze. Clearly, he was not expecting it."

"Yes," commented Alexa. "I saw that on the monitor. He looked shocked, like he'd seen a ghost."

"Kenny couldn't believe that three people in one day communicated with him with out using words or hand gestures or even moving their mouth," Rosi added. "By the time I saw him, he was shocked, totally shocked."

"I'm looking forward to seeing him again. I wonder how he processed that information and I also wonder if he shared this experience with his Dad," commented Johanna.

"I agree," said Abby who had all but finished her beer. "Then there was Lilly. Alexa, I think we have a problem here."

"Tiny Lilly. Yes, I remember her. She looked quite serious and her mother was quite anxious, right?" asked Alexa.

"I'm so sorry everyone. I didn't mean to break down, but what that little girl transmitted was not nice and, well, it brought back some bad memories for me," confessed Johanna. "We have to do something for her!"

Abby turned to her mentor and said straightforwardly, "Alexa, Lilly is a strong telepath as both a transmitter and as a receiver. When she latched on to my mind she let me know that she has been, and is currently being, abused. She projected images that were quite vivid and also sounds that would frighten any adult much less a child. She fears and deplores her mother. Lilly repeatedly pleaded for help."

Rosi chimed in, "I knew Johanna had been tripped up badly, I sensed her pain. When that tiny powerhouse of a child walked in to my room, I immediately sent her a message," Rosi said to Alexa. Lilly told me what Abby just told you. Outwardly she may seem angry, but inside she is very, very scared."

"I don't think I can see her again," added Johanna. "And I think her mother's a bitch. A drugged-out, fucked-up, child-abusing bitch."

Trying to keep the discussion on a professional level, Abby asked Alexa what could they do to help Lilly, although she knew full well that confidentiality was an important part of any clinical intervention, including this noninvasive study.

Alexa's deep sigh made everyone think that she was going to say that there was no way to intervene. They were mistaken.

"I watched all the interviews in real time," Alexa began. "And no one will refute what the video clearly shows. Here is a very small child, perhaps undernourished, who was referred to as a 'runt' by her mother who appeared to be quite nervous and unsteady. She pulled Lilly somewhat violently when they left and this move alone might prompt law enforcement to take action, but for damned sure they will not consider—in any way, shape or form—the messages, images, or anything else you received telepathically. They just won't. It's a nonstarter. What I can do, and what

I will do, is seek advice from the University's Office of General Counsel. They will let us know how best to proceed. Until we hear back from them, please do not discuss Lilly with anyone."

"We couldn't even if we wanted to," commented Johanna. "We have no idea where Lilly lives."

"Right. Just hang on and don't discuss this with anyone. It will be seen as a breach of confidentiality and it could hinder the entire study," remarked Alexa.

"You may want to tell General Counsel that we think it's an urgent matter that should be brought to the attention of enforcement as soon as possible," said Rosi.

"I most certainly will," Alexa stated. "Thank you ladies. Terrific job today."

———◆———

Her small left breast was bare, and the tunic draped over her right shoulder was more tattered and loose fitting than elegant and finely tailored. Her face was not perfect or smooth but lightly scarred in several places. She was neither youthful nor aged; and overall she conveyed a sense of fatigue and desperation. She was kneeling with her back slumped and the earthen clay wine bottle, that was only attached to the index finger of her left hand, was mostly on its side on the ground. The cup held in her right hand, raised up along with her sorrowful eyes, was partly crushed as if it was made of paper. Rosi's gloved hand rubbed the red garnet 120 grit sandpaper on the partially exposed tunic of the four foot tall marble statue located in the corner of her studio apartment.

Johanna and Abby made themselves comfortable as Rosi removed the protective drape from one of her latest works in progress. Carefully, and with purpose, she began to smooth the contours of the soft stone sculpture. It was the first time Abby had seen the piece. Once again she was amazed at her friend's seemingly endless talents.

"Abby, Johanna meet Hebo. I've been working on her for nearly two years," said Rosi.

"Oh my God! She's beautiful," Abby remarked after walking around the pure white statue.

"You mean, 'Oh my Goddess', right?" Rosi asked without looking up.

"Sorry? I'm not following you."

"Greek mythology. Hebe. The Goddess of youth. The daughter of Zeus and Hera. Serves nectar and ambrosia to the Gods and Goddesses of Mount Olympus. Eventually married Heracles, as the myth turns."

"I never got into mythology," said Abby who was still studying the piece carefully. "But obviously, you have."

"Not really but it's been commissioned. Actually my benefactor's friend in Pisa had this piece of Carrera marble shipped over to me to do as I pleased. This marble was quarried from the same mountains used by Renaissance artists. Once this stone arrived I sat and stared at it and I waited until it told me what was hidden inside. Three weeks later, I saw Hebo or maybe Hobe, I haven't decided yet. She's a modern day antithesis of a goddess."

"A beggar," Abby concluded. "A drifter, a hobo. Oh Rosi, that's so clever. She looks so worn, so discouraged. Rosi pointed to the large book on the floor near the sculpture that showed several images of a robust, voluptuous Hebe in paintings, and as statues. Abby looked at the images then back to the sculpture. "I'd say you successfully reversed her good fortunes. Poor thing. How much longer before she's done?"

"Well, without pressure, I'd say about another year, maybe less. Sanding and polishing are time consuming, plus I also have to consider how to complete her face. Wrinkles are doable but they aren't that easy with marble. Maybe I'll keep her face rough, sort of unfinished."

Without asking if they were interested, Johanna handed Rosi and Abby a glass of white wine. She needed one and she didn't want to drink alone.

"Abby," Johanna said as she took another sip, "I don't think I can be a part of your project. Today was too stressful for me and there are so many kids to interview. I didn't know what I expected, but today was just too much. I don't think I can do it."

Johanna's reluctance to continue with the study did not shock Abby. Lilly weighed heavily on all of them, especially Johanna. Olysia had agreed to be an alternate, but Abby didn't want to lose Johanna's involvement. At minimum, she'd need her as a backup.

"I understand completely and I don't want you to do this if you find it onerous," said Abby in between sips of wine. "But when you think about it, most of those kids were easy, even those that were telepathic. We're on again Thursday, in two days. Will you sleep on it and let me know tomorrow morning?" The wine had a soothing effect on Johanna who looked visibly exhausted as if she had just completed a marathon run. She agreed to Abby's request.

Rosi, who had been listening to the conversation while creating a small cloud of marble dust, stood alongside the unfinished sculpture and proceeded to disrobe. She left her chalk-coated clothes and undergarments at the base of the kneeling Hebo, or Hobe, and walked with wineglass in hand across the loft and directly into the shower. The sound of the shower's spray made Johanna, who had become drowsy by the wine and the events of the day, open her eyes and without saying a word, rose from the couch, casually disrobed then joined Rosi in the steamy shower.

No more than a minute later, the three telepaths were helping each other wash away the tensions of the first day of the highly unusual clinical study.

———•———

Rosa was not pleased that her dear cousin roundly refused to bring her to Florence. It was not often that she left the mountain village and it was rare that an opportunity presented itself as perfectly as did Lorenzo's business meeting, which seemed to materialize instantly, out of nowhere. His assertion that he only had to meet a colleague for lunch and that she would be bored if she came with him was less than convincing. He also told her that he was not planning to spend any time in the city; he would return the very same day. Rosa worried that he was getting restless with the confines of their small village and their modest house. She wondered if he sought to return to the faster paced life he once knew. He hasn't been himself lately. He's been resting poorly at night, and spending more time than ever on the computer. His mind was decidedly elsewhere. She also wondered if he was getting bored with her and her simple ways.

So while the professor was in Florence having lunch with the wife of the man who once controlled him from the beyond, his loving cousin spent the day alone conjuring up scenario after wild scenario as to the real purpose of the single day trip. Perhaps her trusted neighbor was right when she speculated that Lorenzo had a paramour in America that had followed him to Italy, and that together they were planning a way—a diabolical and clever way—to rid the famous neuroscientist of his unneeded cousin in order to inherit the mountainside villa. Rosa dismissed the wild idea at first, but then, as her neighbor began to connect irrelevant clues—the extended time on the computer necessary not only to plan with the evil paramour from the past, but also to learn ways to easily kill someone, plus the embarrassing admission by Rosa that he no longer seemed interested in her physically—she began to see that her neighbor's assessment made perfect sense. And with her world crumbling around her Rosa took to her treasured kitchen to prepare a meal that would win the heart of an unmannered ogre, much less that of her treasured cousin. Not only would the stone house be filled with the aroma of stability and adoration, but she would greet him in her finest dress, the same one she wore, and that he liked very much not long ago, when he returned permanently. Once he sees her in that dress, he would have to think more than twice about leaving her for any American vixen.

Lorenzo was in a foul mood when he left the *trattoria* and also when he boarded the outbound train in Florence. When he disembarked at the station near his rural village several hours later, he was still quite upset. He had expected to feel quite differently. Earlier that same day, he boarded the train with a great deal of optimism. He thought he would know with certainty that the dead Dante Paolo had no more claims on him. The stop at the jewelry store in Florence to purchase a gift for Rosa went well. He located the small *trattoria* with little problem and Dante's wife, Laura was quite attractive and a pleasure to have met. But all along he had been taken for a fool. Dante Paolo was more cunning, more sinister that he had ever imagined. From the dark beyond, the dead husband sent two clear messages through his lovely, unassuming wife, "...he is here now...and in everyone I meet", followed by "Don't despair. He's still with us in more ways than you know." Then, in a unimaginable way, Dante Paolo sent the strongest message through the unassuming chef, "*Pere riconciliati.*" Lorenzo Benedetti was aghast with the added abuse he had to endure as the dead man, speaking through a pitiful chef, had to say 'reconciled' in his native Italian tongue, a phrase that had nothing whatsoever to do with fruit or dessert for that matter. It was more than Lorenzo could stand to hear. It was over. The former Dean and esteemed neuroscientist now knew that he was doomed for all eternity.

It was nearly dark when the retired professor walked towards the taxi that would bring him the remaining five kilometers up the narrow switchback mountain roads home. A young man was handing out fliers of some sort that Lorenzo blindly accepted and tucked into the inner pocket of his overcoat without even glancing at it. He simply wanted to get home and go to bed. He was a man possessed, literally possessed, for the rest of his life by the diabolical Dante Paolo who continued to plague him relentlessly.

Should Rosa ever learn of his perpetual ill fortune she would be inconsolable and quite likely she'd be crazed with rage. She would blame herself and wonder how she could love a man who was controlled by *il diavolo*, the devil, himself.

The serpentine road caused Lorenzo to shift from left to right, back to left again in the taxi's backseat. During one of these swings he decided that upon arriving home, he would go directly to bed. He would have no dinner, not even a glass of wine. He needed to rest and to think. In the morning he would wake early and consider his next move with a clear head.

That he all but ignored her completely verified Rosa's worse fears. Lorenzo grunted a lukewarm greeting as he slipped out of his overcoat and placed it not on the hanger in the closet, as was his routine, but draped it haphazardly over the nearby chair. He was altogether indifferent to Rosa. He did not comment on her dress, nor did he acknowledge the aromatic blend of bean soup with pancetta and roasted potatoes with rosemary and black pepper. Rosa watched disheartened as her cousin strode heavily passed the candlelit table set for two and climbed the stone stairs to their bedroom on the second floor. The door to the bedroom closed with a certainty that left Rosa with nothing else to do but to store the uneaten dinner and tidy the kitchen.

When she picked up Lorenzo's overcoat, a pamphlet dropped out of the inside pocket. Rosa picked it up off the floor, sat in the seat by the table and read the words by the light of the flickering candles. The pamphlet detailed plans for a romantic wedding on Italy's famed Amalfi Coast complete with numbers to call to make arrangements for a very special day. Rosa had heard of this beautiful land somewhere south of Rome, but she had never, before today, seen pictures of it. *He's planning a wedding*, she thought thinking back to her neighbor's assessment of Lorenzo's behavior. *He's planning a wedding on the Amalfi Coast with the American vixen.* At first Rosa refused to believe what she was holding in her hands and, in an effort to move the disappointing evening along and to dismiss her thoughts as childish nonsense, she continued to hang up the overcoat in the closet only to notice, in the outer left pocket, the outline of a small box.

———•———

The sunny start to the second recruitment day, a Thursday, did not foretell the coming disaster. Abby had no sooner arrived at the clinical building when someone told her that Alexa was frantically looking for her. Abby found her mentor in the anteroom with the computer screens that showed live feeds of the three interview rooms.

Alexa looked directly into the eyes of her graduate student and calmly said, "Abby, I just learned that Lilly is dead."

4

When Alex was on clinical service at the hospital, Brad was left to experiment on his own. The physician-researcher spent little time in the laboratory because the rotating clinical duty, that occurred every other month for two straight weeks, meant that he was either in surgery or following up with patients who had just undergone a procedure. Alex often chatted with colleagues with expertise in other medical fields during this time. If an infection at the surgical site was suspected Alex would call an expert in infectious diseases, or he'd contact a hematologist if the patient required additional blood assessments or a transfusion. Service lasted a minimum of 18 hours per day, seven days a week for the entire two-week period, a schedule that left no time for anything, let alone research. Brad had seen Alex's state of mind before, during, and immediately following his clinical tour of duty. It reminded him of someone who lived through the ordeal of having wisdom teeth extracted. Alex was quietly tentative at first, followed by a period of pure misery and then, once it was over, he was totally euphoric.

So on his own, Brad added a few twists to the experiment he and Alex outlined before clinical service began. Now, alone in the laboratory, Brad was reviewing the results of those experiments for the first time. The doctoral student could not believe what he was seeing. A mysterious chemical signal, a small molecule perhaps, was present in culture flasks containing brain cells that were nearly dead, but this small molecule was not present in the same flasks sampled only one day earlier. Flasks of newly cultured, healthy brains cells also did not show the presence of this small molecule nor was it seen in flasks of dying brain cells that were rescued and repaired with the adenovirus treatment. But when Brad added filtered fluids from a culture of bacteria commonly found in human intestines to the flasks of brain cells, only those cells that were almost dead made the small molecule. And they made the small molecule in very large amounts. Brad was flummoxed by the results. And to add to the mystery, the small chemical molecule was not detected in the culture of bacteria. How was this possible? What did it mean?

Brad continued to mull over the data when Alex strolled into the laboratory looking eager to get back to the relatively peaceful world of research.

"I see you survived without me."

"Yeah, just barely," replied Brad who turned to face Alex. "You're just in time to help me make sense of these data." Alex sat next to Brad and listened carefully to the design of the recent experiments. He questioned Brad about the testing methods, and he also had several additional questions about the new experiment that had been added since they last spoke. Alex made sure he clearly understood the entire setup before viewing the results.

"Wait, wait," Alex said to Brad who was eager to get to the most interesting findings. "Tell me again. What was the rationale for adding the bacterial fluids?"

Brad explained, "Study after study describes the importance of the symbiotic bacteria that reside in our gut, to just about everything we do from maintaining the robustness of our immune system to controlling overall health and metabolism. And while I know bacteria don't readily cross the blood-brain barrier and therefore don't normally cause brain infections, I thought that there might be some factor, some molecule, that they make that could reach the brain and play a role in the adenoviral neuronal growth and repair function. That's all. I did it on a whim. I didn't think you'd mind if I did the experiment."

"Okay. Show me what you learned," Alex said as he leaned in to examine the graphs and charts more closely. They reviewed the results together. After a vigorous give and take, Alex sat back in the chair and knotted his eyebrows in thought. Then, following a few minutes of silence, Alex asked another set of probing questions.

"At what point during bacterial growth did you harvest and purify the molecule from the culture fluids?"

Brad picked up his laboratory notebook, flipped back a few pages and replied, "It was a mixed culture of bacteria that were growing exponentially at 37 degrees Celsius without shaking. They were growing very rapidly."

"So you collected the culture fluids when the bacteria were at a high growth rate? During a period of time when nutrients are plentiful and their division rate and thus their actual numbers in the culture suddenly explode?"

"Yeah, that would be right."

"And when would you think this condition would happen naturally in the gut? These were gut bacteria, right?"

"Right. Good question. So I guess when one dies—or is just about to die—the body begins to decompose thus supplying bacteria with all the nutrients they need to grow. Unlike the person they inhabited, the bacteria would thrive. You die and the bacteria live better than ever, at least for a short period of time."

"Then," continued Alex, "these bacteria die when..."

"They run out of nutrients," said Brad excitedly who, together with his friend, was starting to make important connections. "So the moment we die, trillions of bacteria that lived in and on us grow wildly. But this unusual nutrient situation alerts the entire bacterial community that they are about to lose their partner in life. Perhaps they then release this type of alarm molecule. They sense, ironically through an influx of nutrients, a dying symbiont that no longer will be able to sustain them. This alarm molecule then makes it way to the brain, probably during the last few heart beats, and..."

Alex continued the line of reasoning, "...the bacterial chemical signal is a last ditch maneuver that traffics to the control center, the brain, and binds to the chemical released by neuronal cells so that the body can try, for one last time, to save the whole system. It's an ultimate, well-coordinated, last-ditch SOS. Each symbiont—the human and the collective bacteria—try to save each other. In our experiments, the adenovirus-containing nanoparticle is a separate thing that triggered the release of some of the brain chemical because it appeared as though there was a final stage event that was taking place when prions were added. It's like a small simulation of the massive injury that the body, along with the bacteria that depended on the body for it's own survival, undergoes at the point of death."

Brad barely heard Alex's last two sentences. His memory brought him back to Dr. Paolo's kitchen. It was his college graduation day when he watched on a computer monitor the brain of his former professor light up like a strobe light. It was the exact moment Dr. Paolo died. Brad said excitedly, "I bet that the dye *RW88* bound to this small chemical. I bet that it was that specific interaction that caused Dr. Paolo's brain to light up." Brad looked at Alex who was still describing how the chemical might be working in unison for the benefit of each organism when he said, "We need to visit Bob Wyle at MIT. There is no doubt that Bob and Dr. Sukawa will be extremely interested in our findings."

"Do you mean *the* Dr. Sukawa?" asked Alex who had extensively read textbooks co-edited by the world-renowned neurologist.

"Yes. Remember he was the senior author on that paper we published?" Brad asked.

"Right. Oh yes, yes. Right. Why of course. Oh this could get very interesting."

———◆———

Although Bob Wyle knew that Amy's boyfriend worked across the river, it wasn't something he wanted to commit to memory. Blocking Brad from his mind made it easier to fantasize about having an affair with Amy even though he knew that realistically such an event was likely never to occur.

Despite these mental games, it didn't take the MIT professor long to place Brad when he read the email message with a request for a meeting.

> Dear Dr. Wyle,
> I am confident that you will be very interested in our most recent data and with the hypothesis we've developed, in light of your own work with RW88.

The pointed email asked for a time to meet and also suggested extending the meeting invitation to Dr. Sukawa.

The meeting between the Harvard and MIT scientists was about to begin and in preparation, Bob reread the week old return email in order to make sure he didn't promise or agree to anything.

> I look forward to reviewing your data. Sukawa is traveling and will not be able to make the meeting.
> See you then,
> Bob

Brad smiled inwardly as he entered Bob's office. Although the location was new the office was as disheveled as ever with piles upon piles of journals, notebooks, discarded computer parts, manuscripts, and newspapers strewn haphazardly from one end of the room to the other. Bob's desk could have qualified as a unique work of modern art that would have garnered the title: Confused. Chaotic. Chaos. Alex watched with amusement as Bob cleared chairs and a small brown leather sofa of papers and magazines so that his guests had a place to sit. Brad introduced Alex to Bob just as Ajay entered the office upon which introductions renewed.

Brad wasted no time ensuring that there would be a "gentleman's agreement" with regard to the confidentiality of the information disclosed at this meeting. No one wanted to waste weeks to arrange formal agreements between the academic institutions to make sure that each would not steal the other's discovery. Instead they all opted to work within the ancient framework of mutual trust and respect, and given that Brad had already worked with Bob and Ajay, and also that Alex was a longstanding admirer of Dr. Sukawa's life work and by association Bob's work as well, there was nothing but collegiality and a sense of teamwork between the four scientists assembled in the cluttered MIT office.

They crowded around Alex's small laptop to see the graphs of Brad's latest results. Alex briefly outlined the adenovirus studies with prion injured brain cells that led to the data with the filtered bacterial fluids. The four slides that Brad prepared for the meeting required about ten minutes to present, but the series of questions and lively discussion that followed made the scheduled thirty minute timeslot for the meeting irrelevant. Bob's questions came in quick succession, one after the other. He wanted to hear everything about the bacterial culture that held the mysterious small molecule that appeared to bind to the brain cells grown *in vitro*.

"That could be an important key. That could be the elusive peptide we've been seeking for a better part of a year. We have some data to show that both *RW88*, and our less toxic version of the tracer *RW96*, binds to something in brain tissue. But the integrity of the interaction, and the tightness of the bond are quite weak and unstable. It's like it attaches then falls off the target like a used stamp on an envelope. It could be that a bacterial peptide is what we were missing. It could be that this peptide makes the entire complex whole and that this new complete structure will allow the dye to bind strongly. I bet you!" said Bob enthusiastically. It was the exact type of comment that Alex and Brad hoped to hear.

"Do you think we could have some of the tracer to do binding studies in our system?" asked Alex.

"Absolutely. We've moved away from *RW88*, in fact we have very little of that tracer left, but we have plenty of *RW96* and sure, I'll share that stuff. I think it's the next logical step. If it works with 96 then we'll do one study with 88 just to again prove that we've increased binding while reducing toxicity," Bob replied. He then turned to Ajay who had been listening to the conversation quietly on one side of the small table. "Ajay do you want to quickly review what you and Amy found recently?"

Ajay was caught completely off guard. He had not prepared a presentation nor had he consolidated his thoughts on the results with the new optical detector and the clinical DNA samples. He also had not discussed the latest results with Amy. Overall he really didn't want to say anything, but all eyes were on him and it appeared as if Bob wanted to share some new data with his colleagues from Harvard.

"Well," Ajay began slowly. "We've developed a rapid way to screen entire human genomes for Xp29.47, the gene that's involved with nonverbal communication. So far we've screened just over one hundred samples and we're now retesting about twenty percent of them to make sure the data are robust but early results are quite interesting." Ajay would have liked to stop there and to withhold his next statement but his boss seemed to be just as eager as the rest of them to hear more. "Preliminary analysis suggests that about ninety percent of all samples tested had at least one copy of the Xp29.47 gene in their chromosome and less than five percent had two copies. It's definitely a dominant trait." He then quickly added, "Brad, I have not had a chance to review these data with Amy so please let me discuss them with her first. I don't want to get on her angry side."

"No problem," said Brad with a chuckle. "No one wants to get on Amy's angry side, that's for sure."

"Ajay, is there a pattern to those that are negative for this gene altogether? Like are they all male, female, old or young? Any association?" asked Alex.

"We don't know. We haven't run those analyses, but we've thought about them and we obviously want to look at a larger database before asking association-type questions."

"What was your target sample size?" asked Bob who realized that he should know the answer.

"At least one thousand. Although we'd prefer two or three thousand to achieve high statistical power."

"If the results for the next one hundred are the same as they were for the first one hundred, then the power will be quite high because the number of positive data points are so numerous," commented Alex who also enjoyed thinking about statistics.

"That's probably true," added Bob. "Great Ajay, thanks. That's exciting stuff. Let Amy know about these data as soon as you can, okay?"

"Sure," Ajay replied.

Alex and Brad left the MIT building with their minds filled with ideas as well as a carefully stowed small vial of the fluorescent red tracer *RW96*. Instead of taking the subway, they decided to walk the three miles across the Harvard Bridge over the Charles River back to Boston to the Medical School.

"Why would the brain make an SOS-type protein and not other organs?" asked Alex who always seemed to be thinking about solving the next part of the puzzle. "And keep in mind that we've only done this work with cultured cells that have been out of the body for quite some time. Perhaps we need to expand our studies to include other types of tissues, like lung, kidney, heart, and liver. Also, we should use the cells as close as possible to the time they were harvested. That way they would better represent how they functioned *in vivo*, in the body. Doesn't that make sense to you?" Brad readily agreed and he found himself again amazed at the clear and fluid thought process Alex exhibited. Why hadn't he synthesized this line of inquiry? Why hadn't he developed these ideas?

"Yes, of course. That's what needs to be done next along with the *RW96* binding studies, exactly," was Brad's simple response.

———•———

Laura requested and was readily granted the window seat on the long, trans-Atlantic flight from Rome to Boston; she wanted to stare aimlessly at the dark, high altitude atmosphere. The noise-canceling headphones reduced the cacophony of sounds that filled the fuselage and in virtual silence; Laura was alone on a full airplane.

Her time in Florence was as revealing as it was refreshing and, in many ways, it was reinvigorating as well. It was hard to believe all she experienced—the art, the people, their culture—in only four and a half weeks. Her eyes welled with tears as she recalled the darkness of the Arno River when she threw Dante's wedding ring into it just before sunrise on what would be just one of many beautiful warm days in Tuscany. Her lips pursed tightly to hold in the sadness as she recalled the parade of trucks filled with men—young and old alike and full of life—as they left for a day at the vineyards. And she had to look down, squeeze her eyes tightly and dab her nose with a tissue to repress an all out cry as she recalled standing alone in front of Michelangelo's captives—unfinished sculptures that Dante had shown her many times in oversized art books that lay underneath the glass-topped coffee table in the living room they once shared. He often said that he couldn't wait to see these powerful works with her someday. A someday that never came.

Laura exhaled to avert sobbing as she turned her thoughts to the sweet and caring Tomasso. From the moment they met, the chef was as kind and as caring as any person she'd known. From his boyish ways when he took her around his lifelong city, right to his insistence that he drive her to the airport in Rome, Tomasso was a genuine person, a true gentleman. At the airport he insisted on escorting her as far as security would allow because, as he said in broken English, "such a lovely woman should not travel alone or at least not without me." Unlike her own, Tomasso's tears ran openly off his soft cheeks as she turned back to wave one final time from the safe side of security. He was heartbroken, but Laura did not promise him anything other than she would remain in touch. Even before they made passionate, rejuvenating love as only those hardened by time could, she made him promise not to fall in love with her. Despite her pleas Tomasso wanted her to remain in Florence with him. He begged her to stay not for a short time but forever. He offered her no more than a simple life rich in food, in culture, in devotion and with a deep sense of purpose. But as enticing as a new start sounded, Laura was steadfast in her decision to return to America and to resume a less than ideal future.

The memory resurfaced as Laura tucked a thin, airline-issued blanket between her right leg and the inside wall of the airplane to guard against the chilly surface. She recalled that she admitted if only to herself, that she gave Dante the lethal injection. It was what he wanted but it doesn't undo the protected fact that she administered the dye. It was at that moment that she recalled the young reporter from the *Rolling Stone*. He asked probing questions that implied that he suspected something awry with Dante Paolo's death. He asked me if there was anything Dante wanted her to do that was unusual. Laura thought: *What was the reporter getting at? Did he want me to come forward and admit to having killed my husband? What was that kid's name again?*

Laura couldn't place the name of the *Stone*'s reporter, but she had to come to terms with her actions or they would haunt her for the rest of her life. She thought about her medical training and of the supportive care given at the end of one's life. Anyone who knew anything about the messy process of dying could have seen that Dante was at the end. And instead of having June administer what would have been the final dose of morphine, she injected the dye as Dante had requested. It was a directive given to her when he was of sound mind. And that's exactly what she did. She injected the dye and, as previously arranged by her clever husband, she completely covered her tracks. His wishes were fulfilled. The experiment was performed as planned and the research paper eventually was published. All good. Nothing bad. Well, almost nothing bad, she reasoned.

Lee. That's his name. Lee King-something. He's certainly not the police or a judge, just a snoopy reporter who is trying to make something of nothing. Is this what I'm returning home to, a whole lot of nothing?

Laura drifted off to a restless nap as her head rested against a cool pillow. In a haze she thought about the strange lunch with professor Lorenzo. *What was the purpose of this guy's visit? He bought some jewelry for someone and he seemed nice, but skittish, if not outright anxious. And his strange and sudden departure was inconsistent with his appearance of being a learned man, well dressed and all together. Did time really get away from him? Did he really have to catch a train? It doesn't matter, Tomasso was so sweet and he prepared a great meal.*

The airplane's massive engines droned on as Laura watched the tops of a few thick clouds pass below in the night. She was alone with her thoughts as photographs of Florence flitted through her mind. *It's been only three hours and already, I miss Italy.*

———•———

Amy was exhausted at the end of the mid November day in Minnesota. And the cold easterly winds that sliced through her down parka didn't help liven her mood. She had not been herself over the past week. She slept right through the alarm clock and for the first time in her entire academic life, Amy missed a class due to something other than an illness. She felt so exhausted that she brought herself to the clinic for an evaluation—another first.

The young physician thought he had Amy's problem pegged even before he shook her hand. *Here comes another overly stressed, high-achieving, type A, strung-out medical student,* he thought. The physician nonetheless began the examination by asking her some probing questions about her current life at the university.

"What are you studying?" he asked.

"Medicine," answered Amy.

"Year?"

"Second."

"Started clinical rotations yet?"

"Not yet. In a couple of months, in January."

"Eating well? Do you have an appetite?"

"Yes. Well, no. Not in the past week or so."

"Stressed?"

"Didn't I say I was a second year med student?"

The physician smiled then continued. "What else is going on in your life?"

"I'm doing research with a group at MIT."

"Oh you decided to play in the small sandbox," quipped the physician.

Amy smiled weakly and added, "Yeah but it's on autopilot. I just review data now and again until I can get back in the lab."

"I see. Are you sexually active?"

"No. I mean yes, just not here. My boyfriend is in Boston."

"At MIT?"

"No, Harvard."

"You do gravitate to those small sandboxes, don't you?" He joked as he asked Amy to lie on the exam table where he began to palpate her abdomen. Amy was relaxed, as he noted no abnormalities with her liver, spleen, stomach, and given that she did not wince at any time during the exam suggested that there was nothing wrong with her major internal organs. With the stethoscope pressed against her lower abdomen to listen for bowel sounds, the physician asked if she had any cramping upon menstruation.

"No. I'm one of the lucky ones."

"When did you last menstruate?"

The simple question stumped Amy. And after some thought, she replied, "Um, I don't recall."

"Taking birth control?"

"Yes. I'm on the pill."

"And the last time you had sexual intercourse?"

"Um...in August. Late August."

"Okay, well I'm going to have the nurse draw some blood to make sure everything is in order there, and I'll also order a hCG test. Until we call you with the results, I want you to eat well, stay hydrated and try not to worry too much."

Amy was more stressed now then before she entered the clinic. The phlebotomy session was a blur as she mulled over the idea of being pregnant. *No, that can't be right, can it?* She thought as she tried to remember the last time she menstruated. *No, I'm pretty sure I had my period in September sometime.*

On the way to her apartment, Amy stopped at the pharmacy and bought a six-pack of a chocolate-flavored energy drink and a home pregnancy test. She was not about to wait for a call from the clinic to learn if she was pregnant; that was one stress she could eliminate herself. Amy carefully read the simple instructions on the single test that suggested using the first urine of the day when the level of the telling hormone would be highest. Amy quickly shunned that advice.

The lines on small dipstick didn't need to wait for the morning either.

———•———

It took a full minute for the statement to sink in, but after Abby processed the words along with the troubled look on her mentor's face did she feel the gravity of the tragic news.

"Lilly. Lilly is dead." Abby said not as a question but rather, perhaps, as stating an untrue fact. "Is that what I heard you say?"

"Yes Abby. That's correct," replied Alexa. "We have to notify the university immediately. One of the study nurses saw the notice in today's newspaper and recognized the picture of Lilly. She told me as soon as she arrived no more than thirty minutes ago. This will be deemed a clinical study adverse event that will require a full investigation. There is no doubt that they will suspend the study. The authorities will need time to gather details about Lilly's involvement in the trial."

Abby was in a stupor and unclear of what needed to be done next. This was unchartered territory for her, but thankfully not for Alexa who served on many safety-monitoring boards that have oversight duties to clinical trials performed at other institutions.

"Abby," her mentor continued, "when something bad happens to a subject enrolled in a clinical study, it is halted to assess whether or not the adverse event had anything to do with the study. Those are standard rules. The trial is now on a clinical hold."

"What happened to her? How did she die?" asked Abby.

"The nurse said that the article mentioned an allegation of child abuse. I've already asked both nurses to send everyone that showed up for today's session home with our sincere apologies. Abby, I think we need to have a chat with Rosi and Johanna. The university will want to talk with each of us, so let's get together to review what went down. I want to get ahead of this story. I don't recall anyone dying in a clinical study at AU. The press will be all over this and we'd better have something to say about what happened during Lilly's interview."

Abby, still shaken, simply nodded.

———•———

Phil worked virtually alone at the Rensselaer Polytechnic Institute. Because of his larger way of thinking he felt as if he was living in a vacuum, totally isolated from everyone else. He felt fortunate, though, to still be able to bounce ideas off of Amy, Brad and Abby so much so that one of the quotes that Phil jotted down in his notebook during their last group conference call was a response to a question posed by Amy:

> Perhaps telepathy is a primitive form of advanced communication that transcends time and space. Main branch perhaps?

In his small office, Phil looked at the complex formulas he had written on the whiteboard. He then looked back at the sentence and the question and thought: *What if the unifying element that connects individuals residing in parallel universes is communication, and that the form of communication is not verbal or written, but pure thought—like telepathy? Perhaps this is the original, uncontaminated form of communication that has existed since the beginning of time and it is, in fact, the nucleus of our existence. That would mean that other forms of our existence are simply different phases of the original energy, like electrons around atoms.*

Phil rose from his desk and began pacing around the small room in total silence. The entire building was empty and he hadn't realized how quiet it was on this Sunday before Thanksgiving when everyone was either generating exam questions, or preparing to answer them before leaving town for a few hectic days off.

Like electrons around atoms, he repeated in his mind before saying it aloud to the empty room, "Electrons around atoms. Electrons in different states. Electrons in different volumes of space occupying different energy levels. Electron orbital maps. Holy crap."

Phil was onto something totally different. With intense focus, he went to the Internet and sought the chemical composition of humans. He wrote the electron orbital map configuration for all the elements in the human body: oxygen, carbon, hydrogen, nitrogen, calcium, phosphorous, potassium, sulfur, sodium, chlorine, magnesium, boron, chromium, cobalt, copper, fluorine, iodine, iron, manganese, molybdenum, selenium, silicon, tin, vanadium and zinc on the whiteboard. He then assigned weights to each one based on the percent contained in an average size adult. Oxygen with an electron configuration of 1s2 2s2 2p4 was assigned a weight of 0.65, as it comprises 65% of all elements. The barely detectable but critically important zinc with a configuration of 1s2 2s2 2p6 3s2 3p6 4s2 3d10 was assigned a weight of 0.003. Phil then went back to the computer and entered the configurations of all 25 elements into a short program. The program combined the weighted electron configurations into one encompassing mathematical array.

Phil's ideas began to gel. He reasoned that the central equation that would describe human energy, independent of where that energy resides, must take into account a person's chemical makeup. If the universal truth states that matter is conserved, then elements that compose that matter must also be conserved. Essentially they would have existed since the beginning of time. The specific atomic arrangement of those elements forms a unique individual, someone with the potential to simultaneously reside in different quantum phases, like the shifting electrons in the elements themselves. It would be the nuances, the almost immeasurable differences in chemical composition, which creates a distinct form.

Phil realized that the discovery of orbital maps to each element was the missing keystone. Now he needed to build the rest of the mathematical archway, the *voussoirs*, piece by piece to support that centerpiece. Phil did not only consider the arch to be a way to visualize his quest, but he also began to realize that each stone was an independent mathematical formula with it's own importance. Each stone, each unique formula was absolutely critical to the existence of the entire arch.

He opened a notebook that contained page after page of mathematical equations that sought to describe multiple universes. He then wrote each equation on a piece of paper and taped it to the wall. Many pieces of paper took the shape of an arch. Now, Phil could easily rearrange each equation as necessary. The topmost piece of paper—cut into the shape of a keystone—was blank. Eventually, it would contain the formula of the orbital maps of each element that composed an individual. The paper keystone awaited the results of the computer's lengthy calculations.

Alone in his office, Phil was mad with deep, original thought.

"Clearly," Phil said aloud. "Nonverbal communication is one stone. But more important than communication was time itself and above that, space. The equations for time and space are known and accepted. Christ! How many stones are there?"

The postdoc stepped back to view the dizzying array of numbers and formulas displayed on the arch. "Each stone, each formula must lead to the next in a logical and mathematically sound fashion. I'm going to assume that randomness is also built into this structure not in each impost or *voussoir, per se,* but as an inherent aspect of the keystone itself. I'm going to consider the human being as a random event."

The only sound Phil heard in the small office as he contemplated the mathematical arch was the low hum of the computer's hard drive as it continued to condense each array of the 25 chemical elements. What Phil did not know was that the program he wrote was so simple in design that the answer could not, indeed would not, be singular. Not even close.

Nexus IV

After they met with Alexa to discuss the grave incident, and after having heard the outline what would be a detailed investigation by American University, the telepaths regrouped at Rosi's studio apartment. Three bottles of chardonnay did little to alleviate the pain they felt over the death of their little subject, Lilly. Although each processed and expressed shock and grief differently, all wondered the same thing—should they have taken the silent pleas of the tortured child more seriously? Should they have broken protocol and acted no matter the consequences?

Johanna was a complete wreck. She was the first one to down a glass of wine. She was inconsolable and repeatedly said through outbursts of tears, "Lilly could have been me. That kid was me. I lucked out. I absolutely fucking lucked out."

Rosi was quiet. She really did not care for Johanna's seemingly excessive wailing. To distract herself from the sorrowful blow, she grabbed a piece of sandpaper and attended to Hebo, or Hobe, whose solid white face seemed a bit more sullen.

Abby, who stayed behind and reviewed the videotape of Lilly's interview with Alexa, joined Rosi and Johanna at the studio apartment just after 1 p.m. with sandwiches. It was unusual for them to drink as much as they did so early in the day, but this was not a typical day. Abby told her friends what she and Alexa had discussed just an hour ago. She opted to speak aloud to her fellow telepaths. Abby needed to hear the words that she may eventually have to say to law enforcement officials, and to university administrators.

"So university officials and others will be allowed to view the video-tape of our interview with Lilly and possibly one or two other children too," Abby started. "We did everything right as per the clinical protocol so that won't be an issue. Lilly's mother..."

"That fucking bitch!" interjected Johanna loudly, an outburst that was all but ignored by Abby and Rosi.

"Her mother's violent actions are clearly evident on the tape and perhaps that's all the officials will need from us. However, there is the possibility that they will ask us what, if anything, was transmitted by Lilly during our time with her. That is where things can get tricky. Everyone will know that this was a telepathy study. It's listed on a clinical trials website so that part is no secret. What will be tough to deal with, how-ever, is what Lilly transmitted to each of us separately, and then whether or not they will believe us. After all, not everyone has even heard about telepathy let alone accept it as a viable form of communication. That's why we're doing this study in the first place, right?" No one was hungry, but they all nibbled on lunch. None held back on the wine.

"We just have to tell the truth. Just tell them what you remember. If your memory is vague, then it's vague. If it is clear, then say what you remember. It's that simple."

Rosi and Johanna had several questions, but they already knew that Abby had no answers to give—all of this was too new. As the first to suc-cumb to the lulling effects of the wine, Johanna rose from the kitchen counter, removed all of her clothes and positioned herself directly into the center of the king-sized bed. Rosi, still covered with a thin layer of white marble dust walked into the tiled bathroom, stripped, then preceded to rinse her slender body in the hot shower. Abby was starting to feel the vague beginnings of a migraine with the all-to-familiar sign of a dull pain at the base of her neck. She thought that the combination of a hot shower and a quick nap would keep the headache at bay. In short order, the three telepaths were fast asleep in a tight, protective spoon formation with Johanna snugly in the middle.

A very thin, middle-aged woman with long stringy hair and wearing an array of white, wispy silk threads appeared through Johanna's portal. All three sleeping women accessed the message. It was as sure as it was reassuring.

Don't blame yourselves, it was fated and it's better this way. Hold no remorse, humans are mostly imperfect.

Through a deep state of repose Rosi responded in her unique way.

Lilly my love your words are so dear/you've come from afar absent of fear/ to calm our troubled hearts/we should have done better right, right from the start/but one question for you/please indulge if you will/you are now a lady so pretty with smile/but last we saw you were just a small child/how could that be/ quite odd to see a grown Lilly.

The middle-aged Lilly, although expressionless, was inwardly amused. She responded through pursed lips as she faded away.

My phase on your earth/to death from birth/is but a physical shell/made for the moment not suited for time/the truth be known/the shell had not grown/ when the energy I am sublime.

Slowly and wearily, Abby awoke from the deep sleep. When she realized that she was safely cuddled next to Johanna who was still asleep, and beyond her Rosi, who was still and breathing softly, Abby closed her eyes and reviewed Lilly's lyrical response.

Abby's Theory

Immediately, Brad noticed that something was different with Amy. She appeared to have aged more than expected since he last saw her only three short months ago. She appeared tired and out of sorts. He thought that her sour mood reflected a nasty combination of an indirect flight path from Minneapolis to Boston, the cold, dark early winter weather she experienced upon departure and again on arrival, and the downright rude holiday crowds that clogged every passageway on one of the busiest travel days of the year, the Wednesday before Thanksgiving. Logan Airport was a zoo. Cars were double and triple parked and limos, buses and taxis snarled entrances and exits. The ride to Brad's family home in Rockport, north of Logan, would have challenged the patience of Zen monks. Their view, for most of the slow trip, was an endless sea of red taillights and countless blinding headlights from cars heading south. It was not a great start to the short holiday break.

He was not used to seeing her sullen, but Brad was nonetheless hopeful that the Thanksgiving holiday with his family, despite its brevity, would be the type of relaxing get-away she needed. For their part, Brad's family embraced Amy although they hadn't seen much of her since she moved to Minnesota.

Finally, after a full day of travel, they were alone in the guestroom suite at the MacIntyre estate. Amy, despite her fatigue, broke the news to Brad in her characteristic straightforward manner. "Brad, I'm pregnant," she said as her eyes welled with tears brought on by a combination of opposing emotions. "I don't know exactly but I'm probably just around the end of the first trimester."

Brad was stupefied. So many questions instantly formed in his mind that he wasn't sure where to begin, but he did know how to approach Amy who was trying hard to hold herself together. He sat next to her and caringly put his arm around her shoulders. As he gently pulled her to his chest she broke down. Brad knew that what he said next was critical not only for the moment, but also for the long-term. He tried to think methodically and rationally. He needed to choose his words carefully. There was no doubt in his mind that he was the baby's father; he had no intention on asking her to confirm it. They relied on the pill even though they knew that it wasn't a totally effective means of birth control. The less than ten percent failure rate was a gamble they were willing to take. But now he had to face the music and live with the consequences of his actions, of their actions. Although it was true that his love for Amy had wavered over the past couple of years, it did so only slightly. He still intended to one day ask her to marry him and to start a family together, just not at this moment. He wanted to wait until they finished medical school. So now what? What was he going to say?

Brad drew a long, deep, breath, exhaled slowly and plunged himself squarely and bravely into the future.

"Amy? Sweetheart?" he started as he shifted himself so that he was looking directly at her.

He cradled her troubled, moist face into his hands. "I love you. I love you very, very much. I want you to know that. We'll be okay." Amy responded with her lovely dark brown eyes.

When the long tender moment passed, Brad asked the question he wanted to ask in the first place. "Have you seen a doctor?"

"No. Well yes, when I went to the clinic. I'm sorry. I haven't been myself lately. I've been so tired. I haven't been able to focus. Anyway, so earlier this week, I don't know, I think it was Monday, I went to the student clinical and they did some blood work that confirmed the result of the home pregnancy test. I know I should have called you right away but I knew I would see you soon and I wanted to tell you face-to-face. Quite a shock, huh? Shocked me too."

"Have you told your parents?"

"No. I wanted to tell you first. We have to think this through. I wanted to see you so we can think about this together. We need a plan, but I think I need to take a nap first. I'm completely wiped. It's been a long day and the thought of going out to dinner tonight with your folks is not sitting well with me. I haven't been very hungry lately. Maybe I'll feel better after a nap."

Brad lay on the bed and Amy curled up next to him. "Don't worry. Just rest now," Brad said trying his best to sound reassuring. In fact, he was not sure about anything other than he loved this woman, who had fallen asleep in his arms, perhaps now more than ever. He was still in disbelief at the news and it's immediate impact. How quickly his life had changed. This very morning he was a second year medical student trying hard to wrap things up in Boston so that he wouldn't be late picking up his girlfriend at the airport for a couple of days off with family to celebrate a national holiday. Now, in an instant, he became a father in waiting; a full-fledged parent-to-be with all the duties and responsibilities endowed by the title. And suddenly he was beside someone who was not just his girlfriend but also the mother of his child.

At this moment, their secret was contained. But soon enough that too would change. His family would be informed and Brad wasn't exactly sure how they would react. His parents seemed to have accepted Amy as a girlfriend, at least in a cordial sort of way, but will they accept her as the future mother of their grandchild? How will they act when they learn that their son will have a child out of wedlock? The concerns kept coming. Although he's a grown man, Brad still relied heavily on his parents. They were paying for his medical school and his living expenses. Will the pregnancy change their commitment to him?

They will have to break the news to Amy's family too. Brad doesn't know her parents that well at all. In fact, he'd never even been to their home in California. How will they take the news?

This is going to be an interesting Thanksgiving, and a challenging New Year, Brad thought as he felt the rhythmic rise and fall of Amy's chest. And as he listened to Amy's breathing, little did he know the magnitude of their New Year's challenge.

————•————

As the train slowly approached Union Station, Phil was beginning to have second thoughts about spending Thanksgiving with Abby and her newfound female lover. Perhaps sex was too much on his mind and his expectations or fantasies of having voluptuous, telepathic women understand and cater to his every need was just that—an overblown, prepubescent-type sexual fantasy. He wasn't an old man, but at 24 he felt as though he wanted a steady relationship with a woman, a real bond like Brad had with Amy. Phil thought, *That lucky dog Brad has such a great relationship with that hot babe. How did he do it? How did he luck out? And forget the women at RPI—done with that thought. Perhaps Abby is the one or she was the one. Maybe she's found her soul mate in Rosi. Maybe I'm yesterday's news and this visit will be my farewell tour.* As random thoughts continued to roll through Phil's mind, the long Amtrak train finally lurched to a full stop, only twelve minutes late.

Abby watched nervously as the train slowly closed in and ground to a halt just five or so yards from the stop bumper. She wasn't sure how she would react to Phil now that she had experienced the touch of women. Would she still have feelings for him? Would he accept her now that he knows that she's attracted to women? When they last spoke he was not very forthcoming about his feelings, but he did accept her invitation to join them for the short Thanksgiving holiday, so perhaps it will not be as strange of a situation as she feared.

Phil stepped off the train looking a bit disheveled after the eight-hour trip, but seeing Abby standing on the platform took the sting out of the ride. Her long, firm embrace warmed him amid the cool, dark November evening. Abby looked prettier than he remembered. There was something about her that made her appear older and oddly, more desirable. Her face looked thinner than the last time they enjoyed each other at Flatbread; her brown hair that matched her caring eyes hung free, and her height hadn't changed, but what Phil should have, but would not notice, is the effect that both time and experience has on a person. Phil hugged an older, wiser Abby than the one he met only a few years ago. Time in graduate school was starting to show benefits, both mentally and physically.

Abby and Phil headed directly to *The Beltway Bistro* where they honed in on the house special: cream of broccoli soup, turkey club sandwich and homemade lemon tart. The two graduate students shared stories about the ordeals of the past year noting both the differences and similarities in their teaching, research and classwork responsibilities. Phil was most animated when he described the universal truth about the conservation of energy, the elemental composition of humans, orbital maps of electrons, atoms, quantum phases, and the entire concept of the mathematical archway.

"Abby," he said. "Nonverbal communication is its own stone, its own *voussoir*, in that archway. I just know it, but I've yet to place it in the hierarchy or to identify it cleanly, I mean mathematically clean."

And Abby described the latest setback with the her research study and the affect Lilly's death had on Rosi and Johanna. "The trial is still on clinical hold and it will likely be that way into the New Year. The only positive thing is that the trial itself is showing an interesting connection between telepathy and sensory loss even if we've only interviewed a small number of children. I think we're on the right track. Hopefully, we'll be able to continue the study someday."

"Yeah, me too and it reminds me why I like what I do," Phil said in a manner that begged a question.

"What's that?"

"I don't have to deal with people. You, Amy, Brad are all the same in that you're in a people business. Your work requires interactions with living, breathing human beings. Me? I prefer to spend time with pencil, paper and dead numbers; I want to interact with as few people as possible. Speaking of people, what's the plan for tomorrow?"

Abby explained that they were expected at Rosi's apartment around noontime. They would spend the entire day preparing and consuming small *tapas*-like meals, drinking fine wines and just enjoying each other's company.

"It will be laid back, stress free and it will just be the three of us as Olysia and Johanna had planned to spend Thanksgiving with their families," Abby said. She then reiterated Rosi's talents as an artist, and the stunning expanse of her apartment that doubled as an art studio.

Their lovemaking on that Wednesday evening before Thanksgiving was tentative at first. But after Abby told Phil that she cared for him deeply, and that she felt that she had the capacity to love both genders equally, their pent-up passion exploded. "My special way with Rosi is just as important as my connection with you Phil," she admitted. "I don't see these feeling as mutually exclusive or divisive. I think that each one of us has a large capacity to love. I am fortunate that I have you and Rosi, and Johanna and Olysia to love."

This was the first time Phil had heard the word 'love' and 'Rosi and Johanna and Olysia' used in the same sentence, and even before he had a chance to comment, Abby filled him in on the details. "We are friends, we are telepaths, and we are caring and loving. It's quite simple really. Admittedly, it's a lot of fun too."

Abby's words enticed and enchanted Phil. Despite the fact that he never really thought about being multiple women simultaneously, nor had he considered making love to a man, he believed in the same principle Abby had just stated. Humans, along with their wide range of needs, desires and emotions, also harbor a broad capacity to love.

Their evening together exceeded expectations. Both the telepath and the mathematician were looking forward to the upcoming holiday with Rosi.

There were no stories of half-hearted gratitude, or market-driven floats parading down the wide, pompous streets of New York City, and no traditional football games. In fact, there were no images at all. No television, no images, no distractions. Instead, overcast skies opaquely lit Rosi's studio and classical music softly filled the single level loft, a setting that made this Thanksgiving unlike any other Phil had ever experienced. Varied plates of food were prepared in short bursts in a team effort and consumed when ready. Drinks, some of which complemented the *tapas*-like meals, were not forced nor encouraged.

Throughout the day Rosi resisted the temptation to work on her art. But she willingly showed Phil some of the projects in progress, including the marble sculpture named Hebo or Hobe—she still hadn't settled on a name. Phil was roundly impressed not only by the combination of the apartment that doubled as a work studio, but also by Rosi's vast artistic talents. He was particularly taken by the description of her wealthy patron and the business arrangement she had with him. "It sounds like something out of the days of the high Renaissance. It seems too good to be true," he remarked. Phil openly wondered if scientists could command attention, commitment and cash from such patrons.

Rosi was as usual, a laid-back, gracious and welcoming host. She had heard so much about Phil that she felt as though she already knew him. His interest in high order mathematics captured the artist's imagination not because she knew something about this abstract field, but just the opposite; it was a subject she did not understand at all. Beyond addition, subtraction, multiplication and division, math was lost on her; that part of her brain, she admitted, was not well developed. Nevertheless, Rosi listened intently and was genuinely intrigued as Phil gave her the short version of his research on multiple universes and the framework of the mathematical arch.

"Nonverbal communication fits in the arch somewhere, but I'm not sure where," he admitted.

"You do not receive, but you transmit clearly, true?" Rosi asked. "You are a 'giving telepath' only, correct?" Phil looked over at Abby for some help.

"Yes, that's true," said Abby aloud. "He's tried but it just won't work. He's also tried accessing the portal, but to no avail. Isn't this true Phil?"

"You told me to access the portal just before I fall asleep and I...well I've tried many times, but I simply pass out as soon as my head hits the pillow. I can't control it. My mind runs so fast when I'm working, but once it's off it just shuts down. Like throwing a switch, I'm off."

Without warning Abby received from Rosi: *No doubt my love for this man/to fully understand/he must go beyond this world/we must execute the plan/perhaps we can take him/both you and I/hand in hand.*

Abby, with only a touch of reservation, escorted Phil to the bedroom. She disrobed and suggested that he do the same. Phil glanced out from the steamy shower clear across the apartment and into the kitchen where Rosi was loading the dishwasher.

Phil was high aroused. So much so that Abby's lathered hands required less than a minute to bring Phil to orgasm. She needed him to be relaxed before Rosi joined them, but the strategy was only partially successful. Once Rosi wrapped her arms around the mathematician's torso his erection returned. The artist's short stature, small firm breasts and closely cropped red hair pressed against his chest as every young man's fantasy came to fruition. Abby kissed Phil deeply as Rosi rotated her body and backed into him. Phil almost passed out when he came for the second time in less than six minutes. The sight of the two telepaths together, their low sounds, and the hot steamy water were simply overwhelming.

Phil laid underneath the down comforter on the large king size bed between Rosi and Abby feeling very drowsy, but not exhausted. Abby told Phil to let his mind relax and to follow their lead. He did as he was told.

Moments later as Phil drifted off to sleep he heard words, but not through his ears. *Follow us young man/you must/you can/to what has been called the other land/and once a time upon/you will be led to the vast place beyond.*

By having just experienced their physical form, Phil was unwittingly in tune with all of the telepath's energy. And without a clear grasp of how it happened Phil was visualizing a form, a strapping fellow with strong Aryan facial features who appeared to be in his late sixties. *Tell your mother it was not her fault*, said the man silently before he disappeared. The encounter was brief, but to Phil it was as powerful as any event he had ever experienced. He instantly understood his grandfather's message. The older fellow did not blame his daughter, Phil's mother, for failing to tell rescue workers that he was trapped in the bedroom beyond the burning timbers of the living room. Firefighters were frantically asking the young mother the whereabouts of others that lived in the house, but paralyzed with fear she could not speak. She failed to disclose the location of her trapped father, a guilt that haunted her ever since. Phil was only a toddler at the time. He was held tightly in his mother's arms as together they watched their house violently burn to its fieldstone foundation.

Phil awoke with a gasp, his eyes damp. It took him a moment to regain his bearings. Then he felt Abby's right hand and Rosi's left hand resting gently on his biceps. "I just had a dream," he stated wearily to no one in particular. "It was my grandfather."

Abby promptly corrected him. "That wasn't a dream and you weren't alone, we were with you. We know that the man was your grandfather. We also understand the meaning of his message."

"Where did he come from? Where did he go?"

"We don't know the answers to those questions," said Rosi aloud. "We've wondered that many times ourselves. Maybe he went to another place."

"How could that be? He died when I was young. The only thing I really remember about him was that he used to cup my face with his big hands and stare into my eyes. Our eyes locked and for what seemed like an eternity. But I was just a little kid. It may have been only a few seconds."

The three young adults lay side by side by side in silence contemplating what had occurred in the past hour since they left the walk-in shower. It was close to 4:30 and the last rays of the day's sun barely illuminated the vast studio apartment.

"Rosi, did you say that you thought my grandfather left to go to another place?" asked Phil who felt like a king between two queens.

"Yes."

"What other place? And what made you think that?"

"Well, he must have come from somewhere. So logically he was headed somewhere other than where we were when we were with him," Rosi replied.

"Where exactly were we?"

"Who knows," answered Abby who was thinking along a completely different line. She rose up on her elbow to look directly at Phil who, along with Rosi, was almost in total darkness. "Did your grandfather hold your face like this?" she asked as she bounced up on her knees and proceeded to cradle Phil's face with both hands.

"Yes. Exactly. His large hands cupped most of my small head. That much I remember."

"Oh my God!" exclaimed Abby. "I think, I think I just made a connection."

Phil grabbed Abby's wrists and guided her hands to his chest as he replied, "Me too."

Rosi lay on her back and stared up at the barely visible ceiling. She knew what the graduate students were thinking and while she understood

Abby's breakthrough she needed a clearer explanation from Phil on his.

2

After a week of sidestepping the issue and trying to ignore him, Rosa finally had to confront her cousin Lorenzo. She needed to be direct. What are his plans with the American mistress he was soon to marry in a lavish ceremony on the rugged hills of the Amalfi coast? Rosa thought that her trusted neighbor was brilliant to have pieced together the clues, including the informative brochure, to conclude that Lorenzo would soon marry his American love. But then, earlier that very morning, the very same neighbor visited Rosa with additional bad news. In the early morning light she told Rosa, in hushed tones, that she dreamt that Lorenzo snuck out of the house in the night and did not return. She also added that there was a wayward goat in her dream. The hoofed beast grazed slowly as if it had not a care in the world. It was a sure symbol that the Lorenzo was not only calculating, but also that he was possessed by *il diavolo*, the cruel and remorseless devil. Anger now topped Rosa's fears. She hadn't spent her entire life longing for Lorenzo only to stand by passively while he abandon's her for another woman—an American at that.

"So now that your soul is possessed, when will the rest of you be taken too?" Rosa asked curtly as she hand-dried the morning cups and plates. Lorenzo, who was seated at the kitchen table scanning the morning news on his laptop, did not know how to react to Rosa's odd question, a question that seemed to have materialized out of thin air. While interactions with Rosa had been off since his day trip to Florence just over a week ago, he thought things had returned to normal. Obviously, this was not the case given her question and outwardly angry demeanor. The professor looked dumbfounded, like a child caught in the act of doing something he was just told not to do. And like that prejudged child, Lorenzo was unsure what to say next essentially because he wasn't sure of his offense.

"What makes you say that?" he asked, hoping that he said nothing in his sleep as he had been prone to do in the past.

"Don't try to deceive me Lorenzo. Although we are not formally married, I consider myself your wife. We have loved each other since we were young children playing together in this very house with our *nonni*. My love for you never wavered even though you went to America and had many women and became famous with all of your important science. Some guys called for me but I refused them. I wanted only you and I knew that you would come back to me someday and that we would finally be together, but now I'm old and defeated. Apparently I wasted my life waiting for the devil himself! Why did you do this to me?"

Overcome with emotions Rosa started for the door but Lorenzo quickly rose and stopped her from leaving. He placed his hands on her shoulders, looked directly in her eyes and asked, "Tell me please, what in God's name are you talking about?"

Rosa desperately tried to hold back tears as she repeated the fabricated words of her neighbor. "I know you met an American woman in Florence," she said. Again, Lorenzo was stunned and confused. Did he tell her that he was going to Florence to meet a business acquaintance or a female colleague? Lorenzo could not recall precisely what he had told Rosa, but he may have said that he was meeting a person named Laura. He did remember that he wanted to go to Florence alone, that much was certain. In no way could Lorenzo have asked Laura about her dead husband's ability to control people from the grave had Rosa been with them. That much was certain. And after what actually did transpire at the *trattoria*, he was glad that Rosa was not present. So Lorenzo needed to bend the truth a tiny bit.

"Yes. You are right. I had lunch with Laura Kean, the widow of an American colleague who happened to be in Florence on vacation."

Just a day before Lorenzo spoke those words, Rosa and her neighbor had prayed mightily to Saint Rita of Cascia, the patron saint of impossible circumstances, that they were wrong. Not only were the two old friends right, but the situation was worse than they had anticipated. The woman Lorenzo met was not just a common vixen, as they had thought, but a widowed one, full of wild, pleasure-seeking ways—a true American whore. Tears shamelessly began to stream down Rosa's soft, chubby face. Through sobs she proclaimed, "And you plan to marry her in Amalfi and give her gold and leave me forever?" Rosa's life had completely unraveled.

Lorenzo was perplexed. Was there a misunderstanding? He never planned to marry Laura. Indeed he hoped he'd never see her again. And why is there this talk of Amalfi and gold? What was she talking about? As Lorenzo's mind tried to understand her words, Rosa elaborated sardonically. "I'm sure that your sex starved American *puttana* will love her gold necklace and that the weather will be just perfect on the Amalfi coast with calm waters and a perfect sunset when the two of you sail away leaving *vecchia* Rosa alone to die, heartbroken, inside these ancient stone walls."

During her tearful rant, Rosa voiced the clue that provided the needed jolt to Lorenzo's aging memory.

"Gold?" he asked.

"*Bastardo!*" she shouted in anger as she freed herself from his light grasp and went to the closet to retrieve both the Amalfi coast brochure and the small box from the pocket of his overcoat. She returned with the evidence.

"Here! Take them and leave. Leave me alone to die in peace. Go! *Va'via!*"

The smile that grew wider on Lorenzo's face seemed to Rosa like the rudest of condescending insults. She looked at him in disbelief. Angry, sad and confused, a defeated Rosa slowly turned to go upstairs, but as she did she felt the unmistakable coolness of metal against the thin skin of her neck. She turned to face her cousin just as he released the now clasped gold rope necklace that assumed its draped form around Rosa's neck.

"I completely forgot that I bought this for you in Florence. I must be getting old. My memory is slipping. It looks even lovelier on such a lovely woman."

Rosa's neighbor, who had been listening to the entire exchange outside just below the kitchen window, raised her head and peered in as the cousins embraced. The protective neighbor made the sign of the cross as she continued to observe the hands of the two cousins wave wildly as the pamphlet was tossed between them amid amusing pantomimes of a wedding ceremony. With a beaming smile on Rosa's still damp face, the neighbor was thankful that her prayers to Saint Rita of Cascia were answered. She knew all along that Rita was the right saint to tap for the task. The neighbor left and returned to her own home to keep the sacred secrecy of the answered prayers to herself, to herself and her other dear friend who lived on the other side of the village.

"So you are not possessed by the devil after all?" asked Rosa flippantly.

Lorenzo laughed hardily as he held her in his arms.

"No, no, no. Well, at least not by the devil," Lorenzo replied, half-jokingly.

———•———

Pappy was an aptly named chimpanzee. As a youngster he was known as Snappy Pappy due to his quick assertive movements around the cage full of toys, swings and other items to keep him fit and active at the Potomac River Primate Center. And as he aged, Pappy steadily slowed down but remained good-natured and well tempered. These traits led Snappy Pappy to acquire a new, more appropriate nickname, Happy Pappy. But now, his current and final nickname, Grand Pappy, reflected both his advanced age of 55 years and his stature in the behavioral research community. Grand Pappy held the record for the greatest number of successfully completed clinical studies. Not only that, the primate outlived his original caretaker and behavioral specialist by more than a decade. The aging chimp was as good-natured as a wealthy, retired uncle. He seemed to welcome any new chimpanzee, or human for that matter, to his jungle-like paradise-in-a-cage.

Dr. Johnson, Jo and Mi-Ok stood outside the large enclosure that held Grand Pappy and another chimpanzee who seemed to be quite younger and the more curious of the two, on this mild, overcast and quiet Thanksgiving Day morning. The caretaker, a stocky middle-aged man, walked into the cage without hesitation as if he lived there and calmly spoke to both chimps about the weather and about the meaning of the holiday. Both chimps sat in front of the caretaker as if they were being tutored and like they understood every word the genial man uttered. The scientists outside the enclosure overheard the man explain to his hominid cousins that a nice young lady was going to do a little procedure on Grand Pappy. He stated that the procedure would be quick and painless. Both chimps tilted their heads slightly to the right and then to the left as the caretaker spoke. When he heard the stocky caretaker say Grand Pappy's name twice in succession, the second chimp scurried to the far side of the vast artificial jungle and sat in a self-made nest of toys and hay where he would watch the upcoming show from a distance.

The caretaker waved to Mi-Ok and motioned her to enter the cage. The thin technician looked up at Jo then tentatively entered making sure to open and close the iron door slowly and quietly. She gingerly walked to where the caretaker and Grand Pappy sat. All three primates in the cage seemed indifferent to Mi-Ok's presence. Having been briefed on the procedure, the caretaker exposed the back of Grand Pappy's neck that, given the chimp's advanced age, had only a thin coat of hair. Mi-Ok had a good view of the base of Grand Pappy's head and neck and with an ungloved left hand she lightly palpated this sensitive area. Grand Pappy was undaunted as Mi-Ok inserted a sterile acupuncture needle with her steady right hand in a specific spot on the upper right side of the chimp's neck. The whisper thin needle was inserted just beyond half of its total length to reach a depth Mi-Ok judged to be adequate to reach the nerve in an animal of Grand Pappy's size. Within seconds the man-size chimp slowly listed to his right side. The animal caretaker guided the amiable chimp to the hay-covered floor of the jungle-like enclosure and watched as the primate's eyes closed restfully. It appeared as though Grand Pappy had laid himself on a comfortable sofa for a mid-day nap. From the far end of the cage the second chimp watched the entire procedure unfold. To imitation Grand Pappy, he also lay on his side and tried unsuccessfully to keep his eyes closed.

Expressionless, Mi-Ok looked out to Dr. Johnson and Jo. After a moment, Dr. Johnson gave a thumbs-up, the prearranged gesture that he was satisfied with the outcome of the quasi-experiment. Now, she could remove the sleep-inducing needle. Mi-Ok then looked at the caretaker who nodded in return. The skilled technician crouched next to the sleeping primate and in a single, sure and swift move removed the acupuncture needle. The chimp did not finch at all but remained asleep. Mi-Ok's heart began to race as she wondered if something had gone wrong, she expected him to awake instantly as mice did when the needle was removed. The caretaker petted the large primate and softly called his name. Slowly, Grand Pappy awoke and groggily pushed himself to a sitting position. The other chimp also sat up and hooted once, a primitive but effective message to the caretaker who readily provided the distant animal a hand signal indicating that he no longer had to stay where he was. The younger chimp immediately returned to Grand Pappy's side as if to ask, *all set old man?*

Later, when they were alone on that memorable Thanksgiving Day, Jo told Mi-Ok how brave she was to be with the large chimps. She looked at him with eyes that made him melt, and said that she felt more fear around Dr. Johnson than the chimps.

Dr. Johnson spent the rest of the holiday with his family completely convinced that part one of his plan was feasible. Now, he had to be sure that the second part would work too.

———— • ————

Alex was more than willing to check on Brad's experiment with the *RW96* tracer on the evening before Thanksgiving, and then again on the holiday itself. The laboratories would be empty during the short break, a situation that left rooms desolate and hallways filled with only the low frequency hum of motors that ran around the clock to keep freezers cold and incubators warm. From experience, Alex knew that if the experiment did not work as planned then his visit to the lab would be disappointingly short. Conversely, if the results were positive, then he would have to spend substantially more time to accurately record the findings, a situation that would be as welcomed as it would be exhilarating.

The clear plastic tissue culture plates used by Brad to grow brain cells had 12 little wells. Each flat-bottomed well was about 22 millimeters in diameter with an area that was less than 4 cubic centimeters. The brain cells adhered to the special plastic well where they grew and divided. The special growth medium supplied to each well nourished the cells. Each culture plate had its own thin plastic cover that fit snugly on top. This cleverly designed cover served to protect the living cells from contaminants in the air while allowing for an exchange of gases that was critical for their survival. Each tissue culture plate was kept in an incubator held at a constant temperature of 37 degrees Celsius—the same as the human body from whence the brain cells originated—and a carbon dioxide level of 5%.

Brad had labeled each of the six plates with a simple code that did not disclose what type of treatment he had performed on the brain cells. Alex's job was to examine a number of wells on each plate under the fluorescent microscope, to document in a notebook what he observed, and also to take digital photographs to record the observations.

It took Alex less than 30 minutes to examine all six plates. Once the plates were returned to the warmth and special atmosphere of the incubator, he ejected the memory stick from the microscope and walked eagerly to his office to view the digital images of the cells on his computer.

Brain cells from three plates had varying degrees of red fluorescence. This meant that Bob Wyle's *RW96* tracer was indeed binding to something on the surface of the cells. The images of cells laced with varying levels of bright fluorescence reminded Alex of a fond childhood memory. For twelve consecutive days, beginning on the evening of December twelfth, Alex's parents added one short string of lights to the tall, blue spruce tree in their living room. It was then Santa's job to place a brilliant bright star on the very top of the tree, and also to leave a single, shared gift for the entire family underneath it.

Alex estimated the degree of red fluorescence for each culture plate and typed a short email to Brad that contained an attached file with the preliminary results. He ended the message by indicating that he would examine the plates again the next day, and closed with a warm wish for a happy holiday. Since Alex did not have the code that corresponded to the letters written on the culture plates, he did not know if the experiment had indeed worked, and so he did not share the preliminary results with Bob Wyle. The MIT inventor of the fluorescent tracer would have to wait until all the data were collected and the code revealed to learn if the experiment was a success.

3

Amy woke from the one-hour nap and felt more alert than she had in days. Brad, who lay next to her awake the entire time, was wracked with fatigue caused by the stress of newfound uncertainty. Before leaving the privacy of the bedroom they devised a plan. Amy decided that she would disclose the news of her pregnancy—their pregnancy—to Brad's parents. Since she and Brad began to date, Joan and Livingston MacIntyre remained on the polite side of neutral towards her. They seemed to neither embrace nor dismiss her. And whether or not they approved or disapproved of Amy's relationship with their son, though it mattered for the sake of family unity, was of little overall concern to her. After all it was Brad, not his parents, who she was committing to. Now, it was all about her, the baby and Brad.

The impromptu meeting took place in the small study in the spacious grand Victorian where Livingston MacIntyre conducted a fair amount of business. Both Livingston and his wife Joan were dressed casually, yet sharply, for their pre-Thanksgiving Day dinner at *Ship-to-Shore* restaurant. Just a few business friends, and close acquaintances attended the annual dinner; the attendance over the years fluctuated as often as the winds of the changing season.

Amy was as direct and as forthright as she'd ever been.

"Brad and I want you to be the first to know that we are expecting a baby. We've learned recently that I am pregnant." Amy continued without hesitation despite the subtle, but real look of shock on the faces of her future in-laws. "I should be able to complete my second year of medical school and I've already applied for a leave of absence for next year. Fortunately, the University of Minnesota has a progressive program that gives women, and men too, a range of options if and when they start families. Brad and I decided to have the baby here in Boston, if possible. When things settle down, we plan to get married. This is all new to us and we appreciate your wisdom and understanding as we chart this new course together. I hope you know that I love your son very much." Amy did well to maintain a firm, solid voice as she spoke to the stoic New Englanders.

After what seemed like an extended moment of silence Brad spoke with as much bravado as he could muster.

"And I love Amy. I love her for her intellect, for her wisdom, and for her drive. She is already a talented scientist; she'll make a wonderful clinician and a warm and caring mother too. I look forward to calling my soul mate, my wife. I do not plan to take time off from Harvard and we're looking into the possibility, a long shot at that, of having Amy transfer her medical studies from Duluth to Boston. We had talked about starting a family, but it was not something we had planned to do so soon." He hesitated briefly then concluded, "I have to admit that the idea of being responsible for a little one is both exhilarating and scary."

Joan and Livingston allowed their son and his pregnant girlfriend all the time they needed to speak before commenting. They were skilled at listening, an art honed through years of interactions with those who made high stakes decisions that affected a countless number of lives. It was trait that served them well in private, family matters as well. From sheer familiarity, each knew what the other was thinking and who best to lead the response. In this case it was Joan, for it was a little known fact that she herself had become pregnant with Brad's older brother just one month before their planned wedding day. An intestinal infection was among the list of false maladies provided to the two hundred guests as excuses for the bride's lack of color and charm on her wedding day; their much-anticipated honeymoon was a month-long, mostly sour event, at a resort on St. Thomas.

Joan admitted that she too was shocked by the sudden prospect of becoming a first time grandmother, but that she was thankful for Amy's forthright and thoughtful presentation of the situation and of their plans to be together for the baby and for each other. Although not a part of her natural demeanor, Joan rose from the small leather couch and gave Amy a warm, supportive hug. She then held Brad's shoulders with both hands and for a solid moment looked at him squarely in the eyes as if to deliver a cautious message on his pending responsibilities before embracing him too. Livingston, who wondered how much this was going to cost him, was right behind his wife in doling out hugs and words of encouragement to the two young medical students.

Brad was relieved and also a bit surprised that the announcement went so smoothly. Perhaps, if had he known about his mother's pre-marital pregnancy he would have been less apprehensive, but he really didn't need to know the still secret undercurrent to appreciate the outcome.

Livingston and Joan left for dinner without their son and future daughter-in-law. Everyone agreed that the next item of importance was for Amy to inform her parents of the news. Although this was a given, the truth was that both sets of adults needed time alone.

———•———

As if it were a daily ritual, the three young adults were completely comfortable lying naked next to each other in a king-sized bed in virtual darkness. Their psyche and pupils had adjusted easily. The faint indirect light that crept through the tall windows was all they needed as the Thanksgiving Day to end all Thanksgiving days drew to a close. Indeed, the darkened atmosphere of the spacious studio apartment lent an added air of privacy, as if to shroud in secrecy what each was about to reveal.

"Your grandfather wanted very much to connect with you, Phil. He did the same thing to you with his hands and his eyes that my mother did to me as a young girl. The difference is that I made the connection right away after her sudden death while you never made the connection with your grandfather until today and with our help," said Abby. "You've always transmitted easily. Over time, I bet you will learn to receive thoughts from others with the same degree of ease." Phil listened and processed Abby's words carefully, but it was Rosi who provided the take home message. "What Abby is saying is that the connection from the beyond is made during one's lifetime by the two individuals together, but that both have to be receptive from the start or else the connection is not made unless it's shepherded by others like we just did with you and your grandfather. That, my friend, is what she's saying. It could, and very well should, be called Abby's theory. I bet it's damn close to being a *de facto* fact."

Phil sat up and leaned back against the cool, white-enameled cinderblock wall that served as the bed's headboard.

"This is fucking amazing! Rosi, when you said that my grandfather came from somewhere, appeared to us, communicated with us, then left for somewhere else, I instantly thought of the archway's keystone and the elemental orbital maps of electrons that move from one defined space to another. Imagine a three-dimensional chess game except that there are many, many more dimensions and instead of pawns, rooks, knights and bishops, you have all of the elements and their respective energies that make you as a unique individual. After we leave this form as humans our energy comes together, coalesces. It is conserved and free to move among any state and take on any form—even human again but in a different dimension, a different universe and a different time. And the probability is not zero that we occur at the same energy state, in the same form but in different places simultaneously."

"Do you think these identical energies could ever come together?" asked Rosi who was still lying flat on her back and staring upward into the dark.

"Identical energies that meet at the same time?" repeated Phil.

"Yeah, like when someone experiences a *déjà vu*? Couldn't that be a situation when the same two energies from different universes come together and time seems to be slightly off, but the experience that is about to unfold is known before it actually occurs?"

"I hadn't thought about that but yes, that's entirely possible."

Rosi found her way to the toilet without the need of light and from that distant spot she asked a question that was as profound and as innocent as any posed by a curious child.

"Are the energies you describe the basis for all religions?" For a long moment no one spoke.

"How?" Phil asked. "I don't see how this ties in at all."

"Oh my god, yes! Yes, I completely understand what Rosi is saying," Abby said as she shifted slightly on the bed. "If you put it all together, what you have is the convergence of three interrelated events, a triangulation of sorts. One is what you've been describing Phil—the ability of energy to move from one state to another and the absolute conservation of energy. The second is the ability to connect with these energies telepathically provided that the third part—the connection—is made when the energies are in the same or a similar state. What we experience as telepathic events with those that have died, like visits to me by my Mom and Lilly and Dr. Paolo, since the dawn of time have been called 'visions' and these visions are the basis for most, if not all, religions. We are, in the absolute purest sense, the creators of our own gods. Our energies, our multiple energies become our own personal, unique intelligent designers. I bet that that's the simplicity that Dr. Paolo was trying to tell me. It's all here within us and based on what Amy said last time we spoke, the programming code to achieve, no, not achieve but to attain this immortality is encoded in our DNA."

The dark room was again silent, this time for three long minutes as each internalized Abby's profound statements. In their own way, the three young adults were attempting to find a flaw with the concept of triangulation and energy conservation.

"Religion aside, I think this is wild; wild, plausible and definitely testable. What you just said could be a part of the mathematical archway," Phil said as he slid back underneath the covers between Abby and Rosi in the pitch-black room.

"Let's see if I have this right," continued Rosi who had returned to her spot in the warm bed to Phil's left. "Each one of us has a unique blend of chemical elements that together form a composite energy and that this energy can reside simultaneously in various dimensions across the vast universe—that's part one. Part two is that we can communicate with other non-self energies telepathically provided that part three occurs and that is that the connections are made when the same energies are in the same dimension, like Abby and her mother did when they were both alive. And what makes this all happen is conserved in our DNA. Oh yeah, and testaments to these events have been documented throughout human history in the form of various spiritual beliefs or religions. Sound right?"

"I think that's correct, Rosi. I also think that all of this can be explained mathematically with my archway model," added Phil who, sensing the excitement of the intellectual exercise rising to an apogee, was again becoming aroused—a condition duly noted by both telepaths.

"From henceforth the postulate will be known as Abby's Theory," declared Rosi who turned to her right and kissed Phil's chest.

Abby, who pivoted to her left and placed her right hand on Phil's abdomen replied, "I like the sound of that. It has a nice ring to it. Will someone please write it down?"

Breakthroughs

1

Alexa was thrilled that the local and federal agencies that oversee clinical trials gave them the go-ahead to proceed with Abby's study. The official letter, addressed to Alexa as the head of the laboratory, contained a few choice sentences that would one day be used by Abby when she defended her Ph.D. dissertation. The first part of the last sentence reflected Alexa's sound stature in the clinical research field.

Enrollment in the study by Lilly's legal guardian followed all required regulations. Despite the testimony by study personnel that they had been made aware of Lilly's abuse, apparently via so-called telepathic exchanges, the committee cannot definitively prove nor disprove these assertions. The committee also cannot definitively prove or disprove that the exchanges, even if they had occurred, would in and by themselves, caused or could potentially have prevented, the child's death by blunt force trauma. However, as this study progresses, should the study personnel sense distress by the minor, by any means including nonverbal communicative methods, they shall inform authorities at the local Department of Social

Services. If the study personnel reports a minor to DSS, he or she would be automatically dismissed from the trial.

That the investigating committee used the word "apparently" in line with "so-called" irked Abby to no end. Obviously, the committee members dismissed the entire premise of the clinical study altogether. They did not even consider the testimony of each of the three telepaths who spoke separately about their nonverbal exchanges with Lilly that included the child's desperate pleas for help.

The entire ordeal, from the moment she met Lilly to the lengthy investigation, was too much for Johanna to bear. She opted not to participate in the study once it resumed. Fortunately for Abby and for the sake of the entire study, Olysia, who was aware of the mishap at the start of the trial, readily agreed to replace Johanna. Olysia too had wanted to explore the mysteries of telepathy.

Cleverly, Abby had also asked the clinical safety committee that investigated Lilly's death, to allow for a small amendment to the study protocol. The readily approved addition allowed for the collection of cheek cells from each young participant with a sterile Popsicle stick. The committee deemed the simple procedure to be harmless to the child. Abby thought that the DNA contained in cheek cells could be tested for the presence of a putative telepathy gene. This idea sprung from the last interaction Abby had with Amy and Ajay. The DNA data combined with their other findings could lead to important connections, thought Abby.

Desperately behind schedule, Abby and the rest of the study staff worked almost nonstop for four full days. They interviewed ten young subjects in the morning, ten in the afternoon and an additional ten for the newly added early evening timeslot. Each member of the study team, from the intake nurses to the interviewers to Alexa, whose role was to control the flow, had become increasingly proficient. The process of transitioning each young subject from room to room to interview with each of the three telepaths progressed smoothly. Olysia enthusiastically embraced her important role in the study. She was comfortable around children and she was also less emotional than Johanna. Overall, the entire process moved along at a faster pace than it had on that ill-fated first day.

By the end of the week 120 young subjects of all ages, shapes and sizes joined Fortune, Javier, Barbara, Kenny and Charlie to yield a total of 125 participants. Sadly, Lilly's involvement would not be a part of the final dataset as all paperwork, notes and the videotape of her interview had to be handed over to the local authorities as evidence in the now-pending murder trial.

Remarkably, all of the parents of the children that had completed the interview part of the study were also willing to submit their child's cheek cells for DNA analysis. And, as an added bonus, parents of ten children allowed their child to undergo a functional MRI analysis of their brain. Alexa thought that this new imaging technology might reveal what parts of the brain are active during telepathic interactions.

An exhausted Abby decided to spend Friday night alone in her dorm room on campus. She needed a large dose of quiet to recover from the nonstop week. Whereas the job of other team members was over, hers had just started. She had a great deal of data to organize, process, condense and analyze including tens of hours of video footage on the young subjects. Abby knew that the clinical study started poorly with Lilly's untimely and unfortunate death, but it ended very well thanks to a dedicated team and also to a unusually warm and mild January in the mid-Atlantic region. Her schedule began to again fill with demands of the new spring semester of classes, teaching responsibilities and now, on top of all of that, data analysis.

———•———

Dr. Richard Johnson stared intently at the syringes filled with a solution of the chemical that Jo had prepared to his exact specifications. He knew that he needed to do a critical experiment by himself and outside the University setting. What he was about to do would never be allowed within the school's rigid, regulatory walls. He was alone at his home, which was located in a Baltimore suburb. There he felt free and unencumbered, just like he was as a child. Ever curious, little Richard experimented with any living thing he could catch with his bare hands or with his homemade traps. Each innocent creature became his personal living laboratory to do with as he pleased. His imagination often resulted in the death of frogs, snakes, earthworms, crickets, field mice, and an occasional bird. Although Richard Johnson was no longer a child, he did use the mouse-ensnaring trap he built when he was ten years old. To his delight, the simple contraption worked last evening as well as it did over four decades ago.

The little brown mouse with its long pink tail and white underside was unable to climb the slippery glass walls of the large pickle jar. It was trapped. Dr. Johnson looked at the small animal for a moment before ensuring that the cover was tightly closed. Then without hesitation, he shook the jar violently. The mouse bounced back and forth between the tin cover and glass bottom as if it were the little ball that clinked inside a can of spray paint. Twenty seconds later the small wild rodent with it's toothed mouth agape was gasping heavily. Suspecting that the mouse was near death, the professor quickly opened the cover of the makeshift torture chamber and dumped the virtually limp mouse onto newspaper. Using his gloved left hand, Dr. Johnson picked up the stunned animal by the scruff of its neck, as he had done a million times before with laboratory mice as a graduate student. There was neither resistance nor a struggle from the mouse as the professor emptied the contents of one of the syringes directly into the poor creature's abdomen. He then placed the still gasping mouse back onto the newspaper. Within thirty seconds, the hind limbs of the mouse began to twitch, followed by its front legs. The clouded beady eyes of the rodent seem to become clear and focused and within a minute the mouse righted itself. Without hesitation the wild animal scurried away as if it had never been caught in the first place. Richard Johnson watched in amazement as the small mammal followed the garden's cement retaining wall out to the edge. Quickly, the feral mouse scampered across a short patch of grass and finally disappeared in the woods.

Mi-Ok's previous experiments showed that the purified chemical was not toxic to healthy laboratory mice. Jo's experiments on the effect of the chemical on tissue cells were done with cultures grown in the laboratory under artificial conditions. But the experiment performed crudely in the privacy of his own backyard with a live, feral mouse conclusively proved to Dr. Richard Johnson that he had discovered an extremely important chemical. The new substance could repair severely traumatic injuries without damaging side effects. Undoubtedly, it was worth hundreds of millions of dollars. Yes, he understood that there were more studies to be done, but what he saw with his own two eyes could not have been a chance event. He was now convinced of the chemical's curative properties. The only thing he needed now was to rid himself of the only remaining obstacle that stood in his way to a lifetime of fame and fortune, the old German.

The little brown mouse scrambled down through a familiar path under a pile of twigs and brush to its nest. Abruptly, it began to violently convulse. Dead, the small mammal rolled downward to its right. It settled face up in a crevice next to the root of a maple tree where it's little body immediately began to peacefully decompose.

———•———

Alex and Brad invited Bob and Ajay to Alex's office in Boston for a lunch-time review of their recent findings with the *RW96* tracer. Bob, who had worked from home that bright yet cold late January morning, walked directly from his apartment to the medical school for the meeting. Ajay had to decline the invitation due to a time conflict. Over lunch wraps and bottled waters the two senior scientists listened to Brad's review of the data obtained with the fluorescent tracer.

Brad showed several slides that summarized the results from four separate experiments—two main experiments each repeated twice. The findings from the first experiment with *RW96* showed clearly that there was something in the bacterial extract that was responsible for the abil-ity of *RW96* to bind to brain cells. "The intensity of the fluorescence increased linearly with the increased amount of sterile bacterial extract added to the cultured brain cells," remarked Brad. "But what we noticed, well to be accurate, what Alex saw over the Thanksgiving Day holiday, was that the fluorescent intensity in all of the plates that contained bac-terial extract increased with time. These are images of the cells taken over time and here, on day ten, the fluorescence intensity peaks but then by the next day the cells are no longer viable and the fluorescence is reduced to low background levels. So something happened when these brain cells began to die that actually increased the binding ability of *RW96*." Brad, who hadn't touched his lunch, didn't hesitate to move to the next slide. "This observation was not specific to brain cells. The same pattern of binding was also seen with human lung, kidney, spleen, liver, and skin cells too."

"Did you look at the strength of the binding?" asked Bob who had subconsciously devoured his wrap.

"Yes, we did. This last slide shows the kinetics of *RW96* binding over time with all of these different cell types. As you can see, there is a sharp rise just before the cells stop metabolizing. Just before they died."

Bob Wyle closed his eyes, grabbed the top of his head with both hands and leaned back in his seat. This was his way of closing out the world to think critically of what he had just heard. Brad used the break to take a bite of his lunch and Alex picked up a notepad in anticipation of Bob's insightful analysis.

Brad had purposefully not said anything about the findings described in the publication he co-authored with Dr. Paolo and the others. As he had mentioned to Alex before the meeting, he wanted to see if Bob would reach the same conclusion as he had regarding the similarities with the images of Dr. Paolo's brain at the moment of death using the older tracer *RW88*, with those he had just presented with *RW96*.

After a couple of moments, Bob Wyle spoke with his hands still on his head and his eyes still closed. "So something made by bacteria is combining with something made by human cells that is expressed specifically at the point of cellular death and the combination of these two substances then binds *RW96* tightly. Could this be what was observed with Cookie and Dr. Paolo in the *Nature* paper? In both cases at the moment of death, their brains lit up like a fourth of July sparkler." Opening his eyes and taking his hands off of his head Bob looked at Alex then Brad and said, "Is this what we're seeing here? Could these data explain what happened *in vivo* with *RW88*?"

Alex looked at Brad and smiled broadly, "Exactly. That's exactly what we were thinking."

Brad opened a new presentation on his laptop and two additional data slides appeared."See this peptide here?" Brad said as he pointed to a small peak among thirty or forty protein fragments that were on the graph. "Watch what happens to it as the brain cells age." Multiple images played like a silent movie clip. While all other peaks remained unchanged, the one Brad had singled out grew in height by several orders of magnitude, an indication that more of it was being made. Bob sat transfixed as the next slide appeared.

"Now watch this bacterial peptide over time," Brad said as he kept his finger aimed at a single peak. The peak also increased in height and thus the amount made by bacteria. "These data suggest that in a living situation, these two peptides—one of human origin and one of bacterial origin—are produced around the same time and combine spontaneously. They also happen to bind to your tracer."

"Have they..." Bob began.

"Yes. Both peptides been sequenced," said Alex having correctly anticipated the question. "There are no matches to them in any national or international database of peptides," added Brad who was clearly animated. "These two peptides are novel, completely new to science. And check this out. I input their amino acid sequences into a protein program and generated a three-dimensional tertiary structure. From the shape of the two peptides and the predicted interactions of the amino acids with each other, we can tell that they can easily and spontaneously aggregate like a bunch of magnetic Lego pieces. No energy is needed to initiate or to complete the assembly process."

"Amazing," said Bob. "Are these peptides similar in size?"

"No," replied Alex. "The bacterial peptide is about 80% smaller. And another interesting finding is when we reverse transcribe this peptide back to its DNA sequence we found that it is in the genome of ten thousand of the most prevalent bacterial symbionts of humans.

"Therefore, virtually all the bacteria that live within us have the genes necessary to make this small peptide. And if that didn't blow you away, this will. We did the same reverse analysis for that brain peptide. We learned that the DNA sequence for this peptide is found in the genes that code not just for brain tissue, but for all of our major organs like the liver, lungs, spleen, kidneys and even the heart. Remarkably, these sequences were in a region that contain so-called nonsense DNA."

"This is absolutely wild," said Bob. "It sounds like something you'd read in a science fiction novel. I mean... all of this is starting to sound strange and bizarre. Just like the stuff in Paolo's paper. We'll have to bring it all together and we'll have to figure out what it all means. All of this must have a purpose. And so much for that nonsense DNA, that junk DNA that was supposed to have some quiescent feedback loops or interference functions. We're blowing those paradigms out of the water. There is actually useful stuff in there but just exactly how useful and for what purpose is another thing. Somehow, it all seems to be coordinated with the onset of death." Bob sat back and again closed his eyes. "Do you have a copy of Paolo's paper?" he asked Brad. Within moments, the electronic version of the paper was retrieved from Harvard's digital library and displayed on the laptop. Brad looked over at Alex with raised eyebrows as Bob Wyle reread the abstract portion of the paper he himself co-authored.

After re-familiarizing himself with the findings, the MIT scientist said, "In Paolo's paper we stated that the findings were 'concomitant with complete DNA demethylation'. Could this self-aggregating protein made from bacterial and human peptides be a universal demethylase, an enzyme that cleaves methyl groups from all DNA no matter its origin? A universal demethylase, now that would be wild."

Alex wrote Bob's question in his notebook and noted the time of the day that it was articulated. He now understood why Brad wanted to let Bob draw the same inferences and articulate the same question. In research, there is nothing as powerful as when scientists, after reviewing the same set of data, independently reach the same conclusion.

"Not only is it a demethylase, and not only does it work on DNA from a variety of creatures large and small, but it is also the most potent one ever studied. It is at least one thousand times more active than any other discovered thus far. This enzyme is like a wildfire in a sea of pure oxygen," Brad said as he showed Bob the data to support his statements. The results Bob saw were still in a raw, handwritten form in Brad's bound laboratory notebook.

"Remarkable. But again, we come back to the same question. What does this mean? What is the purpose of such a global occurrence?" asked Bob. "How do we benefit from this coordinated event?"

"I can't answer that but there is one phrase that Dr. Paolo wrote in *The Atlantic* article that has stayed with me ever since I read it," said Brad. "It was also something he said in class, at least once, when he was getting into his hypothesis: 'to reconcile what was once thought to be irreconcilable—that is, nothing less than our place in the universe'. And I have a hunch that the last part of his statement, 'our place in the universe' is what this demethylase will reveal."

———

Franz Albracht convinced himself that insomnia was somehow linked to Alzheimer's disease. He felt as though his mind was already losing its vitality and usefulness. Two-thirty on a dark winter's morning found the aging neuroscientist awake, alert and for the moment, lucid. He had trained himself not to squander such fleeting moments of clarity and solitude as he made his way to the cherry roll top desk. Sitting in front of his favorite piece of furniture that had served him so well throughout his most productive years as a scientist, he took a moment to run his fingers over the fine dark layers of thin wood that formed the unique flexible cover. Year after year he had locked the cover in the evenings to guard its contents against would be thieves or curious eyes but those days of paranoia were long gone. Now, no key was necessary. Only a gentle upward push on the half-round slates readily exposed the clutter-free desktop and a hibernating laptop.

The subject line of Richard Johnson's email read: Personal and Confidential. But after it was opened Franz was disappointed to see nothing written, no message at all. There was only an odd symbol with the letters m-o-v written below it. The letters meant nothing to the old German. Not knowing exactly what it was or it's purpose, Franz did the only thing he could think of—he maneuvered the cursor arrow over it and clicked several times out of frustration. He leaned back in his chair and briefly closed his eyes. Franz the saw a small black image appear in the corner of the laptop. It began to play on a little screen like a personal peep show from his youth. Franz leaned forward and pulled the computer closer. He watched intently with knitted eyebrows and saw a little brown mouse, trapped in a glass jar, essentially killed by violent shaking, then crudely dumped on the Living section of the *Washington Post*. The shaky video then showed gloved hands grasping the poor creature by the scruff of its limp neck. Dr. Albracht then had a virtual close-up view of the beaten mouse receiving an injection from a syringe filled with clear fluid. The camera panned back as the gasping mouse, having been placed on its side atop the newspaper, began to twitch. Franz was glued to the video image of the little mouse while he contemplated the notion that this movie must be a graphic, symbolic message—one that characterized his own tortured situation as an old man facing dementia and death. But no sooner had he synthesized those self-absorbed thoughts, than the mouse stood and ran with all its might, as if fleeing from pending doom. The video recording ended with shaky images of the mouse darting into dense thicket.

"What in God's name?" he whispered.

Franz looked back at the email message that held no content other than the video. That was when he saw that there was yet another email from Dr. Richard Johnson with the same Personal and Confidential words in the subject line. The email contained a one-word question: Convinced?

That the little mouse seemed to have survived a near death experience after having received the injection was indeed astonishing. But the old neurologist knew that the road from a successful outcome in mice to a medical treatment for humans was a long one that often led to a dead end. He also knew from the literature and lectures on the subject that there was no treatment and, more importantly, no proven measures to avert the onslaught of Alzheimer's disease. Franz decided then and there that he would be treated with Richard's potential miracle potion even if the treatment had not undergone the type of rigorous testing required of a new drug. His options were limited. After all he, Franz Albracht, had worked quite hard to make sure Richard Johnson had the notoriety and the money to do research on brain repair and rejuvenation, so that he would have a fighting chance at this stage in his life. The thought of losing his mind plagued the learned neurologist to the point of irrationality.

Franz again sat back in the chair and looked at the little drawers situated at the back of the sturdy desk. In the nook underneath the drawers was a medium sized yearly appointment book. Franz opened it and flipped to early April to confirm the date when he and his wife would visit Dr. Richard Johnson at Johns Hopkins.

Eight weeks, he thought. *I wonder how much of me will be left by then.*

2

The contrasts could not have been more dramatic. Laura's overall satisfaction with life was low when compared to what she had just experienced in Florence. In the several months since her return to Massachusetts, and to the relentless demands as a physician, Laura came to the realization that the final segment of her life would not be spent in America. Both figuratively and literally, Italy begged for her return. Indeed, besides the steady stream of needy patients there were only two other constants in her life—the handwritten and heartfelt letters from Tomasso that arrived religiously on Wednesdays, and bi-monthly calls from Lee Kingston asking for a follow-up meeting. As much as she adored reading Tomasso's rather poetic sentences that blended English and Italian words, she deplored Lee's dogged efforts to contact her. Laura was convinced that Lee was attempting to make her confess to nothing less than murder, an admission she'd never render.

With smooth efficiency, Laura met with a financial advisor, an accountant and also a lawyer to review what was needed for her to permanently relocate to Italy, or to live for extended periods of time in that country. After carefully weighing the advice of counsel, Laura decided to live in both Massachusetts and Florence, a move that would shield her from excessive financial losses through tax penalties. With ample retirement savings, Laura was free to do as she pleased without financial worries. If desired, she could even purchase her own place in Italy given that she was going to draw income from leasing her condominium while living abroad.

Life was good for Laura and by association, for Tomasso too. But there was one minor issue she needed to put to rest. Laura needed to rid herself of the pesky *Rolling Stone* reporter. She wanted to become a part of the international community free of concerns, and she considered Lee and his motives, to be old baggage that needed to be purged. She decided that to get him off her back she would have to break him once and for all. And, although being calculating and devious was not a part of her general makeup, it took the good doctor only thirty minutes, and a half of a bottle of Chianti, to hatch a plan that would permanently end Mr. Lee Kingston's inquiries. The plan was as simple as it was devious.

———•———

Flatbread, along with other student apartments and the entire RPI campus, was firmly held in the icy cold grip of winter. The weather really didn't matter to Phil as memories of the time spent down south for the most unique Thanksgiving holiday in his life warmed him from the inside out. Indeed, flashbacks to those unbelievable days spent sandwiched between Abby and Rosi were surpassed only by the intellectual insights gained during a return trip to D.C. for the Christmas recess.

On the eve before New Year's Eve, Johanna and Olysia joined, Rosi, Phil and Abby for drinks and a tasty dinner. The vegetarian meal was largely prepared by Abby with help from Phil. Olysia and Johanna brought desserts and several bottles of fine champagne. Because he was now accustomed to being in the presence of telepaths, Phil did not let his mind wander. Not once did he entertain the thought of making love to anyone, let alone with the beautiful women seated around the table. Despite the holiday-like atmosphere, Phil maintained a serious veneer throughout the evening. As an added precaution, he drank only one beer and stayed clear of the bubbly champagne.

What intrigued Phil about his time with the four telepaths was not their individual raw beauty, but their deep intellect. They shared the ability to think critically and collectively. And since telepaths can harbor no secrets, a condition considered to be both a blessing and a curse, they are able to meld concepts from one person's mind into their own on an ongoing, real time basis. They then process the information and generate the next thought or question instantly. But on this evening, out of respect for Phil, the telepaths made the extra effort to verbalize their every thought.

"The problem with Abby's theory is the triangulation part," said Rosi. "It's too simple. It's also too easy to consider telepathy as a key component of her theory."

Abby, who usually followed Rosi's comments in stride, provided a counter thought to rebalance the concept. "It's perfectly logical to try to provide a simple structure to a theory that is so complex and so involved that we are incapable of even defining its vast borders. And as for telepathy being a key component of that theory, well, I'll stick to my initial thought that verbalization of various sounds into structured speech is backwards evolution. Telepathy is significantly more advanced, completely universal, pure and it is truly transparent. Telepaths cannot lie to other telepaths. They are not burdened with the complexities of languages, so it stands to reason that we can communicate with anyone, past or present, living in this dimension or in any dimension, in an honest, direct and clear way."

Johanna was the only one of the four women who was not completely original in her thinking, but she usually provided a statement or a question that pushed the conversation from one sharp edge to another. "What Abby said is right. I can fib all the time to non-telepaths, but you guys get nothing but the truth from me. How does that grab you, Phil? But the part of this whole theory thing that confuses me is the connection part. Let's say I accept the idea that our energies move from one state to another and that being a human here and now is just one of those states. Fine. But the telepathy part to interact with the other energies relies on what exactly? That's the part I don't get. What is it that needs to happen for telepathy to work?"

Olysia, the quiet one who seemed to care little for deep conversation, often added short declarative sentences that punched the air like a clasps of thunder. "That's the key. Find it to open worlds," Olysia said.

Phil listened carefully and made mental notes of the discussion points. Later he'd convert the telepath's spoken words into mathematical equations for his ever-expanding model. He loved how the women turned and twisted and molded a concept as if it was soft clay on a potter's wheel, and it was during that end-of-the-year visit with four insightful telepaths when Phil discovered the last *voussoir* of his great mathematical arch.

The final *voussoir*, Phil realized, was symbiosis—that unique, mutually beneficial association between living entities. He mathematically modeled the absolute requirement of humans to harbor bacteria for survival, as well as important interactions of bacteria with their own viruses, and of viruses with specific prions. Equations associated with this part of the arch often yielded no net energy gain or loss, the hallmark of a true cooperative relationship.

From his second floor perch at Flatbread, Phil's gaze moved from the wind-whipped whitecaps on the mighty Hudson River to the complex, intertwined mathematical arch he continued to build by taping pieces of paper on the wall. The display began to resemble a private detective's office of clues to a murder mystery rather than a scientific experiment.

What puzzled Phil wasn't the logical upward flow of formulas that formed the two sides of the arch but the very keystone itself. The centerpiece represented the individual that inimitably joined each side.

Disappointedly, the computer program Phil wrote to condense the elements that comprised a human gave different results on repeated runs. It took some time for Phil to realize that what caused the variability was not the formulas that connected the keystone to each side of the arch but the keystone itself. That central piece—the individual—was highly variable, erratic, and unstable.

Phil made a comprehensive list of potential human events or conditions that could explain the mathematical anomalies. Life events like the loss of a parent or a child, physical or mental trauma, periods of happiness and joy were included. Conditions such as heart disease, acute infections, and physical abnormalities were also listed. Systematically, and with a great deal of patience, Phil tested each variable until the list was whittled down to one. When he entered the last human trait into the computer program, he was disappointed to see that it too failed to explain the keystone's variability.

Persistence is the hallmark of a sound researcher. Persistence and also knowing when to give one's mind a break from a problem. Even while at rest, Phil's mind, like those of all analytical thinkers, continued to churn away at the intellectual challenge. Subconsciously, he would review the problem until it was solved, or until clues as to how to solve it became apparent.

3

Since he resolved the misunderstanding of what had transpired in Florence during his lunch meeting with Laura, life with Rosa was once again simple and carefree. Even so, the slow pace of retirement wasn't easy on Lorenzo Benedetti. He lacked a challenge. He sought stimulation. He desired intellectual interactions like those he had with colleagues at the Rockefeller University, then as a Dean at Wilmington College. His long career as a scientist, a leader and an innovator in his field, defined him. It made him famous, and it kept him sharp. Retirement, by comparison, was an intellectual wasteland, even amid the utopian landscape of the rugged Tuscan mountains. Occasional requests to review a scientific paper or to consult informally, only served to remind him of those high-energy yesteryears.

On this cool, early spring morning, a pensive Lorenzo decided to send an email to his longtime friend and fellow neuroscientist Franz Albracht. There was no clear reason for writing other than he wanted to know if anyone from his era was still alive and if so, what they were doing. Lorenzo typed the salutation before pausing several minutes to compose the next sentence, which did not come easily because there was no message to deliver in the first place.

> Dear Franz,
>
> It has been some time since I saw you in Stockholm, how have you been? I am now living in Tuscany in my family's home with my cousin Rosa who tends to my every need. My days are filled with walks in the woods where, on occasion and if I'm fortunate, I'll spot a porcino or two. I'll have an early afternoon lunch with Rosa and one of her friends that live nearby. After lunch I have a short nap (imagine that!) before spending the rest of the day reading a few science articles on the web and writing an email to friends or former colleagues like you. Rosa usually prepares a delicious dinner followed by *dolce* with neighbors who happen to pass by. The dinner discussion is usually entertaining but little of it revolves around science. I yearn to speak science with others. Any science would suffice. These days I find myself reflecting back to a time when we were hungry young professors and on top of the world. Remember how nervous we were when we co-chaired a session on neuroimaging at that meeting in St. Petersburg? Little we knew then how much we actually enjoyed those times. Well, I assume you share these warm memories with me. I'm not

worried about dying as much as I am about aging. I feel like I'm becoming an old man, not so much physically but mentally. I sincerely hope this rambling message finds you of sound mind and body.

He signed the email with just his first name and sent it without review. In the past he'd always check his work something but the smell of pasta emanating from the nearby *cucina* meant that *pranzo* was almost ready, and he did not want to be late for the noontime meal.

The old neuroscientist closed the laptop, leaned back in his chair and wondered why he even thought about Franz Albracht. Yes, they had been colleagues. Yes, they were both old and retired and yes, Franz had fulfilled a mission of ensuring that Dante Paolo's paper was published. That publication did little for Lorenzo other than perhaps rescue his soul from perpetual torment from the deceased, vindictive Dr. Paolo. But in truth, Lorenzo wasn't really that close to Franz. In fact, he couldn't even recall if the German was married, or had children, or even where he was living.

The email, however, made Lorenzo wonder if Dante Paolo truly did have designs on him from beyond the grave. Perhaps he would live out his life free of torment after all, and that the many hints and suggestions made by Laura in the *trattoria* were nothing more than vivid bouts of pathetic paranoia. Or perhaps he was losing his mind.

Low gray clouds did not help rouse Lorenzo from his post-*pranzo* nap but the sounds of Rosa rustling in the kitchen made him sit up and start the second half of his day. Instinctively, he opened the laptop cover and was surprised to see that Franz Albracht had already replied to his email.

Lorenzo, what a pleasure and a gift your email was to me. I thoroughly enjoyed reading that you are living in paradise and that you seem to be in a good way with your cousin

Rosa. I fill my days with a walk to my tiny office at LMU where no one bothers to bother me. After reading a paper or two or listening to a seminar on some obscure molecular thing, I have tea then walk back home for lunch with my wife, then a nap (imagine that!). Like you, my friend, I am more concerned with my declining mind than I am with death itself. Aging is cruel while death is compassionate. Would you agree? Indeed, the only science I am now interested in is the work by the Nobel laureate Richard Johnson. Were you not in Stockholm when he received the prize? He has been trying to find the mythical fountain of youth and if I knew how to send you a video clip he sent to me, you would see that he has made progress in this area, but for the life of me I have no idea how to attach things to email. I plan to visit Richard at Hopkins this April and learn what he's been doing. Perhaps he'll have a pill I can take to be young again. Wouldn't that be grand?

Lorenzo noticed the icon at the bottom of the email, positioned below the capital letter F that served as the author's signature. Instinctively, he placed the cursor over the .mov attachment and clicked twice. Within ten seconds, a little video clip began to play on the laptop computer. Suddenly, the scientist inside Lorenzo Benedetti sprang to life. He watched the video intently. He felt as if he was once again reviewing newly obtained data. This vividly presented data was an animal study performed with one little rodent.

What Lorenzo saw made him shake his head in doubt and disgust. If the crude exercise was meant to show that the injection saved the shaken mouse from certain death, it failed. It certainly was no Fountain of Youth. If the video was made to demonstrate how to mistreat an animal or how to do science badly, then it succeeded. In either case, it should be disregarded and the creator should be reprimanded. He wondered if his German friend had been duped into thinking that the video's creator, suspected to be Richard Johnson based on Franz's email, had indeed discovered something important. Was the exercise done to show that there was a way to repair wounds? Or to slow, or even perhaps reverse, the aging process by reinvigorating the entire neural network?

If Franz Albracht was visiting Richard Johnson in April to take the place of the little mouse, then he was a fool on a fool's mission. Lorenzo spent the next few hours wondering whether or not he should warn Franz of the risks and dangers associated with quick fix concoctions. Or rather, should he let the old colleague-of-sorts be comforted by the delusion that he might indeed escape the inevitable cognitive decline that plagues most seniors to the point of reaching a state of carefree bliss?

———•———

The OB/GYN glanced at the blurry, gray ultrasound images and declared with certainty, "Based on the measurement of the femur, you are definitely at the end of the second trimester. Everything looks good. You don't want to know the gender, right?"

"Right," replied Amy who was starting to sport a small belly bulge. It was the only baby decision she had made on her own since learning of her pregnancy. All other decisions, including a short list of boy and girl names, were done with Brad, during their now daily video calls.

"Any other issues or questions? Are you feeling okay?"

"Yes. I'm just trying to stay focused on classes and to get eight hours of sleep each night. I'm eating healthy, too."

"And you're still planning to deliver this baby in Boston? Do you already have an OB there?"

"Yes, I still plan to deliver in Boston and no I don't have an OB there yet. That's on my short list of things to do."

"If you want I can give you the names of some of my OB pals in

Boston. At the minimum we should make sure we could share your medical records electronically. That would make everything a lot easier."

"That would be wonderful."

"On your way out, make an appointment to see me in a month, I'd like to get your vaccines up to date. Are you okay with taking vaccines while pregnant?"

"Absolutely," replied Amy who was feeling quite good on this second day of March, a time when Minnesotans start to think and say that rejuvenating word: spring.

With only three months left in her pregnancy, Amy was indeed busy. Not only was she taking the full load of classes while selling or packing the contents of her apartment, but she was also trying to imagine life with a newborn. She spent many hours wondering how she was going to transition from a full-time, second year medical student and a part-time researcher, to an around-the-clock mother. Until she met Brad, her ambitions were focused inward. She had an encompassing goal of being successful at whatever she decided to do, which turned out to be medicine and medical research. Now, with the reality of motherhood staring back at her from the full-length mirror, Amy would have to summon the nurturing ways of her mother and grandmother, traits that were not a part of her natural being. When it came to maternal instincts she tended to be more like her father. He was loving and caring but straightforward and pragmatic with little patience for drama. If it had been up to her mother, Amy would have had many siblings instead of none. The decision to limit the size of the nest to one was made firmly by her father.

With respect to the location of the baby's birth, Amy was solidly between a rock and hard place. Her parents made a clear and reasonable case for having the baby near them in California. They wanted to help their daughter just before, during and after delivery. They claimed it was their duty. Clear across the country on the other coast was the baby's father Brad, her fiancé. It didn't make sense to Amy to have Brad travel to California for the birth when they were planning to settle in Boston.

After weighing the pros and cons, Amy decided to have the baby in Boston. She considered it a sound choice that allowed Brad to keep his feet firmly planted in both school and work. Of course, they would also need to make some changes to Brad's apartment before the baby arrived, a project that got off to a good start thanks to the willingness of his roommate to move out by the end of April. In short order, the expecting parents needed to make sure they had the essential items in place, including a crib, bottles, diapers, and a plastic baby tub. They sought to be as prepared as possible for when returned from the hospital with a newborn, and a new life as a family. Although they spoke of becoming parents on a daily basis, neither Amy nor Brad could actually envision the moment. They correctly reasoned that this new chapter in their young lives would be quite a challenge, one filled with both glorious highs and disappointing lows.

Other than finding a physician in Boston and packing up her apartment, the other items on Amy's short to-do list included securing a way to Boston in early May, and also to have a discussion with the Dean of Academic Affairs on how to proceed with the paperwork to transfer to Harvard, Tufts or another medical school in Boston at some point in the future. Fortunately, Amy's parents volunteered to fly to Duluth, then rent a car to drive their daughter to Boston. The expectant grandparents were invited to spend the rest of May with their longtime friends, the Kelly's of Winchester, until the baby was born or as long as they wished to stay. Amy's parents readily accepted the kind invitation.

Other than the love of her parents and Brad, Amy also felt fortunate to have Abby's friendship. Ever since she learned of Amy's pregnancy

Abby either called, texted or sent an encouraging email daily. On those down days when Amy was feeling alone and still quite lethargic, days that seemed to have occurred more frequently after she'd returned to Minnesota following the short Thanksgiving holiday, Abby's words made a world of difference.

> Amy,
> I would like you to share your pregnancy voyage with me. I want to feel what you're feeling. In case I never have one of my own I want to know what this is like and I hope you don't mind sharing the good, the bad and the ugly with me. I sincerely hope you agree Amy. I am equally excited and nervous for you. Can I say that? Are you okay with this? Please let me know.
> Love you,
> Ab

Amy thought highly of Abby and since both were sisterless she readily agreed to share details of what she was experiencing as an expectant mother. Over the next few months Amy would openly share her most intimate feelings with her college colleague. So now, other than chatting with Brad about events that would transpire before, during and after the baby's birth, Amy had another person with whom to share the daily highs and lows associated with her pregnancy.

Amy could not have known then that Abby's close, sibling-like friendship would develop into one of the most trusted and vital relationships of her life.

Nexus V

As she lay on the bed in her dorm room on the campus of American University, a place she slept only when necessary or convenient, Abby refused to believe that she was getting sick. It didn't help matters that her mind scrolled rapidly through the endless list of tasks that needed to be completed by the end of the semester. An interruption of any type, for any length of time, was simply out of the question. Perhaps, she hoped, a quick nap was all she needed to overcome the sudden wave of fatigue she experienced during the last class of the day. Wearily, she turned onto her left side, faced the off-white cinderblock wall of the small room, and quickly fell asleep.

They silently passed each other from right to left, and also from left to right. None were familiar to Abby, but they all seemed to be there for the same reason. Something that Abby could not interpret held the group's collective attention. They shared a greater importance than any she had felt previously in this odd world, an importance that was even greater than that Dr. Paolo conveyed when he delivered his simple messages and warnings. Although their faces lacked

265

emotion, they portended a rare sadness that only served to further puzzle Abby. Who are you? Abby pleaded in general to the despondent group. No one seemed to notice her. She received not one response. Suddenly, inexplicably, Abby was overcome with deeply profound sadness. The collective spirit of the strangers suggested that they were preparing for something foreign, something that was obviously painful to them too. Something they'd rather do without.

The ten reduced quickly to one, a short, middle-aged woman with a fair, off-white complexion who shot a quick glance at Abby. On her bare right shoulder was a small square that appeared to have the texture of a soft, woven cloth. Abby noticed that the pale blue patch on the woman's shoulder was the only color in this otherwise insipid world. Then, in an instant, the woman disappeared and all went black. Abby felt like she was standing in the middle of a frozen lake on a moonless and starless night.

With her fever rising, Abby's body shuddered with chill. She turned onto her right side, pulled the covers over her head and returned to a deep sleep.

Dr. Paolo appeared. He sent her strange messages: The opportunity will be golden but sad. Don't miss it. It's simple. Again, Abby had questions for her friend but before she even had a chance to complete a thought, he was gone. All went black. This time she felt hot, like she was standing outside in the middle of a bubbling cauldron on a moonless and starless night.

Abby's cold subsided a week later. Now that she felt better, she recalled the encounters with strangers in the bleak world. She also remembered Dr. Paolo's cryptic messages. It would be a few months later, however, before their meaning came into clear focus.

Spring

1

Lee Kingston leaned back in his chair at the Boston bureau of the *Rolling Stone* and threw his arms up in the air.

"Yes! Yes! Yes!" he exclaimed aloud to the ceiling fans suspended high above the office floor. Since it was late Wednesday afternoon on a beautiful spring day most of the magazine's employees had already left when Lee completed the phone call of his dreams—a chat with Dr. Laura Kean.

"Hello. Is this Lee? This is Laura Kean."

"Um, why hello. Yes. This is Lee."

"Listen Lee, I am ready to finish the interview you started earlier this year."

Caught off-guard, Lee quickly collected his thoughts and opened the calendar program on his desktop computer. "Great. What day did you have in mind?"

"This Friday evening, 7:30. Will that work for you?" she said.

"Yes. That will work."

"We'll meet at my place if that's acceptable to you. I'll send my address by email."

Lee couldn't believe what he was hearing. "Um...yes, that'll be fine. Great. I'll see you soon then."

"Oh Lee? We'll keep this casual. Okay?"

A long sticky thread was released to the prevailing winds.

After the call, Lee left work and headed straight to his apartment for a celebratory beer, and to bask in his good fortunes. This time he was not imagining it. Laura's voice clearly revealed her desire to see him again. Obviously she sought him as much as he sought her. His long held fantasy of spending real one-on-one time alone with the attractive physician in a non-public setting was going to come true. That he had a professional job to do was secondary in Lee's mind, nevertheless he would spend the next couple of days reviewing her file and reconstructing the reason he sought to interview her in the first place.

By the time he finished his second beer Lee remembered that he had hacked into Laura's email to learn that she was recently in Florence. At the same time, he also remembered that he was trying to establish whether or not she murdered her husband, Dante Paolo. He would have to check the files on the hot Dr. Laura Kean when he returned to the office the following morning. He actually could not recall if he had developed a plausible motive. But that little detail would have to wait. Tonight Lee was happy to wade blissfully in his sex-filled imagination for the rest of the evening.

Laura arrived home Friday evening just before Lee was scheduled to arrive. She didn't bother to change out of her work outfit as she sought to maintain her professional appearance in the presence of the young

Rolling Stone reporter. Mentally she was exhausted, but the interview would not require much on her part. Indeed, the plan for the evening would only fail if Lee had no interest in females—a condition the good doctor knew from their previous encounters would not the case.

The anticipation of an evening alone with Laura Kean was almost too much for Lee to bear. The doorbell to Laura's condominium unit buzzed at precisely seven thirty and without acknowledging the caller she released the lock to the main door to the building three floors below. Laura opened the door to her unit just as Lee was about to knock.

The vicious vibrations of the silky threads were easily sensed.

"Lee," she said choosing her words carefully. "Thank you for coming by. Its nicer and more private here than at the hospital. Wouldn't you agree?"

The young reporter didn't know what to say or where to begin. Here he was in a beautiful, but sparsely decorated, condominium with the attractive woman he first met at the hospital just a few months ago. He wondered if she wanted him to tear off her dress and jump her now or later? He was willing at anytime. Or better yet, she probably would take the lead and drag him to her bedroom soon, very soon, probably right after they've had a drink or two. Likely, that was her plan. Lee was convinced that she wanted him desperately and...

"Lee?"

"Oh yes," he said gathering his thoughts. "You have a very nice place and yes it is more private. Much better."

"Can I offer you something to drink?"

"Sure. I'll have a beer," he said as he took a seat on the sofa in the middle of the living room.

Laura returned from the kitchen and handed Lee an IPA and a frosty glass. She picked up her glass of white wine and sat in a cream-colored fabric wingback chair opposite the sofa. Laura slowly crossed her well-defined legs that unequivocally defied her age.

"Um," Lee started. "Thank you for calling me. I've been trying to reach you for months, but the hospital said you were not available."

"I've been out of the country. I was in Italy. And when I returned, I was swamped with work." Of course Lee knew from having hacked into the hospital's email server—a crime that went completely undetected—that Laura was in Florence. He purposely asked a question of where exactly she was in Italy as a test. He wanted to see if she would lie. She didn't.

"Florence. It was beautiful, in every sense of the word."

"Oh, I see. I hope you had a good time. I heard it's a special place."

"You should definitely go someday. Now, where were we Lee?"

Lee reached into his pocket and retrieved the small digital recorder. "Yesterday, I listened to the tape of our last meeting to refresh my memory. Would it be okay with you if I record this session too?" Lee had listened to his first interview with Laura so many times he had all but memorized the exchange. He was so turned on by the sound of her voice that he began to wonder whether he would ever be able to find another woman that could match it.

"By all means," said Laura.

"So last time we sort of ended with June Kennedy, the hospice care nurse that took care of your husband." Lee recalled how badly the last interview ended and he was hoping for a better outcome this time.

"Oh right. You had asked if June was present when Dante passed. I remember now. That June Kennedy. She is such a beautiful woman. Really. She is a lovely, young brunette who is so kind and thoughtful. She's a rare person who carries her own sunshine with that bright perfect smile and those beautiful, deep blue eyes, you know, those with

270

well-defined irises? They go straight to the heart. June was a blessing that came out of nowhere. Both Dante and I were so lucky that she entered our lives when she did."

Lee took another long sip of beer and shifted nervously in his seat.

Twang, went the entire web.

"So she was there, in your house when your husband died?"

"Thankfully, yes and fortunately we've remained friends ever since. In fact, I've asked her to stop by this evening. I thought you'd like to meet her. She's such a delightful person."

Lee was caught completely off guard. Professionally, he should have thanked the investigative reporting gods for the chance to meet another person who was present when Dr. Paolo died, but he hadn't really reviewed all his notes on this story. If he had been well prepared, Lee would have known that he had, in fact, spoken by telephone to June. She easily recalled that Dante Paolo was her patient, but she did not offer any specifics about his illness or death. Personally, Lee felt dejected. With another person in the room, the odds of a sex-filled evening with Laura decreased dramatically. *And things were going so well too*, he thought.

"Oh. It will be nice to meet her," was all the enthusiasm Lee could muster. "Do you think she would mind if I asked her a few questions?" Above all, Lee did not want to upset Laura and eliminate any chance of making love to her as he had done so many times in his vivid dreams.

"Well, I can't speak for her, but I bet she'll be responsive," Laura grinned knowing full well what was about to unfold. "Would you like another beer?"

As Laura headed to the kitchen, the intercom rang. Without bothering to look at the video monitor she pushed the button that momentarily unlocked the main door. Lee watched intently as Laura handed him another IPA, then walk to the door and open it just as a young lady appeared.

June was at the doorway breathing very heavily. Without saying a word, the young lady, dressed in glacier blue running shorts and a matching, form-fitting tank top entered the condominium.

June Kennedy immediately bent over and put her hands on her knees. "Sorry," she panted. "I just jogged here from my place then ran the stairs." After a moment June straightened up. Laura handed June a towel that was instantly used to wipe the sweat off her forehead and neck as well as from her moist, muscular, bare midriff. Lee stood and silently began assessing the young woman's body. He judged her breasts to be perfect Bs.

Suddenly she emerged from her silky corner tunnel.

"June, this is Lee Kingston. Lee, June Kennedy," said Laura.

"Hi," June said as she extended her right hand. "I think we've met over the phone, right?"

There was no denying the truth about June's mesmerizingly beautiful eyes that looked directly at Lee as he shook her hand. He was flustered for the second time in less than thirty minutes. "Yes, um, that's right. We chatted some time ago. Thank you, um, I mean um, thank you for taking my call."

In today's world where everyone should expect the unexpected, Lee was clearly not ready for what happened next. June untied and slipped out of her running shoes, then kissed Laura quickly on her cheek before saying, "I'm going to hop in the shower. I'll be right back." The young hard body then skipped down the hallway towards the one and only bedroom and closed the door behind her as Lee watched in utter disbelief.

Could they be lovers? Lee wondered as he again tried to gather his thoughts. With each passing moment Lee was losing sight of his visit. Of course he would invent any excuse to spend time with Dr. Kean, but now with June's arrival he felt disoriented and confused, like a fly whose wings had suddenly become restricted. He hadn't even noticed that Laura placed a plate of shrimp and cocktail sauce along with a bowl of tortilla chips on the glass-topped coffee table between the couch and the wingback chair. Nor had Lee noticed that the light on his voice recorder was red which meant that it was no longer recording.

"I asked June to join us tonight," said Laura to Lee who found his way back to the far end of the sofa. "I didn't think you'd mind." It was the understatement of the evening as the hacker-turned-journalist was feeling as if he'd won the lottery.

"Um, no. No, not at all. I don't mind. I am surprised, though. I thought it was going to be a one-on-one conversation. I've never interviewed two people at the same time so I hope, um...well, I hope it goes well." It was as professional as Lee could be at that moment.

Laura smiled. "Great, now where were we again?"

Lee opened the top of his notepad, flipped a few pages in to the end, and wrote the date on the top right of the page. "Well, I had... well, I just asked you about June, actually."

"Good timing," Laura said just as June walked barefoot into the living room and sat cross-legged at the opposite end of the couch from Lee. As if her wet hair was not seductive enough, June wore nothing but a white, pullover cotton knit sweater that was too long for the hospice care provider; the bottom reached the middle of her thighs.

Addressing Laura, June said, "I hope you don't mind that I borrowed your sweater, I forgot to bring a change of clothes. Sorry." She then reached over and helped herself to shrimp, a move that caused the top of the V-neck to fall forward thus granting Lee a perfect angle to a cleavage side-view of one perfect B. Leering Lee did all he could to not choke on his mouthful of beer as he wondered if June was wearing anything else under the sweater.

Another vibration and another firm step away from her woven tunnel.

Again Laura silently snuck into the kitchen and brought back a beer for Lee and one for June as well. The widowed physician was now ready to get down to business.

"June," Laura said in a serious tone of voice that was instantly noticed by the reporter. "Lee is investigating Dante's death. Apparently, he's taken with Dante's ability to self-administer the tracer just before he died. Isn't that correct, Lee?"

"Well, um...yeah. Sort of, I guess," Lee said. His broken sentence had barely been completed when June pounced.

"What do you mean 'taken'? Like you're interested in it or what?"

After two beers, and in the presence of a cougar and a hard-body who would be the best tag team duo in his hyper-imagined Wide Wild World of Sex Wrestling, Lee himself started to wonder what he meant by the word 'taken'. Did he ever say 'taken' he wondered?

It was Laura, not Lee, who answered June's question. "Lee thinks I killed my husband and he wants to find out if this is true or not. That would be his story, his exposé. It's that simple."

While Lee never accused Laura of a capital crime, he was in no condition to confirm or deny the statement. He now wished more than ever he had reread all of his notes.

"Is that what you think?" asked June who shifted in the couch to directly face Lee. "You're not serious are you?"

Vibration. Vibration. Twist. Twist. Struggle. Twist.

"Um, well it is a plausible scenario that I was thinking might have happened because he was so sick and..." Lee stammered wildly unsure of the point he was trying to make. Laura sat back, sipped her wine and watched the scene on the couch unfold as if she was at the opening night of a two-person production in a small theater.

"You're goddamned right he was sick. Dr. Paolo was my first hospice patient. Since then I have been with a lot of dying people." June was clearly agitated and her voice grew louder as if the volume itself would make her words more credible. "Men, women, young, old and do you know what? I'll tell you what Mr. Rolling Stone, all those dying people, they're all the same. They were all tired of being sick, they were scared of dying, and they were afraid to die. They were afraid and my job was to make them comfortable and keep them floating on a pain-free, pillow mattress of drugs..."

Rapidly closing in.

"But, it is plausible that Dr. Kean intentionally killed her husband," pressed Lee who again was ill prepared for what happened next.

Kill. Encase.

There were only two things that irritated June Kennedy to no end: condescending people and condescending people that interrupted her. After his last sentence, June had had enough of Mister Lee Kingston. Without hesitation or forewarning, June leapt from her end of the couch like a spring-loaded toy and landed squarely on Lee's lap, firmly straddling him. Her bare backside was squarely on his thin thighs and her nose was no more than five inches from his. June's hands pushed the reporter's shoulders back, effectively pinning him to the couch as she unleashed her fury.

"Listen you motherfucker! I don't know what planet you're from, but here on Earth there are good people and there are bad people. Dr. Paolo was one of the good guys. His wife is one of those good guys too. You, asshole, are one of the bad guys who think they are doing something good when all you do is cause unnecessary problems for no good reason. And frankly, I'm sick of your 'my-word-rules-because-I'm-better-than-you' type of assholes. Everyday, I watch people die and I help them the best I can to have a few good moments with their friends and family before they disappear forever. Most of these poor bastards are so high on morphine that they don't even know that they're still breathing, but Dr. Paolo refused morphine or methadone or anything. Nothing. He didn't even take a goddamned Tylenol. Got that fuck-head? You stub your big toe and take an aspirin, you baby. Dr. Paolo had fucking metastatic cancer eating away at every inch of his body and he refused painkillers because he wanted to do the last experiment on himself. Isn't that what he wrote? Didn't you read that? Or do you only read the bullshit that you write? I was there. Laura was there. His students were there. And those students were in their goddamned graduation gowns because they loved him and they respected what he was doing. You think this lovely person who spent her entire life helping sick people, killed the man she married? What kind of a warped mind do you have? We all cried when the EMTs carted his dead body away. I was there. I signed the papers. And where the fuck were you? I don't know and I don't really give a shit, but for goddamned sure, you weren't there! So give it the fuck up!"

Normally, Lee would have become aroused as soon as June landed on his lap. But she was not in this prized position to make love or even to seduce him. She was there for one reason only, and that was to deliver a stern message. There was no denying her beauty, her lovely eyes or her firm, sexy body. And now there was no denying her persuasive argument. He was a fool to have convinced himself that Laura killed her husband. And to make matters worse, there was no way in hell that he would be making love to Laura, June or to anyone else that evening.

June lifted herself off the startled reporter and headed back to the bedroom with beer in hand. Laura, having again relived the scene of her husband's death, wiped away tears, slowly rose and opened the door that led to the hallway of the complex. Lee grabbed the powerless voice recorder and sheepishly walked out of the condominium without saying another word.

As he walked down three flights of stairs to the lobby, Lee began to wonder how he could become one of June's good guys. That single thought would linger in his mind for more than a month before he came to the decision to research an article on palliative and hospice care providers. Lee's piece, *Saving the Best for Last*, would become one of *Rolling Stone*'s most read articles of the year.

"Was that too much?" June asked Laura as she sat on the edge of the queen-size bed. Laura cradled June's smooth face in her hands, looked deeply into her eyes and said tearfully, "Not for me. No. Not for me."

The two women stood and gave each other heartfelt hugs.

"Thank you," whispered Laura.

"No. Thank your husband," June whispered back.

2

Dr. Jane Kianamann remembers everything.

"Gentleman, I think you know why I've asked you here today," stated MIT's Provost for Research who was seated at a small round table in her corner office that overlooked the crowded streets below. "It's been some time since we chatted and I'd like an update on your progress. Bob, if my memory is true, you told me that your research would lead to improvements in access, communication and intelligence, correct? And that harnessing the full potential of our DNA is somehow involved with our preservation post mortem. Still true?"

Bob Wyle had not kept his former mentor Dr. Jin Sukawa, who was seated next to him, appraised on the latest results. There was just so much to do on a daily basis—both at work and at home—that he simply did not have spare time to chat with his former mentor as he had so often done in the past. And had Dr. Kianamann given Bob more than one day's notice of the meeting, he certainly would have brought the noted professor emeritus up to date on what he had learned. Bob now had to work with the sticky situation as best he could.

"Well, Dr. Kianamann," said Bob, "We've taken a two-pronged approach on this project and we've made substantial progress on both. In one study, we sought to determine the frequency of the Xp29.47 gene in the general population. From the start, the goal of this study was to understand the presence of this one gene in the population. To do this we needed to sequence and probe human DNA samples in a rapid and efficient way. Towards that end, a doctoral student in my lab, Ajay Adani, wrote a computer program and modified existing equipment to quickly analyze DNA to search for the gene."

"Does it work?" asked Dr. Kianamann. Her curt delivery underscored the level of her seriousness.

"Yes, yes it..."

"Have you applied for a patent on the program and the modifications to the instrument?"

"Um, no. Not yet."

"Don't wait. I want you to contact our patent office tomorrow and get them moving on a provisional. After all, that's what we do at MIT. We generate intellectual property from our highly-paid intelligentsia."

Bob knew better than to show it, but he was perturbed by her rude interruption and demand. Highly paid patent attorneys would hound him endlessly until he generated precisely worded documents needed to file a patent on the potential new inventions. Bob has been down this road before, when he was younger and with more time on his hands.

Now, with a wife and child at home, not to mention the demands of the lab, life was very different. The last thing he needed was another massive time sink.

"Right," he replied. "So as I was saying, we were surprised to learn that over ninety percent of the more than one thousand DNA samples tested had at least one copy of Xp29.47 which means that most of us harbor the genetic information to communicate telepathically, at least in theory..."

"You know as well as I do that surveys are for politicians. The important question is: Does this gene exist in telepathic people, whoever or whatever they are?" asked the Provost. The sardonic end of the question was obvious.

Dr. Jin Sukawa sat stone-faced with his thin arms folded at the small table. He listened intently to the exchange between Bob and Dr. Kianamann. From experience he knew when to speak and when to remain silent. Now was the time to keep his thoughts to himself. He knew that his former postdoc was being tested and all Bob needed to do was to keep his emotions in check and to rise above the taunts of the Provost. Dr. Kianamann was a powerful woman at MIT. She was the main liaison for the famed Cambridge institution and D.C. politicians. The Provost was adept at touting the importance of research to federal lawmakers so they would support legislation to fund the biomedical enterprise. She relished high stakes endeavors that led to lofty financial returns, and she wanted to make sure that the young scientist was onto something worthy of her time, as well as the investment and efforts of others with influence.

Although inwardly agitated, Bob was prepared to defend his new laboratory space, academic promotion, funds and research skills with his favorite weapons: data. Despite the fact that they were preliminary and needed to be further analyzed, the results he would share with the Provost would soften her tone. At least that's what he hoped.

"That's right," Bob said in a mild mannered tone of voice. "Probing the general population gives us an understanding of the frequency of the gene but it does not tell us anything about expression. To answer that question we've teamed up with a group at American University in D.C. that has just completed a clinical study with telepaths and non-telepaths. They've agreed to send us de-identified tissue samples for testing. These cheek cells should arrive any day now. They will be coded so we won't know who is telepathic and who is not. The clinical study at A.U. was the first of its kind in the world, so it will be of high interest if a genetic association with telepathy is made."

Bob segued quickly to the next set of results. He did not want to the aggressive leader to interrupt him again. "We've also made significant progress on the molecular end as well. Two docs from Shulman's lab at Harvard wanted to use our *RW96* in their studies on nerve repair. They sought to reveal the molecular activities at the moment of cell death. What's amazing is..."

"So you had a meeting with Harvard scientists?" asked the Provost.

"Yes. It was..."

"And you gave them your tracer?"

"Yes, we agreed..."

"I assume you procured a mutual Confidentiality Agreement, and that there is a Materials Transfer Agreement in place, right?"

Bob loved science, but he despised the type of time-consuming nonsense that Dr. Kianamann embraced, namely these types of legal arrangements. He was walking a fine line when he responded, "Not quite. We've started an important two-way collaboration and thus we're sharing reagents and data as colleagues, not adversaries. I'm not in competition with them nor are they with me. We're interested in the same goals, but we're approaching them from different angles using different strengths. These two scientists from Shulman's lab, Alex Rudman and Brad MacIntyre, used *RW96* on cultured brain cells and showed that the tracer bound to these cells with greater strength when purified extracts from bacteria commonly found in humans was also present. They went on to show that these two small peptides, one human and one bacterial, combined spontaneously and bound the tracer very tightly. Remarkably, these two peptides are expressed at the precise moment of cell death. It is like some sort of last second, all out blitz by all members of the human superorganism at the cellular level. This finding was completely unexpected and it has never before been seen nor predicted to occur in any biological system. Why this final event happens in such a coordinated fashion is the next big question to tackle, but we suspect it has something to do with preservation..."

"Preservation of what?" snapped the Provost. "What exactly?"

Now was the time to end his silence.

"Dr. Kianamann," Jin Sukawa began in his trademark soft, steady voice as he unfolded arms and rested his folded hands on the small table. It first appeared as though he was speaking directly to the tabletop, but by the seventh word he looked up and directly faced the demanding Provost. "Based on what we've just heard, it would appear that Bob and his colleagues are on the verge of one of the greatest discoveries in all of science. It is not the worlds that we already know and understand, but those that we cannot see, or hear, or touch, or smell that remain our greatest challenges. If this research, this line of reasoning and understanding that Bob has described continue its course to a natural end, then there is a high probability that the mysteries that have plagued us for centuries will be solved. What began with Dante Paolo's great sacrifice, his simple revelation, may have pointed the way to this pinnacle."

"Exactly what pinnacle are you describing?" asked the incredulous Provost.

Bob sat back and watched a master at work.

Jin Sukawa unfolded his hands, rested his elbows and grabbed the sides of his head such that he was again looking down at the tabletop. He was in deep thought. "Ancient Greek philosophers began to form concepts relating to the conservation of substances like the earth, air, water and fire. In the 1600s, Galileo and later Leibniz added the conservation of energy as it moved cyclically from potential to kinetic. By the 1800s, Count Rumford made the association between mechanical energy and heat. The understanding of energy conservation continued to rise throughout the 19th century with discoveries made by French and German scientists. Then came mass-energy equivalence and Einstein's famously simple equation."

Dr. Sukawa refolded his hands, looked directly at the Provost and continued. "Space-time, matter-anti-matter, quantum mechanics, and all of the powerful concepts and revolutionary thinking that went into these laws over the centuries did not, Dr. Kianamann, explain how *our* energy, *our* human energy is conserved. Simply asked, when our cells are no longer viable what happens to the energy they once contained? That one answer will end all questions. What you just heard from Bob may very well be that explanation. It is a scientist's dream to answer a question never before posed. You are watching this dream unfold." Having made his points, the agile professor emeritus sat back, and lightly refolded his arms.

The Provost respected the sharp mind of the elderly professor, but she was having difficulty understanding how telepathy tied in with the conservation of energy. Dr. Sukawa knew that it would be a matter of seconds before she asked that question. Patiently, he waited.

"Let's presume for the sake of discussion that telepathic communication is real," said Dr. Kianamann. "How does this line of research—the genetics, the population study, the American University trial—fit into the concept of conservation of human energy?"

Bob was surprised by the Provost's question, as it was one that he himself considered many times. Rather, he thought she would ask about the commercial value of the research. Dr. Sukawa waited a moment to give Bob the opportunity to provide an answer, although he was certain that one would not come from his protégé. After that moment passed and without changing his seated position, the thoughtful professor, who appeared to be both pensive and distant, answered clearly and concisely. "In an absolute, unequivocal, and definitive way."

———•———

The assortment of acupuncture needles available online was overwhelming. Dr. Johnson had not considered the importance of the different types and lengths when he ordered three randomly different sets. Express shipping ensured that the needles would be in hand when his guest arrived. Not once during the purchasing process had he considered asking Mi-Ok for advice. It would be best if she were not involved.

3

Abby realized that the most difficult part of conducting a clinical trial was the initial planning stage, closely followed by the approval stage. The actual test stage, despite its long delay, progressed rapidly after it was allowed to resume. Last, but not least, was the data analysis stage. In essence, no one part of a clinical study was easy or simple.

"And then you have the pleasure of writing the paper that describes the findings, and then submitting it for publication," said Alexa who always forewarned Abby of the challenges that lurked around the next corner. "Actually, you don't just get to write it just once. You write it over and over and over until it's perfect. Until I say that it's ready to go out for review."

Abby's initial goal was to organize the massive dataset. Of the 125 total children interviewed, 51 test cases were deaf from birth, and 48 control cases had normal hearing and normal speech development. A second control group of 26 children were blind, but not deaf, from birth, most exhibited normal speech development. There were an equal number of males and females in each group; the youngest participant was five years old and the oldest was fifteen. Importantly, the age range distribution for all three groups was closely matched, so this variable would not impact the results. Indeed, Abby was relieved to see that all of the basic parameters of age, gender and the number of test and control cases were even, because it meant that direct comparisons of the findings could be made with the use of common statistical methods.

As an added bonus, every one of the participants, whether they were in the test or the control groups and regardless of age, consented to submitting a cheek swab for DNA analysis. Abby had already sent the preserved cheek cells containing the child's DNA to Bob Wyle at MIT for analysis. Abby was also pleased to learn that the parents of 10 children agreed to consider functional MRI analysis, if a future study was launched.

The results of Abby's groundbreaking clinical trial could not have been clearer. All but one of the deaf children were telepathic, a virtually perfect score of 98 percent. In sharp, and quite dramatic contrast, only 11 of the 74 children or only 15 percent with normal hearing were telepathic.

At first glance, Abby was unsure whether or not the differences were significant. She then entered the data into a statistical program.

"Using the Fisher's Exact Test these two groups are statistically different with a probability of less than one percent that they happened by chance," she'd later report to Alexa. Abby would also tell her advisor that blind children were statistically more likely to be telepathic compared to those with normal sight. Only a single child out of 48 that had perfect hearing and vision exhibited telepathic powers.

To back up the numerical results, Abby assembled two short movies from the interviews. One movie showed the responses of telepathic children as they were communicating with Abby, Rosi, or Olysia. The other video showed the responses of non-telepathic children interacting with the three interviewers. Even if one was not learned in how to interpret video-recorded data, the results were clear and obvious. Deaf children of all ages looked absolutely astonished in response to the messages they received telepathically. Their eyes opened wide as if they were in complete disbelief. Their bodies were relaxed and their arms and hands were still. Uniformly, none moved their lips during the entire interview. The ten blind telepaths abruptly stopped speaking, some in mid-sentence, obviously in response to what they were experiencing internally. Clearly, all telepathic children were silently engaged with their telepathic interviewers—a situation that was undoubtedly a rare, and potentially new, experience for them.

The other movie would look more familiar to the everyday person. It could have been a video of any normal child interacting with family or friends at any pizza or donut shop in the country. Each one of the non-deaf, normal sighted children were chatting and answered questions verbally with no hint whatsoever that they were communicating by any other means despite the attempts by all three telepathic interviewers to do so. In one clip, at the very beginning of the interview when telepathic contact was attempted by Olysia, a 7-year-old, dark-skinned little girl turned to her mother and asked, "Why isn't she saying something?"

Abby collected all of the tables of data, graphs and stacks of statistical analyses, and shared the findings with Alexa. The professor was more than impressed. She was ecstatic.

"This is incredibly strong evidence for the existence of telepathy among children of this age," Alexa declared before she began to impart wisdom to her student. "Whenever you present these data, take care not to extend beyond the study design and parameters. This study was performed with children between this age and that age; don't make generalizations like 'every deaf person is telepathic' because you've only studied this small cohort of this very specific age range." Abby readily understood the shortcomings of the trial. She already knew that science was done one small step at a time.

Larger, more definitive studies were in Abby's future. Her research would make a skeptical public, eventually and somewhat reluctantly, accept telepathy as a sixth human sense. Along the way, this line of research would turn Abby into a groundbreaking pioneer. She would be the world's leading expert in the newly described field of Telepathology, the study of telepaths and of non-verbal communication. It would be her lifelong passion.

"In one of our early chats, you thought there may be a trend towards a higher degree of telepathy among young children. Did this pan out?" asked Alexa.

"No. None that we could see with this cohort because all except one deaf child was telepathic, so there was no way to see a trend."

"Oh right. I should have known. And do you have anything on the DNA study?"

"No, not yet but it won't take long, perhaps a week or two. Ajay, my colleague at MIT who will process these samples, said that he'll make it a top priority."

"Well Abby, congratulations to you and to your team too. We'll have to celebrate at *The Beltway* with the gang after you share these findings with the department. You're slated to present in three weeks, on April first. No doubt that the Fool's Day will give you an extra challenge, but I'm sure you'll do just fine. Collecting your thoughts for the seminar will help mold the manuscript. Let's plan a review of your slides in a couple of weeks, and let's go high with your paper. We'll aim for a top-notch journal, okay?"

Additional evidence that confirmed the findings came from an unexpected source: emails and letters addressed not to Abby, but to Dr. Alexa Rudman from parents of the deaf children that participated in the study. All correspondences read as if the same person wrote them. Each had similar observations and comments, and all thanked her for initiating such bold research.

> I had no idea that my Josh was able to communicate any other way then by sign. He tells me often how nice it was to be able to interact with someone so easily and he wished with all of his heart that I could be like Rosi, Abby or Olysia and understand what he's thinking. He also asks if he could come back and visit any of the three telepaths. While he enjoyed being with all of them he often mentions Olysia (a preteen crush?). In any case, I just wanted to express my thanks to you and to your staff for having the interest to study things that are not commonly studied. We've agreed to participate in a MRI study so perhaps Josh and I will see you again if that study occurs. He asks me weekly if that will

happen. Please keep us posted.

Thank you again.

Another read:

> I just thought to let you know that Jackie has been a com-
> pletely different person since she participated in your study
> at American University. She is more outgoing and all around
> she is a much happier person. She's let me know that she
> now is on the 'prowl' as she put it, for others like Abby who
> are telepathic. So far she hasn't mentioned that she found
> anyone but perhaps it's just a matter of time. Thanks for
> doing this study.

Never before had Alexa received feedback from study participants. While healed patients occasionally wrote notes of gratitude to their surgeon or even to their primary care physician, research scientists at the forefront of discovery rarely, if ever, heard directly from the public. The young professor knew that accepting Abby as a doctoral graduate student could lead to something very interesting and significant, or to nothing at all. And there was a possibility that the clinical study could have been a waste of time and effort. However, Alexa also knew that it was important to examine all forms of human communication, including those that resided in left field. One never knows what leads to a breakthrough. Abby's clinical study was Alexa's reward for taking chances.

Abby was beyond ecstatic. Not only did she just nail an important clinical trial, the foundation of her doctorate but the data irrefutably showed the ability of deaf children to communicate effectively without uttering a single word or by signing. In other words, the data supported her hypothesis. She felt extremely fortunate to have taken Dr. Paolo's class at Wilmington College and to have met Amy, Brad, and especially Phil. They've stood by her all along.

She also could not have been more pleased with American University and she felt especially fortunate to have landed in Alexa's world of openness and creativity. And not for a moment did Abby lose site of Rosi's magic. What were the odds that Abby would meet, in the gift shop of an art museum, a telepath as talented, as loving, and as brilliant as Rosi?

Career-wise Abby's future was beginning to take shape. Although she didn't know how the rest of her life would unfold what, she did know was that, for the moment, she was on the top of the world, and it felt damn good to be there.

By any measure Abby's departmental seminar, where she showcased the results of the clinical study for the first time, was a huge success. She also used the date of the seminar to her advantage right off the bat.

"In honor of April Fools Day, I'd like to begin with this quote attributed to Abraham Lincoln," said Abby as she activated the presentation on her laptop. The auditorium filled with faculty, students, and laboratory technicians darkened, and the screen showed a black slide with big yellow letters that read:

> Better to remain silent and be thought a fool than to speak out and remove all doubt.

"Now," continued Abby, "as someone who is about to speak for the next thirty-five minutes this may not be a great quote to use, but let me remove some words and you'll get a preview of my entire seminar." With a tap of a key most of the yellow bolded words darkened to black leaving only:

> silent   thought
> remove all doubt.

These five simple words then ballooned in perfect synchrony, with Abby's next line. "Establishing the existence of telepathy, or silent communicative thought, has been considered a fool's errand, but today I will remove all doubt of its existence." Abby's very clever opening led several members of the audience to smile. Towards the back of the large room, Rosi, Olysia and Johanna beamed with pride.

The entire seminar progressed flawlessly. If there were any doubters or skeptics in the audience of approximately 100 after thirty minutes, they would have been hard pressed to remain that way after Abby presented the results of the DNA analyses. These data were only 48 hours old.

"This graph," said Abby pointing to the multicolored image on the large screen, "shows that 87% of the 125 participants had at least one copy of Xp29.47, the telepathy gene. My MIT collaborators also used bisulfite mapping to measure the degree of methylation in the DNA of all samples from this clinical trial. Recall that all samples were de-identified and coded so that no one but Dr. Goldberg and me knew the source of the DNA. When we received the results from the methylation analysis and after we broke the code, we learned that, remarkably, the Xp29.47 gene sequences from all of the 51 deaf children who exhibited telepathic ability were not methylated. Therefore this gene in these children was not silenced, it was expressed. In other words, gene expression directly matched observed gene function. The same sequence in the DNA from the children with normal hearing was methylated, that is it is silenced, in all children with normal hearing except one, the single child in that group of 26, the single one who was telepathic."

For a moment, the audience of professors and peers sat in quiet disbelief. The genomic data matched the rest of the results exactly. It not only reinforced all of the data collected from the unique trial, but it also provided independent proof of Xp29.47's role in nonverbal communication.

Abby concluded the presentation with a slide that acknowledged the clinical study team including the interviewers, the nurses and all of the study participants. It also noted the patience, wisdom and guidance of her advisor, Alexa Goldberg.

The auditorium resonated with loud applause. And the following question and answer session had almost nothing to do with Abby's results, but it was filled with comments and praise for the boldness of the study itself. Several offered personal stories of family members who exhibited what was commonly referred to as a 'sixth sense'. A Communications Department professor, who was also a member of Abby's dissertation committee, did ask one important question. The question was the last exchange of the seminar and it was one that Abby anticipated, one she had feared the most. How she answered this question could be a defining moment in the eyes of the Department's faculty members and fellow graduate students. Although she rehearsed the answer several times with different approaches, she had not settled on one that satisfied her completely.

"Very provocative, Ms. Lark. Very provocative, indeed," said the dissertation committee professor in his deep baritone voice. "Let us accept your findings as fact and as a necessary and viable form of communication for those that cannot process sound from birth, roughly 1 of every 2,000 births. And also let us accept for the sake of discussion, that by extrapolation of your data, most of us possess the genetic machinery to receive and transmit thoughts telepathically, yet we have no apparent use for this... um... sixth sense. Ms. Lark would you like to speculate as to why we would even have this unique capacity?"

Abby shot a quick glance to the rear of the auditorium and spotted Rosi. Although she had no plans to reveal her theory, Abby nevertheless appreciated Rosi's firm declaration: *No way/don't say.*

Abby paused, walked a few steps to the right of the podium, then a few to the left before returning to the center where the microphone was positioned.

"Why?" Abby said condensing the long question into a single word. "That ageless question posed by children and scholars alike." Chuckles could be heard throughout the large hall and, to Abby's relief, a broad smile could also be seen on the face of the questioner. "I should be satisfied in having unveiled a new way for deaf people to communicate. This is an exciting endpoint on it's own, but beyond these data I haven't a clue why telepathy exists. As you might suspect, I have a number of ideas but they are speculations at best. These speculations can turn into testable ideas that await nothing more than time, will and funding. Could nonverbal have preceded verbal forms of communication? We know that language evolved along with the enlargement of our brain but is it possible that oral communication is a form of de-evolution? That at one time we all conveyed thoughts efficiently? Perhaps it was the universal way we communicated with different species of humans that co-existed at any given time during our evolution? Today, over 300 different languages are spoken in the United States alone, and over 6,000 complex languages exist worldwide. To me, this does not seem efficient. So I can imagine that the gene for nonverbal communication, located in what was once considered 'junk DNA', became quiescent and essentially obsolete as simple sounds morphed into words that created complex languages. Languages that separated us. That's how I'd like to frame these current findings. Would you agree?"

The questioner simply nodded and led the last round of applause.

Afterwards each of the four faculty members that comprised Abby's dissertation committee congratulated her on having performed a groundbreaking study. It was a scene that Alexa had never experienced with prior mentees. There was still a great deal of work to do and by no means had Abby locked up her degree, but she was well on her way to attaining that goal with the successful completion of a very high risk project.

After celebrating a successful seminar with the clinical study staff, hosted by Alexa at *The Beltway Bistro*, Abby lay exhausted but exhilarated next to Rosi in the large bed in the studio loft.

Your world is unique/the academics of new/a big hit today/I'm proud of you/and clever you were/not to tell them more/how to cross over/how to find the door/it would have been too much/they need time to digest/perhaps some-day/you can tell them the rest.

Thank you my love it was great to have you there/with support with strength/to make sure I was aware/and because of you this all came to be/your boldness to engage/to set my mind free to think/to think/to think so differently.

4

First class accommodations on Lufthansa perfectly suited Franz Albracht and Katja, his wife of 57 years. The luxurious flight, indeed the entire trip to D.C to see the spectacular display of cherry blossoms, was a long overdue promise Franz made to his bride on the occasion of their fiftieth wedding anniversary. But as the plane began it's descent to the nation's capital, his thoughts couldn't have been further from cherry trees or from his wife for that matter. Dr. Albracht's thoughts were focused solely on saving what remained of his once agile mind. Initially, the return for delivering science's top prize to Richard Johnson was nothing less than immortality. Now the rapidly aging neuroscientist would settle for a simple reversal, or at least a reduction, in the progression of his Alzheimer's disease. He was unsure how much longer he could hide the debilitating symptoms from Katja who was five years his younger, a healthy and energetic 73. All he knew was that he was about to reverse course.

The plan was set for the day following their arrival. Katja would take a two-hour trolley tour of Baltimore, while he tended to so-called business at Johns Hopkins. They would meet back at the hotel, have lunch, then visit one of the Smithsonian museums and view the cherry blossoms around the Tidal Basin. As with most well made plans—and the majority of the tree buds—events would not unfold as hoped.

Dr. Richard Johnson's spacious laboratory was a beehive of activity. White-coated scientists of various expertise and skill levels darted from one bench to another holding precious samples with gloved hands, or simply conferred with one another over data. Franz Albracht expected this high level of energy and activity in the laboratory of a Nobel laureate.

Richard Johnson made a point to introduce his dear friend, the professor emeritus, to each and every member of his laboratory. He wanted to make sure that everyone greeted the former head of the Nobel Prize committee, so that they all had the same experience. That way, if anyone asked about anything, all would have the same story.

The simple ploy worked.

"Dr. Johnson was beaming with pride as he escorted Dr. Albracht around the laboratory," was a line one postdoc would later give to the police. "I'm shocked. It was obvious that Dr. Johnson was so excited to have him here. It was like he was his father or mentor or something," would be the quote from a senior technician. "They respected and cared for each other. They were true colleagues," would be yet another statement made to the authorities.

Only Mi-Ok, who would not be interviewed by the press or by local law enforcement authorities, was suspicious of her boss's overly polite, affable manners. Indeed, Mi-Ok noticed that Dr. Johnson had been acting rather strange all week. Whereas he never before chatted with her during the many years she worked for him, he stopped not once, but twice, to ask her pointed questions about acupuncture needles. One question had to do with the depth she inserted the hair-thin needles into Grand Pappy. The other question pertained to the actual placement of the needles, and whether or not there was a specific twisting motion during insertion and removal. Dr. Johnson also asked Mi-Ok to remind him how to find the location of the special area where the needles were inserted. Bending down and offering his neck, Mi-Ok pressed her fingers firmly on the two spots making sure to indicate which one was for sleep and which one would be lethal. He replaced her fingers with his own and pushed very hard. He needed to make a good mental image of the locations.

When Mi-Ok saw the elderly Dr. Albracht being escorted through the laboratory like royalty, she sensed that something very odd was about to happen. She acted without hesitation. With gloved hands she stealthily slipped a small digital recorder in the right side pocket of Franz Albracht's brown herringbone blazer just after he and Dr. Johnson turned away from her following the personal meet and greet. She kept the tiny recorded in her desk just in case she needed it someday. Her instincts led her to believe that this day was that day. She watched the two neurologists stroll to the next bench where other lab members took turns shaking hands with the guest of honor. They seemed unaware of Mi-Ok's slick act; whatever happened during the next hour would be recorded in high fidelity.

The door to Richard Johnson's office closed solidly but, as per usual for any normal workday, it was kept unlocked. The Nobelist motioned for his elderly guest to have a seat at the oval table whose glass top contained nothing but a single sheet of white paper placed print-side down.

Both men left their charming public personas in the laboratory. It was time to get down to business.

"Richard, this better be goddamned worth it."

"You saw the video, Franz. That mouse was barely breathing before the injection, then good as new afterwards. And if it would make you feel any better I can show you recovery data with various human cells grown *in vitro*..."

"I don't give a damn about mice and most *in vitro* studies aren't worth a dime, what I want to know is have you tested this stuff, whatever the hell it is, on chimps or monkeys or baboons?"

"No. We've applied for animal approval, but we're still waiting word from the regulatory people," he lied. "Data in mice indicate that the chemical's toxicity is very low. I can assure you that the dose you'll get will not be toxic. It won't kill you."

"Fine then, get on with it. I'll have it with water."

"Pardon me?"

Glancing at his watch the old neuroscientist clarified his request. "I'll take the damn thing with water. Nothing special. Tap water will do."

"The chemical we've purified is not in a pill form, it's liquid. I'll need to give it to you by injection."

Shaking his head with his eyes closed, Franz confessed a life-long embarrassment. "I don't do needles. Never have, never will."

Dr. Johnson couldn't believe what he was hearing. Before that very moment, before he learned that his nemesis hated needles, he wasn't sure how events would unfold. What excuse would he use? Now suddenly the excuse came to him.

"You won't have to worry about seeing a needle Franz. I can momentarily sedate you by acupuncture to relieve whatever temporary discomfort like nausea or injection site pain you may experience. Remember I told you about this painless acupuncture method for temporary sedation?"

"Vaguely. That's exactly the problem and why I'm offering myself as a guinea pig. I can't remember anything anymore and you're my last hope of reversing this dementia, or Alzheimer's or whatever it is. As long as it won't kill me I'm willing to try."

"So you agree to the acupuncture?"

"Fine. Just don't let me see the needles. They're thin right? Not like those huge things they use at the blood bank."

"Right. You won't even know I'm inserting them and I'm going into the back of your neck so you won't see anything."

"Fine. Let's get going on this. I can't be here all day."

"Before I start, I'd like you to sign an informed consent form that we've prepared for the clinical trial we're about to initiate." Dr. Johnson convincingly again lied. "It's right there on the table and essentially it says that this is an experimental..."

"I know what a damn consent form says, just give me a pen and get on with it." Without as much as glancing at the words typed on the paper, Franz scribbled his name on the custom-worded consent form. Without prompting he also dated his signature. One of his longtime habits. Dr. Johnson took the paper and pen and headed towards his large desk. While it appeared as though he placed both items in the top drawer, what he actually did was to fold the signed form and place it in the back pocket of his trousers. It was like an insurance policy he never would look at again; it was merely a safeguard in the unlikely event anyone asked anything.

Richard Johnson's heart rate rose as he instructed the old man to place his arms on the table, look straight ahead and to relax. On the desk situated behind Franz, Richard placed a small plastic case that contained the acupuncture needles. He opened the case and gingerly lifted out a needle with his right hand. He then spoke calmly though the procedure as it was happening so that Franz knew what to expect. His left hand gently held the old man's jaw steady as the little finger of his right hand felt awkwardly for the critical spot. Richard Johnson needed to work fast and sure. Above all, he didn't want to appear hesitant or unskilled. But the old man's neck was thicker and the skin was looser than he'd anticipated and he quickly realized that he was unable to locate the spot with any degree of certainty. Like tossing a dart in the dark, Dr. Johnson twisted the hair-thin acupuncture needle in a random spot in the small of Dr. Albracht's neck.

Almost instantly Franz's head and shoulders hunched forward. Dr. Johnson, whose heart was beating wildly on adrenalin, ensured the safe placement of the German's head on the table. It appeared as though it worked. The old neurologist was asleep with only one small acupuncture needle sticking out of his neck. The second needle, the fatal acupuncture needle was still in the box on the desk.

Now was the time.

With just one more needle, the nagging nemesis would be gone. Forever buried would be the secret of how the Nobel Prize was rigged.

"Fuck you Franz," Richard Johnson said aloud as he reached for the second needle. "This should forever calm your fucking nerves!" But no sooner had he uttered those words then the old man began to violently convulse. The German scientist was thrashing wildly, his thin arms and legs were flaying uncontrollably in what would later be described as a grand mal seizure. Richard Johnson did all he could to steady his one time collaborator. Quickly, he removed the acupuncture needle from the old man's neck and placed it back in the box with the other needles. He slipped the box in his pocket before he yelled for help.

"Someone call 911! Now!"

When the emergency medical technicians arrived they found the old man lying completely still on his back on the office floor. Dr. Johnson, wearing a white, personalized Johns Hopkins Medical School lab coat, was administering CPR. Lab personnel looked on in shock as the revered famous father of the neurology field, a man of high stature that they just met moments ago, now lay ashen and unresponsive to the deep chest compressions administered with renewed vigor by the EMTs.

Dr. Johnson appeared grief-stricken and bewildered as his old listless friend was carted out of the building and into a waiting ambulance. Dr. Franz Albracht would be pronounced dead before reaching the emergency room that was located only five short minutes from the science building.

Although her head was lowered Mi-Ok's eyes looked up at her boss as he followed the gurney out of the laboratory. Unlike the shocked looks of others in the room, Mi-Ok's face was stoic. She was not surprised by the drama unfolding before her. Dr. Johnson had either lucked out and successfully inserted two acupuncture needles or he failed at inserting even one. In either case the end result was obvious. As it turned out for Dr. Albracht there was no difference between success and failure.

Ironically, the cherry trees that lined the Tidal Basin were at peak blossom 48 hours later when the police concluded it's perfunctory investigation into the sudden death of the visiting scientist. Katja Albracht was given her husband's personal belongings—passport, wallet, wedding band, glasses and his brown herringbone blazer—items that fit easily in her carryon bag for the long, lonely return trip home. The new widow also had custody of her dear Franz's cremated remains.

Once home it would take Katja a full week before she could bring herself to unpacking her luggage. The last item she removed from the small, hard shell suitcase was Franz's blazer that had served as a cushion of sorts for his ashes. As she had done so many times over the decades when her husband returned from a trip, she searched the pockets of the blazer for items that may need to be kept or thrown away. In the left pocket she found a sheet of hotel note paper with it's exact address written on it as well as her name and relationship to him: Katja Albracht, *meine Liebe*. In the right pocket she found a small rectangular metallic object that looked like something Franz's would use with his computer. She carried the little electronic device to the roll top desk and placed it in the rightmost inside drawer.

Someone might be interested in this someday, Katja thought as she gently pulled on the half round slats of the tambour to close the desk.

News of the sudden death of the well-respected and revered neurologist Franz Albracht reached Lorenzo Benedetti's computer in Tuscany. The Nobel Committee and the European Society for Neurobiology jointly dispatched a short press release of the news:

> While visiting the laboratory of Nobel laureate Richard Johnson at Johns Hopkins University, Dr. Franz Albracht, Professor Emeritus at Ludwig Maximilian University, suffered a fatal acute myocardial infarction. He was 78 years old. He was in the United States to visit the famed cherry blossoms in Washington, D.C. with his wife of 57 years when the tragedy occurred. A full tribute on the remarkable scientific achievements of Dr. Franz Albracht will be forthcoming.

Lorenzo was stunned.

It was not the first time a colleague had died, but something seemed different with Franz's sudden passing. With walking stick in hand, Lorenzo went for a long trek in the woods to reflect on his times with Franz. He needed space and fresh air to think clearly before returning to review the last emails they exchanged not long ago. Something did not seem right. While Franz complained of memory loss, he never mentioned heart disease or any other ailments. In fact, Lorenzo recalled that Franz looked quite fit at the Nobel ceremonies just one year ago. What did he miss?

In Brief

1

On this warm, early summer's mid-morning, Tomasso recalled the words of his great grandfather, *Quando il giorno è perfetto siamo nelle mani di Dio.* There was no doubt in his mind that on this day, he was indeed cradled in the hands of God. He paused for a solemn moment, as if in prayer, to take in the scene. He then entered the driver's side of his brand new, jet black, two-door Fiat Cinquecento. Laura, the car's first passenger, looked simply stunning in her bright red polka dot sundress. Her mere presence confirmed yet once again that he was indeed blessed. There had been other times when he thought he was in His great palms, but those days now paled in comparison to this one and to this very moment. He worked for this car his entire adult life and he prayed to the Almighty to meet a woman like Laura even longer. *How could such a simple man who has lived a modest life experimenting and manipulating food become so fortunate?* Tomasso thought as they headed northwest on the *autostrada* towards the resort town of Abetone, nested amongst the majestic Apennines.

Laura's only other trip to Italy was the month-long visit to Florence last fall. That entire time was spent within the walls of that splendid city, but today the scenery was different; she was experiencing a whole new part of Tuscany. The *autostrada* was as modern as any four-lane highway in America and, other than the rolling hills dotted with red-roofed villages and vineyards, she could have been traveling through the Green Mountains of rural Vermont.

She was completely at peace with her decision to enter a quasi-retirement and to split time between Boston and Tuscany. And returning to Tomasso was natural and easy, as if they had known each other for several decades instead of a just a few months. He was genuine and polite, caring and doting and most importantly, he was respectful of who she was and of her professional accomplishments.

"Perhaps," Laura said to Tomasso who was still getting use to the feel of his new car, "I'll sign up for a sculpting class. I'd like to learn how to sculpt."

"*È vero?*" asked Tomasso, "Is it true?"

"Yes," replied Laura who meant to speak Italian as much as possible but simply forgot. "As a child I would spend hours making figures by molding clay. I enjoyed it very much. Now I'd like to try my hand at sculpting. It would be fun to try even if I learned that I have no talent."

The turn northward from the *autostrada* towards Pistoia on a *strade statale* meant that the road that connected cities between regions was a bit narrower than the main highway but open nonetheless. They rode in silence, each in their own thoughts, before Tomasso pulled off the road into a small pizzeria. He not only personally knew the owner and his family, but also that they make their own goat milk mozzarella fresh each morning. The two travellers were treated like royalty. Without even asking what they would enjoy for lunch, the friend-owner brought to their table individual Caprese salads, a small round loaf of warm, *pane brutto*, a half-liter of red wine and bottled water.

Before eating, Laura sat back and absorbed the scenery as well as the entire situation. Tomasso, who was already deep into his salad looked up and asked Laura if everything was okay.

"Why yes," she replied. "This is remarkable. I just want to take it in for a moment. Here I am, in Tuscany having *pranzo* outside on a picture perfect day in a idyllic setting overlooking the valley dotted with little red-tiled stone homes and villages sprinkled throughout. I'm here without a care in the world. I just love it. That's all. This may be familiar to you, but for me it's new and it's simply wonderful. It's like I'm in a dream."

Tomasso slowly placed his fork on the plate, took a sip of wine followed by a sip of water. He then wiped his mouth with the cloth napkin he had placed on his right thigh and replied, "You are right. I am familiar with this place, this setting and with the warmth of the summer mountain sun. Yet, with you here with me, I feel reborn in a way. *Il mio cuore*, you know, my heart, is young again and it beats excitedly like a child's *cuore* when something special is about to happen. It beats wildly like a young man's *cuore* just before he gives his first kiss, and tenderly like a father's *cuore* when he see his newborn child for the first time. My *principessa*, you make this old man's *cuore* want to continue beating." He reached for her hand as he stood up, arched over the table and gently placed a kiss on her forehead. "It is me that is living a dream."

Laura felt fortunate to have met Tomasso but she also felt a twinge of guilt. She knew that Dante would have said the same words to her had she spent the time with him when he was healthy. When they had the time. Laura looked down at her still untouched salad as a solitary tear rolled out of each eye, one out of longing for the past and one out of joy for the present. She wiped the tears with the still neatly folded cloth napkin and smiled bravely. Tomasso assumed that both tears were in response to his words. He was only half right.

"By the way," Laura asked in an upbeat voice. "I know we're headed towards Abetone but is that our final destination? In other words, where are we going?"

"We are going to my favorite place *in tutto il mondo*, in all of the world. It's perched high on the side of a mountain like a gem on a necklace. It's rustic but it has modern conveniences like electricity and internal plumbing. It was my grandmother's home and it has been in our family for over three hundred years. I am very excited to bring you there. The roads go straight up and they are very narrow. They coil like a snake that goes this way and that way," Tomasso replied using his right hand to make a side-winding pattern in the air. "So before we continue on per-haps we should take a walk to allow the food to settle a little. I don't want you to get ill from the ride."

"I'm sure I'll be fine."

"We'll both be fine," was Tomasso's reassuring response.

The engine of the Cinquecento alternately roared and exhaled as Tomasso shifted between second and third, before again accelerating uphill on a familiar hairpin curve, along with the downshift to second gear. In Italy driving is more of a sport than it is a means to get from one point to another, and with a responsive new vehicle Tomasso was not just one driver, he felt like he was the entire Grand Prix field. On the serpentine roads that became narrower with each kilometer of altitude gained, Italians were unwittingly not only amateur racecar drivers, but they were also statisticians. They were constantly calculating the odds of encountering a vehicle approaching from the opposite direction as they sped up or down the road from one pull-off area to another. Dirt pull-offs, designed to allow utility vehicles and buses to squeeze over when another vehicle approaches, are predominately positioned on the outside of the road. Most pull-offs, especially those in rural locations in the high mountains lack protective guardrails—why ruin the view of the lovely ravine with ugly steel?

But the jet-black Cinquecento was nowhere near a pull-off when the rugged recycle truck driven by a twenty-year-old, with music channeled loudly through firmly inserted earbuds, forgot the math lesson on risks and odds. The downward-facing truck was positioned squarely in the middle of the narrow road.

Tomasso heard the truck before he saw it.

What the chef saw surprised him. Someone who did not know the etiquette of mountain roads was driving a recycle truck. Not only was it driven without heed to even the slightest chance that someone else would also be on the road but the truck was angled badly on weak shock absorbers to the outside lane and in the direct path of the Cinquecento. The young driver jerked the truck towards the right, the inside of the mountain, as Tomasso tried to maneuver around it by doing what he was taught to do—accelerate—to hit the narrow gap around the truck with power. With the transmission already in second gear, the new engine responded instantly to Tomasso's instincts. The two front tires spun wildly but one had slipped off the narrow pavement and onto the gravel. Due to the torque of the engine and the spinning of the tires, the entire rear of the short vehicle swung outward to the right and over the road's unprotected, rugged edge.

In stunned silence the driver extended his right hand and clasped the left hand of the passenger; events seemed to unfold in slow motion. The headlights aimed upwards as the shiny vehicle dropped precipitously down the rocky ravine as if it was some sort of a sadistic amusement park thrill ride. The sharp impact of the little car against a limestone ledge instantly snapped the passenger's necks as if they were brittle rice cakes. The last thing Laura and Tomasso saw through the front of the Cinquecento's windshield was a narrow strip of a deep blue sky and the rounded top of the rugged mountain where a small stone house that has been in Tomasso's family for centuries stood solidly.

2

In Amy's mind, summer began not on the solstice but on one special day in May. It was that morning when the leaves of the maple and oak trees burst wide open, an event that started slowly at first but progressed quickly resulting in a glorious wave of green. And during this special May Day walk around the neighborhood in Boston she reflected on how transformative this summer would be for her. Amy was in a positively upbeat mood as she counted her blessings. She was to marry a handsome, hard working and smart man, she had caring parents who helped her move from the middle of the country to Boston, and other than a few episodes of morning sickness, she enjoyed an unremarkable pregnancy. Her parents, who now preferred to be called grandparents-in-waiting, have temporarily taken residence with their friends just up the highway in Winchester.

During her stroll she made an effort to balance her front-loaded weight evenly; she sought not to waddle during these final three weeks before her due date. Everyone was in place, everyone was waiting and the only thing she needed to do now was to remain calm, eat well, rest, and to take it easy. But while Amy could easily satisfy hunger and sleep at will, it was more of a challenge for her to relax.

"Abby, the only problem now is that I'm bored out of my mind. I can't just sit around and do nothing but wait. I will go nuts if I don't find something constructive to do. My parents are so nice, but just this morning I had to again refuse another invitation to lunch. I mean there is not much to say, especially since I'm not allowing my Mom to dote on me, and my Dad only yaps nonstop about genetics and medicine. Frankly, I don't want to spend all day having lunch."

"Have you been to MIT?" offered Abby. "I bet Bob Wyle will put you to work."

"You're right, he would but it's not worth the paperwork for just a few weeks."

"Go visit," Abby implored. "I bet he and Ajay have plenty for you to do. They may even have things you can do from home."

Abby was right.

Ajay and Bob had recently compiled data from the population study and they were now in the process of writing a manuscript on their findings. Amy willingly began to draft the results section that concisely described the data presented in the tables and graphs. From the comforts of her small apartment, Amy worked for several hours each day for a week until she was satisfied with what she had written. The work helped her pass the time constructively and it also kept her engaged in the research project she'd started last summer.

With each passing day, as the temperature outside warmed, Amy felt like her fetus was growing at a faster rate than ever. Her last OB/GYN visit confirmed that the baby was in launch position—rear facing, head down and butt up. Sharp kicks and seemingly deliberate pushes against her diaphragm made it difficult for Amy to breathe at times. To relieve these strange pressures, Amy would push the tiny, inside foot away by kneading the top of her bulged abdomen, a maneuver that made Brad cringe. Sleep was becoming increasingly less restful. Her discomfort level reached the breaking point when she told Brad that she was ready to have this baby live on its own. Prior apprehensions related to delivering a child had all but dissipated. Amy was ready to become a mother.

"These are no fucking Braxton Hicks!" Amy clamored to her fiancé through a particularly sharp contraction. "They're... they're... powerful," she gasped. "You're not even due for a couple of days yet and most women usually deliver late the first time," Brad calmly responded recalling the short section on Labor and Delivery covered in OB/GYN class. "There's no need to panic. We're close to the hospital and we should stay put until your water breaks."

Six particularly strong contractions later, Amy was standing in a small puddle in the apartment's small bathroom. She yelled out to Brad, "Is this enough fucking amniotic fluid for you? Call the OB, we're going in." This time there was no hesitation or pushback. Brad did as he was told.

The next twenty-four hours were chaotic for the young couple. Amy was delirious with a building fever, along with wave after wave of painful contractions. A large needle was inserted in her arm and IV fluids administered to her stressed body. Several people voiced medical terms—febrile, distress, hypoxic, ascending, PROM, resistance—that Amy heard but could not comprehend through the tumultuous storm of madness that flooded and dulled her every sense.

Brad, the once calm observer, was starting to feel the gravity of the situation increase with each passing hour. The emergency room lights were ablaze like a camera's flash stuck on. The gurney that carried his beautiful wife-to-be was whisked down a hard-tiled hallway by a skilled response team with the speed and efficiency of Olympic bobsledders. Despite his medical school training he felt bewildered at all of the questions he had to answer and the many decisions he had to make on the spot. Familiarity with the hospital itself did not ease Brad's anxiety. His parents were also not particularly useful. They arrived to show support only to ask seemingly mundane questions about legal issues since he and Amy were not officially married. Thankfully though, Amy's parents were more reasonable and for the most part stayed within arms reach of Brad. They quietly monitored every medical move being made on their only daughter.

The highly anticipated birth was anything but the joyous moment Amy and Brad had envisioned. The lethargic and quiet little boy, instantly named after his father, was briefly shown to both parents before being placed in a portable ICU positioned across the delivery room. Amy could barely keep her eyes open. They stung due to beads of salty sweat that seeped in from her oft-wiped forehead. She repeatedly asked about the baby although she was no longer allowed to see her son. Yet, through bouts of delirium she kept asking.

When he saw the off-color newborn, Brad's knees went weak. He had to hold on to the bed's side rail to keep from collapsing altogether. That uncanny feeling of losing control had never happened before to Brad nor would it happen again in his long productive life as a medical doctor. It was as if this singular moment was the very worst he could encounter as a physician, nothing else could or would compare. In that instant, he had entered the lowest ring of medical and paternal hell.

Brad's short text message to Abby was cryptic yet clear:

Baby Brad in septic shock. On vent. Dire.

Abby sat at the counter in Rosi's kitchen and reread the desperate message.

Their baby is dying. He's dying.

In an instant Abby was transported back to her childhood. She relived the moment when told of the accident and sudden death of her mother. She also relived the whirlwind of activity that began at her college graduation ceremony when she received the text message from Laura stating that her former professor Dr. Paolo was fading quickly.

The mere thought of her dear mentor-friend, Dante Paolo, instantly unleashed a very specific message that had been stored in the recesses of her memory.

The opportunity will be golden but sad. Don't miss it. It's simple.

Within seconds, bits of stored thoughts flashed in her mind and spontaneously assembled into the most important and enduring message of Abby's life. What emerged from her every dream, everything she had ever read, seen, heard or thought of, suddenly and concretely coalesced into one sharp message. Even her once wild theory now made perfect sense.

Abby's skin erupted in a wave of goose bumps as she recalled her mother's soft hands as they loving cradled her young face. It was that simple gesture, the opposing hands held apart by the very flesh of her own flesh, that created the stillness necessary for Abby's mother to focus, unabated and directly, into her daughter's soul—a gaze that formed a permanent pairing.

It's simple.

Abby silently looked at Rosi. *The opportunity will be golden but sad/I now know/they were preparing not just for anyone/but specifically for little Brad/I must go.*

Within three hours Abby was on an airplane heading northeast on a direct flight from D.C. to Boston.

She stood only momentarily in the brightly lit corridor of the L&D ward just outside the private hospital room and peered at the intensely sad scene inside. Brad was by Amy's side with her parents standing guard by the shaded window. Amy's head slowly turned towards the hallway and spotted her friend.

"Abby! Oh Abby! My baby is dying. He's not going to make it. They just took him off the ventilator and gave him to me to hold for one last time," the new mother said through heavy tears.

With precious little time left Abby ignored everyone else in the room and went directly to Amy's side. Gently she lifted and angled the little child so that mother and child were only inches apart.

"Amy, listen to me carefully," she said in a firm, business-like voice. "Let me support him while you cradle his face with your two hands. When he opens his eyes, look at them deeply and tell him how much you love him. You don't have to speak it just think it. And before Amy had a chance to react to the odd, heart-wrenching request she did as she was told. The exhausted mother was face to face with her son who was now bluish-gray and breathing shallowly.

Abby's mind was focused on a single appeal.

Open your eyes little one/your time here is not yet done/you must open them now to see what you see/it will make a difference now and for eternity. Abby silently repeated the short phrase until little Brad's eyelids began to quiver.

Do it/open wide/we're here on this side/do it/open wide.

The simple reflex seemed to take all of the energy left in the tiny, diseased-riddled body. A third. A third of the way opened. Halfway. Halfway more the eyelids opened. Fully opened. His deep blue eyes were staring directly ahead.

Amy gazed deeply into the eyes of her firstborn. The trio of Abby, Amy and the little dying child were oddly united as if they were suspended in both space and time. They were unaware of their surroundings and of the intense stares of the small audience gathered in the private room. Then, after what seemed like a suspended, yet fleeting, moment baby Brad's eyelids ever so slowly began to droop, as if they were following the path of his heartbroken mother's stream of tears, until they closed for the final time. Abby softly placed the now lifeless, limp child in his mother's arms, and then she brushed Amy's black hair back and solemnly kissed her warm, moist forehead.

Spent, Abby turned away from the bed and went to Brad. As they hugged, he felt her tears moisten his shirt while she felt his soak hers. They held each other tightly for quite some time; there was nothing else left to do or to say.

Thank you, Abby. Thank you.

En route to D.C., Abby used the airline's Wi-Fi to understand more about the disease that so rapidly and ruthlessly killed little Brad. Never before had she heard of GBS bacteria nor had she ever heard the nonsense phrase 'orphan vaccine'. The more she searched and the more she read the vast scientific literature base on this disease of newborns, the angrier Abby became. It was the type of anger that rose from the gut, and it rose all the more as she read first hand accounts of mothers and fathers who lost their babies to the vaccine-preventable disease. The vaccine remained useless on a pharmaceutical giant's shelf because profit margins would be too slim to produce it. She wondered how many newborns would die—how many more parents would suffer irreparable pains—as the deadly group B *Streptococcus* continued to evolve and laugh at the antibiotics it once feared. She also wondered how large a profit margin was acceptable to the pharmaceutical company's executives who looked beyond the tiny caskets to focus on their bottom line.

Abby couldn't shake her anger as she stared out of the airplane's window at the array of lights that created the intense nighttime view of New York City from 30,000 feet. She thought of vaccines and medicines and of viruses and bacteria and of Amy and Brad alone back in Boston surrounded by little things for a tiny one that was ice cold in the hospital's morgue awaiting the next day's pickup by the mortician. While she knew that the young couple would survive their ordeal she couldn't help but wonder if human beings—in spite of their advances and complexities—are spun in an irreversible and perpetual cycle of pettiness; a self-aggrandizing species, guided by an ever-expanding array of twisted, perverted priorities.

Perhaps it isn't only language that has devolved, she thought.

3

Phil was usually awake at 11 p.m. but rarely did he get a phone call at that late hour. He smiled when he saw that it was from Abby who was too wound up to sleep following the late night flight back to D.C., and the subsequent subway ride to campus. The last thing Phil knew about his friends in Boston was that Amy's due date was sometime soon, but he was unsure of the exact date. He had been working hard these days and had not kept up with anyone. So the mathematician sat in stunned silence alone at Flatbread that overlooked the dark Hudson River as Abby recounted what had recently happened in Boston.

At times Abby's voice was steady while at other times it cracked as she described the many exchanges she'd had with Amy throughout her pregnancy, and especially during the final weeks leading up to the birth. She then told Phil about the short text message from Brad, and the sad events that transpired at Amy's hospital bedside.

After Phil had a chance to recover from the shock of the unbelievable story, and after Amy had answered dozens of questions to the best of her ability, only then did she tell him about her dreamlike experience. She told him about the unrecognizable people that conveyed profound sadness, anguish so palpable that it made her cry in her sleep. Abby told Phil about a particular middle-aged woman in that strange world with a little blue patch of fabric on her bare right shoulder.

"Phil, I knew all along that Amy and Brad would have a son. The blue patch symbolized little Brad. And I also knew that he wouldn't live long because these people were preparing to receive him. What I didn't know was how long he would live. Did they appeared to be sad because they knew that little Brad wouldn't have a chance to live a natural life nor die a natural death? They knew he would die physically first, a situation that is not right. Phil, I knew. I saw and I knew that this was going to happen, but I didn't understand the symbolisms nor did I appreciate the messages. But now I do. And now I realize why Dr. Paolo appears like a young man in this other world. Can you guess why?" she asked without giving Phil a chance to answer. "It's because we die not one but two deaths: a physical human death and, for the sake of a better term, a metaphysical death. In Dr. Paolo's case, his metaphysical death occurred at a relatively young age compared to his actual physical death so that's how he appears now in this other world."

Phil was taken with Abby's novel concept. He was completely engaged and he wanted to make sure he understood exactly what she just said.

"So let me see if I can repeat all of this back to you, okay?"

"Okay. Go on."

"My grandfather was a wrinkly, creaky old man who shuffled more than he walked when he died at the age of 78. He was once a heavy-set man who lost a lot of weight when he got cancer. When he died he looked terrible—pale, drawn and tired. So let's say he died the metaphysical death or whatever you called it, when he was a young man enlisted in the

Navy. The photograph on the coffee table at my grandparent's house was of my grandfather as a 22-year-old, new enlistee dressed in uniform and standing on the deck of a big ship. If I saw him now in this other world he would be like the young 22-year old in the picture, and not the old man he was when he died the regular type of death. Right?"

"Exactly."

"Wow. Abby, this is wild."

"I'd say, but it explains what I've been experiencing when I visit this other world. In that other world both my mom and Dr. Paolo appear younger then they were when they actually, physically died."

"So what about little Brad?"

"Right. Little Brad, in all likelihood, died a physical death before the metaphysical one so I don't know what will happen. Will he be seen as a child, young man, or an old man in this other world? Good question. But if my theory is correct and Amy and little Brad made the connection, then Amy may see him again. And if I'm right, he will not be a newborn but a child or a young, middle-aged or even an old man, but probably not an infant."

"You're saying that because they looked deeply in each other's eyes in this world they will be able to communicate across worlds?"

"Yes. That's right. That's absolutely right. Does it sound too simple?"

"Frankly, yes it does. I mean isn't looking into each other's eyes commonly done between two people who love each other?"

"Maybe. But it may not be done sincerely or with deep love. Or, if it is done sincerely and with deep love, and the connection is made, it still may not work. The telepathy part may be missing or it is underdeveloped or outright ignored. Speaking of underdeveloped, have you found the portal?"

"No. I've tried, but it's impossible. I'm asleep the moment I lay down."

"You're not always asleep when you're laying down," said Amy in a teasing, suggestive voice that immediately lightened the serious conversation.

The next morning, while in the shower, Phil reflected on his conversation with Abby. He recalled an interesting fact she mentioned about the bacteria that killed little Brad. "Group B Strep can live on women without causing any harm, but if it gets into the baby's blood stream during birth, it could be fatal." It was that sentence that made Phil realize that the mathematical arch he developed hadn't accounted for everything that made human's human. He completely dismissed the bacteria and all of the other microbes that co-exist with humans. The more he thought about these microbial symbionts the quicker his heart raced in excitement. He was onto something. Still damp, Phil walked out of Flatbread's small bathroom and into the living room. Taped to the wall were sheets of paper filled with formulas and arrows that formed his mathematical arch.

Phil stared at the keystone of the arch, the human being—the source of his intellectual angst and confusion. The computer program he wrote that incorporated the very elements that comprised the human body into a mathematical formula worked well with one exception, the results were wildly inconsistent. It was like following a recipe to make white bread only to have different batches taste like dark rye, pumpernickel or cinnamon. Why was this happening? What was responsible for this variability? Phil tried to mathematically assess many conditions such as gender, birth order, place of birth, lifespan, eye and hair color, as well as life choices including level of education, career path, marriage, becoming a parent, and risky behavior, but nothing seemed to account for the variability. He also tried to test those devastating and unexpected life-altering events like accidents that left sensory deficits, sudden loss of a parent or a child, and again, nothing seemed to account for the variable results.

But now, from one of those unexpected, life-altering tragedies just described by Abby, came the answer. Phil searched the medical database to learn that bacteria alone account for up to three percent of a human's weight—a huge amount when compared to some of the metals and other elements present in trace amounts. So with renewed excitement, Phil added an algorithm to the computer program to take into account the composition of the most abundant bacteria found in human gut, as well as on the largest organ on the human body, the skin. He then reran the program and waited patently for the computer to do the calculations.

Four days later, on a late Friday afternoon, Phil taped the new formula for the keystone to the wall. The aberrant results constantly present before he accounted for the bacterial inhabitants of humans now occurred only rarely. He chided himself for not immediately making the connection between the last *voussoir*, dedicated to symbiosis, and its relevant and obvious segue to the keystone positioned just above it.

Months later, when he was writing the manuscript on his findings, Abby again provided a clue to a possible second reason for those infrequent deviations in the keystone results. Phil would realize, and then go on to prove mathematically, that they occur when energies from different universes collided. What Abby described as *déjà vu* episodes are actually collisions we experience in this universe. They are uniquely personal rare intersections of energies from different parallel universes.

When he stepped back and viewed the grand archway, Phil must have felt as content as any visionary scientist. He had one of those rarely encountered, satisfying moments in life when he saw something, knew something, discovered something that no one else had seen, or knew, or had unearthed before. Regardless of the starting point to each archway, no matter the type of variables added to each *voussoir*, the sum total of the keystone human was null, a net zero. The energy of the individual were gone but not consumed. It simply shifted from one state to another that left the keystone an empty relic, like a fossil in limestone.

"The other states are right here. The parallel universes are right here. They exist all around us," he said aloud to the empty room in Flatbread overlooking the Hudson River. "They are right here. It's simple. Like Dr. Paolo said. It's so simple."

4

"This came for you this morning," Ajay said as he handed Bob a small padded envelope. The return label had no address, town or zip code; it showed only two letters: an uppercase J and a lowercase O; the postmark read: Baltimore, MD. It was mailed two days ago. Bob watched Ajay leave the office and thought for a moment until he remembered his former postdoc. He opened the light brown envelope to find a smaller, sealed white envelope with a short handwritten message that read:

> Do not open content. I see you on Milky Way this Friday
> noon.

And it was signed 'Jo' without a closing. Inside the white envelope was a sealed pink pouch that looked like a sugar substitute. Bob placed the little pink pouch back inside the white envelope, then placed the white envelope back inside the padded one and tucked the whole thing in his top desk drawer. He locked the drawer with a little key he kept on a ring along with the key to his apartment. Bob looked at his appointment calendar to see that he already had a noontime meeting scheduled for that Friday. After considering who was scheduled to be at that meeting, he made no changes. *Perhaps the stars are aligning*, he thought.

Brad and Alex were the first to arrive to the noontime meeting. Although Bob gave a great deal of thought as to what he would say to Brad, the only words that rang true were, "I'm so sorry. How is Amy?"

"She's getting there, but slowly. The infection was difficult to treat and the whole ordeal has taken a toll on her both physically and mentally. But she's getting better. Thank goodness her parents are around. Thank you for sending flowers to the apartment. It meant a lot to us," was Brad's low-key reply.

"Sure thing. Everyone here has been very concerned for Amy and for the both of you."

Brad just nodded.

"Before we get started I want to let you know that we're going to have company today. This was dropped on me at the last minute and instead of trying to rearrange everyone's schedule, I thought we'd all meet and here's why." Bob Wyle went on to explain the brilliance of a former postdoc named Jo Jung-Zoo, a molecular chemist who helped develop *RW88* and the early variations that eventually led to *RW96*. Bob also described Jo's strange and sudden departure to work in Richard Johnson's lab at Hopkins.

"So I don't hear from Jo again until the other day when I get this little package in the mail. I'm not sure what he sent, but I have a hunch that you will be very interested in it. But that's only a guess based on something else that came out of left field recently."

Alex and Brad listened intently to Bob's lengthy prelude to their meeting, but their interest was piqued because it involved the tracer, and they had invested a great deal of time and resources in this special chemical.

"So then—bam! The day after Jo's package arrives, as if on some cosmic cue or something, I get an email out of the blue from Tuscany. Brad, you remember Lorenzo Benedetti, right? Alex, I don't know if you know this guy, but he and Dr. Paolo had some kind of strange relationship that I really don't know the details of, nor do I care to know, but I guess he was a leader in the neuroscience field and now he's retired and living in Italy. Anyway, this email is not one of those 'howdy-do' emails, but it describes some research that Richard Johnson, yes, the same Richard Johnson, Nobelist, Hopkins guy is doing with—now get this—chemicals made by animals at the time of death. He even includes a video clip of a freaking mouse that has the bejeebers shaken out of him in a glass jar. It looked like the thing was almost dead, then the mouse gets an injection with something and the mouse twitched, then springs back to life like some hocus-pocus, raised-from-the-dead miracle."

"What?" Brad asked. "Are you kidding me?" As usual Alex's response was more measured. In a calm voice he asked, "Would it be possible to view that video?"

Just as Bob opened his laptop where the short video resided, there was a quick knock on the small conference room door and in walked Jo and Mi-Ok.

The two out-of-town guests were surprised to see other people in the room—they were expecting a private audience with the MIT scientist. After quick introductions, Bob explained to Jo and Mi-Ok that it was fortuitous that they were present for this all-important meeting with his trusted collaborators from Harvard. In broad strokes Bob divulged the unpublished data with *RW96* making sure to leave out critical details, especially the part about the peptides found in bacterial extracts.

Jo nodded as if he understood everything Bob said, while Mi-Ok sat quietly and assessed the various personalities in the room. It was the first time Jo and Mi-Ok travelled together; it was her initial visit to Boston, a city that she had heard so much about since she began dating the bright chemist.

"So, Jo. I see that you sent me a gift. It looks like a packet of sugar or something," Bob said as he handed the padded envelope to Jo to reopen. Jo sheepishly took the package and placed it on the table without opening it.

"Aaa...I wanted to come to talk with you about what I did at John Opkins," Jo said hesitantly, unsure of where to begin. The bright Korean carefully explained to the small group that he had isolated a chemical that was expressed in mice at the exact moment of death. He credited Mi-Ok and her special acupuncture technique that made it possible to harvest tissue from mice at the precise moment that the animals expired. He explained how this critical advance led to the eventual isolation, characterization and synthesis of a unique chemical. He also divulged that the chemical extended the life of cells grown in the laboratory, and also that it was not harmful to mice.

"Do you know the mechanism of action at a molecular level?" asked Alex.

"No. We just test *in vitro* with culture cells."

"And did you say that this chemical prolonged the viability of cells in culture?" asked Brad.

"Not only does it extend viability, but it also can rescue cells that appear to be undergoing apoptosis, programmed cell death," clarified Mi-Ok who had by now assessed everyone in the room and judged them to be trustworthy individuals.

"But why? Why would cells express this particular chemical at that defining moment? It doesn't seem logical," reasoned Bob who decided it was time to open up this discussion. "Have you done any rescue studies in animals? Would this chemical be able to help an animal recover from injury? Have you done that experiment?"

Both Jo and Mi-Ok shook their heads. "No, we have not done this study."

"Someone has," replied Bob as he opened his laptop and showed everyone in the room the video sent by the old neurologist from Tuscany.

No one in the small conference room knew how to react as they watched the odd scenes unfold. Mi-Ok closed her eyes in disgust when the little brown mouse was shaken violently in the jar, but afterwards her eyes opened widely to study the details of the scene—the type of protective gloves, the size of the syringe, the color of the needle's hub, the newspaper, the scenery—in an effort to identify the pathetic person who performed this cruel act. Jo and Mi-Ok looked at each other when the little mouse twitched then righted itself after it had received an injection, responses they knew quite well from the toxicity studies in mice they performed together. They had no doubt who belonged to the hands that shook the jar and injected the contents of the syringe into the feral mouse.

"I received this video from Dr. Lorenzo Benedetti who claimed to have received it from Dr. Franz Albracht, who apparently received it from Dr. Richard Johnson. Does any of this make sense to anyone?" asked Bob.

Brad and Alex shook their heads just as Jo began to speak.

"I prepared syringes of the chemical for Dr. Johnson. He asked me to make syringes of the chemical, but I didn't know why."

"It is likely that Dr. Johnson made that video on his own," said Mi-Ok in a firm, sure voice. "The behavior of the mouse—the momentary twitching—after it received the injection is what we've seen in the lab when we did the toxicology study. I don't know what to say about its recovery. We've never done an experiment like that before. It would never be approved. I would never do it."

"So you think Johnson did this to the mouse and made this video?" asked Bob pointedly to Mi-Ok.

"Yes," she responded. "And I wonder why he sent it to Dr. Albracht? Not long ago Dr. Albracht visited our lab, but he had a seizure and died in Dr. Johnson's office." Mi-Ok let the sentence sink in as she closely watched the expression on everyone's face.

"He died right in the office?" asked Brad in disbelief. "How bizarre."

"I thought so too, especially since Dr. Albracht looked quite well when I met him just moments before he met with Dr. Johnson privately," added Mi-Ok who noticed that Alex was nodding quizzically as if he had something to ask, but thought better of it. Instead it was Bob who asked the obvious question; the same one Alex had formulated.

"And no one suspected foul play?" offered Bob who recalled the odd part of Dr. Benedetti's email related to a concern for Dr. Albracht's well-being. The old Tuscan worried that his German friend would submit himself to Richard Johnson as a human guinea pig, to test the healing powers of the newly discovered chemical that looked like a miracle, fountain-of-youth-type cure.

"Aaa...the police came but nothing happened," offered Jo to which Mi-Ok added, "They questioned quite a few of us in the lab and even Dr. Johnson and as far as we know there were no issues. He must have had a great seizure."

As a physician, the described events did not add up to Alex, but because he wasn't there to witness the events, he kept his thoughts to himself and instead turned the discussion back to science. "Sometimes things happen so suddenly. I'm sorry. I bet it wasn't a nice situation for anyone. If I may, I'd like to ask you some questions about the toxicity studies. First, did you do acute or chronic studies or both? And the second question is relates to the health of the mice. Were they young and healthy, or old and diseased? In other words, what was the general health and age of the mice?"

Mi-Ok sat upright and promptly answered the questions in Amy-like rapid fire. "All mice were young, disease-free, 10-week old, Balb/c inbred females. Acute was the 24-hour timepoint. Although chronic is usually quite long, like 90 days, we ended the study after just 30."

Alex was making his way through a line of questions towards a goal like a child angling through a crowd of adults for a better view of the parade. "You mentioned that the *in vitro* studies seemed to rescue and reverse cells from dying, right?"

"Yes, that's correct."

"That suggests to me that these tissue cells had already completed their life cycle and were in decline. It mimics what happens in animals and plants too, I suppose when they are in later stages of life or when there has been acute trauma. If indeed your chemical was used on that feral mouse, it may have worked because the mouse experienced acute, severe trauma not necessarily because it was healthy. Therefore, one would think that critical experiments on the potential therapeutic properties of your chemical require the use of old animals near their end of life. For example, if mice that are old and ailing—arthritic, feeble, inactive—appeared healed or rejuvenated after receiving the chemical, as what appeared to happen to the acutely injured mouse in the video, then it may explain to some degree how the chemical works. It may be involved in a universal cellular repair mechanism."

Jo, who was very impressed with Alex's line of inquiry and sound, rational reasoning said, "Aaa...that why I send some to Bob. That's why."

"What? That's what you sent? You sent this chemical through the mail? Does Johnson know?" asked Bob who smiled at the thought of having some material to test while worried about the vast legal implications. He could already hear Dr. Kianamann's outrage should he make a marketable discovery with this chemical without having procured a formal material transfer agreement. But Jo had yet another bomb to drop on the group.

"Aaa...I want to come back to MIT and with Mi-Ok too. We want to work with this chemical here with you. I...aaa...we...me and Mi-Ok do not like Dr. Johnson."

"Jo and I are no longer happy working in his laboratory. We think he can be dangerous with this chemical. If you'd like, we can discuss this issue after this meeting," added a composed Mi-Ok.

Bob knew that Mi-Ok was right. This unexpected tangent didn't directly involve Alex and Brad so he decided to bring the meeting to a close. In any case, Alex had already described the next set of important experiments. It was just a matter before they would be performed.

———•———

He couldn't remember the last time he took a Friday off, but Richard Johnson decided that this glorious early summer day with temperatures in the mid-seventies was the perfect time to take a much-needed breather. He agreed to humor his friend with a round of golf, a sport that he neither played well nor one that he particularly enjoyed, however he was upbeat and ready to do something different.

He realized that he skirted a disaster last month. Franz Albracht's death could have unfolded much differently. His planned use of two acupuncture needles bordered on insane, yet by all indications he would have gotten away with killing the old German with the little sharps because no one noticed the entry site of the one needle he did insert. In any case, what counted was that Franz Albracht is dead and the bullet of his stupidity whizzed by without causing harm. Now it was onto a new level of fame and fortune with the power and prestige of the Nobel Prize as an unshakable base. The newly discovered chemical would reap hundreds of millions of dollars in royalties for its remarkable healing powers and all he had to do now was enjoy his worthy existence. Life was more than good for Richard Johnson, but in this life, every successful rise must be followed by a precipitous fall.

His movement on the golf course was remarkably simple. With a gloved right hand, Dr. Johnson stooped to balance the hard, shiny white golf ball atop the red plastic tee he had just inserted in the ground. That was when the pain exploded and radiated outwards with equal intensity in all directions from the center of his lower back. Kneeling on the soft, perfectly manicured grass, Richard Johnson let out a muted, but forceful groan, as he grabbed the small of his back with his free left hand as if he sought to extrude the crippling pain from his body. With teeth gritted he was helped into the golf cart and taken directly to his car where he insisted that he was capable of driving himself home safely.

Ever so gingerly the Nobelist eased himself from the car into his empty home. Through streaks of pain he carefully made his way down to the finished basement where he had hid a second syringe originally prepared for a repeat animal experiment. Richard Johnson was unaware that the little feral mouse had long since died of starvation in the Keep-Me-Alive trap placed behind the shrubs next to the foundation of his house.

Dr. Johnson gave little thought to the chemistry behind the rapid synaptic firings of the nerve bundles that crippled his every movement as he removed the protective plastic cap from the thin tuberculin syringe and jabbed the small 27 gauge, one-half inch needle past the skin and dermal layers, to an area deep in the muscle of his right thigh. Every drop of the one-milliliter, colorless synthetic chemical diffused in a steady manner through the muscle fibers and into the arteries. In short order, the chemical dispersed to every part of his body. Seated awkwardly in the leather office chair with his right leg extended, he exhaled fully, closed his eyes and waited for the miracle to occur.

After he relaxed for several moments Richard hesitantly thought to attempt to tilt his hip slightly upward—a move that had been prohibitively painful ever since he knelt on the golf course. And when he did his eyes widened not in pain but in the unmistakable absence of it. There was no pain at all. None in his hip or lower back. Pain did not shoot down his leg nor was any discomfort when he stood upright and walked across the room. With natural, pain-free movements, Richard Johnson even bent over to pick off the carpeted basement floor the thin plastic cap that once covered the syringe's needle. No more then fifteen minutes ago he could barely get himself out of the car and now he felt loose, limber and, if he dared to think it true, he oddly also felt younger. He could have been a man half his age, full of vigor and life. *Franz would have died to have felt this young again. Poor Franz*, he thought. *Poor fucking bastard.*

While he marveled at his good fortune he also recalled the rapid, miraculous effects that the synthetic chemical had on the badly injured feral mouse. Then in a moment of clarity he realized that he had just become the first human being ever to benefit from a discovery made in his own laboratory. It was a self-experimentation moment in medicine that would mark a new age of therapy.

What an advance! I'm a goddamned genius after all!

Richard realized that he had to document this historic moment. He had to record for the sake of accuracy, the day's events—the serendipitous occurrence of his unfortunate and extremely painful injury, the solid forethought to have prepared the purified chemical ready to inject at a moment's notice, the bravery to self-administer the injection, and his willingness to risk his very life, not only to alleviate his own pain, but also to lead the way to eliminate the agony from the hundreds of millions that suffer from terrible diseases and ailments worldwide.

Had anyone won the Nobel Prize twice, he wondered? *Surely I will be crowned again for the discovery of this miracle chemical.*

With events of the important day duly documented Richard Johnson went outside to unload the rarely used golf clubs from the trunk of his car. As he did, he felt a renewed determination to complete what he started not more than eight hours ago. With a tee, a ball and what he assumed was a driving iron in hand, Richard went into his small backyard that abutted a large swath of wooded conservation land. He placed the red tee into his lawn with ease. Without hesitation he placed the little, dimpled, white hard ball on the tee's cupped top. He then twisted his torso from left to right and back to left again to make sure he was still pain-free before lining up to swing. He felt limber and strong as he recalled the mechanics of the powerful stroke. Richard watched as the golf ball popped off the tee at a steep angle and, as luck would have it, struck a large limb of a tall oak tree. Like a Ping-Pong ball off a solid paddle, the golf ball was propelled back towards the yard landing harmlessly at the edge of the property where the manicured grass met the decaying woods. Determined to let one rip through the forest, Richard went to retrieve the white ball, but this time as he bent towards the ground, he landed headfirst into it.

Two exited from the left armhole, three from the right sleeve. Four scampered out from the inside of the plaid golf pants. Four other mice stopped gnawing on the exposed fingers and scurried safely to underground tunnels of the forest floor as first responders approached the now cooled and relatively stiff body of Dr. Richard Johnson.

5

The defining experiments with the four key chemicals—the tracer $RW96$, the bacterial peptide, the human peptide, and the newly labeled 'Hopkins Compound'—were obvious to Alex, Bob, and Brad, as well as to Jo and Mi-Ok. The Korean chemist and the animal expert had relocated to Boston just prior to the disbandment of Richard Johnson's laboratory in Baltimore. They now held research positions in the Wyle laboratory.

The first set of experiments with the combination of chemicals was performed *in vitro* using a variety of cells from humans and mice. The sequence of events, that is the addition of each compound, was the most critical part of the experimental design. First, cells were grown and given nutrients necessary to allow them to undergo their natural, and well-defined life cycle. On day 10, when the once vibrant cells began to die, the Hopkins Compound was added and the cells, as expected, recovered and were again vibrant. Once the cells appeared vibrant, a result that took only hours following the addition of the Hopkins Compound, the combination of bacterial and human peptides was added along with $RW96$. The cultures were then immediately placed in an instrument that recorded the intensity of the fluorescence.

The results of these preliminary studies followed the predictions of the experimenters. The greatest level of tracer $RW96$ binding—the most fluorescence—was measured with cells that were first rescued or revived with the Hopkins Compound followed by the addition of the two peptides. No other sequences worked. Taken together, the data suggested that the Hopkins Compound worked at the cellular level to repair any damages, after which the two potent demethylases—one of bacterial and the other of human origin—removed methyl groups from cellular DNA. These powerful enzymes triggered all genes to be instantly activated just before death of the organism.

"It's as if the body repairs itself for an all out expression of genetic information for one last, highly orchestrated event," Brad offered as the team met to review the new data.

"That's a huge leap, from tissue culture to whole body, isn't it?" Bob asked Brad.

"It certainly is," replied Brad. "And I'll bet you a round of beers that's exactly what will happen when we do this experiment in animals. I say this because it's exactly what happened with Cookie, and with Dr. Paolo too."

Mi-Ok saw the opportunity to add much anticipated news to the meeting. "Just this morning we received approval from MIT to do the experiment in monkeys provided that they are examined by an outside veterinarian and deemed to be terminally ill and ready to be euthanized."

"You know," added Brad who was reaching into his backpack. "Sometimes the timing of events is uncanny. I have here the galley of a just accepted manuscript that will appear next month in the *International Journal of Theoretical Physics and Mathematics,* research performed by our friend Phillip J. Hess at RPI. I am not a mathematician, or a computation expert so you'll have to help me out here, Ajay. What I took away from Phil's research, and what I understood from the chat we had last evening, is that he's derived a mathematical hierarchy that predicts what happens to the chemical action potential of the human body during it's life and at it's death. Phil's model shows that all energies are not consumed, but that they shift, in total and all at once, to another state. This event leaves the body empty, without energy. He proposed a framework for the existence of multiple universes and a plausible mechanism for how one's energy can move from one verse to another. If you'll entertain me for a minute, I'd like to postulate that the biological signals we've discovered, and the endgame that we've discussed, could be the way the human body readies itself to move out of this verse, this state, and into another. Repair, express, collect, and transmit in that order; the transmission part, the decisive act, is visualized by the tracer *RW96*."

Alex followed Brad's line of reasoning. "Every living cell has electrochemical action potential. Every specialized cell like neurons, cardiomyocytes, indeed every muscle cell works by moving electrical charges along chemical chain reactions—action potentials and membrane potentials. These reactions happen a billion times each second of each day in our body until we die. It's how we move, think, feel, smell, and see. It's how we function. If I recall, we can generate 100 watts of power on a 2,000 calories diet, so if the conservation of energy is a universal law, then what Brad just described is an astounding way for our it to be harnessed and transported."

"Ah," said Bob who had anticipated Alex's ending. "Transported where and how?"

Just then the door of the small conference room opened. Several in the room were glad that Brad had forewarned them of the possible late addition to their meeting.

"Amy!" exclaimed Bob. "Come in. So good to see you! We've missed you."

It was the first time Amy ventured out of the apartment since the heartbreaking loss of her son. With Brad's encouragement she made the decision to move beyond the long weeks of tormented grief. It took some time for Amy to arrive at the decision to make the trip to Milky Way, but she knew that it would be good for her to see familiar faces as a way to peak out from inside her protective shell. Living in a shell was foreign to Amy, and she really didn't care for it.

Amy stood in the doorway and looked around the room, the pain on her face still evident. Ajay, who was surprised to see his research partner nodded and smiled from the far side of the table. Jo Jung-Zoo rose and bowed his head as he shook her hand, then he introduced her to Mi-Ok who also shook Amy's hand. Alex left his seat and gave Amy a quick hug, as did Bob. Brad then pulled a chair to the table next to him and gave his wife a kiss on her left cheek; as he did he whispered in her ear, "I'm proud of you."

Appropriately, Bob updated Amy on the discussion at hand and he left off by repeating the question he had posed moments ago, "So then I asked 'transported where and how?'" Brad was shifting nervously in his seat as he wondered if all of this discussion about death was too much for his wife, but it didn't take long for him to get his answer.

Having listened intently to Bob, Amy kicked into science gear like her old self.

"I'll be direct. I think the expertise in this room can address the 'how' and leave the 'where' for quantum physicists who have studied this exact part of the question for decades. I think we can make an assumption that the energy leaves the body through the braincase based on what we already know. *RW88* and *RW96* showed us in dramatic fashion with Cookie, then with Dr. Paolo, that the brain bursts with activity before going dark just like a cosmic supernova. Why would energy follow anything other than a path of least resistance? Upward and outwards seems reasonable."

"This kind of reminds me of the halo effect, like those you see on a lot of Christian icons," remarked Bob.

"Exactly," said Amy. "Kind of makes you wonder, doesn't it?"

"Aaa...I read in MIT newspaper that MIT astrophysicist has an instrument to measure low energy from distant stars. Maybe she could help us?" Jo asked.

Bob's mind accelerated. "Holy cow. Could you imagine if we were able to measure an external energy spike at the moment of death that followed the brain's supernova? Perhaps we can build this into the animal study. Ajay, would you and Jo and Amy get in touch with this astrophysicist and see if this is at all feasible? And Mi-Ok, would you informally ask the animal folks if additional approvals are needed if we use an external instrument that does not touch the monkeys during the experiment?"

Each person in the room took notes and readily agreed to follow through with their given tasks.

"If this works, if we actually measured external energy around the head of a chimp, or a person at the precise moment of death, then it would be the cream on top of the frosting of our research cake," commented Alex. And with a broad smile, he quickly added, "It would send shockwaves around the entire globe. Perhaps even the entire universe."

Nexus VI

There was nothing unusual about the early summer day Abby had just lived. Grad school days were moving along at an exciting clip, and her relationships with everyone in her immediate and extended circles were supportive of her work and quite pleasant to be around. Her relationship with Rosi had become stronger over the past few months and neither partner questioned the others devotion and love. Even sharing time and affection with Phil, or Olysia, or Johanna seemed as normal as seeing the moon in the evening sky. And this night, like most, ended with Rosi cuddled up to Abby who was at the brink of a sound sleep. Indeed, Rosi's cool hand on her bare shoulder was the comfort moment that sent Abby to sleep.

It was dark and empty, that is until young Dante appeared from somewhere just below her line of site. They recognized each other but unlike the other visits, this time it seemed like there was nothing to share, that is, until Abby sensed a mixture of emotions from her friend. Then from Abby's left appeared a young woman, perhaps in her twenties. She was beautiful. Abby was shocked. She now realized that the two in her midst knew each other very well. Once they were husband and wife, a union now insignificant. Abby felt her heart race in confusion. The three stood as questions and answers raced silently between them.

You see, relayed young Laura, it really was simple. To bond eternally all one needs to do is to cradle in your hands the face of the one you love and look deeply into their eyes. Say silently, firmly and with conviction that you love them. And when you say farewell—no matter the length of time apart—say it sincerely and also with a smile for now you know that a goodbye, like a sound hypothesis and even like a brilliant theory, is only temporary.

Abby awoke with a gasp. She positioned herself upright and looked straight ahead into the soft light of the studio. There was no doubt that it was Dr. Paolo's wife. Abby was trying to recall the last time she contacted Laura and the context of the exchange, but she simply could not remember. Without disturbing Rosi, Abby slipped out of bed, put on a light robe and went into the living room. She sat on the couch and opened her laptop computer.

Oddly, the most recent hit on the search for 'Dr. Laura Kean, Boston' was from the United States Bureau of Consular Affairs. The notification of Laura's death on the Bureau's link read as if written by a lawyer who followed a standard fill-in-the-blank-type template. Date, approximate time of death, mode and location of death were detailed in exactly ten words. Below those ten words was a line: Next of kin? Not Applicable.

Abby went to the website of Myer Memorial Hospital and searched for Dr. Laura Kean in hope that there was some sort of mistake. But there was no match. Dr. Laura Kean was no longer listed in the hospital's staff directory.

Abby closed the laptop and stared straight ahead at the brick wall. Laura died about two weeks ago and tonight she paid me a visit to deliver a simple message. Abby closed her eyes and thought about the first time she met Laura when Dr. Paolo told everyone that he had cancer. She met Laura again on her graduation day. Abby recalled how she held Laura's saddened face and relayed a message from her just deceased husband.

Now, with her mother long gone and her father somewhere outside of her circle, with her champion deceased and now his lovely wife gone too, Abby realized that there were few older folks to lean on. She felt too empty to cry, so she just lay on her side on the sofa and thought of Laura Kean, and of Dante Paolo too. She thought about their times together until she fell back to sleep.

Epilogue

"Hello, my name is Trevor Wicke. May I please speak with June Kennedy?"

"Speaking. I'm sorry I don't want to be rude, but I don't like solicitors," June answered. But before she could end the call, the man on the line rapidly said, "I represent the estate of Laura Kean and it's imperative that we speak. Please don't go." June was confused at the odd request by a complete stranger.

"Could you tell me what this is about?" she asked.

"The only thing I can tell you over the phone is that I am an attorney. I represent the estate of Dr. Laura Kean. I would like to arrange a time when we can meet. You were obviously very special to her."

June froze. She did not know how to react. Everything sounded on the level, but he spoke nervously as if he didn't care to do what he had to do. It was as if something has happened to Laura, but June, ever the optimist, also considered the possibility that it was just some legal formality that her friend forgot to mention.

"Um, yes. Thursday at noon will be fine."

And with the address to Mr. Wicke's office scribbled on a napkin, June ended the call. Immediately, she tapped the number to Laura's cell phone, her hands shaking. By eleven that evening, June had lost count of the number of voice messages she had left on Laura's phone. The last one was a plea through desperate tears and a cracking voice, "Laura, please for fucking Christ's sake, call me."

"Please have a seat, Ms. Kennedy," said Laura's baby-faced attorney.

In the privacy of his small office, Mr. Wicke sat at his modest-sized oak desk and opened the sole folder that was on the black blotter. After momentarily reviewing the top page, he removed his glasses and looked directly at June who was seated across from him in a comfortable captains chair.

"Ms. Kennedy, I'm very sorry to inform you that our office was notified last week by the United States Bureau of Consular Affairs that Dr. Kean died in an automobile accident in Italy. Since she has no next of kin, we were notified as her legal representative."

June sat stone-faced.

Since receiving the initial call from Mr. Wicke, the hospice care provider made repeated attempts to reach her friend by phone, by knocking on the door to her condo, and even by going to Laura's hospital where she worked. Every attempt proved futile; it was as if Laura simply disappeared and no one knew what had happened to her. Over those three long days of searching for her friend, June slept little while holding on to the slim chance that the glass was, somehow, still half full.

"Ms. Kennedy, Dr. Kean left this letter for you. It has been sealed in our safe since it was deposited earlier this year. I've been instructed to deliver it to you personally, and then to follow your wishes." Mr. Wicke handed June a white business envelope with 'June Kennedy' typed on the front and on the back was Laura's signature written across the flap's seam. If it had been opened, June would have easily seen that the cursive lettering did not align. The envelope had not been opened. June held the handwritten letter with both hands.

Dear June,

As you know Dante and I were childless. Shortly after we were married I lost twins, late in my one and only pregnancy—a loss that we never overcame. We did not speak of the loss nor did we entertain the 'what-ifs' of having had children, that is, until you came along. Dante realized that you would have been about the age of our child (he didn't know until shortly before he died that I miscarried two children—a boy and a girl).

Dante spoke with such love and affection for you, June. His interactions with you, as well as with his dear students (particularly Abby) were special to him. It was as if he was trying desperately to compress an entire lifetime of fatherly love in the remaining weeks he had left. He spoke of you at great length—your intellect, your enthusiasm for life, your noble career choice, your desire to help others during their time of need, your endless energy, and your infectiously positive spirit—and he repeatedly made me promise that I would keep his admiration for you private because he feared that if you knew, you might be frightened away.

When Dante spoke of you I listened stoically, but then afterwards, when he slept and I was alone, I cried. I wept for this deep void in his life—in our lives—and for the experiences forever lost.

June, you have been a treasure to Dante and to me. I've

enjoyed our times together without exception. Should any-thing happen to me, I want you to have my condominium and some money to pay taxes, fees and other expenses for five years. Mr. Wicke, or an associate of the firm, will pro-cess my Will and then he will transfer the title of the condo to you unless you decline accept the offer. The decision is totally yours to make. I think Dante would have approved of what is written in this Will.

Keep smiling, keep loving, and remain true to yourself, because you are one of the best.

With undying love and admiration,

Laura Kean

June sat stunned and saddened. She looked up at Mr. Wicke and slowly handed him the letter.

"I've taken a quick look at Dr. Kean's Last Will and Testament that was signed earlier this very year," the attorney started as he flipped through the several pages of legal-sized paper in his hands. "It appears that she left you her homestead along with five-years worth of money towards expenses. If I may ask, what do you do for work Ms. Kennedy?"

"I am a hospice care provider. I work for a nonprofit that deals with hospice and palliative care," she replied as tears began to roll off her cheeks.

"Interesting," he replied. "Would it be: The Hospice and Palliative Care Center of Greater New England?"

June sniffed and wiped the tears from her eyes as she wondered how he knew or why he cared. "Yes, that's it. Why?"

"Well it appears as though Dr. Kean left one-half of the rest of her estate to that organization. It's quite a sizable donation."

"That's great," June, replied clearly not understanding the full value.

"Don't you want to know about the other half?"

"Not really. It doesn't matter. I can't believe any of this."

"The other half is going to fund a Chair in the Science Department at Wilmington College in the name of Dr. Dante Paolo. The only provisions are that the course must be called *Teach the Professor* and be limited to six seniors per semester. Those are quite odd stipulations, wouldn't you agree Ms. Kennedy?"

June hesitated for a moment as she processed the question. The hospice care provider recalled the Wilmington College students Laura referred to in the letter she had just read and replied in a sure voice, "Not odd, Mr. Wicke. Obvious."

2

The preparatory sketches done in pencil and charcoal were simple enough. There would be one carving made with a perfectly sized piece of pure white Carrara marble. Virtually vein-less, the Italian stone was leftover from a prior project; it measured eleven inches cubed. Even though Rosi was quite comfortable carving marble, the delicacy of the piece tested the limits of her skills and patience.

Rosi dedicated the rare, spare time she had to this piece; she worked on it secretly for the better part of two years. She constantly evaluated and rethought the lines, its shape, its bends and folds, its protrusions and its pulse. This creation would represent the many highs and lows of a special person's life. As such, Rosi sought for the creation to be transcendental and transformative, subtle yet mysterious, highly personal and deeply provocative. She poured her very heart and soul into ensuring that the privileged stone achieved these goals with conviction. Rosi sought for the piece to be worthy of its recipient. It would be as perfect as any piece of art she'd ever create.

———◆———

The function room at *The Beltway Bistro* was hopping on this early Friday evening. Beer, wine, along with a wide assortment of tasty hors d'oeuvres zigzagged across the room from person to person that came to celebrate the lofty achievement. At times it seemed like the hostess, Alexa Goldberg, who was in high party mode, had just defended her own dissertation instead of her prized, now former, graduate student and the soon to be officially hooded, Dr. Abigail Lark.

With near universal praise for the two outstanding and highly original papers she co-authored and published in respected journals, her Ph.D. committee voted unanimously, in a closed-door meeting following the defense of her dissertation, to nominate Abby for the highest degree offered by the university. It seemed like everyone loved this young researcher for tackling an issue that had long been dismissed as being too subjective to perform definitively. It also seemed like everyone in both Alexa's and Abby's inner academic circle attended the high-energy celebration. Most departmental faculty made an appearance to offer continued success to one of American University's newly minted doctors, and its most highly rated graduate teaching assistant. This time, Olysia, Johanna and Rosi, invited guests of the hostess and doctor-of-honor, blended easily with the jubilant academic crowd.

It was close to midnight when Alexa, Abby and Rosi, the last celebrants standing, left the bistro. It had been quite a day that began with high drama and anxiety, but ended with a grand celebration that made all other student attendees just that much more driven to complete their own research program.

Abby and Rosi walked Alexa to her car that was parked at the faculty lot on campus. Although it was a pleasant evening, Alexa insisted on driving them to the center of Georgetown, only one block from Rosi's studio. From the center the two telepaths walked hand-in-hand, in silence, as they usually did. Abby was drained, yet elated. Rosi was cool, yet apprehensive.

The single beam appeared as a focused column of soft moonlight that emanated from the ceiling high above. It was the only light in the otherwise dark studio apartment. There, on a round white marble base, was Rosi's creation. Two opposing wrists and hands carved of marble with thin, ring-less fingers splayed open; thumbs connected side-by-side. The polished stone hands with their veins and tendons visible appeared ready to receive something tender, something precious.

It took a moment for Abby's weary eyes to comprehend the powerful piece.

With all my heart, my love.

Abby placed her knapsack on the floor and slowly, silently approached the delicate, life-size sculpture. She viewed it from every angle, transfixed on its tenderness and beauty. And as the meaning and power of the artwork coalesced in her mind, Abby's eyes welled with tears. Tears that came along with vibrant memories of her mother, Dr. Paolo, and of little Lilly, of baby Brad, and of Laura Kean. All of them, together—focused on the space inside the marble hands.

Tears of joy and exhaustion, and of gratitude and love, left Abby's face, which was firmly buried in Rosi's nape. The stream of tears left a moist trail down the center of the artist's narrow back.

I call it InfinitUs.

3

After months of anticipation, both travelers could not believe the day had actually arrived. They were heading due north from Milan on Scandinavian Airlines flight 6901 to Stockholm. It was the first time she had flown in her life and Rosa would not have agreed to join her cousin on the week-long winter trip if he had not convinced her that she would feel welcomed by others that attended the Nobel Banquet. The highly formal affair would only be for one evening and then they could explore Sweden's natural beauty during the rest of their stay. The trip that included a stay at a four-star hotel, daily excursions and delicious seafood, would be the only one of Rosa's lifetime. It would also be Lorenzo's last.

Earlier in the year, Lorenzo had been asked by the current Chair of the Nobel Ceremony Committee to present a 15-minute tribute to the former Secretary General of the Nobel Committee, the late Professor Franz Albracht. It was an honor he neither anticipated nor sought, but it was one that he accepted for two reasons. The first of which was to provide an adventure for his cousin.

Rosa was awestruck from the moment they entered Milan's vast Malpensa airport. Never before had she seen such a sea of seemingly endless people hustling and bustling to and fro, or just standing stoically in an endless serpentine-like line waiting for something that could only happen after something else happened before it. Fortunately, Lorenzo knew what to do and where to go and before she was overcome by the foul smells of diesel and re-circulated human exhaust, they were airborne and moving faster than she had ever moved before in her life. Rosa looked out the window in amazement as the plane cut through the fog and rose above the clouds that hid the sun from the ground. They were so high in fact, that she was sure that she was closer than she'd ever been to heaven, and to almighty God Himself.

The entire city of Stockholm, the *Venice of the North*, as seen from the window of the airplane was just one shock Rosa absorbed in the early stages of the voyage. The big black car drove them to the opulent hotel on roads with names that meant nothing to her. Rosa could not understand how Lorenzo knew how to maneuver through the complexities of travel. And it was upon landing in the capital of Sweden that she first heard her cousin converse fluently in English.

In some ways, however, she already yearned for the well-worn stone paths and well tended grape vines that surrounded her house in the village. Yet, in other ways, she quickly realized that what she assumed she knew about the world beyond her Tuscan village was hopelessly flawed. Preconceived perceptions that she was well read and thus knowledgeable of worldly matters quickly vanished.

And the excursion from her home to the hotel in Sweden was just the beginning. Although the tribute to Dr. Franz Albracht occurred on the evening before the main Nobel Prize event, the ostentatious dinner gathering was nonetheless as lavish and as extravagant as any fairy tale ever written or read. Like a honeybee on snow, Rosa felt stunned and frozen with fright as many seemingly important people, mostly men, made their way to shake hands with Lorenzo, and to her by association. She acknowledged their presence with a poorly recycled smile, a light handshake, and a required nod. But the entire situation and everything she had to endure was worth it as she was seated in a place of honor, at the head table near the stage. She heard what she reasoned to be a laudatory introduction followed by applause for her cousin who looked as relaxed and as confident in front of the large crowd as he did sitting on a stone wall, walking stick in hand, passing time with neighbors in the village. Rosa did not speak nor did she comprehend English, the universal language of scientific meetings. Nevertheless, she could tell from the crowd's laughter that Lorenzo began with an amusing anecdote. But then his delivery turned solemn and sincere. He chose to use only a few choice vintage pictures of Franz Albracht as a scientist that loomed large on the two white screens at the front of the great hall. The pictures of the neurologist working in his wooden laboratory table of long ago were not scripted or posed or produced, they were worn black and white photos taken with natural light such that blurred areas denoted movement. Later, he would tell Rosa is that when he showed the last of the low-resolution images of his longtime colleague, he reminded the audience that scientific advances are made not by those who see the world as black and white, but by those who take the time to dissect the vast seas of gray, with simple common sense and sound intellect.

A second dignitary would replace Lorenzo at the podium and memorialize Professor Richard Johnson, one of last year's laureates. As Lorenzo sat politely and listened to the excessive words, accompanied the numerous slides on the relatively few achievements of the late Dr. Johnson, he couldn't help but wonder if the two deaths were, other than temporally, related.

Rosa smiled politely at others at their table during the multi-course meal. Several toasts were made to those they had just memorialized, as well as to the two speakers who delivered the remembrances. Other than the rich chocolate pie, Rosa was not impressed with the quality of the dinner. At one point during the multi-course meal, she leaned close to her cousin's ear and whispered, *"tanto da insegnare,"* to which he smiled in agreement that there was indeed was so much to teach.

The crowd thinned as the late hour pointed to a new day. And with Rosa fading quickly it was time for Lorenzo to fulfill the second reason for accepting the invitation to return to Sweden.

"As you probably already know, one of the greatest scientific discoveries of this new millennium is revealing itself through a series of separate, but interrelated findings," Lorenzo said to the Nobel Committee's Secretary General. "Research closely followed by Dr. Albracht and myself since it's inception has now fully matured. These advances will dictate the future of our species. The disciples of Dante Paolo have surrounded themselves with wise people in environments that foster creative thinking and exploration. Collectively, these scientists have led the way to reveal how an individual's energy is ultimately conserved and how that energy becomes our place in the universe—our immortality. They have also described how one communicates with these energies, a discovery that will be studied by scientists, theologians, historians and philosophers for the rest of time. In short, they have explained life and, simultaneously, they have conquered death." For emphasis, Lorenzo leaned forward and thus closer to the Secretary as he reached into his shirt pocket and produced a plastic holder containing a small SD card. "Here are the papers, and the data: the mathematics, the genetics, the telepathic method of communication and lastly, the one from MIT and Harvard that will be published early next year. Not only does that paper describe how the human body repairs and collects its energy, but it also proves that this energy exits the body through the cranium at death."

The Secretary General took the small package and looked at it as if it held special powers. Lorenzo stood, as did the Secretary General. As the two men shook hands, Lorenzo stated clearly, "If I were on the Nobel's selection committee I'd make history while history is being made."

"I'm not following," remarked the Secretary General. The comment came as no surprise to Lorenzo.

"While it is well known that the Nobel Prize is a high honor, it is also well known that the Nobel Prize in Medicine proclaims 'Eureka!' an hour after everyone else. By that time the cheering has ended, the lights are off and the discovery has already left its mark on mankind. Many times, you've completely missed the boat. It reflects poorly on your ability to recognize the real-time impact of new truths. The visionaries that

351

made the discoveries you are now holding in your hand deserve the rapid blessings of your Committee. These young scientists are the ones who have reset the height of the scientific bar. Their collective works should be acknowledged for what it will do for humanity—that is, it will liberate us from our innately conceived limitations. There can be no greater achievement."

The Secretary General again looked at the small package still held in his hands. He thought for a moment and nodded in understanding. He harbored the same thoughts on the passé nature of the awards, especially those given in the biological sciences.

Lorenzo looked at Rosa who was by this time more than anxious to leave the large ballroom. As the two started to leave, Lorenzo turned once more to the Secretary General and said, "Stated simply, they've reconciled what was thought to be irreconcilable."

4

Amy was beyond exhausted. At the end of each day she had not a calorie's worth of energy to spare. She loved her husband and she enjoyed being a pediatrician. But more than anything, Amy felt absolutely joyful as a mother to her eight-month old son, Jonathan.

She lay in her bed, the sheets cool, and the baby asleep, and with her husband spending yet another night on call at the hospital Amy drifted off to a deep slumber. Delicately, she stumbled through the once elusive door. At first she just felt silence, pure peace, but then from a position that could have been straight ahead, she saw a young man who was perhaps twenty. He looked directly at her, his baby blue eyes showing through his jet-black hair. *Mom I am sorry for your pain I meant it not. Please know I love you. I know you love me too. Amy did not know how to respond, she just felt the thoughts that any parent would have in this situation. You are so beautiful, so handsome I think of you everyday all the time and even now, with little Jonathan I think of how you two would have been brothers. Together. My sons. Mom, I am with you and the others more than you know or realize. Thank you for making the connection. I'll always be here now and forever.*

And just as quickly as he appeared, young Brad, vanished.

Amy slept through her tears. She did not want to wake up.

Several days later, on a Friday afternoon, when baby Jonathan did something just slightly different than he had done the day before, Amy recalled the unusual encounter with her first son. She froze in place as the memories flooded back.

Immediately she picked up her cellphone.

"Abby," she said through pursed lips that tried to hold firm against an onslaught of emotions. "It happened just as you said it would. I saw little Brad in a sort of a dream, but he was not a baby anymore. He was a young man and so handsome, so beautiful and he... Abby," she continued through tears. "Abby, he let me know...he thanked me, Abby. He thanked me for making the connection and he said that... he said that we would always be together. Forever. Oh Abby!"

The End.

Acknowledgments

A sincere thank you to those who took time to read and to provided critical feedback, corrections and advice not only to *Abby's Theory* but also to *The Last Hypothesis*. I am indebted to Robert Angerer, Richard Blakemore, Nicole Bloor, Laurie Comstock, Philip DiNuovo, Patricia Gerard, Christopher Jennings, Wilma Lange, Bonnie Lawrence, Leslie Linkkila, Michael McInnis, and Jane Trenaman.

Also, special thanks to Hannah Lane who did the page and cover layouts of this novel as well as *The Last Hypothesis*. Without a doubt, her talents made both books look "pretty on a shelf."

www.ingramcontent.com/pod-product-compliance
Lightning Source LLC
Chambersburg PA
CBHW030636260626
47157CB00007B/2349